I0659381

Girls Without Gods: The Final Revised Edition

A Dog Among Thorns, Volume 2

Joshua Fields

Published by Joshua Fields, 2023.

Table of Contents

Preface

"WHAT I HAVE WRITTEN I have written." ~ Pontius Pilate, The Gospel of John 19:22.

This work, now under the title *Girls Without Gods*, is the final edition of *Thirtyfolder*. My sentiments towards it are the same as my sentiments towards the first book in the series, *A Dog Among Thorns*. "I will not rewrite it again" and "it is now in the best form possible given limited time resources, competing projects, all manner of interruptions and my waning interest."

The preface to *A Dog Among Thorns* gives a brief explanation as to why it and *Thirtyfolder* needed improvements in both plot and prose. The latter, published in 2014, was in need of a rewrite as opposed to a mere revision. Several characters in *Girls Without Gods*, for example, have been removed, replaced or merged with other characters, the most notable instance being the replacement of Lydia Rogers with Sophie.

I do not know if I will return to the series to write a third book. Another project beckons and I expect it to take years to complete. That said, I hope this rewrite makes a difference and I sincerely hope you enjoy it.

Joshua R. Fields

ENRAGED BY JACOB'S dismissal, Marcion hurtled recklessly and desperately through the spirit world. His fury fueled his speed.

"Fucking bitch!" he snarled as he accelerated. Cursing the trouble Miriam's treachery caused him, he barked, "Fucking traitorous bitch!"

Departing the realm of the spirit, Marcion exploded into Stonechurch with a bone-jarring scream. His horrific screech echoed off the cobblestone walls as he swiped at the air with his claws and vented his vitriol in a crazed display of charred, twisted flesh. Baring his rotting, jagged teeth, the demon howled like an angry gibbon and leapt onto a column erected of irregular, earth-toned rocks and whitish-gray mortar.

"No wonder the humans view us as ignorant, violent savages," said a deep, masculine voice, its words ending Marcion's outburst. Hopping off the column, he landed on the ground and stood emotionlessly with his arms hanging at his sides. The voice thoughtfully added, "But I suppose your kind has its uses nonetheless."

Marcion's black, bulging eyes searched the room. They rolled over two rows of four support columns that ran through the center of the chamber. His jet orbs then jumped from stained-glass window to stained-glass window. Each one was ensconced in the cobblestone walls and slathered in black, viscous paint that obstructed the sunlight outside.

"What the fuck are you doing here?" Marcion sneered, the pitch of his voice increasing with annoyance. He shifted and squirmed as his hatred flourished.

"To unfuck Gottschalk's temptation, of course," said the voice with disapprobation. The silhouette of a tall, well-built man appeared at the far end of Stonechurch.

"Fuck you, *Aaron*," Marcion snarled. He failed in his attempt to appear undaunted by Aaron's presence but managed to utter, "Go unfuck something else."

"You've raised our Master's ire, Marcion," stated Aaron sharply. He approached Marcion with steady, confident footfalls and revealed himself while saying, "He has little confidence in your abilities as of late."

Marcion squinted his distended eyes. Aaron, a study in masculine perfection, stood six-foot-five-inches tall with a lean, muscular frame and brown, stylishly-mussed hair. He possessed the sharp facial features and the prominent cheekbones of an excessively-handsome model, his brown eyes penetrating and seductive. Stubble covered the lower part of his face, the modest growth adding just the right amount of ruggedness to his polished exterior.

"Then why haven't I been recalled?" Marcion inquired smugly, the reasonableness of his point helping to assuage his fear of his Master. He leapt onto one of the wooden support beams. Enjoying the higher vantage point and the false-yet-reassuring sense of superiority it provided, Marcion paced back and forth along its surface.

"You still have a part to play despite your recent incompetence," said Aaron matter-of-factly. Marcion dropped below the beam and hung upside-down from it with his gnarled arms and legs.

"*A part?!*" griped Marcion. He dropped in front of Aaron and glowered at him, repeating angrily, "A part?!"

"Take the younger one," ordered Aaron, his patience fraying ever-so-slightly "and leave Kaiser."

Marcion stroked his chin and pondered the command while Aaron indulged his delay. A contemplative expression arose on his horrid face.

"It won't work. He'll balk at her age," advised Marcion. The gears of his warped mind spinning and his twisted thoughts developing as he spoke, he explained, "But he'd give in to the older one. *Yes.* He already desires her. She's a younger, sluttier version of her mother. Yes, yes. I'll take her instead."

"You'll do no such thing," Aaron replied in disgust. He shook his head and glared at Marcion with contempt, saying, "Seduction is *not* your specialty."

"Then what the fuck am I supposed to do?!" shouted Marcion, the demon hopping up and down with clenched fists. He punched one of the columns and knocked chunks of rock and mortar out of it, the strike sending debris in all directions. Aaron exhaled in frustration.

"*Be you,*" he said bitterly.

• • • •

ELIZABETH LIFTED THE cigarette to her lips and inhaled, the Constable indulging in the way the nicotine rushed through her body. Exhaling, she folded her arms while carefully holding the cigarette between the middle and index fingers of her left hand. The nicotine meshed perfectly with the adrenaline coursing through her veins, the stimulant keeping her wide awake despite the late hour.

Standing alone on the stone balcony of her mansion, her dusky, muted green eyes caressed the entire Kaiser Valley from the multitude of lights shining at the city's center to the dark peak of Mount Baldwin. She shivered as she acutely sensed her husband Jacob's absence from the valley. Despite wearing one of Jacob's jackets over a Laurel green sweater and thick jeans, she failed to ward off the nippiness in the morning air.

Her sister, Darby, abruptly exited the glass security doors leading to the balcony and slammed them shut in an attempt to startle her. Seemingly impervious to the chill in the air, Darby wore only a tight black t-shirt and black jeans. Holstered at her side was her beloved, fifty-caliber pistol.

"We've got Sarah," advised Darby, the irritation evident in her voice as she approached Elizabeth. Standing shoulder-to-shoulder with her, she added brusquely, "They're bringing her in now."

Elizabeth remained motionless. The smoke from her cigarette floated upward over her coffee-hued hair before being dispersed by the early morning breeze.

"Care to explain *why* they're bringing her in?" Darby grumbled, her wild, light-blue eyes shimmering. The stench of whiskey on Darby's breath tickled Elizabeth's nostrils.

"Perhaps if you stopped clogging your mind with alcohol you could discern the answer on your own," replied Elizabeth disapprovingly. She puffed her cigarette and folded her arms again while holding the smoke in her lungs longer than usual.

"Fuck off," Darby barked as she angrily whirled around to face Elizabeth. Displaying an uncharacteristic unwillingness to defer to the Constable, she grumbled, "You're not my fucking mother."

Elizabeth exhaled and kept her eyes on the vibrant city lights. Darby's alcohol abuse was the least of her problems.

"Unfortunately, the spiritual world has taken notice of my city, and, more importantly, my daughters," explained Elizabeth dryly. Darby froze as she continued, "I never anticipated such a threat but I intend to neutralize it. Sarah appears to be the foremost authority on that world, other than my husband, and I need her knowledge of it."

"What do you plan on doing?" Darby asked slowly, her pact with Marcion foremost in her mind.

"Forming a task force to handle *spiritual* problems," responded Elizabeth. She took a final drag from her cigarette and heedlessly tossed it off the balcony.

"That little demonic bitch's not coming back," reasoned Darby, "so why go to the trouble?"

Elizabeth turned to her sister with determined eyes. Darby gazed on her quizzically.

"Jacob will be my only loss in my war with her and I'll protect my chil-," Elizabeth's voice wavered before she composed herself and continued, "*children* at all costs. If he returns to the city, his demon whore will undoubtedly be at his side. It may only be a matter of time."

· · · ·

JACOB STARTED AS HIS eyes popped open. His mind and heart raced while a searing, burning pain radiated up from the pit of his stomach and into his chest cavity. Instantly and bizarrely cognizant of Elizabeth's absence, an acute panic struck him. His legs tingled with paresthesia as fears of her infidelity plagued his reeling consciousness.

Due to his disoriented state, several seconds passed before he realized that he dozed off while sitting against a gnarled tree. A nocturnal chorus of boisterous insects filled the air with a multitude of chirps, clicks and calls. Blowing in a strange manner, the wind rushed amidst the tree tops before dying completely and then rushing forward once again. Darkness reigned.

A rogue gust of wind swirled around Jacob and ushered in a new sense of trepidation. He sensed another presence lurking in the star-tinged darkness, an oddly-inviting yet chilling centripetal force. Ba'al Zeboul, the Lord of Demons, had moved another pawn into the game and Jacob knew it.

"'What is your name?'" Jacob demanded in the words of Jesus as his heart anxiously thumped within his chest. (Excerpt from the Gospel of Luke 24:39). He scanned the vicinity but his eyes detected nothing. The absence of physicality confirmed his suspicion that a demon prowled the blackness around him and he demanded again, "'What is your name?'"

Several tense seconds of silence passed. Jacob shivered.

"How do you know that I'm a demon?" replied a seductive-yet-sinister female voice, its tone both youthful and wise.

"'. . . a spirit does not have flesh and bones,' and your appearance is not 'like lightning,' nor your clothing as 'white as snow,'" Jacob said knowingly as his fear lessened. (Excerpts from the Gospels of Luke 8:30 and Matthew 28:2). He demanded a third time with burgeoning confidence, "'What is your name?'"

"*Assarion*," admitted the wavering voice reluctantly. Jacob's initial astonishment at the demon's obedience prompted a bemused smile. His fear completely subsiding, he rose to his feet, dusted himself off and gazed in the direction of the voice.

"So, are you worth two sparrows?" Jacob queried.

"Are you worth many sparrows?" sniped Assarion in reply. Jacob's smile widened. He was intrigued by her familiarity with the Gospel of Matthew but his smile evaporated when she quoted the exact Gospel passage, the demon stating with conceit, "Or should I say 'So do not fear; you are more valuable than many sparrows.'" (The Gospel of Matthew 10:31).

"It doesn't cause you any pain," Jacob remarked. Dumbfounded and frightened at the comfort with which Assarion referenced the words of Christ, he said aloud, "That's not good."

"We may hate Him but we're obedient when He requires it, just like the Gerasene demoniac who bowed before Christ," answered Assarion. She continued in a conflicted tone, "And that obedience sometimes comes with abilities not possessed by others of our kind. Your precious Miriam possesses such abilities, does she not?"

The image of Miriam arose in Jacob's mind. He contemplated her inimitable nature as well as the jealous rage that would ensue if she knew of his demonic encounter. Wary but intrigued, Jacob decided to briefly delve deeper into the enigma that was Assarion.

"So that which is holy causes you no pain?" Jacob inquired with great interest.

"None whatsoever," said Assarion, "and, in that way, I'm unlike Miriam. By the way, how's Miriam's . . . *instruction* proceeding?"

Jacob looked away.

"She'll find her way. . . eventually," Jacob assured Assarion though his tone betrayed his uncertainty.

"Of course," said Assarion, "but then again, remember your Lord's words, Jacob:

> 'Do not give what is holy to dogs, and do not throw your pearls before swine, or they will trample them under their feet, and turn and tear you to pieces.'" (The Gospel of Matthew 7:6).

A stunned Jacob shivered as another rogue gust of wind rushed past him. "Assarion?" he called out. Shaken, he bellowed, "*Assarion!*"

Doubt crept into Jacob's troubled mind as he realized he no longer sensed Assarion's presence. He searched the vicinity with quick, side-to-side jerks of his head but saw nothing.

"Fuck!" he uttered in frustration.

• • • •

THE COMMOTION OF AN unseen creature stumbling clumsily through the forest chased Assarion from Jacob's mind. He swiftly ducked behind a tree.

"Mother fucker!" cursed a male voice with a pained groan. Jacob peered around the tree guardedly as a pot-bellied man staggered into view holding his lifeless left arm. He wore only a stained white t-shirt and tattered jeans. Perspiring, blood-stained and battered, he labored to breathe.

"Come here, widdle pigwet," Miriam called out wickedly, her voice so chillingly evil that Jacob shuddered. The man whirled around, lost his balance and plummeted to the forest floor.

"AHH! Fuck!" bellowed Miriam's victim as he landed on his broken left arm. He moaned in agony and struggled to stand.

"Oh, widdle pigwet fell down," Miriam mockingly pouted, her demonic voice interspersed with her human one. She materialized next to the man, the *daimoniou* perched upon a rock despite wearing knee-high, black-leather boots. Reaching down, Miriam deftly plucked out the man's left eye. He screamed and applied pressure to his eye socket with his right hand.

"Don't be so fucking dramatic," Miriam admonished him as if he carped about a paper cut. She brought the man's eyeball to her face. Wiggling it about on her clawed finger, she accidentally flung it to the forest floor. She giggled like a child and exclaimed, "Oh, shit!"

"Mirry!" scolded Jacob as he approached her purposefully. Surveying Miriam's handiwork with abhorrence, Jacob stated, "That's enough."

Miriam hopped off the rock and landed next to the man. She grabbed him by the hair and lifted his head as he screamed.

"Jake, meet Kirwan," Miriam said. Jacob turned his head slightly and grimaced in disgust. Blood trickled down Kirwan's face from his oozing, empty eye socket as Miriam explained, "This is the fucker who Agatha wanted to take you to Hanahan. Isn't that right, widdle pigwet?"

Miriam shook Kirwan harshly but he lapsed into unconsciousness. Perturbed at his lack of cooperation, Miriam shoved him face-first into the dirt.

"Then why the hell are you torturing him?" queried Jacob in irked disbelief. Miriam grinned devilishly and spun like a top into Jacob's arms.

"Because he works for Agatha and I don't trust that cunt," Miriam snarled in her full demonic voice. Tapping her fingers rhythmically on Jacob's cheek, she added in her human tone, "Besides, I know evil, Jake, and *he* is evil."

Jacob took Miriam by her arms and pulled her into his body, his serious eyes entrancing her. Startled by his conviction, she failed to resist.

"'But love your enemies, and do good and lend, expecting nothing in return; and your reward will be great, and you will be sons of the Most High; for He Himself is kind to ungrateful and evil men,'" Jacob said firmly. (Excerpt from the Gospel of Luke 6:35). Disheartened by Miriam's inveterate descent into violence, he urged her, "'*Be merciful, just as your Father is merciful.*'" (The Gospel of Luke 6:36).

A suddenly-enraged Miriam screamed hideously, popped out of his arms and raised her hand to swipe at him with her deadly claws. She froze before connecting and Jacob, dumbfounded by her sudden hostility, stood wide-eyed yet still before her as his heart pounded. Assarion's words echoed portentously in his mind.

" . . . do not throw your pearls before swine, or they will trample them under their feet, *and turn and tear you to pieces*,'" she warned. (Except from the Gospel of Matthew 7:6).

Silence prevailed as neither Jacob nor Miriam moved. Stinging remorse wracked her and she looked away guiltily.

"She hasn't seen this fuck in a long time," Miriam explained while hoping to squirm out of the tension of the moment. Looking back to Jacob, she continued, "His little *cabin in the woods* no longer exists."

"So?" asked Jacob. Agatha's suspicious designs distracted him from Miriam's vitriolic outburst and he heard her parting words in his mind:

"I wouldn't trust anyone from this point on," Agatha advised.

"Not even you?" Jacob asked.

"Not even me," replied Agatha.

"So fuck you," Miriam snarled. She watched Jacob with a nervous, expectant expression much like a loyal dog uncertain of its master's intentions.

Kirwan abruptly rose and readied a desperate strike but Miriam whirled around to meet his advance. She nonchalantly ended his maneuver by grasping the top of his head with her right hand and quickly turning it one-hundred-eighty degrees. The nauseating crack of Kirwan's neck rippled past Jacob and disintegrated amidst the trees as he succumbed to a severed spinal cord. His body plunged to the ground.

"Well, so much for moral arguments today," conceded Jacob while assessing Kirwan's gruesome corpse. He exhaled in defeat, looked to the night sky and asked, "How the hell to we find Hanahan now?"

"Don't worry," Miriam droned peculiarly as if hypnotized. Jacob shot her a perplexed look. Pointing to the southeast, she uttered, "An ungrateful and evil man has shown me the way."

• • • •

ELIZABETH STRODE CONFIDENTLY down the hallway leading to the main elevators though her walk lacked its usual brisk pace. Trailing a few paces behind her sister, Darby treaded heavily with an emotionless face.

Armed guards standing on either side of the elevator door watched their approach as the doors opened. Standing in the elevator was the short, wiry Sören Walter with his intensely-blue eyes and ruddy complexion. He held a single dossier in his hand.

"Ah, Sören. I see you sleep as little as I do," Elizabeth greeted her Chief of Staff. She observed the dossier with disapprobation and said, "I take it you have the candidates for my new task force commander . . . though I certainly hope there's more than one."

"One candidate's qualifications are exemplary," responded Sören matter-of-factly. He glanced at Darby quickly before adding, "Though there may be one small problem."

Turning her head to view her sister in her peripheral vision, Elizabeth waited patiently for her to depart. Darby stared at her and stood motionless.

"Darby, would you be so kind as to excuse us for a moment?" asked a perturbed Elizabeth.

"I'll take the fucking stairs," grumbled Darby as she rolled her eyes. Elizabeth stepped onto the elevator with Sören and, seconds later, the doors closed. He offered her the dossier but she raised her hand to refuse it.

"Darius?" Elizabeth inquired with a slight grin. Sören watched the light dance in Elizabeth's eyes as she conjured up old images of Darius in her mind. Her cheeks flushed faintly.

"He's currently commanding officer of the exterior zones," answered Sören. Tucking the dossier under his left arm, he said, "He prefers the anonymity and the less stringent oversight of operating outside the walls."

"I know, very much like my husband," Elizabeth remarked flippantly with a sigh, the thought of Jacob's exploits outside the city shattering the images of Darius. Sören absorbed her comment but failed to respond. Elizabeth then queried in a businesslike manner, "Have you spoken to him yet?"

"Yes, and he is amenable to reassignment," said Sören. The elevator doors opened as he added, "He will be in your office at 10:00 a.m."

Elizabeth held out her hand. Sören retrieved the dossier from underneath his arm and handed it to her.

"Make it 1:00 *p.m.*, please," she instructed respectfully. She grinned weakly and said, "I intend to have breakfast with my daughters later and, hopefully, get a little sleep."

. . . .

ELIZABETH SPUN HER wedding ring around her pale finger as she fondly recalled memories of her relationship with Darius. His dossier lay on the table in front of her with several pictures of him scattered on its surface. Her uglier battles with Jacob occasionally kindled a desire to reconnect with Darius though she successfully squelched the urge.

Reclining in a black, leather chair in her situation room, she allowed herself to relax and drift into her younger years. She wallowed safely in the bosom of the Mount Borgia bunker complex like a bubble bath, the Constable protected from the outside world by layer-upon-layer of impenetrable steel.

Dusky, blue neon lighting ran the circuit of the room and eerily illuminated the floor, walls and ceiling. Two flat screen televisions lined the walls on either side of it, their screens alternating views from cameras placed throughout Kaiser. A projector unit hung from the ceiling above a large, rectangular black table surrounded by smaller leather chairs.

Daydreams of Darius vanished as the locking mechanism of the reinforced-steel doors clunked and buzzed. Elizabeth quickly shoved the pictures of Darius into the dossier and closed it as the doors methodically slid open.

A guard dressed in full tactical gear entered with Sarah attached to his muscular right arm. The Ursuline was shockingly attired in a black Gothic uniform, her outfit consisting of a tight, ankle-length skirt, leather gloves and a battered, ripped leather jacket with two parallel rows of ruffles running down its front. Black leather straps, complete with silver buckles and rings, wrapped themselves around her arms above and below her bare elbows.

Sarah slicked back her hair and concealed her olive skin with white makeup. Black lipstick and eye shadow on each eyelid starkly contrasted with her artificial pastiness.

"Why on earth are you dressed like that?" chastised Elizabeth. Inexplicably unsteady as the guard guided her behind the Constable's chair, Sarah's deep, blue eyes, now dilated and inert, stared forward as if she were blind. The guard seated Sarah at the table to Elizabeth's right and departed. She errantly attempted to place her arms on the arm rests, her arms finally sliding inward and onto her lap.

"As I once told you, Constable, the slums are rife with the sick," Sarah answered brusquely. Turning her countenance towards Elizabeth but seeing only a hazy, blue blur, she continued, "The Gothic gangs only allow their own kind in their neighborhoods. If I wish to preach the Gospel there, I must dress as the Goths do, so to speak."

"I see," Elizabeth said with disinterest. The women sat in silence for thirty seconds with neither one venturing a single word. Altering her tack, Elizabeth broke the silence first by saying, "Given our history, this isn't easy for me to admit but . . . I'm in need of your services."

"*You* are in need of *my* services?" queried Sarah in disbelief. Blinking repeatedly, she grinned and said, "I assure you, I'm of no value to you."

"Oh, I beg to differ, Sarah," Elizabeth countered, "because I have a demonic problem and you've proven yourself quite adroit at dealing with demons."

Sarah leaned back in her chair. Her smile dimmed and she sighed heavily.

"I don't know where they went," Sarah stated while defiantly staring forward. She steeled herself against the beating certain to follow.

"But I do," broke in Agatha arrogantly with a sly smile, her abrupt appearance causing Sarah to tense. The nun's eyes anxiously darted to Agatha despite her obscured vision. She said nothing.

Agatha stood alone in the situation room doorway. Clad in a shiny, lime-green sport coat, a black blouse and black slacks, her eyes mimicked the apparent blindness demonstrated by Sarah. She entered the room with surprising steadiness given her obscured sight and bulk and seated herself in the chair to Elizabeth's left. Agatha asked glibly, "Ever heard of Bernie Kunar?"

The situation room doors closed. Elizabeth shot Agatha a dirty look.

"Bernie Kunar," Elizabeth repeated with irritation. Bitterness rolled off her tongue as she elucidated, "Beloved former city councilman, absolute fool and hopeless alcoholic. I imprudently accepted him into my administration to appease the public. But Bernie Kunar is dead. What could he possibly have to do with my husband's whereabouts?"

"You were never regaled with his tales of the 'hedonistic haven at Hanahan?'" laughed Agatha boisterously. She rolled her chair out from the table and spun it around once. Elizabeth sighed in mild frustration but smirked.

"Oh, yes,' Elizabeth said, "many, many times. He claimed Hanahan was a small town just outside my territory that supported a huge casino long before the fall and, amazingly, was still in operation. Naturally, I didn't believe him. His little disappearances were blackouts and benders, *not* visits to Hanahan as he insisted."

"Well, Liz, I gotta tell ya," interjected Agatha. She indulged in a pregnant pause before uttering, "*It exists.*"

"Of course it does," Elizabeth muttered while rolling her eyes.

"She speaks the truth," interjected Sarah solemnly. Agatha's smugness evaporated as the color drained from her pudgy face. Puzzled, Elizabeth scowled.

"How would you know?" Elizabeth snapped while glowering at Sarah.

"I've been sifting through my sister's lies for decades," Sarah replied as Agatha winced at the revelation.

"Sisters. How fascinating," Elizabeth commented blithely. She glanced sidelong at Agatha, noted her chubby countenance, narrowed her eyes and then looked back to Sarah's lean face. She taunted disinterestedly, "Let me guess, *half*-sisters."

Agatha fumed but remained silent. Sarah merely stared at her blurry form.

"You're both wasting my time," Elizabeth complained, the Constable brushing aside her newfound knowledge of the kinship of Sarah and Agatha. Her patience wavering, she tersely queried, "Where's my husband?"

"I sent him to Hanahan," Agatha explained with renewed smugness.

"And you did so why?" Elizabeth asked while pushing the fingertips of her left hand into her forehead. Weariness weighed on her heavily and diluted her ire.

"You may not like your husband, but I do," replied Agatha. She gestured and said, "I thought I'd do that poor drunken bastard a favor, especially given that he paid me two grand to do it."

Sarah's demeanor chilled, an unexpected negative energy rushing over her like an unforgiving arctic wind. Elizabeth and Agatha felt troubled as her dark mood washed over them.

"It would be best for all of us if he never arrives there," Sarah warned.

2

ELIZABETH, FOREVER seeking ways to ensure the loyalty of her officers and VIPs, transplanted an entire upscale Irish pub onto the grounds of the mansion. Maintaining the dark wood interior but removing the Irish elements of the tavern, she established the Kaiser Officers' Club. Works of colorless or deeply earth-toned art replaced its former Irish memorabilia, the paintings and sculptures flavoring the room with class and sophistication.

The center of the rectangular, one-room pub housed its sizeable kitchen and storage areas. Great, dark wood walls enclosed the kitchen with immense mirrors and lighted, glass liquor shelves affixed to their outward faces. Interrupted occasionally by entryways leading into the kitchen, a bar surrounded the kitchen structure. Beyond the rows of high-backed bar chairs, square, four-person tables dominated the remainder of the room. Tinted windows of bulletproof glass permitted filtered sunlight to illuminate the pub.

A drunken Darby, currently the club's only patron, clumsily grabbed the whiskey bottle in front of her and filled her glass again. Most of the remaining whiskey spilled onto the bar but she managed to fill her glass three-quarters full. Closing one eye, she lifted the bottle and peered into it. The realization that it was empty prompted her to grimace and hurl it over the sea of tables. The bottle struck a window and shattered.

"Get mea . . . a-anotha' . . . fuckin' boddle!" she demanded, Elizabeth's sister barking slurred orders to an audience of assorted liquor bottles on the wall behind the bar. Nearly toppling over, she rotated her chair towards the windows.

"Well aren't we a crunken dunt," snickered Marcion mockingly, the demon appearing on top of the bar wearing a ridiculous bartender's outfit complete with an orange vest, a white dress shirt and an orange bowtie. Darby fell out of her chair and barrel rolled before leaping up as she drew her fifty-caliber pistol and aimed it at Marcion. Standing on the bar, he meticulously polished a beer stein with a white towel. He cackled and added, "And in the morning no less!"

Darby searched her mind for the vilest possible words while she squinted and attempted to focus on Marcion's blurry image. She struggled to hold her firearm stationary.

"Wha' the fuck . . . d'you want?" Darby responded with difficulty. She stifled a belch and then hiccupped. Frustrated with her inability to hold her pistol steady, she clumsily holstered it and uttered, "Fucker."

Darby stumbled back to the bar, slumped into her chair, grasped her glass and took a long drink. Marcion sneered. Hurling her drink at him, she demanded, "When're we killin' J-Jacob?"

Marcion remained motionless and let the glass pass innocuously through his body. It shattered on the mirror and left behind a large crack.

"Soon, very soon," Marcion said coldly as he set the beer stein down on the bar next to him. Throwing the towel over his shoulder, he urged her, "But we, and by *we* I mean *you*, need to get the ball rolling by getting Lady Lizzie to Hanahan."

"She ain't goin' tuh H-Huh," Darby said before suppressing another belch. Her eyes narrowing, she managed to say, "Hanahan."

"What?!" chirped Marcion in a high-pitched whine. He kicked the beer stein which tipped over on its side, rolled off the bar and hit the floor with a thud. Marcion griped, "Why not? Isn't she going after Gottschalk?!"

"*No*," answered Darby. She yawned. Poorly imitating Elizabeth's prim and proper mannerisms and speech, Darby said with waning success, "She is, is waitin' for *him* to come to *her*. And she, she dudn't believe it, it exists . . . either."

Marcion lowered his head and wobbled as if he would fall. His countenance became bleak, the *daimoniou* seemingly feeding on and dimming the light in the pub. Darby quivered uncomfortably as negative spiritual energy inundated her. Recovering and standing up straight, Marcion quietly considered his options before a slow smile came to his face.

"*I'll* get her to Hanahan," he ordered in a peculiar demonic tone. Darby furrowed her brow as he directed her, "*You* just have that accident ready to go."

• • • •

TRAILING MIRIAM AS she meandered into the burgeoning dawn, Jacob let his mind meander into the past. He could no longer play the memory as if it were a recording: he simply recalled the image of a pretty face, an engaging smile, the romantic tension and the exhilarating, gentle touch of teenage breasts on his forearm. Jacob failed to act at that pivotal moment, to risk all and make a play for the most popular girl in high school.

"*Risk all*," he rebuked himself while remembering the alluring charm of that buxom, blonde girl and how she overwhelmed the awkward, insecure teenager that he was. He coveted those adolescent feelings of insecurity and wished to substitute them for the adult feelings of insecurity he possessed now.

"Am I beautiful," Miriam cooed before her tone dipped sorrowfully, "or am I hideous?"

Miriam's treacherous words shattered Jacob's reverie. She continued to walk forward, the demon feigning a lack of concern over his reply.

"So how much farther is this fucking place?" asked Jacob while pretending that Miriam's words never reached his ears. Exhausted, he grumbled, "We've been walking for hours."

Miriam shrieked, lunged to her right and punched a tree, its trunk exploding like a shattering toothpick. The upper portion of the tree plummeted to earth and crashed to the ground between them. Awestruck, Jacob stared blankly at Miriam as she glared at him.

"You fucking heard me and you fucking know it," snarled Miriam, her monstrous voice bleeding into her human one. She bounded onto the fallen tree with demonic precision and looked down upon him. Recovering from his shock, Jacob defiantly yet unsteadily climbed onto the trunk. He managed to stand and retain his balance.

"What the fuck's your problem?" queried Jacob as he gestured angrily. Steadying himself, he barked, "Ya' wanna can the rage for a while?"

Miriam lowered her head and watched Jacob with immoral eyes. She smirked deviously.

"Am . . . I . . . beautiful?" she demanded in her demonic tone.

Jacob's umbrage vanished after several tense, quiet seconds. He stifled a grin.

"Not right now," he quipped. A quizzical expression flashed across Miriam's face and she lifted her head. Fighting off an embarrassed grin, she turned away from him to hide it. Jacob chuckled and wisecracked, "Eh, let's just fuck and get it over with."

He tensed as Miriam whirled around to face him. Wild glints of elation and fear flashed in her jet eyes and intensified into two brilliant pinpricks of light.

Miriam and Jacob watched each other with great uncertainty, the pair simultaneously fearing and yearning for their first sexual tryst. The opportunity, though an imperfect one, was nonetheless real: they were alone and without threat of interruption.

Miriam stepped forward first and then Jacob followed suit. A few seconds passed before they moved closer to one another, Jacob affectionately placing his hands on the curves of Miriam's hips. She, in turn, lovingly placed her hands on his chest. Hesitant but steady, they moved their faces ever closer. Miriam tilted her head to the right, not in her usual, animalistic manner, but in a fluid, sensual motion. Closing her eyes, she raised herself onto her tiptoes and prepared for their lips to caress.

Jacob suddenly became conscious of the weight of his wedding ring on his finger. Pangs of guilt instantaneously riddled him and he aborted their kiss. Miriam's eyes popped open.

"Mirry, I can't do this, not now," confessed Jacob. He loathed the thought of hurting Miriam but was unable to break his wedding vows. Troubled by the prospect of irrevocably marring his marriage to Elizabeth, he said, "I'm just not ready yet."

Miriam's left hand grasped Jacob's shirt as she placed her right hand on the back of his head. She forcibly and unemotionally pulled him towards a kiss. Jacob struggled against her advance to no avail.

"Damn it, Mirry, no . . . *please*," pleaded Jacob. Holding him fast, she avoided his lips at the last possible second. Sliding her cheek against Jacob's face, she lightly nibbled his ear with her teeth and then increased the pressure of her bite. Jacob ceased struggling and whispered, "*Stop.*"

Miriam nuzzled his neck and bit it gently but failed to break the skin. Chills rippled down Jacob's spine as Miriam embraced him.

"You're *mine* now, Jake," Miriam cooed into his ear, the demon seducing Jacob with a honeyed tone. Her demonic voice interspersed with her human one, she said determinedly, "I love you, and no one will ever take you away from me. *Ever*. If Elizabeth tries to get you back, I'll crush her fucking pelvis so she can't walk, and while she lies there, screaming, bleeding, I'll start cutting open her veins, one by one. I'll watch her bleed to death while I slowly slice open her eyes, and tear off her fingers and toes, and peel off her skin."

Miriam nuzzled Jacob's neck again and cuddled into him. Horrified and nauseated by Miriam's vehement malice, he trembled.

"Your marriage ended when you left Kaiser," Miriam advised firmly. Taking his chin in her right hand, she guided Jacob's frightened gaze to her loving countenance and stated slowly, "You don't have to be faithful to her anymore."

The dazzling light of the morning sun clawed its way through the foliage. Miriam glanced to the East before looking back to Jacob and patting him on the cheek.

"You'll have to wait, though, my love," she explained, her intensity inexplicably waning. She hopped off the tree trunk and said, "We need to go a little farther today."

• • • •

ELIZABETH SUNK HER teeth into the buttery toast and savored its warmth and its flavor. Conscious of her diet to a fault, she rarely indulged in unhealthy eating. She feasted this morning, however, the Constable celebrating the special occasion of her first meal with her daughters in many days.

The smell of bacon, sausage, eggs and pancakes wafted throughout a breakfast nook which exhibited the charm and decoration of a farmhouse kitchen. Country knickknacks titivated the shelves and walls while the window dressings resembled colorful quilts. The nook, the antitheses of Elizabeth's tastes, mimicked a soothing remnant of her own childhood. She, Vanessa and Mallory occupied three of four chairs surrounding an antique table.

Elizabeth ordered the construction of the nook to provide her daughters with a homey, normal place to eat, the family often forsaking the lavish and cavernous dining rooms of the mansion. Built on the second level, it faced Mount Borgia. The positioning allowed in the light of day while shielding it from the threat of ranged attacks from the city.

"I need to speak to the both of you," volleyed Elizabeth after sipping her coffee. Jacob's departure was foremost on her mind.

"This room is ridiculous," Vanessa inquired bitingly before popping a piece of bacon into her mouth. Vanessa, Elizabeth's nineteen-year-old daughter and a carbon copy of her mother, rolled her eyes and asked, "Why the fuck do we still eat in here?"

"Vanessa!" scolded Elizabeth while setting down her coffee cup in its saucer with a clank. Conveying her displeasure via a withering look, Elizabeth stated, "*Unacceptable*."

Mallory, Elizabeth's petite and precocious seventeen-year-old, watched her mother in anticipation of her answer. The olive-skinned teenager possessed deep brown eyes and wispy, light-brown hair.

"I'm an adult, mother," Vanessa grumbled while being unaffected by her mother's criticism. Letting her ire fade and with an odd gleam in her eyes, she inquired, "Where's Jake?"

Elizabeth's heart bled. She knew she balanced precariously at the edge of her daughters' adulthood. She expected them to react strongly to the news of Jacob's departure. Pressured by her daughters' emotional distress and feeling trapped, she resorted to one of her specialties: propaganda.

"I didn't want to tell you this but Jacob is missing," Elizabeth expounded while funneling her inner turmoil over Jacob's departure into her deception. The gleam in Vanessa's eyes became fear and two worried faces studied Elizabeth carefully. She elaborated slowly and gravely, "There've been several terrorist attacks recently and I believe the insurgents were targeting Jacob. It's possible he was kidnapped."

Vanessa's worried expression deepened but Mallory successfully fought off her concern and became stone-faced. The untruths Elizabeth told her children undoubtedly hurt them. Those untruths, however, were necessary evils and shields to protect them from the horrible reality of a crumbling marriage and a usurping denizen of the spiritual realm.

"Why would they take Jake?" asked Vanessa with the slightest hint of tears in her eyes. She trembled.

"You're lying," Mallory said while lifting a glass of orange juice to her lips and gulping from it. Setting the glass on the table, she bitingly stated, "You two broke up and you kicked him out of the city. I know *all* about Lady Lizzie and her drunken fool."

Elizabeth abruptly rose to her feet, nimbly rounded the table and smacked Mallory across the face. Vanessa flinched as Elizabeth's palm connected with her sister's skin.

"Don't ever use that name again," snarled Elizabeth. She scowled and demanded, "Where did you hear it?"

"From me," remarked a robust female voice, its tone mature and saturated with immodesty. Tara Nicks strode into the room with Elizabeth's supreme confidence and Darby's intimidating aura. The sisters clearly derived their height from their mother as Tara stood a svelte five-foot-nine-inches tall. Her daughters possessed more defined musculature but Tara still sported a long, lean physique that defied the ravages of the aging process. She stated with a smirk, "Of course, your dalliances are certainly no secret in this city. Everyone knows about Lady Lizzie and her penchant for cycling through men."

Elizabeth fumed, her face turning red due to wrath and embarrassment. Her mother reveled in her response.

"Given recent events, I thought you could use a little help from Mommy," said Tara. Her vibrant eyes did not penetrate those upon whom she gazed but instead her corneas served as veils obscuring the machinations of her cunning mind. Tara's countenance was an exquisite painting, beautiful yet static, with an elegant nose terminating in a quaint point. She shared Elizabeth's soft, pale skin but her hair was dirty-blonde.

"You're supposed to be in retirement, Mother," Elizabeth chastised her. Tara ignored the rebuke.

"Is that so?" countered Tara as flames erupted in Elizabeth's eyes. Spreading her arms in anticipation of her granddaughters' eager embraces, Tara said, "Now, girls, how about a hug for the sexiest grandma on earth?"

• • • •

THE CLANG OF JACOB closing the cumbersome metal door boomed like thunder and rumbled down the defunct, cylindrical drainage tunnel. He and Miriam stood on a platform at its head, the chamber comprised entirely of rectangular, gray stone blocks. Many of the blocks were discolored, some of them greenish with moss and others blackish with water damage.

Two flights of eight steps on either side of the platform led down to narrow walkways that hugged the walls. The tunnel, which encompassed a stagnant river of murky, green water, eventually curved to the left and out of sight.

A rectangular shaft set in the ceiling permitted sunlight from the surface to dimly illuminate the tunnel. The air, though dank and musty, lacked the overwhelmingly-unpleasant smell of a sewer.

"This tunnel leads right to Hanahan," said Miriam proudly. Jacob chewed the inside of his mouth and emitted several clicks that echoed faintly down the tunnel. The prospect of journeying through it vexed him but at least, in his mind, it would shield them from prying eyes. Miriam provocatively slithered into Jacob's arms and said, "And now that we have a little more time . . . ."

Jacob acquiesced and, much to her surprise, leaned towards her. He halted a mere inch from her lips.

"What?" demanded Miriam bitterly, the demon irritated by Jacob's aborted advance. Looking over her right shoulder, he saw a thick, rusted metal door set in the discolored stone at the base of the stairs.

"Did you hear that?" Jacob queried.

"No," lied a perturbed Miriam as she tugged his arm. She felt a human presence in the room beyond the door but concealed that fact, saying in a snarky tone, "You're just hearing things. Probably alcohol withdrawal."

Jacob resisted and listened carefully. A nearly inaudible voice wafted into his ears and he nodded toward the door.

"Someone's in there," he stated firmly.

"The itsy, bitsy spider crawled up the waterspout," sang a haunting female voice, "down came the rain, and washed the spider out."

Intense curiosity welled up within Jacob. He continued to eavesdrop on the song while a frustrated Miriam pulled free of Jacob's grasp to view the door. The references to "spider" chilled her spirit and caused her to reflexively massage her spider charm between her right index finger and her thumb.

"Out came the sun and dried up all the rain," continued the voice, "and the itsy bitsy spider went up the spout again."

Jacob rushed around Miriam, descended the stairs and heedlessly approached the door. Turning the handle, he found it to be locked and rattled it. The singing ceased.

"Fucking locked," he muttered angrily with traces of desperation in his voice. He searched determinedly for a key and ran his hands over the mossy walls in an attempt to locate a false brick.

"*What in the God damn mother fucking fuck are you doing?*" asked Miriam while clenching her fists in annoyance. She knew otherwise but added nonetheless, "It's probably a fucking demon trying to sucker you in there."

Jacob ceased his search. He then glanced at Miriam.

"Mirry, I need you to open this door," Jacob said. His distress melted her resistance.

"Fucking NO!" barked Miriam incredulously, the *daimoniou* bristling and suspicious of who lurked on the other side of the door. Jacob's brilliant blue eyes caused her to scowl yet concede, "Fine. *Asshole.*"

· · · ·

PATIENTLY WAITING FOR Miriam while standing on a platform step, Jacob leaned against the wall with his arms folded. She gripped the door handle tightly with her right hand and it buckled under the immense pressure she applied to it.

"Thanks, Mirry," Jacob said with a wry grin. Miriam glowered at him before returning her attention to the handle.

"Fuck you," muttered Miriam under her breath, the *daimoniou* imagining the sound of Marcion's laughter at her newfound submissiveness to Jacob. She thought, "Little burnt bastard'd *love* this."

Miriam placed her left hand on the door just above the handle and, with a jarring, abrupt jerk, she ripped out the locking mechanism. Tossing the hardware into the river with an echoing plunk, Miriam looked to Jacob.

"Happy?" inquired Miriam as Jacob approached her with deliberate steps. She wilted under his adoring gaze as he moved to embrace her but the woman's call interrupted him.

"Who's out there?" she shouted. Jacob lifted his index finger to his lips to request Miriam's silence. She begrudgingly nodded in assent and, knowing he would wish it, she made herself invisible to all other human eyes.

"My name's Jake," Jacob replied. Warily inserting his fingers in the hole where the handle was once affixed, Jacob pulled the door outward. It creaked and caused him to pause briefly before he continued to open it. He added, "We're not going to hurt you."

"Speak for yourself," mumbled Miriam as she slithered around him and blocked his advance, Jacob's paranormal protector prepared to slaughter any creature that dared assail him. She sensed a human presence to the right side of the door and added quickly, "*Don't move.*"

Suspecting a trap, she stepped into the room. A baseball bat welcomed her but passed harmlessly through her body and hit the wall.

"Whoa!" Jacob shouted as he jumped back and nearly toppled off the walkway and into the river. Miriam hesitated for a fraction of a second due to her surprise that the wielder of the bat detected her. Deeming it coincidence, she leapt out of the room, grabbed Jacob by the sleeve and kept him from tumbling into the water. He cursed, "Fuck!"

A young woman armed with the bat appeared in the doorway, her tired eyes looking through Miriam to warily survey Jacob. The contours of her face were soft and inviting, her visage framed by unkempt, pale-blonde hair that hung just above her shoulders. She wore light-blue jeans and a snug, beige t-shirt with "◇◇◇◇ LOUNGE" printed on it.

"Go away," warned the whey-faced woman. She spurred Jacob's libido with her lean-yet-untoned frame, her curvaceous hips topped with tiny deposits of baby fat and her full, round breasts. Whirling around to depart, the woman inadvertently displayed her impeccably-sculpted-yet-squishy buttocks. Jacob's gaze dropped to her alluring posterior.

"Well, hold on a minute," objected Jacob. He stepped forward and asked, "What's your name, kiddo?"

"It's not kiddo," the woman sardonically countered. Jacob attempted to enter the room but Miriam snagged his arm and halted him.

"Where the hell do you think you're going?" protested Miriam incredulously.

"Take it easy," said Jacob as he squiggled free of Miriam's grasp and entered the room. He conducted a perfunctory scan and deadpanned, "Nice place. Live here by yourself?"

Two fixtures of long, fluorescent lightbulbs brightly lit the punctiliously-swept and cleaned room and a non-operational boiler and furnace occupied its far wall. A broom and dust pan leaned against the right wall several feet away from a narrow door that led to a tiny bathroom. Deep purple curtains hung on the left wall and a matching shag rug adorned the floor.

"I never said I lived here," the woman stated. Jacob's eyes lingered on her bosoms as they struggled against her t-shirt. Miriam seethed and skulked behind Jacob.

"Let's try this again," said Jacob while watching the woman place the bat in the corner formed by the bed and the wall. He continued, "My name's Jake. And you are?"

"Not interested, so get lost," Sophie replied while retrieving a worn backpack from under the bed. Miriam squirmed restlessly. She acutely perceived the sexual attraction Jacob felt and it enraged her.

"It's pretty dangerous out there," Jacob reasoned as he subtly nodded in the direction of the door, "and it probably wouldn't be a bad idea for you to tag along with us, at least for a little while."

The woman stopped packing her backpack with her belongings and looked to Jacob. Making no effort to hide her curiosity, she narrowed her eyes and examined his face.

"*Us?*" the woman inquired carefully. She leaned forward as she attempted to peek out the doorway and catch a glimpse of Jacob's mysterious companion.

"Don't you fucking dare," growled Miriam while rapidly shaking her head in a flurry of loose, blonde curls. She snarled, "She's *not* our problem."

"I've got a friend with me," Jacob continued despite Miriam's umbrage. Encouraged by the woman's piqued interest, he asked with an encouraging grin, "Would you like to meet her?"

• • • •

"LET'S GO, *dick bag*," ordered Miriam. Painfully aware of her foul mood, she scurried out of the room and into the tunnel with Jacob in tow.

"We're not leaving her, *vag hole*," Jacob argued in a harsh whisper intended to shield the woman from his debate with Miriam. His mind on the apparent proximity in age between the woman and his stepdaughters, he said, "She's just a kid."

"Damn it, Jake!" shouted Miriam as she shoved Jacob, the push causing him to stumble back. Her ire stoked by his dubious decision-making, she excoriated him, "Who's gonna take care of her? *You?* You can't even fucking take care of yourself!"

Jacob's countenance dimmed as the guilt of abandoning Vanessa and Mallory prickled him. He stared off into the darkness at the far end of the tunnel.

"You're absolutely right," Jacob concurred, his concession surprising Miriam. Raising his eyes to the skylight as if the light shining through it were a manifestation of God, he said, "But *He* will . . . *through* me."

"I swear, if you start that 'with God on my side' bullshit again," warned Miriam while glowering at Jacob. She slowly and angrily shook her head.

"'Truly I say to you, to the extent you did it to one of these brothers of Mine, even the least of them, you did it to me.' *I'm not leaving her*," Jacob responded staunchly. (Excerpt from the Gospel of Matthew 25:40). He paused and then added with less conviction, "And I'm going to help her. Alone if I have to."

Enraged by the content and implication of his words, Miriam smacked Jacob while lightly dragging a single claw across his face. The cut instantly bled.

"There is no *me*. There is no *you*. There is only *us*," Miriam scolded him. Her black eyes oozing with fury, love and pain, she demanded, "Don't you *ever* fucking say that again."

Sobered by Miriam's strike, Jacob raised a knuckle to the cut on his cheek. He let one drop of blood rest upon it and then pulled the knuckle away from his face to study it. A subtle grin came to his lips.

"Okay, then, you win," conceded Jacob, the thirty-five-year-old encouraged by Miriam's passionate commitment. She smugly wrinkled her nose at him to revel in the illusion of victory but he quickly shattered it by saying, "*We* are not leaving her. Now go convince her to come with us."

"What?!" exclaimed Miriam with wide eyes.

"We're negotiable," Jacob said tenderly while placing his arms on her shoulders and planting a sizzling kiss on her forehead. A stunned Miriam allowed him to maneuver her towards the doorway. Nudging her gently, Jacob added, "Taking her with us is not."

· · · ·

MIRIAM MATERIALIZED as she passed into the room, the demon feeling woozy with lovers' elation. Jacob's kiss still burned on her forehead.

"*You're* his friend?" the young woman asked. She took great interest in Miriam but was unfazed by her demonic traits.

"Yeah," muttered Miriam. The woman's acceptance of her appearance brought her out of her funk.

"I've never seen eyes like yours before," the woman stated bluntly as she moved closer to Miriam and scrutinized her demonic orbs. Reaching out as if to touch them, she caused Miriam to recoil. The woman gradually withdrew her arm.

"They used to be blue," replied Miriam while fidgeting. Despite her discomfort, the odd gravity of the woman's presence drew the truth out of her and Miriam explained as if to a child, "But I was very bad, and God punished me, and made them black."

Neither of them spoke for several seconds as the young woman pondered Miriam's account. She then stirred.

"Would God make my eyes black if I was very bad?" the woman asked with a desirous voice. She took Miriam's left hand and studied her claws. Furrowing her brow, she inquired, "Would he give me claws like these?"

Miriam repressed a smirk, her ego stoked by the woman's bizarre admiration. The tiniest shred of fondness for her arose in Miriam, the *daimoniou* momentarily forgetting her usual loathing of social interaction.

"I don't know," admitted Miriam. Never had a human expressed a desire for any of her demonic traits. She suddenly remembered the purpose of her visit and urged, "Jake wants you to come with us."

"No," the young woman stated as she shook her head in the negative. Releasing Miriam's hand and returning to her bed, she resumed packing and said without elaboration, "You should leave before Kirwan gets back."

"Kirwan?" asked Miriam with a chilling sneer. She fondly recalled her torture and slaughter of Agatha's associate. The thrill of his murder caused her spirit to tingle.

"He's my uncle," the woman advised while stuffing a flashlight into her backpack, "and he'll kill your boyfriend if he finds him here."

"I wouldn't worry about that," said Miriam in her hybrid tone. Nonchalantly walking over to the doorway, she punched a stone block in the wall adjacent to the doorframe. The force of her strike pulverized it and tore chunks out of the surrounding blocks.

"Safety in numbers, I guess," the woman said thoughtfully. She offered Miriam a quick, awkward grin, her smile simultaneously touching the good and aggravating the evil within her. The young woman reached for the baseball bat and added, "For now."

"You won't need that, uh," said Miriam, "what *is* your name, anyway?"

"Sophie," the woman answered while picking up the bat. Miriam scowled.

"Well, get your shit together, *Sophie*," Miriam demanded with bitterness on her tongue. She nodded to the door and grumbled, "We're leaving."

3

WHITE WALLS, BLACK shelving units and black marble flooring dominated the landscape of Elizabeth's office, the room able to be entered through double doors of tinted, bulletproof glass. Situated upon a sizeable rug of black-and-white concentric squares, an elaborate sitting area contained a low, square table constructed of glass and black, metal legs. Matching ergonomic chairs, two to a side, framed the long table.

Elizabeth and Tara sat across the table from each other. The Constable maintained proper posture while Tara was turned to the side with her legs crossed and her right elbow resting on the back of her chair.

"I appreciate your concern, Mother," Elizabeth stated with faint traces of suspicion in her voice. Her misgivings disappeared as she discussed her daughters, however, and she conceded, "Vanessa and Mallory would be much more accepting of my departure if you were to stay with them."

"Then there's nothing holding you back," Tara argued.

"I'm not going after Jacob myself," scoffed Elizabeth. Gesturing to make her point, she said, "I have special operations units that are quite capable of retrieving him. Besides, I'm not completely convinced you're able to govern a city of over 900,000 residents."

"It's funny how you have no problem leaving your beloved children with me but you're uneasy about placing me at the helm of your precious city," sniped Tara with a smirk. She uncrossed her legs, shifted her body to the left and crossed her legs again. Placing her left elbow on the back of her chair, she asked in a mock wounded tone, "You don't trust your own mother?"

"Managing the criminal underworld of a city is very different than managing the city itself," Elizabeth retorted, her eyes boring into Tara to underscore her seriousness. She uttered with distaste, "You can't simply 'whack' problematic citizens when your city depends on their labor. They tend to revolt. And how often have you dealt with basic sanitation, commercial development or-."

"I can play fucking Constable for few weeks," interjected Tara with a muted sneer and a feigned tone of politeness. She engaged Elizabeth in a brief optical battle before relenting with a chuckle, "You're such a hard ass, my dear."

"Frankly, I don't understand what Darby's concern is here, Mother," Elizabeth said. Peeved by Darby's interference and skeptical of her intentions, she continued, "She detests Jacob. It amazes me she wants to send *anyone* after him. But for some strange reason she believes I must participate in the operation . . . she even wants to accompany me. It's bizarre and I *don't* like it."

"Yes, it is," Tara admitted. Elizabeth, prickled by the thought of her love for Jacob, rose to her feet and walked towards the glass balcony doors. She stopped in front of them and gazed out onto the city, saying, "Though she was adamant that you should go, she couldn't give me a plausible explanation as to *why* you should go."

"Then why should I?" queried Elizabeth as she rotated around to face Tara and folded her arms. She looked to her mother expectantly.

"Something's weighing heavily on Darby, Liz," Tara explained. Uncrossing her legs and sitting up in her chair, she postulated, "She may hate Jacob but she knows you love him. Perhaps she feels partially responsible for your break up."

"As touching as that is," said Elizabeth resolutely, "it's an insufficient reason for me to leave my children and my city. I'm not going anywhere."

• • • •

AIMING HER SEMIAUTOMATIC pistol down range, Tara squeezed off three rounds. Each bullet struck the center of a target resembling the black silhouette of a man. Taking a moment to survey her accuracy, she placed the gun on the counter in front of her. She turned around and slid her ear protection down around her neck as Mallory did the same.

"There's really nothing to it, Mal," Tara explained matter-of-factly, the Constable's mother dressed casually-yet-neatly in a red, long-sleeved top and skintight black jeans.

"Mom said no fucking guns," advised Mallory gruffly. Attempting to conceal the fact that guns unnerved her, she folded her arms in defiance.

Elizabeth's disapproval of her daughters' use of firearms proved a convenient smokescreen for Mallory's dread of Tara's pistol.

"You've got quite a mouth on you," Tara remarked with a reminiscent expression and muted grin. She meticulously examined Mallory's youthful face and said with disdain, "Just like Jacob."

Suddenly retrieving her pistol, Tara ejected the magazine and thrust the gun towards Mallory. She flinched.

"You're not quite as courageous as your mother thinks, are you?" taunted Tara with a chuckle.

"Fuck you," snapped Mallory as she shoved Tara's arm away from her, the teenager embarrassed by the revelation of her fear. Tara laughed again and returned the pistol to the counter. She nonthreateningly shook the magazine at Mallory who watched her with wary eyes.

"Your mother believes - correctly, I might add - that 'fear is for those without destinies,'" Tara stated as she opened a box of bullets sitting on the counter. Pulling out three rounds, she reloaded the magazine as she spoke in a critical tone, "Yet she engenders fear in you and your sister by shielding you from the outside world. That only makes you fear it more when it arrives on your doorstep . . . and arrive it will."

"'Do not be afraid any longer, only believe,'" recited Mallory while hearing Jacob speak the words in her mind. (Excerpt from the Gospel of Mark 5:36). Despite her interest in doing so, discussing the outside world often frightened her and Christ's words soothed her young spirit.

"Another one of your mother's parenting mistakes," Tara rebuked her with a scowl. Failing to understand that Mallory's words were not meant for her ears, she uttered, "Allowing Jacob to fill your heads with that Jesus bullshit."

Tara lifted the pistol, swiftly reinserted the magazine into it and cocked it. Mallory squirmed uncomfortably as her grandmother holstered her weapon.

"Your mother thinks you're safe inside this mansion, Mal," continued Tara, "but she can't keep the outside world at bay forever and she can't keep her eyes on every threat. You must be able not only to defend yourself against those threats, but to anticipate their advances and strike at them before they strike at you."

Mallory shivered. Tara placed a reassuring hand on her petite shoulder.

"The world was a different place when you were born," Tara explained, "and, in *that* world, you could've lived the idyllic life that your mother wants for you. The world is infinitely more dangerous now. There are dangers without and dangers within."

Mallory's trepidation succumbed to her curiosity at Tara's mention of "dangers within." She cocked her head to the side.

"Dangers within?" questioned Mallory as she preyed on her grandmother's desire to shatter Elizabeth's utopian façade. Tara paused in brief contemplation of Mallory's request before grinning subtly and deviously.

"One round," Tara negotiated, the grandmother drawing her pistol, flipping it around and offering the handle to Mallory. Glancing at the gun and then back at Tara, Mallory hesitated. The deal stoked her anxiety but piqued her curiosity.

"One round," agreed Mallory. Sliding on her ear protection and steeling her will, she moved forward fluidly, whisked the gun out of Tara's hand and braced herself. Tara positioned her own ear protection.

Turning her head slightly in anticipation of the blast, Mallory pulled a trigger for the first time in her young life. Simultaneous with a muzzle flash, the pistol leapt in her tiny hands and nearly broke free of her grasp. A boom rolled down the range.

Mallory's heart thumped wildly in her chest and her entire body trembled. Setting the gun down carefully on the counter, she turned to Tara.

"*Your turn*," Mallory uttered stoically.

· · · ·

JACOB RETRIEVED AN old power bar from his jacket, partially unwrapped it and bit into it. Miriam "borrowed" a few of the chocolate-and-peanut-butter bars from Kirwan prior to torturing and slaying him. Jacob gobbled it down rapidly despite his desire for a more substantial meal and, after meticulously folding the wrapper several times, he returned it to his jacket.

He shoved his hand in his pockets and wandered down one of the walkways running along the murky river. Examining the dingy walls of tunnel and listening to the scratching and squeaking of rats just beyond his field of vision, Jacob looked back. He could no longer see the platform.

Thoughts of Miriam numbed the prickling pain of the cut on his right cheek and caused him to ignore the blood trickling from it. He sensed himself unmooring from Elizabeth, the tempest of Miriam's fierce infatuation forever dragging him into a sea of infidelity.

Guilt welled in Jacob. The bow lines connecting him to his wife frayed but he refused to permit them to break. A *thunk* echoed towards him from the head of the tunnel.

"Fuck," cursed Jacob while carelessly kicking a stone into the river. He complained, "I never should've kissed her."

"I take it you weren't expecting her to slice open your cheek in return," Assarion chimed in arrogantly, her elusive voice failing to echo or betray her location. Jacob cautiously removed his hands from his pockets and flattened himself against the tunnel wall, the intrusion chasing the *thunk* from his mind. Assarion chuckled softly and said, "I warned you."

Jacob scrutinized the tunnel and searched for physical evidence of Assarion. He found none.

"The question is, *why* did you warn me?" uttered Jacob, his words pregnant with suspicion. He stood up straight and returned his hands to his pockets. Annoyed and amused, he rocked himself onto the balls of his feet.

"That's a nasty little cut," Assarion commented with apparent concern, "and I'd hate for it to get infected."

Jacob's cut tingled and then burned, the wound corrupted by an infection that arose in seconds instead of hours. He touched it lightly and flinched. Feeling a twinge of pain and viscous pus, he instinctively wiped off his hand on the wall. His efforts only served to mix the pus with dirt and he tried to shake off the disgusting mixture.

"Fucking cunt!" snarled Jacob defiantly, his head swiveling to acquire Assarion in his vision and strike her.

"Such decadent wrath," Assarion cooed, the *daimoniou* enticed by Jacob's enragement. The evil in her tone dumbfounded him and allowed several tense seconds to elapse. Assarion then spoke in an oddly remorseful manner, saying, "My apologies, Jacob. Sometimes the evil gets the best of me. I can't help you but I know someone who can."

Assarion's presence vanished just as the overwhelming power of the Holy Spirit filled the tunnel, its appearance followed by a dazzling white light. Jacob thrust up his arm to shield his eyes. The light waned and revealed a young child with traces of a familiar, classic beauty hidden behind her adorable, childish traits. Her hair and eyes were dark but of an undeterminable hue.

Inexplicably trembling, Jacob knelt and perceived the hard, unforgiving stone pressing into his patella. The child walked forward while watching him with a virtuous precociousness and then touched his cut. The press of her small finger immediately mended the wound.

"Are you . . . ?" asked Jacob, his frail humanity unable to force the remaining words from his lips.

"'No one can serve two masters; for either he will hate the one and love the other,'" said the child, "or he will be devoted to one and despise the other.'" (Excerpt from the Gospel of Matthew 6:24).

The child and the light simultaneously disappeared.

"What the hell are you doing?" queried Miriam distrustfully. Jacob jerked his head up and glanced at her with a pale countenance. Sophie stood next to her, her baseball bat clutched in one hand and her backpack thrown over her shoulder. Perceiving Jacob's shock, Miriam rushed to him, grasped his shoulders and lifted him to his feet. She anxiously inquired, "What happened?"

"Nothing," Jacob muttered. Still awed by the apparition of the child and bewildered by her words, he trembled and stated, "Just a rat. Scared the shit out of me."

Judging by the severity of his reaction and the absence of the wound on his cheek, Miriam knew Jacob tangled with the spiritual realm. Deeming it imprudent to push the issue, she repressed her usual impulsiveness.

"Sophie's decided to come with us," advised Miriam reluctantly. Sophie showed no emotion but kept her gaze on Jacob.

"Good," uttered Jacob with difficulty.

"So let's get the hell outta here," grumbled Miriam, the demon frustrated by the circumstances. She impatiently ushered them forward and griped, "I hate this place."

• • • •

THREE EIGHTEEN-INCH, white candles, each placed in a gold candle holder on the table, flickered volatilely and then stabilized. They cast warm, inviting light around the dining room, their glow complementing the illumination provided by the dimmed, gilded chandelier. The room was dubbed the "Christmas Room" by Mallory and Vanessa in their younger years, the name prompted by its maroon walls, red maple floors and golden embellishments.

Tara sat at the head of the dining table with Mallory to her left and Vanessa to her right. The trio dined in silence, their meal interrupted only by the occasional scrape of a utensil on a plate or clink of a water glass.

"If you're finished, Vanessa, you're excused," stated Tara pointedly while watching her disinterestedly shuffle the remnants of her meal around her plate. Vanessa's eyes darted to Mallory.

"What about Mal?" Vanessa asked suspiciously, the teenager anticipating a terse response from her sister. No such response came as Mallory solemnly stared at her plate.

"Your sister and I are going to have a little talk," advised Tara. She lifted a short, stout glass to her lips and partook of its clear contents. Mallory remained silent and continued eating.

"It's about Jake, isn't it?" Vanessa questioned distrustfully, her voice quavering and her face flushing. Her body tingled.

"Of course not, Vanessa," assured Tara with a sympathetic grin. She dabbed the corners of her mouth with a red cloth napkin and returned it to her lap. Vanessa engaged in an optical battle with Tara, the nineteen-year-old brooding over her grandmother's reassurances. Tara clenched her jaw in frustration and barely restrained the verbal lashing brewing on the tip of her tongue.

"It's okay, 'Ness," Mallory said with an unusually serious and empathetic look. Speaking with the authority of an adult, she added, "Just give us a little while. I'll be up in a bit, I promise."

Mallory glanced at her sister with a look that conveyed a full report on the conversation would be forthcoming. Vanessa considered her sister's expression and then returned a muted grin.

"Fine," conceded Vanessa as she rose to her feet and tossed her napkin onto her plate. Sauntering off in a tiny jean skirt and a sleeveless blue top that revealed her cleavage, she soon vanished through the dining room doors. Tara watched her depart in disgust.

"And now that the slut is gone . . . ," Tara said with a sneer. She focused on Mallory and, absorbing her granddaughter's stinging, disapproving glance, asked, "Why don't we discuss the *dangers within*?"

• • • •

VANESSA SQUIGGLED OUT of her little skirt, tossed it to the floor of her bedroom and plopped onto her four-poster bed. She neglected to turn on her lamp, the teenager content with the light shining into her bedroom from the living room of her suite. Her skimpy, black panties clung to her pale skin and revealed most of her buttocks.

Quiet permeated the second floor of the mansion, the silence interrupted only by the faint footfalls of mansion guards traversing the stairs and the occasional gurgle of her dinner digesting. She reached out and grasped a blue pillow, pulled it to her chest and embraced it.

"Grandma's such a cunt," Vanessa complained, the nineteen-year-old disregarding her mother's constant preaching on the subject of profanity. She muttered, "Now I know where Aunt Darby gets it."

Rolling onto her stomach as she flung the pillow to the floor, Vanessa closed her eyes and sighed. The haze of sleep engulfed her as she stewed over Tara. Her thoughts turned to Jacob, her conscious mind passing her desire for him into her unconsciousness. Vanessa's nipples hardened and she became wet as they rendezvoused in her dreams.

Marcion appeared on Vanessa's bed, the demon ominously looming over her and inspecting her attractive body with his malicious, bulging eyes. His arms hung harmlessly at his sides, one half of his horribly burned body obscured by shadow, the other half dimly illuminated by the light filtering into Vanessa's bedroom. The weak glow crept into the nooks and crannies of Marcion's charred flesh.

"Fucking Aaron, always meddling, always seeking the Master's favor," Marcion growled. He stood perfectly still and continued to observe Vanessa for several minutes as she slept. A wellspring of selfish pride arose in him and he announced shrilly, "I'll do it *my* way! They'll see. *My way!*"

Marcion abruptly pounced on Vanessa. Using his momentum to drive her into the bedspread, he wrapped a disfigured arm around her head and covered her mouth with his hand. Vanessa's eyes popped open and she screamed in terror but Marcion's hand muffled her cries.

Undulating his body like a serpent, Marcion forced himself upon Vanessa as if raping her. She continued to scream through her tears and struggled to escape. Unable to break free from Marcion's demonic grasp, she hyperventilated.

"That's it," Marcion encouraged Vanessa, the *daimoniou* feigning compassion. He continued to rhythmically slam his body downward and use the force of his thrusts to discombobulate her. Consumed with panic and fright, Vanessa's hyperventilation intensified and she lost consciousness. Marcion plunged into her three additional times before ceasing his assault and gently guiding her face-first into her comforter.

"You're going to help me knock Aaron from his pedestal," uttered Marcion chillingly as he allowed his body to descend onto Vanessa. Attaching himself to her with his arms and legs, he added, "And it'll be a long fall."

Marcion's gruesome body rapidly swelled and contorted, his burnt flesh blackening and decomposing with outlandish hisses and sizzles. His mouth gradually opened, his maw widening so far beyond human capability that the joints of his jaw snapped. A brown, viscous substance oozed from his mouth and nose.

Marcion's body hissed a final time as Vanessa's eyes opened. They resembled polished, black marbles. Throwing off the corpse like a blanket, she stood up and examined herself with delight. Vanessa desirously ran her pale hands over her nubile teenage form.

"No more fucking burnt jokes, *bastards*!" Marcion squealed happily in his own voice, his smile revealing jagged-yet-healthy teeth.

Marcion's head quickly snapped to the side as the suite door opened. A deep, powerful male voice summoned his victim.

"Vanessa? You all right?" it called out.

· · · ·

ELIZABETH PERSONALLY selected her mansion guards with great care, the Constable meticulously investigating their qualifications, backgrounds and personalities. She subjected them to exhaustive interviews and never made a final decision without first seeking Sören's unbiased opinion. She even permitted Darby to intimidate the guards with veiled threats as, to her, Darby's unrelenting retribution seemed an effective insurance policy against treachery.

Blake Gustuvson passed Elizabeth's gauntlet with unanimous approval. Darby found it unnecessary to indirectly coerce him and even Jacob maintained a cordial relationship with him. A handsome, masculine and married father of two children, Gustuvson guarded Vanessa and Mallory as if they were his own daughters and often doubled in the role of concerned caregiver. Elizabeth, therefore, assigned him permanently to the mansion levels where she, Jacob and her daughters lived.

Gustuvson peered around the suite's entry door, the Constable's minion worried by Vanessa's failure to respond to his initial inquiry.

"Vanessa?" he called out again.

"I'm in my room," answered Vanessa after a long pause. A few more seconds passed before she added in a blatantly-seductive tone, "You can come in if you want."

Gustuvson's intuition prickled him and he laid his hand on his firearm. He entered the suite and slowly closed the door. Looking into Vanessa's room, he saw no one.

"Everything okay?" asked Gustuvson with a troubled expression. He cautiously walked down the hallway towards Vanessa's room, his hand still on his semi-automatic pistol. Faint traces of a putrid smell entered his nostrils.

"Yeah," Vanessa answered with uncharacteristic curtness. Gustuvson stopped in her doorway. She sat at her dressing table and methodically brushed her hair.

"Why're you sitting in the dark, kid?" inquired Gustuvson, the guard puzzled but attributing Vanessa's weird behavior to teenage hormones. He let his hand fall from his weapon. The nauseating smell burgeoned inside her room and prompted Gustuvson to inquire, "And what's that smell?"

"Why do you ask so many stupid fucking questions?" Vanessa queried sharply. Gustuvson thought he detected an atypical whine in her tone. Vanessa continued brushing her hair.

"Hey, watch your language, young lady," chastened Gustuvson, his patriarchal instincts flaring. He flicked on the light switch and marched over to Vanessa to further rebuke her. Her disheveled bedding momentarily distracted him as he walked closer, the bedspread appearing as if it concealed someone. Regaining his senses, he questioned, "Are you hiding someone in here?"

Gustuvson froze when he saw two obsidian-hued orbs staring into the mirror adhered to the wall. Vanessa glanced up at him via the mirror and smiled evilly to reveal her razor-sharp teeth.

"Oh, you're good," Vanessa said in Marcion's voice, the demon feigning that he was impressed. He continued, "You're very, very good!"

Marcion lunged at Gustvuson with blinding speed, grasped his shirt collar and tie and thrust the hairbrush into his throat. Gustuvson gagged on the hairbrush for several seconds and struggled wildly before Marcion impatiently thrust it through the back of his skull. Retrieving his hand, Marcion allowed Gustuvson to slump heavily to the floor.

"Nothing like a murder and a kidnapping to get the ball rolling!" cried Marcion amid hideous cackling. Viewing Gustuvson with contempt, he tossed the bloody hairbrush onto his chest and shuddered as if attempting to shake off the violence to which he resorted. He then dematerialized and ventured back into the spiritual world.

• • • •

"HOLY FUCK!" EXCLAIMED Darby while holding her shirt over her nose and mouth to avoid the abhorrent smell of decomposing flesh. Breaking free of her astonishment, she rushed to Gustuvson's dead body. She lamented, "Aw, fuck, not Gustuvson."

Looking to Vanessa's bed, she observed a swollen, blackened foot protruding from her bedspread. Panicked and disgusted, she swiftly ripped it off the bed and revealed Marcion's former, grisly host. A sudden hiss of gas expelled from the horrid body briefly paralyzed her.

"Marcion, you fucking asshole," Darby grumbled. Looking to the ground behind her, she noticed that she left boot prints in Vanessa's carpet. She turned back to the corpse and shouted, "Fuck!"

Darby's gaze fell on Vanessa's white, wooden dressing table which contained a surfeit of candles, aerosol sprays and cosmetics. Hurrying around Gustuvson, Darby charged to the table and began dumping contents of bottles onto the carpet and bed. The corpse hissed and sizzled as Darby poured a full bottle of nail polish remover on it and threw the comforter over it.

She grabbed a can of hairspray and a candle lighter, clicked the lighter to life and sprayed hairspray through the flickering flame. Vanessa's bedding ignited. Chucking the hairspray can and the lighter into the blaze, Darby then upended the dressing table. She leapt over Gustuvson with an expression of grim determination on her face. The blaze intensified.

"I'll assign the worst forensic unit to investigate this mess," she thought while retreating down the hallway. The hairspray can detonated. Realization struck Darby like a thrown rock and she said aloud, "Holy shit. He took Vanessa."

Behind her, the fire spread to the walls and flames licked the ceiling. Darby, with incredible celerity, sprinted into the living room and pushed the intercom button.

"Get fire containment to Vanessa's suite, now!" commanded Darby. She flinched as another aerosol can exploded in Vanessa's bedroom and barked, "And lock down the mansion! Someone's kidnapped Vanessa!"

The inferno grew, tendrils of smoke wrapping around the edges of the door frame like searching fingers. The hallway fire alarm wailed as Darby fled the suite.

4

THE TWO TRIANGULAR halves that formed Vanessa's rectangular room told two very divergent stories. The near half remained relatively unscathed by Darby's arson and the firefighters' efforts to quell the fire save for some small debris and spots of moisture.

The far half of the room, however, fared much worse, the walls, ceiling and carpeting charred and drenched with water. The blaze also incinerated Vanessa's dressing table and bed. A blue, flame-retardant tarp, framed by remnants of her possessions and other rubble, covered the remains of Marcion's former host. Several feet away, another tarp covered Gustuvson's burned body.

Elizabeth burst into the room and shoved a firefighter in full yellow gear to the side. Rushing to the tarp covering Marcion's former host, she flung it aside and gasped. The firefighter quickly exited.

"Vanessa!" she cried, the Constable wracked by grief and nearly vomiting. Darby and Sarah entered the room, both women gazing on the body with disgusted horror. It suddenly emitted a hiss as it expelled gas, the noise causing Elizabeth and Darby to flinch. Sarah remained unmoved but grimaced.

"That isn't your daughter," Sarah chimed in unexpectedly. Elizabeth lunged towards Sarah and threateningly grasped the fabric of her dress.

"How do you know?!" demanded Elizabeth, her eyes wild with desperation. Darby took several cautious steps backward while warily watching Sarah. Elizabeth shook the Ursuline and snarled, "*How?!*"

"I've seen Vanessa very briefly, Elizabeth, if you'll remember," Sarah said sympathetically as she took Elizabeth's hands in her own. Lowering her arms and looking at her reassuringly, she added, "Your daughter is nearly as tall as you and that corpse is the size of a small child."

Elizabeth momentarily pondered Sarah's words and composed herself. Glancing over her shoulder, she confirmed the size of the singed body and exhaled in relief.

"Besides, I don't believe this is a normal corpse," Sarah indicated gravely. Releasing Elizabeth's hands and approaching the body, the nun was unable to tear her gaze away from Marcion's former host. Elizabeth turned towards it and, upon further inspection, noticed the cadaver suffered hideous disfigurement and bloating.

Sarah crouched down to examine it more closely and maneuvered herself to prevent her dress from touching the floor. Her eyes scanned the vicinity of the body and finally rested upon a dingy toothbrush. She quickly picked it up with the tips of her fingers and used it as an instrument to inspect the carcass before her.

"I've heard of corpses like this before, though, with one historical exception, the reports were only rumors," Sarah explained pensively. She probed the carcass in several places. Lifting a flap of burnt flesh and wrinkling her nose, she commented, "Or at least I thought them to be at the time."

Sarah studied the head of the corpse, the mouth of which was still opened unnaturally wide, and the barely discernible traces of a hardened, unrecognizable substance around its mouth and nostrils. She poked the substance to test its solidity. Darby, now standing in the entryway to the room, lost all the color in her face.

"And?" inquired Elizabeth sharply, her grief overwhelmed by impatience.

"In 1503, Pope Alexander VI died, allegedly poisoned by accident while attempting to poison his enemies," Sarah continued as she inspected the body. Prodding it, she said, "He was a particularly evil, immoral man and one of the worst Popes in history - nepotism, fornication, incest, political intrigue, greed. It's said his corpse rapidly decomposed and swelled while his nose and mouth emitted brown foam and his body hissed gasses. Demonic possession has been suggested as the cause, but only suggested, mind you."

Sarah gasped as she recognized Marcion's cavernous eye sockets.

"God help us," Sarah prayed aloud. She said softly and slowly, "I know who this is."

Darby swallowed hard.

· · · ·

WALKING PURPOSEFULLY down the grimy hallway, Sarah held her Bible in her left hand and focused intently on the door at the end of the hall.

Ignazio, a young man to whom she ministered, occupied the apartment to which the door belonged.

Confined to a wheelchair and blind since birth, Ignazio possessed an indubitable spirit and zest for life. His unquenchable passion for playing the violin inspired her and she kindled that same passion for the Lord within him. His deceased parents frequently patronized the Church of Saint Cyril until their deaths.

Sarah, however, became increasingly concerned about her spiritual ward as he plummeted into an unexplainable depression. He weathered the storms of his disabilities, the fall and his parents' demise with his ardent love of life, the violin and God intact only to mysteriously fall emotionally and spiritually ill.

She arrived at the apartment entrance and raised her fist to knock but paused when she noted the silence. Sarah gazed at the tarnished "5G" affixed to the door and pondered the absent melody of Ignazio's violin. She knocked.

"Ignazio?" she called out. The silence returned. Sarah turned the door handle and, when it moved, she experienced a slight twinge of fear: Ignazio always locked his door. She called out again with a wavering voice, "Ignazio?"

Sarah reluctantly pushed the door open, the hinges creaking eerily as it moved. She entered the apartment.

"Ignazio!" Sarah cried, the nun crumbling to her knees in utter shock. The young, dark-haired man laid face-down and motionless on the floor of his cramped, cluttered living room. It appeared he fell forward onto his violin bow, the force of his fall thrusting it into his throat. Oddly, however, he still held onto the bow with both hands.

Crying and unable to stand, Sarah pulled herself along the edge of Ignazio's couch towards his body. Miriam appeared in Ignazio's wheelchair, the *daimoniou* seated upon it as if she were an evil queen upon a throne.

"Who the fuck are you?" asked Miriam in her human voice. Astonished, Sarah fell backward and sat down with eyes wide. She hesitated but then steeled her faith and stoically rose to her feet.

"Sister Sarah Russo, servant of the Lord Jesus Christ," Sarah stated defiantly as she absorbed Miriam's demonic qualities. Miriam screamed upon the mention of Jesus. She leapt to her feet, snatched up the wheelchair and launched it at Sarah. Diving onto the couch, the nun barely avoided the wheelchair as it hurtled past her. It struck the door forcefully, the impact slamming it shut and causing the wheelchair to burst into several pieces.

Sarah calmly stood up and straightened her dress. Miriam snarled at her.

"And who might you be, my little harpy?" Sarah inquired with a trace of hostility in her tone. Miriam readied herself to pounce but was interrupted by a shrill, whiny voice.

"Don't be so hasty, *Miriam*, don't be so hasty," ordered Marcion as he materialized in front of her. She glowered at him while Sarah's face contorted in disgust at the sight of his burned physique. He admonished Miriam slowly as he ogled Sarah, "The Master is watching."

Miriam squirmed with discomfort and deferred to Marcion. He grinned at Sarah with jagged, decomposing teeth.

"I didn't realize that demons were involved in simple murder now but I suppose these *are* strange days," Sarah said.

"He killed *himself*," replied Miriam sharply, her girlish voice tinged with her demonic one. Marcion waved her off as Sarah furrowed her brow in response to her remark. Miriam seethed but obeyed.

"Regardless, you've accomplished that for which you came," Sarah stated. She lowered herself to the floor to compassionately take Ignazio's head in her hands. She added forcefully as she attended to him, "Please leave."

"Good bye, Sister Sarah," Marcion said mockingly with a devious smirk on his face. He dematerialized but not before muttering under his breath, "For now."

Miriam hesitated, the demon feeling an unfamiliar emotion flare within her as she watched Sarah gently close Ignazio's eyelids. The Ursuline sensed Miriam's attention and glanced at her. Observing the uncertain expression on her face, she offered her a compassionate mien. Miriam hissed at her and swiftly disappeared.

· · · ·

DARBY HASTILY UNDID her thick leather belt, unzipped her pants and pulled them down. Her holster hit the ground with a clunk. She seated herself on the toilet and immediately began urinating in a powerful, steady stream. The painful pressure on her bladder subsided as the sound of the urine forcefully hitting the water echoed throughout the bathroom.

"Holy fuck," she sighed in relief. Continuing to urinate, she retrieved her flask from her jacket and drank from it. She closed her eyes, bowed her head and let her elbows rest on her thighs, groaning, "Jesus Christ that feels good."

Marcion, now inhabiting Vanessa's teenage body, materialized in front of Darby.

"Why would Jesus care?" asked Marcion in his usual sniveling tone. He disrespectfully spat on the ground and repeated, "*Why?*"

Sensing a threat, Darby's eyes popped opened and she ceased urinating. Dropping her flask, she reached for her gun but abruptly stopped. The flask clattered on the floor tile.

"Vanessa?!" she exclaimed with bewilderment. Vanessa now possessed the black demonic orbs and claws common to all *daimoniou*, her once pale skin now awash in the pallor of death. Her eyes scrutinized Darby and seemingly protruded from their sockets.

"Whaddaya think, Darbs, whaddaya think?" asked Marcion, the demon twirling around to display his new host.

"You evil, evil fuck," Darby growled in a furious, venomous tone. She lunged towards Marcion but aborted her attack, partly because she realized she sat on a toilet with her pants around her ankles and partly because she realized that to strike Marcion was to strike Vanessa. She returned to the toilet seat.

"Contract was up! Due for an upgrade!" Marcion sang while examining his new host with satisfaction and a chuckle. He danced a peculiar dance.

"You piece of shit," reproached Darby angrily. She retrieved her flash and demanded, "Get the fuck outta my niece."

"Fuck you, cunt!" Marcion snapped as he thrust a finger at Darby. Slapping the wall and causing the drywall to crumble, he expounded, "I told you to get Elizabeth to Hanahan but you fucked it up! So now we do it my way. *My way!*"

"Bullshit. I'm out," Darby insisted. She whisked up her gun and let it rest on her lap, saying with ire, "Possessing Vanessa was *never* part of the deal."

"Bullshit? *Bullshit?*" Marcion queried rhetorically. His expression grew cold and he warned, "Convince your sister she needs to go to Hanahan to retrieve her brat or I might decide to keep her."

Darby fumed but did not respond. Marcion massaged Vanessa's young breasts yet, instead of engendering rage in Darby, it caused her anger to evaporate.

"Sorry about this, kid, but the little bastard has it coming," apologized Darby matter-of-factly.

"What?" Marcion asked. Darby tilted her pelvis forward, partially covered her urethra with her finger and sent a stream of urine into Marcion's face.

"Ahhh! Fuck!" Marcion bellowed as he retreated and raised his arm to ward off Darby's assault. Dematerializing, he shouted, "Cunt!"

Darby settled back on the toilet seat and watched Marcion disappear. She then finished urinating as if nothing out of the ordinary occurred.

"I just pissed on my demon-possessed niece," commented Darby blithely. She scooped up her flask and drank from it, adding in an odd tone, "That's definitely a first."

· · · ·

PACING RELENTLESSLY in front of her desk, Elizabeth alternated between sobbing and fuming. Her mind churned, her brain sifting through Sarah's account of Marcion and planning Vanessa's rescue. The sequestering of Mallory and Tara in the bunker complex under heavy guard provided her with a small measure of comfort.

Sarah remained silent and patiently waited in the sitting area. Darby suddenly entered the room to the expectant gazes of the Constable and the nun. She squirmed uneasily under their eager stares.

"There's not a fucking thing on the cameras except Gustuvson entering the suite," Darby said in an agitated tone. The disappearance of Vanessa, however, prevented Elizabeth and Sarah from perceiving the true cause of her angst. She walked forward and grasped the back of one of the sitting area chairs with both hands. Her knuckles turning white, Darby explained, "And no one came in or out of the mansion complex between the time he went in and the time I locked it down. They're still tearing this fucking place apart."

"She's not here," advised Sarah cautiously, the Ursuline remembering the two sisters' penchant for responding to unfortunate news with violence. Elizabeth ceased pacing and suppressed a sob while Darby glared at Sarah.

"Yeah, and how *the fuck* do you know that?" Darby barked in opposition. She moved threateningly toward Sarah and asked, "Why the fuck are we listening to you, anyway?"

"Enough, Darby," Elizabeth scolded, the rebuke causing Darby to abort her advance. Turning her attention to Sarah, she calmly asked, "Why do you say that?"

"I've been thinking. Demons are spiritual beings who do not die," explained Sarah. Staring forward as her eyes glazed over, she continued, "The physical host that Marcion left behind was clearly dead but his spirit undoubtedly survived. Either he remains just that, a spirit . . . or he found a new host."

Elizabeth faltered and burst into tears. Both Sarah and Darby raced to her, one on either side, and comforted her. Shoving her sister away, Elizabeth grabbed Sarah by her arms and bore into her with bleary, fraught eyes.

"How do I get her back?" Elizabeth sorrowfully begged Sarah as tears rolled down her pale cheeks. Darby remained quiet and looked ill as her sister mewled, "How do I get my baby back?"

"Jacob," answered Sarah while looking on Elizabeth with pity. Darby perked up.

"Jacob?" Elizabeth questioned incredulously. She appeared as if she might faint.

"To find your daughter, you must find Marcion," expounded Sarah, "but the only one we know of who can find him is Miriam . . . and only your husband can convince Miriam to help you."

Elizabeth contemplated Sarah's words carefully. Jacob may not have been a model stepfather but Elizabeth knew he would give his life for her daughters. Miriam, however, posed a significant problem. Elizabeth wondered if she could cooperate with the demon that stole her husband and threatened her life.

Darby, meanwhile, observed Elizabeth with great anticipation. She hoped her sister's decision would obviate the need for her to reveal Vanessa's fate.

"Then I'm going to Hanahan," Elizabeth stated with conviction and a darkening mood. Darby exhaled in relief through her nostrils.

• • • •

ULTRAVIOLET LIGHTS whirred to life and cloaked the holding cell in eerie, bluish illumination. Clad in all black, Darby's and Elizabeth's entire forms melded into the darkness and the ultraviolet waves gave the contacts they wore a bizarre, purplish glow. The sisters stood before Agatha who, while unharmed, was tied with cords to a metal chair.

"What the fuck is all this, Elizabeth?" demanded Agatha, the crime lord straining forward against her bonds and lifting the chair off the ground. Darby stepped between Elizabeth and Agatha.

"Sit down, cunt!" Darby barked with a murderous expression. Agatha glowered back but failed to daunt Darby as the latter warned, "Or I'll fuck you up in ways you couldn't imagine."

Elizabeth nudged Darby to her right and pushed Agatha back onto the legs of her chair.

"You will behave yourself, Agatha," ordered Elizabeth while holding up her right index finger in Agatha's face. Turning to Darby, she instructed, "And you, dear sister, will never use that word in my presence again."

"*Cunt* or *fuck*?" Darby inquired with mock uncertainty. A biting glance from Elizabeth prompted Darby to deferentially lift her palms in surrender and state, "All right, all right."

"This is Darby's shtick, not mine," Elizabeth explained as she turned to address Agatha once again. Annoyed, Darby moved to the wall, leaned her back against it and folded her arms. Elizabeth said, "I'm simply testing its effectiveness."

"I was talking about the jail cell and the restraints," replied Agatha bitterly, her teeth glowing in the ultraviolet light as she spoke. She complained, "This bullshit is pretty fucking ballsy, even for the Queen."

"Where is Hanahan?" Elizabeth queried, the Constable ignoring Agatha's grievances.

"Your hospitality sucks as of late," replied a defiant Agatha with a supercilious smile. She attempted to stand again and said, "Let me the fuck outta here and maybe we'll talk."

Darby moved to strike Agatha but ceased her attack as Elizabeth drew her semi-automatic pistol and fired a bullet into Agatha's left thigh. The muzzle flash temporarily lit the cell and she cried out in severe pain. Her chair dropped back to the floor.

"Perhaps you didn't hear me the first time," Elizabeth said while letting her shooting arm fall to her side. Stunned by her sister's uncharacteristic aggression, Darby observed the situation silently. Elizabeth asked again, "Where is Hanahan?"

Agatha moaned and shuddered, blood saturating her pant leg around the bullet's entry point. Breathing heavily, she gathered herself and spat at Elizabeth. The Constable adroitly dodged Agatha's spittle and fired a bullet into her right thigh.

"Fuck!" shouted Agatha while still breathing heavily and beginning to sweat. She shuddered as her wounds bled and moaned in agony.

"I have thirteen more rounds, Agatha," Elizabeth advised as she again let her arm fall to her side, "which is, most likely, more than you can survive, but I promise I'll do my best to keep you alive as long as possible."

"O-o-kay, okay," capitulated Agatha while sweating and bleeding profusely. An unimpressed Elizabeth cocked her firearm, the threat prompting Agatha to say, "Okay! I-I've never been there, but there's . . . ya' gotta take the East Road . . . out-outside of your territory . . . and take it for a long fucking way, even when it takes you southeast along some mountains."

"I know the area," Elizabeth interjected impatiently. Laboring to breathe, Agatha shivered and coughed repeatedly.

"Ya' used ta' be able to take other roads south but ya' can't anymore . . . they're impassable," Agatha continued. Steeling her will to speak clearly, she continued, "The East Road will twist and turn and ramble in all directions . . . and there's a spiderweb of other dirt roads along the way to confuse the hell outta ya' . . . and nothing's marked. But . . . if you pay attention, you'll know the main road . . . and it leads you right to Hanahan."

Elizabeth searched Agatha's face for any sign of deceit as she waited for a pardon. Satisfied with her veracity, Elizabeth lifted her weapon one last time and fired a round into the center of Agatha's face. The criminal overlord of Kaiser was no more.

"Holy shit!" exclaimed Darby. Utterly shocked by her sister's resort to violence, she stood up straight and asked, "What're you gonna tell the nun?"

"Nothing until I have my daughter back," Elizabeth answered, her eyes on Agatha. She lowered her firearm.

"That was pretty fucking hardcore," said Darby as she walked up to Agatha and examined the bullet wound in her disfigured face.

"I'd kill you if it meant saving Vanessa's life," Elizabeth uttered callously. Holstering her weapon, she turned on a dime and exited the cell, the Constable failing to see her sister's hurt, angered mien.

• • • •

DRESSED IN A SLINKY, black silk robe, Elizabeth sat upon her king-sized bed, her hair still wet from a hot, relaxing shower. The four posters of the bed, made of a polished, black wood, supported a myrtle-green canopy.

Vanessa's and Mallory's youthful smiles shined out from hundreds of pictures scattered atop Elizabeth's myrtle-green comforter. She sifted through the photographs, the proud mother meticulously inspecting every image of her daughters' faces with loving eyes. A cup of green tea steamed in a saucer next to her.

Tara dramatically threw open the heavy, wooden doors to the bedroom suite. Elizabeth watched her mother circumvent the free-standing fireplace located between the doors and the bed and walk up to the granite dais on which it was situated.

"Mother!" Elizabeth rebuked Tara with a trace of panic as she knocked her teacup and saucer off the bed. They plummeted to the dais and shattered. Ignoring the clatter, Elizabeth demanded, "Where's Mallory?!"

"Oh, settle down," replied an irked Tara as she stepped onto the first layer of the dais. Elizabeth glared at her mother until her displeasure prompted Tara to confess, "She's with Darby and that fucking nun."

"That *fucking nun* is going to help me rescue your granddaughter," Elizabeth brusquely informed Tara, "so you may want to show her a little respect."

"It's creepy enough having her skulking about the mansion," complained Tara. Noticing the pictures scattered about the bed, she asked, "Do we really need to take her with us?"

Elizabeth lowered her eyes and pretended to shuffle through some photographs. Ascending the next dais step and seating herself on the edge of the bed, Tara picked up a recent picture of Vanessa and Mallory laughing as they posed for the photograph.

"You certainly made some beautiful babies," commented Tara proudly, "and they get along better than you and your sister did at that age."

"You won't be accompanying me to Hanahan," Elizabeth blurted while dreading a battle with her mother. Tara carelessly tossed the photo onto the bed, Elizabeth's mother spinning it with a flick of her wrist. She rose to her feet.

"I was looking forward to an assignment with a little more action," objected Tara curtly. She glared at her daughter.

"I need you here with Mallory," Elizabeth pleaded, the Constable bracing for stout resistance from Tara. She implored her mother with sad eyes, "There's no one here that I fully trust to protect and care for her in my absence."

"Darby'll love to hear that," replied Tara with a chuckle. Her countenance softened.

"I trust Darby to protect her," Elizabeth stated, "but it's her parenting skills, or lack thereof, that I don't trust."

Elizabeth sighed.

"Relying on Jacob to help raise the girls is a luxury I no longer have," Elizabeth said heedlessly before she realized the import of her words. She withdrew into herself to consider her former reliance on Jacob to care for her children. A picture of the girls, Jacob and Elizabeth drew her attention. She picked it up and gazed on it with conflicted emotions.

Jacob, with a lighthearted, goofy smile on his face, wrapped his right arm around Elizabeth and his left arm around Vanessa as he posed for the picture. Mallory, standing to Elizabeth's right, forced a smile. Elizabeth and her daughters looked elegant and stunning, their hair and makeup a study in perfection, while Jacob seemed out of place in an unremarkable ensemble of a navy-blue sport jacket, a blue-and-yellow tie and tan slacks.

"He was intoxicated in that picture and we were in the middle of an ugly fight, though the girls didn't know it," Elizabeth expounded. Entranced by the picture, she said, "He didn't want me riding alone with Steven in my limousine and I refused to acquiesce to his insecurities. He completely ruined the entire evening."

"You certainly cast a spell on that drunken fool," remarked Tara with a devious grin. Her comment stirred Elizabeth from her reverie and, realizing its impact, she added, "You just never learned to take full advantage of it."

Elizabeth let her eyes linger on the photograph for a few more seconds before setting it face down on the bed. She looked at Tara somberly.

"Sören is quite capable of running this city in my absence and he's done so on several occasions. I'll expect you to defer to him on most matters," Elizabeth explained firmly. A dubious expression arose on her face and she said, "That being said, he can't handle Darby. The last time I left she threw him out of a moving vehicle."

Tara guffawed. Elizabeth, unmoved by her mother's laughter, exhaled.

"Thank God they weren't traveling in the helicopter," she said.

"That's my crazy, impulsive little girl," commented Tara fondly while grinning from ear to ear. She queried, "But isn't Darby going with you?"

Elizabeth paused and, with her mouth closed, ran her tongue over her upper teeth. She craved a cigarette.

"To Hanahan, yes," Elizabeth said, "but once I locate Jacob and Miriam, she and the rest of the team will be returning to the city."

"Why is that?" queried Tara in mild, amused disbelief.

"I've been in a demon's clutches before, Mother," Elizabeth replied chillingly. Tara's smile faded as her daughter expounded, "I've experienced Miriam's supernatural strength and felt the bite of her merciless claws. I was powerless and only Jacob's intervention saved my life. Darby's skills and lethality mean *nothing* in that world, Mother, *nothing*. I won't sacrifice my sister to it, or anyone else for that matter."

"Then it looks like you'll have to rely on Jacob one more time," counseled Tara. She added in an odd tone, "You and Vanessa, that is."

Thoughts of Vanessa stirred in Elizabeth's mind and she failed to perceive Tara's strange manner of speech. Moving to Elizabeth's side, Tara used her foot to clear away pieces of the teacup and saucer and placed a reassuring hand on her left shoulder. A single tear ran down Elizabeth's right cheek.

"Bring her back, Liz," Tara encouraged her. She continued softly in an unsettling manner, "Mommy has *everything* under control."

• • • •

"IF I LED THE INSURGENCY, I'd have sniper rifles trained on this balcony at all times," Darius stated reproachfully. The six-foot-three-inch, sinewy black man who approached Elizabeth wore a rugged, dark-grey jacket, a purple t-shirt and jeans. He shaved his head but sported a thin Van Dyke which he stroked as he said, "I can't believe Darby lets you come out here."

"She'd keep me locked in prison cell if she had her way," responded Elizabeth, her skin unexplainably crawling as the words fell from her lips. She quickly changed the subject. Turning around to face Darius and smiling affectionately, she asked, "How's life on the other side of the walls?"

"Dangerous as ever and getting pretty fucking bizarre," responded Darius. They shared an awkward embrace, both of their bodies tingling with ardent remembrance as they touched. Elizabeth pulled free and forced an uncomfortable grin.

"This is awkward, I know," Elizabeth conceded. Fidgeting with uncertainty, she said, "We never really talked about it, and then you left, and-."

"No worries, Liz," interrupted Darius with a raised palm. Elizabeth hugged herself as he assured her, "My bruised ego healed when I realized that you're out of my league."

"I beg to differ," Elizabeth corrected him, her cheeks flushing ever so slightly in response to Darius's flattery and his handsome face. A thought struck her. Cocking her head to the side, she asked, "Who exactly *is* in my league?"

"Only the men you choose to be in it," stated Darius flatly. Guilt struck Elizabeth as she remembered Vanessa's abduction. Her mood dimmed.

"The situation is grave, Darius," Elizabeth said. He shifted and frowned.

"I figured as much when you cancelled our meeting," replied Darius. Sensing Elizabeth's palpable distress, he asked, "What is it, Liz?"

Elizabeth struggled to speak but no words fell from her lips. Retrieving a pack of cigarettes from his jacket, Darius pulled one half-way out and offered the pack to her. She sighed, greedily whisked the cigarette out of the pack and placed it in her mouth.

"Thank you!" Elizabeth gushed with relieved gratitude.

Darius swiftly produced a lighter and lit the cigarette for her. She inhaled, indulged in the nicotine rush and then exhaled a cloud of smoke.

"This will be difficult to believe," Elizabeth began grimly as Darius stuffed the pack and the lighter back into his jacket, "so I won't mince words. The spiritual world has turned its attention to Kaiser, specifically the *demon* world."

Darius, in both confusion and disbelief, watched Elizabeth speak with rapt attention. She leaned against the balcony railing and puffed on her cigarette.

"Several months ago a 'female' demon preyed upon Jacob and I's marriage with the intent of inducing him to commit suicide," Elizabeth continued, the Constable smoking as she spoke. She stated acrimoniously, "Instead, she fell in love with him and stole him from me. She fled the city with him and I've not seen or heard from him in days."

"My God, Liz," Darius said in astonishment, Elizabeth's former lover still uncertain if he believed her.

"God has abandoned us," Elizabeth snapped with a flash of anger. Composing herself, she said, "Unfortunately, Miriam was not our only demonic visitor."

Elizabeth paused. Balancing on the verge of tears, she used her hatred and wrath to smother them.

"Another demon has kidnapped Vanessa," Elizabeth stated, her voice cracking as she spoke her daughter's name. Darius grimaced as she said, "And, unfortunately, Jacob's demon whore is the only one who can find her."

Darius chewed on Elizabeth's account for nearly a minute while she studied him keenly. She tucked her left arm, rested her right arm upon it and held her cigarette away from her body. Darius shrugged.

"I'll have a team together and ready to move in three hours," stated Darius in businesslike fashion. He reached for his cell phone.

"There won't be a team," Elizabeth informed Darius. He pulled his hand out of his jacket as she said, "I'm taking only you, Darby . . . ."

Darius furrowed his brow and, taking umbrage with Darby's inclusion, he scowled. Elizabeth moved as if she laughed briefly yet no sound came from her lips.

"I'll keep her under control, I promise," Elizabeth assured him, "and we'll also be taking along a civilian."

"A civilian?" scoffed Darius. Prickled by curiosity and Elizabeth's peculiar strategy, he inquired, "May I ask why?"

"She knows demons, and particularly Jacob's demon, very well," Elizabeth answered while rotating around to observe Kaiser and puffing on her cigarette. Darius perked up and smirked.

"Who is she?" inquired Darius mischievously.

"She's a Catholic nun, pervert," Elizabeth said with a wounded, disapproving glance over her shoulder.

"That just makes it better," retorted Darius while mockingly pressing his hands together as if to pray.

5

THE CASINO AT HANAHAN burst forth from the earth, a fantastical, spectral skyscraper bathed in psychedelic purple light and partially shrouded in dense, ghostly mists. The towering glass building gleamed brilliantly against the backdrop of night, its tubular body terminating with a truncated apex. Starting from zero degrees at its southern edge, the apex rose and gradually formed a one-hundred-thirty-degree angle at its rounded pinnacle.

Jacob, Miriam and Sophie observed the building from the northwest. They stood on a large ridge of land that separated the small, abandoned town of Hanahan from the skyscraper. Its immense base was partially concealed by fog and sat at the foot of a small range of mountains which shielded it from all but southern observation.

"What the fuck is this place?" Jacob asked as he stood awed by the sight before him. Miriam's tight grip on his hand was the only evidence that he remained in the material world.

"Chinese Peak Casino," answered Sophie. The skyscraper failed to entrance her as it did Jacob. She stepped ahead of him and Miriam and added, "At least that's what Kirwan called it."

"You've been here before?" Jacob asked while gazing on the casino as if in a trance.

"No," replied Sophie.

"Tell me we didn't cross over," Jacob murmured while touching Miriam's right triceps muscle.

"It doesn't work that way, idiot," advised Miriam, the demon focusing just as intently on the casino as did Jacob. She backed into him, snuggled into his body and wallowed in the feel of her back against him. Miriam stated worriedly in her hybrid voice, "This place is crawling with demons, Jake. I can feel them . . . they're *everywhere.*"

"Everywhere?" queried Sophie, her peculiar tone conveying her piqued interest. Miriam threw her a sidelong glance.

"We'll have to risk it," Jacob said. Uncertain yet committed to his decision, he clicked the callous inside his mouth and explained, "There wasn't anything left to scavenge in town and the power bars are gone. Sophie and I gotta eat something. Besides, who the hell knows where the next settlement is?"

"Don't worry about Sophie," the young woman said as she began her descent down the southeast side of the ridge. Using her baseball bat as a walking stick, she called back, "This is where she gets off your crazy train."

"I'll handle the demons, Mirry," Jacob whispered in her ear. Reassuringly placing his hand on Miriam's waist, he added, "You just handle whatever the hell else is in there. *And keep an eye on Sophie.* She has no idea what the fuck she's getting into."

"Oh, and you do?" Miriam snapped with a sour expression. She felt a tingling pain in her hip as he spurred her forward with a squeeze and a nudge.

"If this is a bad idea, now would be the time to tell me," Jacob silently prayed as he raised his eyes to the starry heavens. He begged earnestly, "*Please tell me.*"

• • • •

THE ENVIRONMENT WAS soundless and still and not even the breeze disturbed the eerie quiet on the grounds of Chinese Peak Casino. Sophie walked through a foggy parking lot dotted with the occasional luxury car or SUV while Jacob and Miriam trailed at a distance. The vehicles, cold to the touch and coated with moisture, had been parked there since before nightfall.

The luminosity emanating from the skyscraper provided enough light for them to navigate their way to the entrance. They stepped out of the fog after several minutes of walking and arrived at a pristine, white-cement walkway, the small grains of its shimmering minerals reminding Jacob of the sepulcher on Mount Borgia. Trimmed with miniature fountains molded into nude, shapely women, the walkway bifurcated into two paths and encircled a great fountain. The paths reunited on its far side and led to cement steps.

Sophie strode up the fountain, its center the head and neck of a stern-yet-beautiful woman with her hair pulled back tightly into a bun. Water trickled from her piercing eyes as jets encircling her head launched streams of water into the air. The jets suddenly fell silent.

Standing atop the stairs as if she had awaited their arrival for centuries, an attractive black woman with straight, raven hair and smooth, rounded facial features observed Jacob, Miriam and Sophie. She exuded a convivial aura, the woman smiling invitingly and holding her clasped hands in front of her stomach.

"Welcome to Chinese Peak," greeted the woman. She wore a glittering gold dress with full sleeves and a collar concealing her neck. Her grin fading into a neutral expression, she said, "We've been expecting you, Mr. Gottschalk, though we were unaware you were accompanied by guests."

Miriam emitted a guttural growl, the demon irked by the sight of eyes identical to her own. Jacob noticed them as well but failed to react.

"Well, Agatha's words make a little more sense now," he said while placing his hands on his hips. He pondered the situation as he studied the woman and then let his arms fall to his sides. Jacob smirked, and, indulging in his newfound power, demanded, "'What is your name?'" (Excerpt from the Gospel of Luke 24:39).

The woman battled against an abrupt shudder and glared at Jacob briefly before regaining her poise. He offered her a haughty sneer.

"There's no need for such hostility, I assure you, Mr. Gottschalk," the woman stated. She once again clasped her hands in front of her stomach and said, "My name is Adedewe and -."

Miriam unexpectedly shrieked and charged into the main fountain. Letting the water drench her as the jets again launched aqueous streams, she rounded the left side of woman's head. Jacob attempted to move Sophie behind him but she shoved him away. Adedewe remained motionless.

Reaching the far side of the head, Miriam lunged forward and grasped Marcion. He screamed pathetically as she effortlessly flung him at one of the smaller fountains and sent Vanessa crashing into a female statue. The impact pulverized the top half of the woman's body.

"Fucking cunt!" Marcion screamed in a high-pitched whine as he leapt to his feet and swept up a stone breast in his hand. He chucked the breast at Miriam but she snatched it out of the air.

"Your girlfriend's pretty bad ass," said Sophie while tapping her bat on the cement. Miriam hurled the breast and it hit Marcion's forehead. He responded with a sickening yelp in Vanessa's voice.

"*Ness?*" Jacob said in astonishment as he realized his stepdaughter stood before him. He froze.

"I'm gonna end you now," announced Miriam, the demon smiling with delight. Sharp pains rippled through Jacob's chest like hundreds of tiny knives plunged into his flesh.

"Miriam!" he beckoned desperately. Miriam stopped and fell silent in response to Jacob's commanding tone. Her wrath subsiding, she recognized Marcion's new host.

"You sick fuck," uttered Miriam. She felt a twinge of pity for Vanessa.

A powerful rage exploded within Jacob and he charged Marcion without fear of claw or tooth. Retreating with great speed before his oncoming wrath, Marcion fled.

"Come out of her!" Jacob commanded. Marcion screeched and Jacob watched in horror as Vanessa tripped and fell, the possessed teenager disappearing into a low bank of fog. He shouted, "Vanessa!"

· · · ·

JACOB PAUSED HIS SEARCH on the spot where Vanessa disappeared. He breathed with difficulty as his head spun and he absorbed the events of the past twenty minutes.

"Jake?" Miriam called tenderly, a worried expression on her pallid face. Jacob stared off into the darkening fog on the edge of the skyscraper's glow and failed to acknowledge her. Miriam grasped his arm and shook him, the *daimoniou* calling out, "*Jake!*"

"Why the fuck would he go after the girls?" asked Jacob. Becoming agitated, he attempted to march off into the fog while declaring, "She's gotta be here somewhere."

Miriam halted Jacob's flight by grabbing the lapels of his jacket and pulling his face down to her level. She captured his attention with her stern gaze.

"I can't sense her anymore, Jake. I can't sense either of them," Miriam said softly. Moving him to within an inch of her face, she said with sympathy, "*They're gone.*"

"Why don't you ask Adedewe?" suggested Sophie as she emerged from the fog. Enraged by the intrusion, Miriam glared at her.

"I don't know, bitch. Get lost, will ya'?" scolded Miriam. Ignoring her anger, Sophie stood motionless and unafraid.

"According to Adedewe, Jake's my ticket inside," answered Sophie, "so I'm stuck with you two for a while."

Jacob took Miriam's hand and, without saying a word, walked back to the casino. Escaping the obscurity of the fog, the trio returned to the fountain area and arrived at the base of the stairs. Adedewe remained in her original position.

"So, golden cunt, where's the girl?" snarled Miriam. She threw a hateful glance at Adedewe who returned the favor. The two demons engaged in a bitter optical battle.

"I have no idea," Adedewe advised. She looked to Jacob and said, "Marcion is known here but he is not one us."

"Lying bitch," sneered Miriam as she and Adedewe continued to exchange malicious stares. She growled threateningly, reached out to a nearby statue and scratched it with the claws of her left hand.

"'Put the sword in the sheath,'" said Jacob with resignation as he contemplated Vanessa's possession, the towering demonic haven before him and his fateful journey from Kaiser. Miriam turned to view him with listless eyes as he asked, "'The cup which the Father has given Me, shall I not drink it?'" (Excerpts from the Gospel of John 18:11).

· · · ·

THE ENORMITY OF THE Chinese Peak's luxurious and visually-stunning lobby momentarily overwhelmed Jacob as he stared upward with mouth open. Ascending four stories, the rear of the seashell-shaped chamber formed five huge alcoves in the undulations of the shell.

"This'll do," said Sophie while wondering off to the right. Miriam inveterately shadowed her as she moved through the bustle of sharply-dressed patrons and provocatively-clad workers. Jacob stopped in his tracks.

A colossal waterfall centered the room, its structure set in the middle alcove and constructed out of concentric rings of smooth, polished stone. The rushing water passed over hundreds of light fixtures emitting Capri-blue light, the bulbs casting the entire lobby in a welcoming, comforting radiance. Two parallel lines of cylindrical fountains, each lit like the waterfall, ran from where Jacob stood to a tunnel. It bisected the waterfall and led patrons further into the building. A lounge was built into the fourth level above the waterfall.

The two alcoves to the right housed the customer service desk on the first level and windowed offices on the second while the two alcoves to the left formed a two-story restaurant, the modernistic and chic "Vitoria." Suites occupied the four side alcoves from the third floor upward and formed a giant honeycomb of balconies which terminated at the bottom of the fifth story. A thicket of coffee and end tables, sofas and chairs formed sitting areas in the remainder of the lobby.

"How the hell do you maintain all of this?" Jacob queried in disbelief as he scanned the spectacle before him. A leggy brunette in a purple, sequined mini dress crossed his path, her ample, exposed cleavage instantly drawing attention.

"I don't believe I'm the one to answer that question for you, Mr. Gottschalk," replied Adedewe as she twirled around. Jacob averted his gaze to her face though not before she caught him ogling the brunette. She assured him with a smirk, "But don't worry. You'll meet someone who will, *that* I promise you."

Miriam failed to appreciate the lobby's grandiosity, the demon still fuming over Jacob's acquiescence to Adedewe's invitation. She watched her own kind lurking all around her, their presence both infuriating and frightening.

"Forgive the intrusion, but you're *gorgeous,*" said a flamboyantly-homosexual man as he sashayed up to Jacob. The pale, willowy man wore a white, silk suit with a fuchsia ascot. Touching Jacob's chest playfully and tossing his longish blonde hair, he added, "Your eyes are like beautiful little blueberries. Scrumptious!"

"Uh, I .. I'm, uh, not really into . . . *that*," explained Jacob uncomfortably yet politely. He backpedaled, the move catching Miriam's attention, and said, "But, uh . . . thanks?"

"Well why not, honey?" he inquired impishly. Undaunted, the man pursued Jacob and placed his hands on Jacob's shoulders. He massaged his muscles.

Miriam growled as Jacob untangled himself from the man's grasp and fought off his pawing. She tensed herself to attack but aborted her assault when she noticed an attractive, suit-clad man in his forties flirting with a disinterested Sophie in one of the sitting areas. She heard Jacob's admonishment in her head: "*And keep an eye on Sophie.*"

"Fuck," Miriam cursed while throwing down her arms like an ornery toddler. The nagging of her usually-silent conscience vexing her, she griped, "This is such bullshit."

Winking out of material existence, she travelled through the spirit world and reappeared next to Sophie. Her unexpected entrance startled the man and caused him to back up and trip over a chair. A glare and a growl from Miriam sent him swiftly on his way.

"I thought you were gonna stick around for a while," Miriam chastised Sophie. She leaned closer and leered at her.

"I'm inside now," deadpanned Sophie. She glanced over to Jacob, the homosexual man still fawning over him while Adedewe attempted to intercede. Nodding in the direction of the commotion, Sophie said with flat affect, "Looks like your boyfriend's got a boyfriend."

"Don't fucking move," Miriam threatened with a pointed finger. She wrinkled her nose and vanished.

• • • •

MIRIAM COMPLETED HER ritualized, spiritual examination as she did with all her victims and swarmed over the homosexual man in mere seconds. She absorbed his nature, breathed in his essence and inspected every inch of his body. Her spiritual perception washed over his thoughts, emotions and memories.

Flashing into the field of Jacob's vision with astounding speed and precision, Miriam forcefully poked a single claw into the homosexual man's trachea. She then turned his body to face her and pushed the man backward with her finger. Patrons scrambled to avoid the violence as the man coughed and struggled to breathe.

"This one's taken, cock breath," warned Miriam in her hybrid voice.

"Damn it, Mirry, no!" Jacob scolded while trailing Miriam. Her demonic strength was all that kept the man on his feet. Adedewe observed the situation as if Miriam spilled a drink. Jacob demanded, "Stop it!"

Wrapping his arms around Miriam, Jacob tried to yank her away from the homosexual man. She effortlessly shrugged him off and shrieked at him before flinging the man to the floor with a flick of her finger. Jacob rushed to his side and took his hand.

"Get help!" Jacob shouted at Adedewe. She remained still and watched Miriam grab Jacob by his jacket.

"We have *other* problems, Jake," argued Miriam impatiently as she hoisted him to his feet. She sneered, "Remember Vanessa?"

"I must agree with Miriam, Mr. Gottschalk," Adedewe advised with veiled bitterness, the demon loathing any concurrence with her. She examined the gay man and expounded, "This man's life is insignificant and we have important matters to attend to."

His hand clutching his throat, the man gurgled in agony as he slowly suffocated to death. Many eyes surveyed Miriam's handiwork, the demonic ones without pity and the human ones with measured disgust.

Jacob struggled with Miriam. She shoved him further away from her dying victim.

"Fuck you, Mirry!" Jacob barked. Infuriated by Miriam's callous violence, he shouted, "It's all bullshit, isn't it?"

"Doesn't God hate fags anyway?" questioned Miriam in response to Jacob's vehement reprimand while the scrutiny of the other demons intensified. Miriam abruptly panicked. She fell upon the man and tore out his throat with her teeth. Looking up from his corpse with a gory face, she appeared much like a lion feasting on a fresh kill.

"Mark twelve, twenty-nine through thirty-one," Jacob stated authoritatively while disregarding the wild, abhorrent stares from the surrounding *daimoniou*. He reasoned gravely, "The two greatest commandments are love God and love your neighbor. It's that fucking simple, Mirry. Stabbing someone in the fucking windpipe is *not* loving your neighbor, gay or not."

Jacob shook his head in disgust.

"You told me you'd accept His will in your life, Mirry," Jacob chastened her.

"I relieved his pain," Miriam stated while nodding to the homosexual man's corpse. Raising her defenses to ward off Jacob's stinging displeasure, she walked away and licked the blood dripping from the points of her teeth. She tossed Jacob a careless glance and added, "God should thank me."

Jacob, uncertain of Miriam's sincerity or her stability, nervously chewed the inside of his mouth. He felt the emptiness of solitude yet again and it terrified him.

"Wait," he said abruptly while his anger evaporated. He scanned the crowd and asked, "Where the hell's Sophie?"

. . . .

SITTING HEEDLESSLY in front of an enclosed bubble fountain illuminated in the same blue light as the lobby, Sophie watched the bubbles ascend. She sat at a cocktail table in the bar area of Vitoria with an elaborate, silver candle fixture in front of her. Jacob sighed in relief as he entered the bar and saw Sophie was safe.

Vitoria's bar was an amalgamation of black wood and white, translucent glass tainted blue by strategically-positioned lights. Silver fixtures dotted the tables and bar, the blue light occasionally glinting off their metal surfaces. A comely, raven-haired bartender with sharp facial features watched Jacob closely as he dried cocktail glasses.

"I can't believe you fucking let her come in here by herself," Jacob grumbled while ignoring another suspicious glance from the impeccably-dressed bartender.

"I can't believe a man with such a small penis is such a giant dick," retorted Miriam. She nudged him with a sharp elbow and added, "She'd not a kid and she's not our problem."

"You a drinker, Sophie?" Jacob asked as he and Miriam arrived at her table. She shot him an unamused look as he sat down and added, "You look old enough, though here it probably doesn't matter."

"I don't have daddy issues," responded Sophie matter-of-factly, "so you're wasting your time."

"Hey, what the fuck's your problem?" Jacob sneered as he leaned over the table and pointed at Sophie. Glowering at her, he ranted, "What are you, fucking nineteen, twenty? You're still a kid and if it wasn't for us, you'd still be locked in that shitty boiler room singing your stupid fucking songs. I'm just trying to help ya' outta the ass-end of the civilized world. So how about a little mother fucking gratitude?"

"I don't think you could speak with if I removed the word 'fuck' from your vocabulary," said Sophie while remaining cool and collected. Miriam, standing behind Jacob, stifled a snicker.

"Fine, ya' know what?" Jacob snapped. Standing up and angrily pushing his chair away, he said, "I'm out. You're back on your own. Go wherever the fuck you want."

Jacob stormed off towards a hallway to the left of the bar that purported to lead to the banquet halls and restrooms. The bartender continued to surveil him.

"He's got quite a temper," commented Sophie as she observed Jacob depart. She then focused on Miriam as if measuring her and said, "The two of you seem to have that in common, at least."

Miriam's eyes darted to Sophie. She snarled.

"We should've left you in that shithole," Miriam said.

· · · ·

MIRIAM FOLLOWED JACOB down the uninhabited hallway, the demon puzzled by his suddenly cold, distant behavior. He glanced over his shoulder as he walked. Sophie was gone.

"What the fuck's the matter with you?" Miriam queried in annoyance, her insecurity fueling her discontent. Jacob abruptly stopped and whirled around towards her.

"'You unclean spirit!'" he exclaimed ferociously without provocation as he pinned her to the wall. He bellowed, "'What is your name?!'" (Excerpts from the Gospel of Mark 5:8-9).

Jacob's spiritual command bankrupted Miriam of her power. She shrieked at him in a hideous, mind-numbing pitch and recoiled in terror from the dazzling, spiritual light emanating from him.

"Miriam!" she confessed against her will in her demonic voice. Her body wracked with pain and bereft of her demonic abilities, she wilted under his spiritual power and anger.

"Were you in on Vanessa's possession?!" asked Jacob with fierce determination. Unaffected by her screech, he pushed his body against Miriam to smother her against the wall. He twice pointed a finger in her face and snarled, "And don't you fucking lie to me! Were you?!"

"No!" answered Miriam monstrously while struggling against Jacob. Her strength rekindled while his waned and she managed to thrust him away with a bitter, "Fuck you!"

"Fuck me?! Fuck me?! Fuck you, you fucking cunt!" he shouted while gesturing emphatically. He continued to berate her as his spiritual light winked out, yelling, "I left my fucking wife for you, and two teenage girls who'd already lost their real fucking father! Liz may not've fucking loved me in the end but it was still just enough to stick around. Now all that's gone. If you're not it, I'm *fucked!* Hear that! I'm *fucked!* So either jump on the mother fucking Jesus train or get the fuck outta my life!"

Jacob punched the wall next to Miriam's head, screamed "Fuck!" and stormed off down the hallway. She trembled and her jaw dropped as she watched Jacob stomp away. Regaining her senses, she collapsed to the floor and bawled.

"I'm sorry," Miriam whimpered while sobbing without tears.

• • • •

DESIRING TO HIDE FROM the world, Jacob found a small, isolated booth nestled in a far corner of Vitoria. Ostensibly a place for the restaurant staff to take breaks, it was tucked behind a wall near the kitchen. A bottle of whiskey and a one-quarter-full glass sat in front of him.

"At least I'm still breathin'," Jacob said as he imbibed the contents of his glass. He grasped the bottle and poured himself another drink as he mused, "If that's even a positive anymore."

Sophie stepped out from behind the wall, the young blonde holding her baseball bat like a cane. She, as was her wont, observed Jacob without emotion; however, he sensed for the first time the astuteness of her observation. His face hardened.

"What's the deal with that bat?" asked Jacob as he lifted the glass to his lips and gulped from it. Studying the bat closely for the first time, he noticed its worn, splintered surface and inquired, "I mean, is it like a security blanket, or a doll, or did your dead dad play baseball with you when you were six or what?"

Sophie released the bat and it hit the floor with a clatter. She stepped over it as it rolled away.

"It's just a bat," replied Sophie blithely. Picking up the bottle of whiskey, she topped off Jacob's glass and said, "I use it to hit people."

Sophie set the bottle down. Leaning forward with her forearms resting on her thighs, she placed her bulbous bosoms on the table. Jacob struggled to maintain eye contact with her but his gaze inadvertently fell to her breasts. He panicked.

"So, ever been to the One-Two-Three-Four Lounge?" Jacob asked quickly while raising his gaze to Sophie's face. Her slender nose was prominent and pointed and, with her steady blue eyes, it gave her the type of inimitable look that always ensnared Jacob. An intoxication-like buzz bubbled up within him and lifted his sexual spirits and his penis. He warded off the feeling with another gulp of whiskey.

"No," answered Sophie. She failed to react to Jacob's poorly-veiled attraction and added dryly, "I took it off a dead girl a few years ago."

"Why?" Jacob asked with a grimace. His skin crawled.

"Because I liked the shirt," said Sophie without the slightest trace of concern or remorse. Her callous response further blunted Jacob's newfound interest.

"You're so fucking weird," uttered Jacob before taking another drink of his whiskey. Sophie's earlier rejection prickling him, he bluntly inquired, "So, given that you don't have *daddy issues*, why are you back?"

Sophie languidly blinked and tilted her head to the right. Jacob furrowed his brow as several quiet seconds passed.

"I saw your little dustup with Miriam," explained Sophie, "and I realized I needed a new baseball bat."

Jacob sat up straight and smirked. He then chuckled.

"Ah, looking for a spiritual bodyguard," Jacob said in a sardonic tone. He folded his arms and stated, "Well, I'm feeling a little less charitable now, *kiddo*. So, if I agree, what're you willing to throw on the table? The bat? Your dead-girl t-shirt?"

"Sex," said Sophie matter-of-factly. Jacob laughed.

"That's a little presumptuous, don't ya' think?" countered Jacob despite the adrenaline coursing through his veins and the blood engorging his penis.

"Not when you've got a hard-on like that," shot back Sophie. Discomfited by her penetrating awareness, Jacob's smile disappeared and he squirmed in his seat.

"*Mr. Gottschalk,*" beckoned Adedewe as she appeared from behind the wall.

"Uh, yeah . . . hey," Jacob stammered as he scooted further under the table to hide his erection.

"I'd like to take you to your suite, now," advised Adedewe. She clasped her hands in front of her stomach and queried, "Will your *friend* here be joining you?"

"Uh . . . yes," Jacob said. He bit his lip while feeling the alcohol in his bloodstream and the pull of Sophie's youthful allure. Shaking his head in the affirmative, he stated, "Yes, she will."

• • • •

JACOB AND SOPHIE SILENTLY followed Adedewe to their suite. Their host turned a final corner and stopped in front of large French doors with elaborate panes of translucent glass. She thrust them open and turned to address her guests.

"Compliments of my Master," she said while welcoming them with a warm smile. A short, wide hallway lined with huge mirrors opened into an immense great room centered on a fountain and its circular basin. A leather sectional surrounded the fountain, its sections separated by two entrances into the fountain area and regularly-spaced cocktail tables. Water leapt out of the fountain, splashed into the basin and gurgled as it churned and flowed against the basin's exterior wall. Each side of the room contained high arches, the right arch leading to bedrooms and the left arch leading to a dining area. A center arch led to a windowed chamber containing a large hot tub.

"Look, Jake, a hot tub," Sophie said while peering into the chamber. Jacob remained in the suite's entry hallway and chewed the inside of his mouth nervously. He expected Miriam to appear any minute and slaughter he and Sophie.

"Is the suite satisfactory?" Adedewe asked politely.

"No, it's not," said Miriam as she appeared in the entry hallway. Lunging toward the mirror to her right and punching her hand through the glass, she reached into a once-concealed observation room and yanked a man in a suit through the broken mirror. Lifting the man to his knees and holding him by his maxilla, she slowly pressed her claws into the soft palate of his mouth. Shards of glass littered the floor.

The man's face bled from multiple lacerations. He attempted to scream in pain as Miriam penetrated his soft palate but she immediately withdrew her hand and grasped his mouth to stifle his cry. Glowering at him and shaking her head in the negative, she shoved him to the floor.

"So we'll need a different room," demanded Miriam demonically. She punctuated her sentence with a threatening growl.

"But of course," Adedewe replied though her contempt for Miriam bled through her diplomacy. Miriam flung the man into the hallway, waited for Adedewe to depart and then slammed the doors closed behind them.

"Nice work," commented Jacob casually. Miriam whirled around to face Jacob.

"Even for a fucking cunt?" she queried bitterly. Human and demon engaged in an optical battle for several seconds before Jacob mischievously grinned.

"Even for a fucking cunt," answered Jacob. Miriam rushed him but fell harmlessly into his embrace. Looking over his shoulder, she noticed Sophie standing in the hot tub room's archway.

"What's *she* doing here?" Miriam inquired in her hybrid voice. Sophie stared at her with the faintest trace of a grin on her face. Miriam growled.

"Easy, Mirry," scolded Jacob. He, without further elaboration, added, "She changed her mind."

6

ELIZABETH GAZED THOUGHTFULLY out the window of a M1114 Humvee as it departed from a security outpost outside of Kaiser. Bereft of dopplegangers after the murders of Elsa and Angela, she traveled to the outpost by switching vehicles numerous times in locations throughout the city.

Thickening clouds ambled in from the West as they ushered a morning cold front to the area. Light rain soon fell, its drops littering the Humvee with dots of water as a strengthening wind arose behind it. Daylight faded.

Elizabeth sat in the rear passenger seat behind Darby, who insisted on driving, while Darius sat behind Sarah. Darby clicked on the windshield wipers as the rain intensified.

"Jesus fucking Christ," griped Darby due to the arrival of precipitation. Squeamish of her blasphemy, Sarah winced but kept her eyes on the road ahead. Reaching into her jacket, Darby removed her silver flask with the words "Fuck You" engraved upon it. She drove with her knees while unscrewing its top.

"Put it away, dear sister," Elizabeth ordered. Darby threw a glance over her shoulder, the motion causing a string of light-brown hair to pull free of her ponytail and dangle near her right eye. She lifted the flask to her lips.

Elizabeth drew her pistol with blinding speed and pushed it into the back of her sister's neck, the barrel even with the top of her spinal cord. Darby froze while Darius and Sarah watched in disbelief.

"Put it away or you'll end up in a wheelchair or a coffin," instructed Elizabeth coldly before cocking the gun. Darby hesitated for a few seconds. Swallowing her ire instead of her whiskey, she screwed the top back onto the flask and stowed it in her jacket.

"You weren't kidding," she stated while recalling Elizabeth's murder of Agatha. Elizabeth holstered her weapon.

"My daughter may already be dead," said Elizabeth without emotion while looking into Darby's eyes through the rearview mirror. She then looked to Sarah and warned, "There's no margin of error for *any* of us."

Last of all Elizabeth turned her attention to Darius who nodded his head in solemn, supportive agreement. His steadiness bolstered her and fed her sexual attraction to him. She offered him a thankful, muted grin and returned her gaze to the outside world. Retreating into herself, Elizabeth remembered Darius's powerful embrace during lovemaking. His sexual prowess rendered her pleasurably-satiated every single time.

Jacob suddenly crawled into Elizabeth's mind like a perverted cockroach. His depraved sexual appetites always discomfited her, his fetishes causing her to crave the slower, more passionate occasions they rarely shared. Preventing herself from looking at Darius, she compared and contrasted Jacob's devious, sex-focused coitus and Darius's tender-yet-masculine lovemaking. Her cheeks reddened in shame.

"You're still a married woman," she admonished herself.

· · · ·

ADEDEWE CONFIDENTLY entered the banquet room, the demon turning around and walking backward for her final few steps. Raising her arms up to present the elaborate chamber, she smiled proudly.

"As you requested, a romantic setting perfect for star-crossed lovers," she proclaimed.

A huge waterfall constituted the far wall of the banquet room, a thin sheet of water running down a camel-brown, stone wall into a shallow pool at its base. Lust-red curtains hung on either side of the waterfall, each curtain backlit by prominent white lighting that, when shining through the curtains, created a red, romantic ambiance. Stained, mahogany-wood panels, some austere and some ornate, seamlessly covered the walls and ceiling.

A round banquet table, ornamented with a lust-red tablecloth, sat in front of the waterfall. Eight chairs surrounded the table, an elegant place setting before each one - white plates, polished silverware, crystal glasses and lust-red napkins held in circular, mahogany-wood bands. Several off-white candles and a mahogany base formed the centerpiece.

Two high-topped beverage tables at which dinner guests could congregate to imbibe cocktails flanked the banquet table. A lamp under each table emitted a bright white light which shone through the floor-length, red tablecloth. Black-and-red-brindle carpeting blanketed the floor.

"The lights will be dimmed and the candles lit with romantic music playing in the background, of course," Adedewe explained while sauntering around the table. She stopped and straightened an errant spoon.

"Impeccable," remarked a smooth, male voice. It, with deviousness in its tone, said, "I believe it's time to prepare our guests for dinner."

. . . .

JACOB ENTERED THE MAIN room of the new-though-identical suite while squirming uncomfortably within the tight fit of his black tuxedo. The sound of the gurgling fountain drew his attention, in the basin of which floated pieces of two blue, broken shoes. A defiant Miriam sat on the sectional with her legs folded beneath her.

"What the fuck did you do?" Jacob inquired. A pile of blue, shredded dress material sat next to Miriam.

"I'm not going," snapped Miriam with a glare. She rose to her feet and paced uneasily, her disheveled red dress fluttering with each dramatic turn. She grumbled, "This *dinner* is just the opening act in some fucking evil scheme. *I* should know."

"You're going," Jacob shot back. Recalling the last time he wore a tuxedo – at the wedding of Sören's daughter – Jacob fiddled with the jacket and complained, "I fucking hate these things."

"Then take it off," demanded Miriam impatiently in her hybrid voice. She approached him and complained, "It's fucking weird that she wants us to dress up anyway. We should just get the fucking hell outta here. I hate this place."

"And go where?" Jacob countered as he approached her.

"Not to some fucked-up, demonic dinner party," replied Miriam bitterly. Pouting, she looked away.

"Look," Jacob said. Taking Miriam's chin in his left hand and gently guiding her eyes back to his own, he explained, "This isn't the opening act in some scheme, Mirry. It's the second act in the temptation of Jacob

Gottschalk. But this 'Master' of Adedewe's is going to have to show at least a few cards tonight, and the more of his cards we see, the better."

"What about Vanessa?" asked Miriam. Jacob's face contorted.

"That wasn't Vanessa," Jacob answered quickly. Gnawed by doubt, he said, "Just a feint."

Miriam pondered Jacob's words with a disturbed frown. She disagreed with his assessment but a knock at the door interrupted her thoughts. Jacob and Miriam looked to one another and then the door.

"Yeah, who is it?" Jacob asked suspiciously.

"Adedewe, Mr. Gottschalk," answered Adedewe. She added cordially, "I've come to escort you to the banquet room."

Glancing at Miriam, Jacob raised his eyebrows in a "here we go" manner. She growled at him with a sneer though her hostility was intended for Adedewe. Jacob proceeded to the door and opened it.

"Good evening," greeted Adedewe with a nod to Jacob. Looking to Miriam with disapprobation, she added, "I take it the dress was not to your satisfaction."

"Fuck. You. Cunt," Miriam replied. Her dress fluttering with an abrupt turn, she returned to her seat on the sectional. Adedewe bristled at Miriam's enmity.

"*Mirry,*" Jacob scolded lightly. She threw up the shreds of her dress in the air, the pieces drifting to the floor like leaves. Adedewe looked beyond Jacob and to the hallway leading to the bedrooms.

"I see that your dress *was* to your satisfaction," Adedewe commented, a pleasant smile of approval coming to her face.

"Holy shit," Jacob gushed as he turned around. Sophie donned a long-sleeved, strapless dress of thick, black cloth that wrapped around her shoulders like a cloak. It hugged the contours of her sensuous body and stylishly bunched up in different places as she moved. Eyeshadow of the faintest blue and light, pinkish lipstick graced her face but her hair remained in its usual, mussed condition. Jacob's eyes guiltily absorbed every inch of Sophie's picturesque physicality and he uttered, "You look . . . *very nice.*"

"Thanks," said Sophie as she walked to him. Miriam sensed Jacob's physical reaction to her and scowled. She popped up and moved to his side, the demon interjecting herself between Jacob and Sophie.

"Are we ready?" Adedewe asked. Sophie fiddled with her small, black purse.

"As we'll ever be," replied Jacob. He chewed the inside of his cheek, popping the callous several times as he contemplated the dangers inherent in dealing with demons. Jacob nudged Miriam and said, "*All* of us."

"*Fine*," sneered Miriam. Intertwining arms with Jacob, she forcefully led him forward. Sophie, studying the interaction between them, followed in their wake.

• • • •

LEANING ON HIS RIGHT elbow on a high-topped table, Jacob imbibed his cocktail greedily. His impending meeting with what he presumed to be a high-level demon unnerved him regardless of his developing talent for exorcism. He prayed for strength and courage.

"They're fucking everywhere, Jake," grumbled Miriam as she leaned into him. She planted herself between Jacob and Sophie, the young blonde sipping from a glass of water but remaining silent. Miriam squirmed and complained, "I've never sensed so many demons in one material place. This is really fucking bad."

"Jesus fucking Christ, Mirry, knock it off," Jacob blurted in annoyance. He took another swig of whiskey and then massaged his eyes with his right index finger and thumb, saying, "I never thought I'd meet someone who's more negative than I am."

Boiling inside, Miriam tensed to unload her wrath on Jacob. Adedewe ceremoniously opened the banquet room doors, however, and interrupted Miriam's burgeoning vitriolic upsurge.

"I would like to introduce Mrs. Elizabeth Nicks, Ms. Sarah Russo and Ms. Darby Nicks," announced Adedewe graciously as she entered the room. She halted at the door and motioned for the trio to proceed into the room.

"*Oh, shit*," Jacob muttered. Miriam snarled to register her displeasure with him. He, however, ignored her and stood mesmerized by the majestic beauty of his wife as she glided into view. She wore a strapless, carmine-hued ballroom gown with a broad sash tied just under her bust. Her hair was styled in a flawless French twist and her lips were painted with matching lipstick. Twinkling diamond earrings adorned her ears.

"Hello, Jacob," she said with a loving yearning, the Constable realizing how much she missed her husband. Her muted green eyes shimmered with intense emotion. Passion welled within Jacob as his love for his wife overwhelmed him.

Sensing Jacob abruptly slipping from her grasp, Miriam roared ferociously and accelerated through the air. She barreled towards Elizabeth with her arms outstretched and her teeth bared. Sarah, outfitted in Ursuline garb, appeared from behind Elizabeth and interposed herself between human and demon.

"Miriam, no!" she yelled harshly. A heretofore-absent spiritual force field raged around Sarah, its contours seen only by those with spiritual vision. Darby, wearing a black, unembellished militaristic uniform, followed on Sarah's heels with gun drawn. Pausing due to her position, she considered simply shooting Miriam through Sarah's body regardless of the morality of such action.

Miriam, meanwhile, hurled herself backward against her forward momentum to evade Sarah's holy tempest. She turned a somersault in the air and landed on her feet. Livid, she screeched hideously at Sarah with murderous intentions burning in her spirit.

"Enough!" bellowed a male voice, its compelling, commanding tone paralyzing Miriam, Sarah and Darby. It lowered its volume and said, "Ms. Nicks, please holster your weapon."

Darby reluctantly complied while an aberrantly-sheepish Miriam averted her gaze like a mischievous schoolgirl with a hopeless crush on her judgmental teacher. Sarah remained still though even she could not tear her attention away from the man.

"Who the fuck are you?" Jacob bluntly inquired of the tall, tuxedo-clad man. Every female, human and demon alike, desirously watched him and eagerly absorbed his presence. Proving to be the lone exception, Sophie quietly observed the entire scene with keen eyes.

"Now, Miriam, you will go with Adedewe and change into proper dinner attire," instructed Aaron firmly. Jacob's heart plummeted into his stomach as

Miriam lowered her head in shame and obediently followed Adedewe. He trailed them before Aaron blocked his path.

"I must insist that you remain here, Mr. Gottschalk," said Aaron. Jacob fumed as he explained, "Miriam will return shortly, I assure you. Now, if you will all take your seats, everything will be explained to your satisfaction as soon as she returns."

"Not good," Jacob thought, humiliated by the way the man entranced both Elizabeth and Miriam, "not good at all."

• • • •

JACOB SAT NEXT TO SOPHIE at the table with the waterfall to their backs. The rest of the counterclockwise circuit was comprised of Sarah, Darby, Elizabeth, Aaron, an empty chair and Adedewe. Romantic music floated through the banquet room as its candles flickered. The humans ate their salads while empty plates sat in front of the demons.

"The one throwing daggers at me," said Sophie as Elizabeth sized her up from a distance, "that's gotta be your wife."

"Yep," answered Jacob as he shoveled in a forkful of salad. He felt his heart tugged in different directions as it simultaneously yearned for Miriam and Elizabeth. He and his wife shared quick, uncertain glances at first but he ceased looking at her when she and Aaron began conversing about Kaiser

"'No one can serve two masters,'" counseled Sarah quietly, "'for either he will hate the one and love the other, or he will be devoted to one and despise the other.'" (Excerpt from the Gospel of Matthew 6:24).

"Yeah, I've heard that before," Jacob said under his breath without looking at Sarah. Spooked by her quoting of the same verse as the "light" child, he glanced at Elizabeth and then the empty chair as he chewed another bite of his salad. A scrape of Sophie's fork on her plate wrested him from his thoughts and he said softly, "If you wanna help, tell me which one I should love and which one I should hate."

"I appreciate your patience," Aaron said as he noticed Sarah's and Jacob's side conversation. Looking back to Elizabeth, he stated, "I know we have many critical issues to discuss."

"My patience is grounded in your assurance of a swift resolution to my . . . *problem*," answered Elizabeth, the Constable carefully crafting her words. Despite her compliance with Aaron's request to delay the discussion of Vanessa's abduction, her words piqued Jacob's interest and he pounced.

"What problem?" he questioned with narrowed eyes.

"All in due time," cautioned Aaron with a stern expression, "so please, no further discussion until Miriam returns."

"Fuck you, demon," Jacob snarled. Hating to be left out of the loop for any period of time, he griped, "This is bullshit."

"Jacob, please," chastised Elizabeth, "there's more at stake here than you realize."

"Fuck you, too," Jacob barked while leaping to his feet and knocking over his chair. Darby began to rise but Elizabeth squeezed her arm and she aborted her planned action. Jacob gesticulated wildly and ranted, "You can sit on this guy's cock later, right now I wanna know what the fuck's going on! I've had enough of this cloak and dagger bullshit!"

Sophie struggled with laughter during Jacob's rant. The others remained silent.

"Sit down, Mr. Gottschalk," ordered Aaron with the slightest traces of a demonic tone in his voice. Adedewe's black eyes rebuked Jacob and Elizabeth scowled at him.

"Oh yeah, douchebag?" Jacob asked haughtily though he still exhibited a slight tremble. Drawing himself up and calling on the Holy Spirit, he inquired with conviction, "'What is your name?'" (Excerpt from the Gospel of Luke 24:39).

Aaron cringed but withstood the pain while Adedewe demonically screamed at Jacob. Elizabeth, Darby and Sarah shuddered in agony as her cry pierced their eardrums. Aaron composed himself.

Another figure just outside the banquet room door caught Jacob's attention before he could complete his spiritual assault. His jaw dropped.

"Mirry?"

• • • •

GRUDGINGLY PLACING one open-toed, high-heeled shoe in front of the other, Miriam cautiously entered the banquet room. She wore a slinky, strapless dress, the black garment cut just above her breasts and just below her mid-thigh. A black choker encircled her pale neck with an obsidian charm suspended from it by a tiny, three-linked gold chain. The soulless blackness of the obsidian resembled the voids of Miriam's jet eyes; it seemed as if someone plucked one of her demonic orbs from its socket and set it in the necklace. Two gold filaments encompassed the spherical charm and connected it to the gold links.

A black hair band collected Miriam's curly hair into a bottle neck before dispersing it again onto her back. Never in her life as a *daimoniou* had makeup graced her deceptively-youthful face.

Jacob studied her with captivation and a newfound appreciation of her beauty. Elizabeth's eyes darted to her husband, the Constable surveying his adoring countenance before slowly returning her attention to Miriam.

"Please be seated, Miriam," Aaron directed as he motioned to the chair next to him. Miriam complied, her atypical deference concerning Jacob. She failed to even acknowledge him.

"Hello, Miriam," greeted Elizabeth with great effort, her hatred for Miriam making her uncomfortable in her own skin. Her welcome of the *daimoniou* stunned Jacob and he gaped at her as she elaborated, "Our host has suggested that we try to resolve our differences and avoid any violent confrontations."

"You are a fucking cunt," Miriam stated with fake civility. Sarah cringed. Miriam smiled joyously and lifted her water glass in a mock toast, saying, "Here's to me tearing out your fucking throat and watching you suffocate and/or bleed to death, bitch."

"That is no way to speak to guests at a dinner engagement," corrected Aaron quickly as Miriam lowered her glass. Looking to Elizabeth, he offered, "You'll have to excuse Miriam. Apparently, Mr. Gottschalk's horrendous manners and language are impairing her judgment. Now, Miriam, apologize to Mrs. Nicks immediately, please."

Miriam instantly crushed the glass in her hand, her efforts spraying tiny shards of glass everywhere and startling Jacob and Sarah. Darby and

Elizabeth instinctively reached for their pistols while Miriam glowered at Aaron. She finally relented.

"Sorry," apologized Miriam without looking at Elizabeth. Servers abruptly entered the room. Deftly sweeping up the debris of Miriam's display and distributing the entrée of lamb chops, they derailed the lingering tension.

"Now, if we can avoid any further outbursts, we may begin," Aaron said. He waved his upturned hands at his guests and explained, "You have all converged here at Chinese Peak, certainly not by *my* design, however-."

"Bullshit," interjected Jacob bitterly. He fumed and said, "We're all here so your Master can finish the job that Miriam started."

"Mr. Gottschalk, you must learn to control your emotions," Aaron chastened. Mustering a rare earnestness for a demon, he said, "I have nothing to do with you or your temptation, other than the fact *you* arrived at *my* doorstep. As I understand it, you were sent here by Agatha Moriarty, who informed your wife of that fact, which is why she's here."

"Is that true, Liz?" inquired Jacob. Elizabeth looked to Aaron for approval. He nodded to indicate his assent.

"Yes," she said but nearly faltered as she thought of Vanessa.

"What is it, Liz?" Jacob questioned. Elizabeth covered her mouth with her hand and fought back tears as he asked, "What the hell's going on?"

"S-Sarah, p-please," she muttered before squelching a sob.

"Of course," replied Sarah compassionately. Pausing briefly to collect her thoughts, she addressed Jacob and Miriam. Speaking with the utmost gravity, she explained, "Marcion possessed Vanessa and absconded with her two days ago. We've come to seek your help in rescuing her."

• • • •

NO ONE SPOKE AS THE air in the room became brittle. The crushing news of Vanessa's abduction shocked Jacob to his very core. Miriam watched him closely and wondered if he would reveal their earlier encounter with her.

"We've seen her," Jacob announced, his words piercing the silent tension like the ringing of a bell on a frigid winter night. He clicked the callous inside his mouth twice.

"What?!" asked Elizabeth desperately. Brushing off Darby, she demanded, "When?!"

"Last night, by the main fountain," Jacob confirmed while nodding in the direction of the casino entrance. Swallowing his distress, he added guiltily, "I tried to cast Marcion out of her . . . but he got away."

Elizabeth buried her face in her right hand and wept softly. Darby, risking revelation of her ties to Marcion, slammed her fist down on the table.

"We're fucking wasting time!" snarled Darby. Her angry eyes darting to Miriam, she demanded, "Where the *fuck's* Marcion?!"

"I don't know," answered Miriam, her voice tinged with bitterness. She maintained her composure but still returned Darby's glare.

"What do you mean you don't know?" Jacob and Elizabeth queried simultaneously, both spouses surprised by Miriam's reply.

"I mean I don't fucking know," grumbled Miriam, the demon annoyed and hurt by the spouses' emotional connection.

"Perhaps you should explain *why* you don't know," Aaron suggested. Jacob furrowed his brow as he observed Miriam squirm under Aaron's direction. She lowered her gaze and stared into her empty plate.

"Marcion can conceal himself from me," admitted Miriam begrudgingly. Scowling, she continued, "He can conceal himself from most demons. I can't find him if he doesn't want to be found."

"Awesome," Darby complained. She rolled her eyes and said, "This whole trip was a big fucking waste. Just fucking awesome."

"To the contrary," interjected Aaron. Standing up, he walked slowly around the table and stated, "Miriam may not be able to locate Marcion, but I most certainly can."

"Who the fuck *are* you?" Jacob demanded. Aaron rolled his eyes to Jacob, their brown hue turning to a soulless black, and smiled deviously.

"Enough, Jacob," chided Elizabeth. Frustrated by Jacob's constant interruptions, she said, "Control your anger, *for once*, because I would like to find my daughter."

"Miriam, tell Mr. Gottschalk who I am," Aaron ordered, the *daimoniou* taunting Jacob with his snide tone. Miriam, unable to look at Jacob, struggled to speak before complying.

"Aaron," Miriam confessed with difficulty. Her human voice barely perceptible, she muttered, "He's Aaron."

"Oh, fuck this," said Jacob, the hybrid emotion of anger, fear and embarrassment erupting within him. Sophie kicked him under the table but he ignored it. Standing up and addressing Miriam, Jacob stated determinedly, "You're getting your wish. We're bailing."

Expecting Miriam to defend him against any human incursions, Jacob rounded the table towards the doors. She, however, remained motionless and, before Jacob passed Aaron, Elizabeth leapt up and pistol-whipped him on the base of his skull. Losing consciousness, Jacob saw no more.

7

TINY, ACUTE PAINS RIPPLED through Jacob's chest as he abruptly regained consciousness. His anxiety spiked as the all-to-familiar burn steadily grew in his stomach. Complete darkness enveloped him. The base of his skull throbbed.

Struggling, Jacob felt the bite of tough, inflexible cords on his torso, which was firmly affixed to the metal chair in which he sat, and his wrists, which were tightly bound behind his back. The chill of the chair's cold, hard touch radiated through his clothing.

"Well, this fucking sucks," Jacob commented blithely while ceasing his struggle against the unyielding cords and relaxing his body. He leaned his head back and gazed upward into the blackness. Thoughts of Elizabeth and Miriam tiptoed into his mind and raised his ire. Their quick, bizarre obedience to Aaron troubled him while their veiled surrender to his wily charms shamed him. His cheeks reddened and warmed.

"I need a drink," he said loudly and carelessly. Pink, neon light suddenly blinded Jacob, its luminance jarringly bathing the entire room in a fresh, vibrant glow. He closed his eyes and jerked his head to the side to avoid the visual onslaught. Squinting as his eyes adjusted to the pink light, he surveyed his surroundings.

Constructed entirely of smooth, perfectly-formed concrete painted a reflective white, the austere room starkly contrasted with the opulent luxury of Chinese Peak. Banks of neon tubes adorned the walls, the fixtures ostensibly running the entire circuit of the chamber. Jacob strained to turn his body and see the remainder of the room but the area lying directly behind him remained a mystery.

"Who the fuck comes up with this shit?" Jacob asked aloud. Disoriented from his recent unconsciousness and the transition from total darkness to the overpowering pink light, he started when footsteps rang out from behind him. He quickly turned his head to the left, acquired a lean female form in his peripheral vision and questioned in disbelief, "Liz?"

Jacob watched his wife stride past him wearing a wig of short, pink hair and a pink, latex seduction dress, the skirt of which contained equidistant ruffles and terminated at her upper thigh. The cap-sleeved, open-collared bodice covered her entire torso save for a circular cutaway on her chest, the opening revealing her ample cleavage.

Jacob's gaze dropped to his wife's buttocks as she circled around him, her posterior barely concealed by her skirt. Leather, knee-length boots, latex, elbow-length gloves and shuttered sunglasses – all of a pink hue – rounded out her strange-yet-enticing ensemble.

Elizabeth passed behind him and returned to his left side. Grasping Jacob's shoulder and throwing a leg over him, she seated herself on his lap. He winced, the contact tweaking his healing bullet wound. Bringing both hands to his face, Elizabeth tenderly pressed her fingertips into his cheeks and longingly focused on his countenance. She slowly moved in to kiss him but Jacob evaded her lips.

"Babe, what the fuck's going on?" Jacob inquired in bewilderment. Remembering his predicament, he struggled against the cords and demanded, "Untie me, damn it."

A familiar face pierced Jacob like a flaming arrow launched into his heart. Examining the countenance of the woman before him, he realized she was not his wife.

"*Vanessa?*" he asked hoarsely. She smiled slyly and slid her hands upward to affectionately grasp Jacob's head.

"Hi, Daddy," cooed Vanessa before planting a sultry kiss on Jacob's mouth and briefly sucking on his bottom lip. She released it with a soft "pop" and queried playfully, "Did you miss me?"

Revulsion stemmed the tide of Jacob's rage long enough for him to realize that Marcion no longer possessed his stepdaughter. He leaned his head away from Vanessa's mouth.

"There's no one else in there?" Jacob asked.

"No, Daddy," remarked Vanessa fondly as she ran her right hand through his hair. Wrapping her arms around his neck, she happily continued, "*You saved me.*"

"It's really you?" Jacob inquired as a tremor of doubt rocked his mind. His stepdaughter seemed foreign to him.

"You don't believe me?" asked Vanessa while wiggling on his lap and pouting. A chill trickled down Jacob's spine and caused him to shiver as his eyes glazed over.

"How'd you disappear so fast?" he inquired. Vanessa grabbed Jacob's hair in her right hand and directed his eyes to her sunglasses. He stated, "I looked everywhere for you."

"I heard your voice," explained Vanessa while shivering. Jacob pulled his hair from her uncomfortable grasp as, with a quivering bottom lip, she said, "But then the demons came."

"Is that so?" Jacob responded rhetorically. He chewed the inside of his mouth as he focused on her absurd sunglasses and said, "Why don't you tell Aaron to go fuck himself? I'm not falling for this bullshit."

Vanessa, with a muted grin, removed her sunglasses with her right hand and casually flung them aside. They struck the cement floor with a crack and skidded to a halt.

Her eyelids raised and revealed demonic eyes, each hollow orb jet-black and evil. Stunned despite his suspicion, Jacob attempted to recoil to no avail as Vanessa held him fast. He gaped at her in astonishment for twenty seconds before she released him and rose to her feet.

"We can still play, though, can't we?" asked Vanessa. Pulling off her left latex glove with a resounding snap, she flung it over Jacob's head. She waved to a horrified Jacob, his stepdaughter wriggling her clawed fingertips to emphasize her demonic transformation. Vanessa then removed her other glove with a devious grin and tossed it aside.

"So you've come to take Miriam's place," Jacob said grimly, his insides churning and his skin crawling. Vanessa's resemblance to a demonic Elizabeth nauseated him but he continued with contempt, "This won't work so you might as well let her go."

Ignoring Jacob's disdain, Vanessa rotated around. Grasping the hemline of the dress's skirt, she gracefully lifted the dress and began slithering out of it. Uncomfortable, Jacob looked away from her shapely buttocks before glancing at her again.

"Put that back on," Jacob uttered with a look of sorrowful disgust on his face.

Vanessa turned back to Jacob clad only in a miniscule pink thong. She folded her arms and teasingly concealed her full breasts. Jacob warred against his awakening sex drive.

"You're still married to my Mommy," Vanessa admonished licentiously with a satisfied smirk, the demon within her perceiving the growing lust in Jacob's eyes and the growing erection in his pants. Subtly altering the manner in which she spoke, she stated, "I have long desired to speak with you, Jacob Gottschalk."

Instantly recognizing the hint of Assarion's seductive-yet-sinister tone in Vanessa's voice, Jacob glowered at her.

"Come out of her!" demanded Jacob. Vanessa's body started as if jolted by electricity and then shuddered. Lunging towards Jacob but keeping her arms folded, she screamed at him hideously and bared her pointed teeth.

"Stop!" Assarion shouted in a terrifying demonic voice.

"Come out of her!" Jacob demanded as he felt the Holy Spirit surge within him. Assarion roared in excruciating pain and slammed Vanessa's body to the ground. She convulsed but continued to keep her arms folded.

"Stop or she dies!" bellowed Assarion amid her convulsions. Jacob halted his spiritual assault.

"You're coming out of her," threatened Jacob, the ire boiling in the depths of his spirit. Assarion rose to her knees and watched him with cold attention as he asked, "So why don't you make this easy and just do it yourself?"

"What if I told you that coming out of your dear, sweet Vanessa would be unspeakably tragic for her?" Assarion cryptically queried. Jacob's anger cooled as he prepared for the propaganda to come.

"Really?" he responded. He chuckled and added derisively, "Let's hear it then, *daimoniou*. And you might wanna throw in what the fuck you want with me, too."

Jacob's distrustful eyes chastised Assarion. She nodded in agreement.

"Of course," Assarion acquiesced with a kind smile. She stood up and said, "If you care to humor me, I'll explain to you why yet another demon of the Abyss has taken an interest in Jacob Gottschalk, as well as the plight of poor Vanessa Nicks."

The Holy Spirit moved Jacob at the very second Assarion spoke his name though It did so in a subtle, fleeting manner. He heard Sarah's voice in his mind just as he heard her on a rainy night not so long ago: *"It is not those who are well who need a physician, but those who are sick.'"* (Excerpt from the Gospel of Luke 5:31).

Jacob bit his lip and warily surveyed Assarion. He decided that his immediate future, for better or for worse, involved the mysterious *daimoniou*.

"This setting is so uncomfortable," said Assarion, "so let's go somewhere a little more pleasant."

Assarion used Vanessa's mouth to place an ardent lip-lock on Jacob. The pink neon lights then died and the kiss ended as Assarion left Jacob alone in the darkness.

. . . .

"A WORD, MIRIAM," REQUESTED Aaron, the demon overtaking her with long strides despite her hurried pace. Jacob's detainment worried and agitated her and she hoped he would soon be returned to the suite.

"It's never just a word with you," she rejoined with a sneer while quickening her steps and marching down one of the massive hallways of Chinese Peak. Aaron matched her speed with little effort. He snatched her arm, halted her and spun her around to face him. His touch made her woozy and she shivered.

"Let go of me," Miriam uttered feebly though she failed to deliver her message with the forcefulness or profanity she intended.

"Despite its interference with my diplomatic efforts, I'm truly enjoying your caustic personality," commented Aaron, his cunning eyes twinkling as he examined her.

"I'm not the weak-willed, starry-eyed girl you seduced anymore," Miriam replied as she tugged lightly against Aaron's grasp. He released her.

"I know," said Aaron with hauteur. Offering her a heart-melting smile, he expounded, "I bestowed upon you the gift of demonic immortality and all its attendant powers and abilities. And, with the exception of your recent dalliance with Gottschalk, you've made exceptional use of them."

Miriam's head reeled, every fiber of her being pulled by the charismatic gravity of Aaron. Reminiscing on her past temptations and demonic exploits, she felt a selfish elation bubbling up within her. Aaron moved closer to her and she, drawn in by his masculine magnetism, moved closer to him.

"Tonight I negotiated a deal that will give me Kaiser," said Aaron. Reaching out to her with his left hand and motioning that she should take it, he continued, "That city teems with fragile, downtrodden humans ripe for temptation. A significant rise in suicides might persuade our Master to overlook certain transgressions on your part."

"*Never*," Miriam stated with great difficulty. The hallway darkened and the temperature dropped.

"I find it very peculiar that the Master has permitted you to spurn him, abandon your purpose and join one of the elect," remarked Aaron grimly as he withdrew his hand. Viewing her with contempt, he said, "I wonder if his tolerance will continue after Gottschalk's temptation is complete."

An alarm sounded in Miriam's spirit which caused her to spring backward. Aaron straightened up, Miriam's former tempter stone-faced but obviously peeved by her retreat.

"Perhaps he'll summon you back," threatened Aaron, his ire rising. Miriam tensed to shriek and flee but thoughts of Jacob truncated her fright.

"I'm going to my suite, if you'll excuse me," Miriam snarled as she whirled around and departed. Aaron smiled with satisfaction.

"As you wish," Aaron replied politely, his words causing Miriam to halt. He advised her, "You are *not* to leave your suite until further notice."

Miriam bristled at Aaron's command but accepted it. Swiftly rounding a corner, she disappeared into the immensity of Chinese Peak.

* * * *

EXHAUSTEDLY TOSSING her purse on her luxurious, king-sized bed, Elizabeth slipped off her shoes and sighed. She then retrieved her purse, unzipped it and pulled out her small semi-automatic pistol. Her cavernous bedroom, part of a suite in which she, Darby and Sarah resided, included an immense bathroom with a state-of-the-art hot tub.

"Forget about briefing me on your little dinner party?" inquired Darius while leaning against the doorframe with arms folded. Elizabeth slumped into a sitting position on the bed and offered him a weak, tired smile.

"No, I was planning on getting out of these shoes and this dress first," Elizabeth said with a trace of irritability in her voice. She gestured with her pistol as she spoke, expounding, "Then I was going to brief you, and then I was going to relax in a hot bubble bath with a glass or two of wine."

Elizabeth nearly broke down again but wrested herself back from the brink of despair. Darius offered her an expression of sympathy.

"They will be my only consolation in the next twelve hours," she said forlornly.

"Let's do it all at once," suggested Darius puckishly, her former lover adept at easing Elizabeth's tensions. She blushed and grinned.

"I'm still a married woman," Elizabeth objected though in a suggestive tone that did not match her words. She pondered her options while absorbing every inch of Darius's body with her eyes. Elizabeth also contemplated Jacob's dilatory outbursts during dinner, how he unwittingly admitted the demonic world into the lives of her children and how powerless he was to help save Vanessa. All his faults flooded her mind including his anger, his jealousy, his foul mouth and his bizarre brand of Christianity.

"Liz?" called Darius delicately, his words waking her from her funk. She smiled a sad, sheepish grin and motioned with her right index finger for him to approach. Darius entered her bedroom and closed the door behind him. Her decision made, Elizabeth surrendered her love for Jacob forever. She fell into Darius's arms and wept.

• • • •

MISBEHAVING WITH THE insolence of a spoiled child, Miriam tore the suite doors off their hinges and effortlessly hurled them down the hallway in a destructive, cacophonous display. Sophie, who sat on the fountain wall, glanced up at her without concern as she marched into the suite.

"Your lack of self-control is epic," said Sophie. She repeatedly ran her hand through the turbulent water of the fountain and, with a knowing smile, added, "It's one of the only things you and Jake have in common."

"Tell me why I shouldn't drown you right now," Miriam threatened in her hybrid voice. She displayed her fearsome teeth with a hiss and a sneer.

"Because if you do, and if Jake ever escapes this place, he'll face the world alone," replied Sophie with an eerie vibe. Her assertion discombobulated Miriam and blunted her homicidal intentions. Shifting her weight, Sophie said, "And we both know you don't want that for him."

"What the hell are you talking about?" Miriam asked with a shiver. She warily approached the fountain, the demon fearing Sophie's revelation like a human would fear her claws.

"You're not getting out of here with Jake . . . but you're already aware of that," advised Sophie while gazing into Miriam's eyes. She patted the fountain wall next to her and explained coldly, "Aaron's not going to let you leave. You're his again. So who goes with Jake? The wife who hates him? The sister-in-law who wants him dead? The nun who finds herself in a den of demons?"

Sophie chuckled. Miriam felt woozy so she accepted Sophie's direction and sat down.

"She'll never make it out of here alive," said Sophie as her mien hardened. The gears of Miriam's mind whirred.

"How does she know?" thought Miriam as panic crept over her.

"You love Jake, right?" asked Sophie. Miriam trembled.

"That's right," Miriam replied with a smug jealousy. Fueled by possessiveness, she scowled at Sophie and added, "*He's mine.*"

"Your love didn't help him much back there, did it?" inquired Sophie, her tone measured but her words biting. Miriam delayed her answer for nearly a minute.

"*No,*" Miriam confessed with a bowed head. Her deathly pale skin turned a shade of grey, her failure to protect Jacob shaking her very spirit. Sophie placed a reassuring hand on her shoulder but, to Miriam's surprise, it did not burn her skin.

"The best thing you can do for him now is to help him, *to help us*, get out of here," urged Sophie. She squeezed Miriam's shoulder.

"Do you love him?" Miriam inquired, her entire face twitching and quivering as she fought off sobs and rage.

"Does it matter?" countered Sophie with raised eyebrows.

"*Yes,*" the *daimoniou* whispered forlornly. Sophie's hand fell as Miriam dematerialized and limped into the material world.

• • • •

ELIZABETH SOAKED IN a hot, soothing bubble bath, the Constable nestled between Darius's powerful legs. Choosing the regular bath tub over the hot tub to experience greater intimacy, she cuddled into his body and felt his engorged penis press into her lower back. A multitude of candles illuminated the bathroom like a starry sky and instrumental relaxation music played over the bathroom's sound system. Two semiautomatic pistols, a half-empty glass of wine and an uncorked bottle sat on the floor.

"Feeling better?" asked Darius while wrapping his muscular arms around her. Elizabeth closed her eyes and wished she could remain in the safety of his embrace forever.

"Words cannot describe it," Elizabeth said with a peaceful sigh as she felt the satiation of an hour of passionate lovemaking. She pinned her hair up to keep it dry but strings of it fell and intermingled with the bubbles and bathwater. Despite desiring sleep, she instead addressed the demands of the Constabulary and said, "I suppose you've waited long enough for a briefing."

Elizabeth broke out of Darius'ss embrace and retrieved her glass of wine. She drained it and set it back on the bathroom tile.

"I exchanged Kaiser's criminal underworld for the safe return of Vanessa," Elizabeth stated. She scooted back into Darius. Recognizing her signal, he encompassed her in his arms once again. Elizabeth, content with his affection, then explained, "Aaron will deliver Vanessa to me, *alive and unharmed*, and in exchange he wants to harvest the fertile fields that are Kaiser's slums."

Elizabeth chuckled.

"He wants access to all my demented castaways," she continued. A single bead of sweat crossed her left temple and rolled down her cheek as she said, "In addition, Aaron agreed to keep all demonic activities *outside* the walls, permanently."

"We've heard that before," said Darius skeptically. He recalled her administration's constant efforts to extricate criminal operations that crept over the walls and into the city streets.

"With Agatha's demise, I needed to swiftly fill the power vacuum to avoid any disruptive, armed conflicts among her underlings," Elizabeth answered in irritation. Brushing it aside, she expounded, "Aaron also consented to the maintenance of the same terms as Agatha operated under. This deal will allow me to keep the underworld flow of cash and goods moving which is especially important given the opening of the overseas markets."

"Dealing with the devil is always dangerous," counseled Darius, the concern evident on his face. Elizabeth threw him a stinging glance.

"I'm not dealing with the devil," Elizabeth admonished angrily. Darius lifted his hands in surrender. Her ire quickly melted, however, and she added playfully, "I'm dealing with a *demon*."

"All right, all right," relented Darius with a grin. His tone turning serious, he said, "The slums are dangerous enough as it is. With all those damn demons running around, we're putting our people at significant risk."

"I'm not concerned about that," Elizabeth responded, "because Aaron understands it's beneficial for all involved that his minions operate in the shadows. Most citizens will never know of that dark world. Those who do will forever be a part of it or die."

"I pray you're right," said Darius as he lifted his knees and draped his arms over the edges of the tub.

"Speaking of prayer," Elizabeth said. She ran her hands from Darius's knees down to his ankles and grasped them, saying, "I'm assigning Sarah to your command. She'll be tasked with masterminding our spiritual defenses . . . whether she likes it or not."

"So, then, what's our next move?" inquired Darius as he digested Elizabeth's pact with Aaron. She reached back with her right hand, grasped the back of Darius's neck and pulled him into a passionate French kiss.

"Back to the bedroom, of course," she replied with a lustful smile.

• • • •

AROMATIC AIR, WARM and humid, brushed Jacob's face as his guards thrust him forward. He stumbled briefly but managed to steady himself despite his sore, stiff muscles.

Several hours after Assarion's abrupt departure, the guards whisked him from his concrete prison and hurriedly escorted him to a new destination.

His vision obscured by a tightly-tied blindfold, he now smelled the appealing scent of a particularly-fragrant flower and heard the soothing sounds of multiple fountains.

"Untie him and leave," ordered Vanessa's voice curtly, its tone far too sagacious for its age. Jacob heard the click of a locking mechanism and felt the cords around his wrists loosen. The guards pulled the cords from his hands and dutifully departed, their exit punctuated by the thuds of two heavy doors and an unusual, electronic whirring noise.

"You can remove the blindfold, Jake," offered Vanessa's voice amiably though it was undoubtedly infused with Assarion's distinct tone.

Jacob cautiously lifted the blindfold from his face. Dumbfounded by the way Vanessa watched him with licentious, twinkling eyes, he dropped his hands to his sides and the blindfold to the floor. His stepdaughter wore a revealing chemise of lavender silk festooned with images of oriental flowers and matching stiletto heels. He soon realized she wore nothing else as her lingerie revealed the outline of her taut, ample breasts and pert nipples.

"Her body pleases you," Assarion commented with delight and a wry smile. She shifted her shoulders and provocatively let the chemise's left strap fall. Glancing at her flawlessly-shaped breasts before returning her seductive gaze to Jacob, she continued, "Especially these."

An embarrassed Jacob's cheeks warmed as he averted his eyes from Vanessa's breasts. Assarion's earthly form pleased him indeed.

Overcoming his embarrassment, Jacob momentarily ignored Assarion and observed his ostentatious surroundings. He stood in a massive pentagonal chamber with a vaulted ceiling and white-tiled walls. Stretching out from Jacob's feet, a walkway of the black marble extended into the center of a large pool of water and provided access to a square island also constructed of black marble. Columns arose from each of its four corners and ascended into the ceiling.

The island contained a sitting area of posh, black chaise lounges and end tables surrounding a rectangular, fully-stocked bar. Fountain heads shaped like black flowers and affixed to each column gently poured water into the pool, its surface dotted with floating black lanterns titivated with bouquets of lavender flowers. Large, colorful koi swam in its waters

"This is opulent even for Chinese Peak," remarked Jacob as he studied the bizarre chamber. Assarion reclined in a chaise, the demon lying on her left side with her left arm on the back of the lounge. She held a glass of rosy-pink wine in her hands and appeared very much as if she were relaxing at a day spa. Jacob sat down across from her on another chaise lounge with his elbows on his knees and his hands folded in front of him.

"It was once a den of human decadence and iniquity," Assarion answered with a sexy smirk. She sipped her wine.

"What is it now?" asked Jacob bluntly, his eyes glazing over and falling to the floor.

"A den of demonic decadence and iniquity," Assarion retorted, her smirk widening.

"I noticed," uttered Jake in annoyance.

"Please forgive my earlier appearance, Jake," she said. She sipped more wine and admitted, "I never should have disgraced Vanessa's body like that."

Jacob winced. The surrealistic nature of a demon possessing his stepdaughter vexed him.

"You must understand," continued Assarion convincingly, "evil and deception have been my modus operandi for millennia. As the cliché goes, *old habits die hard.*"

"Does that include possession of the innocent?" Jacob asked impatiently. Assarion sneered.

"Yes, yes it does," confirmed Assarion, her words tinged with frustration. Composing herself, she candidly expounded on Vanessa's plight, "Most of the mortals at Chinese Peak are prostitutes, Jake, utilized by Aaron to entice and seduce his victims and achieve his evil ends. If Vanessa isn't freed, she'll be destined for a life of sexual slavery. As long as I inhabit her body, however, she'll be spared a life of such degradation. There are many who want her already and, if I leave her, they will *all* have her. Is that really what you want?"

A single tear emerged from Assarion's left eye and rolled down her cheek. She ignored it.

"Maybe I'll just cast all you demonic fuckers into the Abyss and walk out of here with her instead," Jacob sneered, his ire fueled by Vanessa's tear. Fully cognizant that his threat was an empty one, he said, "Mirry loves to kill. I'm sure she'd be happy to clear out Aaron's mortal minions for me."

Assarion chortled.

"'Or do you think that I cannot appeal to My Father, and he will at once put at My disposal more than twelve legions of angels?'" recited Assarion eloquently in a mockery of Jacob's faith. (The Gospel of Matthew 26:53). She rose and set her wine glass on a nearby end table. Walking to Jacob and unexpectedly plopping down on his lap, she wrapped her arms around his neck and cooed, "Even if you succeeded, there's the little issue of Vanessa's Brugada Syndrome."

Jacob grabbed Assarion forcefully to thrust her off his lap. He aborted his contemplated action when he realized it would only truly affect Vanessa.

"Just spill it," Jacob snarled. He wriggled uncomfortably underneath his stepdaughter.

"Her Brugada Syndrome," replied Assarion with hauteur. She caressed his cheek and said, "There are cells in her heart which generate electrical impulses, impulses which cause her heart to beat. Miniscule pores on those cells, called channels, direct those impulses. Unfortunately, Vanessa's channels are defective, which makes her heart beat abnormally and puts her at risk for sudden cardiac arrest. When I entered her, she was seconds from a massive heart attack. Marcion's possession and expulsion were just too traumatic for her young body."

"Bullshit," Jacob snapped. He lifted Assarion's slight form and set her on her feet.

"If it's bullshit, then cast me out," taunted Assarion while gazing at Jacob earnestly. She batted her eyelashes at him.

"Fuck," Jacob muttered as he looked away. Assarion had won the round.

· · · ·

ASSARION GAVE JACOB several minutes to contemplate the new information before launching another sensual salvo. She attempted to return to his lap but he shoved her away and stood up.

"Ya' know, contrary to popular belief, I don't think with my cock *all* the time," Jacob stated brusquely. Pushing past Assarion, he muttered, "Fuck this."

Jacob marched onto the marble walkway. Assarion turned to watch his departure with a muted grin. She then called out confidently to him as he crossed the halfway point.

"'But love your enemies, and do good and lend, expecting nothing in return; and your reward will be great, and you will be sons of the Most High; for He Himself is kind to ungrateful and evil men.'" (Excerpt from the Gospel of Luke 6:35).

Jacob aborted his exit. Whirling around to glare at Assarion sternly and uneasily, he remembered how he recited the same verse to Miriam the night she slaughtered Kirwan. He wondered if she eavesdropped on their conversation that night.

"What do you believe, Jacob?" Assarion queried, her gaze riveted on Jacob. He nervously glanced at the floor to avoid her scrutiny as she asked, "Is He kind to the ungrateful and the evil?"

"Jesus fucking said it, right?" scoffed Jacob, his nervousness subsiding. Firing a suspicious glance at Assarion, he inquired, "But why the hell would you care?"

"For thousands of years, I've been ungrateful and evil," replied Assarion, the sorrow in her voice sparking pity for her in Jacob's spirit. Her countenance sad, she walked to him and said, "And now I seek His kindness . . . and yours."

Jacob's head reeled. The gamut of demonic personalities he experienced since Miriam simply astounded him, their varied natures both confirming and dispelling his preconceptions regarding *daimoniou*. Now Assarion sought him out for the spiritual guidance which he still sought himself. He keenly felt the weight of her expectations and the pressure scared him.

"Jesus Christ," Jacob snapped. Choosing instead to believe that Ba'al Zeboul tossed in Assarion as another wrinkle in his plan, he deflected her apparent sincerity and asked, "How many demons does BZ have on this?"

"To my knowledge, three," answered Assarion pointedly, "Marcion, Miriam and Aaron."

"Mirry's not in on it anymore," Jacob admonished Assarion with a look of disappointment.

"Perhaps not wittingly," stated Assarion without heed for his disapprobation. She moved to within inches of Jacob and, lording Vanessa's beauty over him, she allowed her sweet scent to tickle his nostrils and kindle his libido. She said, "But I guarantee you she's still serving his purpose or he would've recalled her by now."

"Well, thanks for the warning," Jacob said while tearing himself away from Vanessa's enticing form and retreating towards the door. He tried to open it to no avail before throwing Assarion a stinging glance over his shoulder and requesting, "You wanna open this fucking door, please?"

Assarion exhaled and resigned herself to temporary failure. She glided to the door and traced a series of symbols on a glass wall panel with a single claw. Jacob heard the electronic whirring noise yet again and the doors opened.

"'I do believe,'" Assarion desperately pleaded. She begged, "'*Help my unbelief.*'" (Excerpt from the Gospel of Mark 9:24.)

Struggling with uncertainty as to Assarion's motives, Jacob examined her meticulously. He was doubtful as to her credibility but also unwilling to dash her faith should it be genuine.

"You'd better be damn sure," Jacob cautioned darkly. He added with a grim smile, "You might just find yourself on the pinnacle of the temple some day with your boss yelling, '''Jump! Jump!'''"

"My faith is growing," stated Assarion proudly, "and I know God won't let me fall."

"Oh, He'll let you fall," Jacob corrected her hauntingly. He maintained eye contact with Assarion long enough to underscore his point and uttered, "Just never from a height you can't survive."

8

EXHAUSTED FROM HIS long, emotionally-draining day and craving a soft, comfortable bed, Jacob carefully treaded down the darkened hallway towards his bedroom. He hoped to avoid all entanglements whether they be human, demon or otherwise.

Proceeding down the hallway, he nearly jumped out of his own skin upon seeing Miriam standing in front of him. The shadows obscured her face much as they did the night she flushed Jacob out of The Last Place. Sophie spied on them from the shadows of her bedroom but neither Jacob nor Miriam acknowledged her presence.

"Jesus, Miriam!" Jacob exclaimed in a harsh whisper. He muttered, "Ya' trying to give me a fucking heart attack?"

Grasping the arm of his tuxedo jacket, she dragged him forward and into his room. Jacob wriggled free of Miriam's grip, quietly shut the bedroom door and fumbled for the light switch. She finally reached out and flipped it upward after watching him unsuccessfully grope for it in the dark.

"Where've you been?" demanded Miriam angrily. Her question reminded Jacob of Elizabeth's usual inquisition after one of what she termed his "jaunts."

"Oh, didn't you hear?" Jacob replied. Gesturing wildly, he said, "Ya' see, Liz pistol-whipped me and knocked me unconscious because someone in this room left my ass hanging out in the breeze tonight for no fucking reason. So I spent the night in demonic custody and then got molested by my demon-possessed stepdaughter. And, get this, the demon possessing her just happens to have found Jesus."

Miriam's eyes widened to inhuman proportions and she trembled with unadulterated rage.

"What do you mean she's 'found Jesus?'" inquired Miriam in her demonic voice.

"Oh, she wants me to be her spiritual guide, too," Jacob stated with a skeptical chuckle. Miriam convulsed and suddenly vanished. Exhaling and rubbing his eyes, Jacob prayed, "You want me to seek righteousness but all you keep sending me are girls without gods."

· · · ·

BARRELING INTO THE spirit world, Miriam screamed a horrendous scream. She attacked the spiritual space around her, her claws and teeth harmlessly flashing with dizzying speed. Her futile attack stormed on for what would have been hours in the material world as she furiously vented her enragement and jealousy.

She abruptly plummeted without warning, her spirit thrust downward by some unseen force of great power. It mercilessly buffeted her before ejecting her into the material world. Miriam crashed into a hard surface, the darkness blotting out any natural light but failing to impede her demonic vision.

Remaining on the ground, Miriam swiftly crawled like a spider towards a wall. Marble expanded out from beneath her and rose from the floor to a height of four feet. A cream-hued stone comprised the remainder of the wall up to the arched ceiling. Wooden benches, resembling old church pews, lined the walls as did various paintings. Miriam recognized her surroundings: the concourse of Agatha's headquarters.

"Must you crawl on the floor like an insect?" Aaron chastised Miriam who looked up and froze. He sat on a bench directly in front of her, his arms folded in displeasure as he said, "Our kind is rivaled in their penchant for descending into savage, uncivilized creatures only by humans. *Stand up.*"

Obediently rising to her feet with poised grace, Miriam curtsied respectfully to Aaron. She then spat in his face.

"I didn't realize your breed of demon could generate saliva," Aaron commented disinterestedly.

"Either did I," replied Miriam. Removing a handkerchief from his suit jacket pocket, Arron wiped away the spittle.

"You do realize I have the authority to order you to lick my face clean with your tongue, perhaps with your precious *Jake* as a spectator," he said. His face dry, Aaron returned his handkerchief to his pocket. Miriam leapt onto the wall above him and again mimicked the movements and stance of a spider. She scurried in a circle, positioning her head closer to Aaron. She then tilted it to the side in an animalistic manner and growled at him.

"Very amusing, Miriam," Aaron remarked, the demon leaning his head backward to observe her. He waved his hand in front of him to present the surroundings to Miriam and stated ambitiously, "This will soon be our new material home, our base of operations as we pillage the unwashed masses of Kaiser."

"I'm not working for you, cocksucker," answered Miriam sweetly in her human voice. She leapt off the wall and landed in front of Aaron.

"Most evildoers assume that they must be the sole victors in their schemes, viewing the formation of true alliances as weakness," Aaron said, "even when those alliances would often allow them to reap the same benefits far more efficiently. Their greed and overconfidence blind them."

"What the fuck are you talking about?" asked Miriam. Aaron's words baffled and irked her.

"My agreement with the Constabulary, for example," Aaron poignantly replied. Undaunted by Miriam's hostility, he continued, "I could've started operations in Kaiser without official permission or notice, but sooner or later the humans would have learned of my activities and sought to stamp them out. Yet instead, I turned something Elizabeth greatly desired into a sanction of my efforts. We *both* benefitted."

"So what do you have that *I* want?" inquired Miriam, her interest piqued despite her attempt to appear unimpressed.

"A way for you to save face with our Master and still win the heart of Jacob Gottschalk, all while 'working for' me," Aaron said in a strong, clear tone.

Miriam, indubitably intrigued, made no further effort to hide her feelings. She shook with anticipation.

"It would be premature to reveal my plan yet but I have a goodwill offer to tide you over," Aaron advised. He stood up, moved to within inches of Miriam and expounded, "After Jacob's removal from the banquet room, an ambassador of our Master took him into custody for several hours. She won't reveal the purpose of her visit but I'd wager she has a special interest in Mr. Gottschalk."

Miriam seethed, dropped her hands to her sides and clenched her fists.

"Her name," Aaron added, "is Assarion."

"She told him she wants him to be her 'spiritual guide,'" snarled Miriam jealously. She tilted her head and uttered, "Fucking bitch."

"How clever," Aaron stated while ruminating over Assarion's presence. Several seconds later he said, "She's probably offered herself as a more willing convert than you. *You're being tested against competition, Miriam.* And Assarion has been given a significant advantage."

"What advantage?" asked Miriam, the *daimoniou* terrified and furious at the same time.

"The Master's given her Vanessa to possess," Aaron answered gravely, "and we both know who she resembles."

Miriam shrieked in emotional agony. Aaron remained unmoved.

"Have faith, my dear," Aaron said with a sly smile. He laughed and uttered, "I have everything under control."

• • • •

MATERIALIZING ON THE unoccupied half of Sarah's bed, Miriam lay on her back parallel to Sarah and closed her eyes. She folded her hands on her stomach and did not make even the slightest movement.

Fifteen minutes later, Sarah rolled over from her right side to her back, the nun barely on the verge of consciousness. She sensed a presence in the room, stirred and opened her eyes. Sarah started but, before she could scream, Miriam's hand flashed to the right and covered her mouth.

"Be quiet," Miriam ordered. Languidly pulling back her hand, she assured Sarah, "It's just me."

"Miriam!" whispered Sarah as her eyes adjusted to the darkness and she recovered from her sleepy daze. She attempted to rise but Miriam draped her arm over her body and held her fast. Sarah queried, "What in God's name are you doing here?"

A fearful Miriam expected to be attacked by one of Ba'al Zeboul's minions. The attack never materialized, however, so she settled herself and again folded her hands on her stomach.

"Things are getting . . . *complicated*," Miriam stated in an odd, distressed tone. Remaining otherwise motionless, she entreated, "Jake and I didn't come here alone. Her name is Sophie and I don't trust her. If I don't make it out of here, you have to get Jake out."

"What are you talk-?"

"Swear it!" barked Miriam in a demonic voice audible only to Sarah, her fervor shaking the bed. Regretting her tone, she said hoarsely in her human voice, "*Please*. Swear it."

Sarah, utterly bewildered by Miriam's appearance and compassion for Jacob, gazed on her with pity. She nodded in assent.

"I swear it," Sarah stated with conviction.

Miriam, without speaking, conveyed her gratitude by reaching out and grasping Sarah's hand. She squeezed it affectionately, her claws softly pressing into the Ursuline's skin. Sarah returned the gesture before Miriam's form faded and disappeared into nothingness.

Closing her hand into a fist to be certain that Miriam vanished, Sarah shut her eyes. Disturbed but unable to fight off sleep, she rolled back onto her right side and drifted into strange dreams.

• • • •

MIRIAM RETURNED TO her suite via the spirit world. Completely dark save for the lights illuminating the perpetually-flowing fountain in the living room, it showed no other signs of motion. Miriam quietly floated down the hallway leading to the suite's bedrooms.

She lingered momentarily at Sophie's doorway and sensed that she slumbered tranquilly. Entering the room and remaining material, she glided to Sophie's side and seated herself on the bed. The young woman shifted, her movement resulting in a stray strand of hair falling into her face. Miriam, using the lightest touch of a single claw, brushed the strand aside.

"If I only I could trust you," Miriam thought. Leaving Sophie behind, Miriam continued to Jacob's room. Phasing into the spiritual world and entering through the wall, she saw that Jacob slept deeply. His heavy breathing occasionally ascended into a soft snore before descending back again. He stirred and shifted himself from his stomach to his side.

Miriam tilted her head quickly, her old defenses screaming at her to retreat from Jacob. Hopeless love for him flooded her spirit, however, and washed away her doubts. She dematerialized and reappeared next to him. Carefully easing her body into Jacob so as not to wake him, she pulled his arm over her like a blanket and closed her eyes.

Miriam relaxed her body as Jacob reflexively embraced her. She reveled in his touch.

"You'll *always* be mine," Miriam whispered aloud.

. . . .

LOUNGING ON PLUSH, bronze chaise in front of a Romanesque fountain, Elizabeth held a black saucer in her left hand and a matching coffee cup in the other. Aaron's assurances that he would locate Vanessa and a restful night's sleep in Darius's arms served to numb her pain if not alleviate it. Clad only in a white silk bathrobe, she waited impatiently and attempted to visualize Vanessa's return to her.

Darby, clothed once again in her black tank top and dark blue jeans, entered the living room of the suite. She held a cell phone to her ear, and, as she spotted Elizabeth, stopped in her tracks.

"Yes, that's the deal," Darby said quickly, "but I gotta go."

Darby punched "End Call" on the cell phone and stowed it in her pocket. Taken aback that Elizabeth remained in her bathrobe so late in the morning, she watched her sister gaze into the fountain for thirty seconds before speaking. Hatred for Jacob burned within her as she blamed him for the demonic incursions against her family.

"So, can I finally kill Jake?" Darby inquired bluntly.

"Excuse me?" responded Elizabeth. She froze with her saucer and coffee cup in midair.

"Well, now that you've ditched him for Darius and Aaron's gonna help us find Marcion, it looks like douchebag has outlived his usefulness," Darby said coldly. She gestured and added, "His demonic cun-."

Darby paused as Elizabeth lifted a disapproving eyebrow. She recalled her sister's explicit instruction not to use a certain profane word.

"*Miriam's* jumping ship for Aaron so she's no longer protecting him," Darby explained. She caressed the handle of her fifty-caliber pistol and suggested, "Now's the perfect time."

Elizabeth placed her coffee cup in its saucer and set them both down on a small, thin-legged table next to the chaise.

"Darby, why are we here?" questioned Elizabeth with poise despite the irritation that Darby's bloodlust caused her.

"To get 'Ness back," Darby replied with a confused expression.

"Precisely," stated Elizabeth, "and what must we combat in getting her back?"

"Demons," Darby grumbled as she rolled her eyes in annoyance.

"And who has demonstrated the greatest prowess in combating demons?" inquired Elizabeth. Turning over her sister's argument in her mind, Darby's eyes glazed over and fell to the floor. Elizabeth retrieved her cup and saucer and enjoyed another sip of coffee while she waited for her sister to grasp Jacob's importance.

"Damn it," Darby cursed while folding her arms in frustration.

"As much as you hate Jacob, he *is* still my husband and will always be special to me regardless of what happens to our marriage," said Elizabeth. She sipped her coffee again and then continued, "You will *never* have my permission to kill him. He may have failed in most areas as a husband and stepfather but protectiveness is not one of them. You and Jacob are the only people I trust to give their lives for the girls, and he's my Plan B to get Vanessa back."

The emotion drained from Darby's face. She lifted her chin gradually.

"Even if I can't pull the trigger, you still have to," Darby wisely observed. She kept Elizabeth squarely in her vision as her sister's mien dimmed and she stared into the bubbling fountain.

"Soon," answered Elizabeth weakly with a troubled expression, "very soon."

• • • •

JACOB'S BLUE EYES POPPED open and he started. Darkness prevailed in the windowless room with only a miniscule amount of light intruding on it from the hallway. Jacob expected to see Elizabeth snoozing beside him but soon remembered that he spent the night in the comforts of Chinese Peak.

He often studied Elizabeth in the mornings as she slumbered peacefully and memorized the few imperfections of her face. A wistful expression washed across his countenance as he thought of the barely perceptible laugh lines around the corners of her mouth. He cursed his yearning to hold her in his arms again.

Banishing the ghost of Elizabeth from his mind, Jacob remained still as he studied his surroundings. He recognized the indentation in the bed next to him, its general size and shape closely resembling Miriam. Jacob lifted his head and surveyed the entire room for his demonic paramour. Failing to see her, he dropped his head back onto his pillow, rolled onto his back and drifted into a light sleep.

An unseen force grasped Jacob by his t-shirt and thrust him upward. It slammed his back into the wall above the bed's headboard and left behind a Gottschalk-shaped depression. Disoriented, Jacob groaned and writhed, sharp pains shooting through his back as two unseen hands pushed him further into the wall.

"What happened between you and Assarion?!" demanded a monstrous voice, a voice which Jacob heard in his mind but not in his ears. His senses reeling, he struggled to regain control of himself as he felt invisible hands wrap around his throat. Attempting to peel the hands from his neck, he groaned as the voice roared again, "What happened?!"

Sophie appeared in the doorway, her usual unflappable demeanor cracking as she watched the spiritual assault. Focusing on her, Jacob rallied. He feasted upon his unseen assailant with an emboldened gaze.

"Leave!" Jacob rebuked the evil spirit forcefully while projecting the Holy Spirit through the conduit of his faith. He recalled the Gospel of Mark 9:25, grinned maliciously and snarled, "Into the swine, mother fucker."

Jacob perceived the evil spirit's sudden fear and panic and, despite his inability to see its retreat, he sensed its presence vanish. He harmlessly plummeted forward into the mattress but felt the pain caused by his encounter with the wall. Sophie approached him and, after helping him up, abruptly embraced him.

"Demon?" she asked. Jacob reluctantly returned Sophie's unexpected embrace. He exhaled and contemplated his next move.

"Yeah," Jacob replied. Speaking with a conviction that surprised himself, he stated determinedly, "Go get your shit. We're gonna fix this right now."

. . . .

BOTH ELIZABETH AND Darby jumped and drew their pistols as someone pounded heavily on the entry doors to their suite. Exchanging wary looks, they quickly moved out of the line of any weapons fire coming through the doorway.

"Liz!" Jacob yelled while continuing to slam a fist on the door. Recognizing her husband's voice, Elizabeth holstered her firearm, and, with a puzzled glance towards her sister, hurried towards the entrance. Darby lowered her weapon but failed to holster it. Jacob shouted again, "Liz!"

Elizabeth threw open the doors. Jacob rushed past her into the suite, his charge causing Darby to aim her pistol at him with uncanny speed. Jacob ignored her, placed his hands on his hips and turned towards Elizabeth.

"Where's Sarah?" Jacob demanded, his eyes sparkling with intense energy.

"Jacob, what's wrong?" inquired Elizabeth, the Constable deeply concerned by Jacob's impromptu entrance and fierce determination. His possible discovery of her infidelity struck her like lightning and her face whitened. Noticing that Darby still pointed her gun at Jacob, she waved her off and admonished her sharply, "Put that away."

"I need Sarah. Where is she?" Jacob asked impatiently as Darby reluctantly complied with Elizabeth's order. He took a step towards her.

"You'd better settle *the fuck* down, asshole," warned Darby while pointing a finger at Jacob. He, in response, whirled around and swiftly whipped out a SIG Sauer P226. Darby, dumbfounded by Jacob's use of a weapon, stared at him in shock. Elizabeth remained calm and still.

"Fuck you, cunt," Jacob growled while wielding the firearm with unexpected authority. He thrust the gun at her and said, "I don't have time for any of your fucking bullshit right now so drop your gun, sit the fuck down and shut the fuck up."

Darby recovered and glowered at Jacob. Unimpressed, he thrust the gun at her again.

"Do it!" he barked.

Elizabeth tilted her head to indicate that Darby should obey Jacob's command. Carefully lifting her pistol out of her holster with two fingers, Darby lowered it and then dropped it to the floor with a dull thud.

"You too, hon," Jacob instructed Elizabeth without looking at her. Walking over to where Darby stood, she drew her pistol and laid it down. She then motioned to Darby to proceed to the sectional. Both women sat down as the fountain gurgled boisterously.

"Thank you," Jacob stated, his angst slightly cooling. Still aiming the gun at Darby, he questioned, "Now, where's Sarah?"

"She went for a walk, and, in fact, I expect her to return shortly," advised Elizabeth, her tone conciliatory. She crossed her legs and leaned back. Darby seethed. Seeking to determine if Jacob knew of her tryst with Darius, Elizabeth queried, "What's troubling you, Jacob?"

"I'll explain later," Jacob said, the gears of his mind turning as he relentlessly chewed the inside of his cheek. Elizabeth's anxiety subsided as she observed him. She knew how to read her husband and his reaction belied any knowledge of her infidelity.

"Is the gun really necessary?" asked Elizabeth. Jacob's uncharacteristic behavior deeply concerned her.

"Can you keep her under control?" Jacob shot back with a quick nod towards Darby. Elizabeth nodded in the affirmative, the gesture prompting Jacob to lower his gun halfway.

"Now what's going on?" inquired Elizabeth worriedly.

"Perhaps I can explain," Sarah's voice rang out. All eyes turned to the suite's doorway where she stood solemnly. Wearing her traditional Ursuline garb, Sarah folded her hands in front of her. She wore her hair in a ponytail draped onto her right breast, her familiar bun absent.

"Go ahead, Sister Sarah," Jacob responded as he lowered his pistol the rest of the way. Darby immediately noticed and attempted to rise but Elizabeth restrained her with one arm and guided her back to her seat. He asked with a furrowed brow, "But what the hell could you possibly know about it?"

"If you'll kindly put your firearm away, I'd be happy to tell you," suggested Sarah pointedly. Jacob watched her with uncertainty for several seconds, snapped his mouth callous three times and then stuffed the pistol into his waistband.

"Thank you," said Sarah earnestly. She then called out, "Sophie."

Sophie entered the room, inspected it meticulously and then stood shoulder-to-shoulder with Sarah. She wore her beige t-shirt and jeans and her backpack was strapped to her body. Her gaze fell on Elizabeth.

"Hey, there, Mrs. Jake," Sophie greeted Elizabeth with a smirk.

"Hello," replied Elizabeth. Bewildered, she watched Sarah in anticipation of her promised explanation.

"This young lady's name is Sophie," said Sarah while placing a reassuring hand on Sophie's shoulder. She glanced at her and then stated, "I sought her out this morning on the advice of Miriam. You see, Jacob and Miriam rescued her on their way here and they've been taking care of-."

"They're not taking care of me," Sophie interrupted. She made sure to meet every gaze in the room and said, "We're just helping each other out during the shitstorm we're all in."

"In any event," continued Sarah, the Ursuline undeterred by Sophie's correction, "this morning Sophie witnessed a violent demonic attack on Jacob. I believe, because of that attack, he's seeking my help in protecting her."

Elizabeth observed Sophie closely. Sarah's account garnered her pity for the young woman but, oddly, she sensed no distress in her.

"How may I help?" asked Elizabeth, her husband's compassion for Sophie rekindling an intense spark of love for him in her heart. She, as had Jacob, thought Sophie to be close in age to her daughters.

"I'm getting a new room for Sophie and me," Jacob expounded gravely, "and I want Sarah to stay with us."

"Of course," replied Elizabeth. She forced a compassionate smile to hide her reservations and her jealousy.

* * * *

LATE MORNING TRUNDLED towards early afternoon, the sun's rays increasing in intensity as they hit the shimmering minerals in the white cement walkway leading to the entrance of Chinese Peak. Miriam appeared on the west side of the large, central fountain while remaining invisible to human sight. Water trickled from the eyes of the woman's head as the jets encircling it launched streams of water into the air.

The smaller fountain into which Miriam hurled Marcion no longer resembled a nude, shapely woman, the denizens of Chinese Peak repairing it into the form of a repulsive, pigheaded demon. Its arms extended out with fearsome claws and its screaming maw displayed jagged teeth.

"That's new," Miriam commented blithely. Glancing around her, she beckoned, "Marcion! Where the fuck are you, you little cocksucker? Marcion!"

Seating herself on the edge of the main fountain's three-foot-high retaining wall, Miriam grasped its edges and clicked her claws against the cement. Marcion failed to appear despite her summons so she gazed out into the parking lot. No longer blanketed in fog as it was at the time of her arrival, the lot contained more vehicles but no signs of activity.

Miriam sighed and laid on her back with her knees bent and her feet flat on the top of the wall. She let her right hand fall into the basin and wiggled her fingers in the water while she tucked her left hand behind her head.

Marcion entered the material world an hour later. Bereft of a human host, the demon swirled around Miriam and examined her for several minutes.

"What do you want, *traitor*?" whined Marcion. Mimicking a vampire sitting up in its coffin, Miriam rose and slowly turned her head towards him. Her expression became emotionlessly dark as he taunted her, "Where's your precious Gottschalk?"

Miriam spun her legs to the left, dropped her feet on the cement and hopped off the wall. Strolling in a straight line to the nearest statue, she punched its head and pulverized it. A spray of dust and stone debris flared outward from the point of impact as the neck crumbled.

"Aaron wants to talk to you," Miriam responded. She sauntered to the next statue and punched its head. She continued around the circle in the same manner.

"About what?" sniveled Marcion suspiciously as his spiritual form followed her. She pummeled another stone head.

"Elizabeth's younger daughter," Miriam said, the taste of her nemesis's name bitter in her mouth. She loathed Elizabeth and her offspring and wished to be rid of them. Wrecking another statue, Miriam explained, "Aaron wants you to possess her and take her as far away from Kaiser as you can. Ya' know, like you were supposed to in the first fucking place."

"Why?" Marcion snapped. The malicious aura he projected caused Miriam to fire him a contemptuous, sidelong glance. The glance became a wicked, scalding glare.

"It doesn't matter," stated Miriam in an acerbic tone. She arrived at the last unmolested statue - the pigheaded demon.

"What do I get?" Marcion asked. Miriam's anger oddly subsided as she studied the demon statue. She wound up to strike it and swung her fist but halted just before it connected.

"A new material body to start, asshole . . . and a full pardon for your recent fuckups," replied Miriam. She studied the demon statue, ran her clawed fingers over it and then asked, "So are you in or out?"

"In," Marcion grumbled.

"I like this one," she said thoughtfully while caressing the stony hairs of the pigheaded demon's chin. Leaving Marcion behind, she departed into the spiritual world.

9

A STUDY IN GRANDIOSITY and opulence, Aaron's office might have been characterized by some as more of a museum with its regal furniture, painting of diverse genres and numerous other works of art. An ornate entrance built into one corner loomed opposite Aaron's immense desk. Tinted, wall-length windows comprised two sides of the office, one to the desk's left overlooking the mountains to the south while an identical window to its right overlooked Chinese Peak's massive lobby. The wall to the desk's left housed a bank of flat screen televisions overshadowing a sitting area.

"Thanks for the loaner!" Marcion said with an evil cackle as he leapt onto Aaron's desk. He landed in a squat with his elbows resting on his knees and his arms hanging down in front of him. Looking on Aaron with smug contentment, he thoroughly enjoyed the seventeen-year-old body of his new host. Aaron leaned back in his chair and viewed Marcion with utter contempt.

"Perhaps you could try sitting in a chair," Aaron suggested, his tongue dripping with disdain.

Marcion's temporary host was a darling girl with cute, almost-cartoonish eyes of bistre. She appeared Caucasian but her olive skin and the dense raven hair that tickled her lower back exhibited a hint of ethnicity. She dressed in skinny jeans and a tight, pink-cotton top.

"Perhaps you could stop wasting my fucking time and let me go get the girl," complained Marcion while watching Aaron with bulging eyes. Examining his host's healthy arms and hands, he smiled in satisfaction and exclaimed, "I love these! I love these!"

"You're not to go back to Kaiser," Aaron warned as he ignored Marcion's incessant cackling and the bizarre, disjointed dance he performed. Waiting for him to regain his focus, Aaron demanded, "*Get off my desk*."

Straightening up and ceasing his disturbing dance, Marcion narrowed his eyes and then hopped off the desk. A suspicious expression washed across the woman's youthful face.

"You will remain here until the opportunity for her possession presents itself," Aaron sneered with wavering patience.

"Presents itself?" inquired Marcion. Conveying his captivation with Aaron's scheme by slamming his palms down on the desk, he queried, "She's coming *here*?"

"It's all part of the downfall of Jacob Gottschalk," Aaron answered while leaning backward in his chair with his elbows on its armrests and his hands folded in front of him. Aaron expounded, "The perfect storm is brewing in his life. He will soon learn his wife has given up on their marriage and abandoned him for another lover. Her betrayal will induce him to leave Kaiser. He is also losing his bid to turn Miriam to God and, in fact, she is turning him towards us. *Gottschalk is weak.* The pressure will eventually consume him and he will surrender his faith. As the humans say, it's only a matter of time. But we must pressure him on every front."

Marcion squinted and contemplated Aaron's words. He twitched and paced in front of the desk.

"Unfortunately, Vanessa Nicks is no longer under our control," Aaron said with considerable angst. He paused to let his wrath simmer and then continued, "So we will use her sister as I originally planned. You will bait Gottschalk down ever darker and more dangerous roads, roads that lead him farther and farther away from Kaiser, from his home. Am I understood?"

"Yes, yes," said Marcion hastily in the young woman's tender voice. His form already fading, he added with a pointed finger, "Just keep Miriam out of the way."

. . . .

SOPHIE SAT IN A LARGE recessed sill and stared out the window. She watched flocks of birds swirling back and forth in the mountains.

"She doesn't say much," Sarah commented concernedly while returning her attention to meal preparation. Slicing a tomato, she said, "She's just been watching the birds all day."

Jacob, with Adedewe's reluctant assistance, commandeered a small, two-bedroom apartment used for staff quarters and moved Sarah, Sophie and himself into it. Sparsely decorated and furnished, it lacked the lavishness of Chinese Peak's suites and resembled the abode of a bachelor or college student.

Jacob leaned against the hallway wall leading into the apartment. He exhaled and rubbed his face while feeling cautiously optimistic that he and Sarah could shield Sophie from any further demonic incursions. The spiritual assault still weighed heavily on this mind, however, as he wondered if Miriam had truly turned and attempted to tear him to pieces.

"She's got some rough miles on her," said Jacob while observing Sophie, "and I think she's learned she can't rely on anyone."

"But now she has *us*," Sarah replied. Her eyes, tinged with admiration, lingered on Jacob until another form moved into her view. Her gaze caused him to squirm in discomfort.

"I see everyone's settled," stated Elizabeth, the Constable forcing a pleasant grin. Sophie remained oblivious to her presence. Subtly leaning into Jacob with her shoulder, she asked softly, "May I speak with you for a moment?"

Jacob stood up straight and turned around while viewing his wife with a furrowed brow. The peculiar tone of her voice concerned him and his heart palpitated nervously. Sarah pretended to be immersed in meal preparations but listened intently.

"Sure," responded Jacob. Elizabeth whirled around while folding her arms and proceeded into the hallway outside the apartment. Jacob hesitated but soon followed.

Elizabeth rotated back around upon exiting the apartment. She offered Jacob a cordial grin though Jacob sensed she concealed negative information from him.

"How is your head?" asked Elizabeth gingerly. Her remorse was palpable.

"Little sore," Jacob replied with a dismissive expression, "but no real harm done."

"I apologize," said Elizabeth. "It's just-."

"Mommy adrenaline, I know," Jacob quipped. Forcing himself to act normally and changing the subject, he queried, "So, what's up?"

"I was wondering if you'd have dinner with me tonight," said Elizabeth with feigned composure. Jacob perceived the uneasiness that bubbled beneath her collected emotional surface as she explained, "We haven't had an uninterrupted conversation in a long time and we *are*, for better or worse, still married."

Jacob considered the efficacy of informing Elizabeth about Vanessa's new possessor. The thought of revealing her daughter's fate to her caused his stomach to burn.

"Sure, sure," he acquiesced though unable to meet her gaze. He reached into his interior jacket pocket and fiddled with its contents.

"Perhaps Vitoria," suggested Elizabeth, "maybe sevenish?"

"Might I suggest The Thin Dolphin," Adedewe interjected, the demon appearing out of nowhere. She wore a stylish, navy-blue pants suit, glasses and her hair in an Ursuline-like bun. She added, "It sits at the pinnacle of Chinese Peak, both literally and figuratively. It's our finest restaurant."

"Is there any news on Vanessa?" questioned Elizabeth desperately. Forgetting everything but her daughter, she restrained tears and trembled. Jacob instinctively buttressed her by wrapping his arm around her waist, and, to his surprise, she accepted the gesture.

"Unfortunately, no," Adedewe confirmed while placing a reassuring hand on Elizabeth's shoulder. An alarm screeched in Jacob's spirit as he observed Adedewe's clawed hand. He felt his wife press into his body.

"She didn't mention Marcion or Assarion," Jacob said to himself. He squeezed Elizabeth and thought, "Oh, what a tangled web . . . ."

· · · ·

JACOB CLOSED THE DOOR of the apartment and sighed in relief. He relished the hiatus from Sarah's veiled fawning and Sophie's redoubled emotional distance. Miriam's extended absence also provided a measure of solace.

Dressed in a borrowed black suit, dark-red dress shirt and black tie, Jacob proceeded to the elevator. Butterflies filled his stomach as he anxiously anticipated his "date" with Elizabeth and the imminent revelation of whatever bad news she harbored.

He pushed the "UP" button and the doors slid open. Jacob, looking down at his black, polished shoes, failed to see Miriam's clawed hand spring forth from the elevator. It grasped him by the collar and flung him to the floor. His head spinning and his vision blurred, he watched the elevator doors close and Miriam hit the emergency stop button with the claw of her index finger.

"Where the fuck are you off to, dick bag?" demanded Miriam in her human voice. Jacob lifted himself into a sitting position with his palms pressed into the floor. He blinked several times and shook his head to correct his vision.

"To dinner," Jacob answered. Aiming to wound Miriam with his words, he added nastily, "With my wife."

Shrieking wildly, Miriam spun around and swiped at the elevator doors. Sparks jumped off the metal as her claws shredded it like paper. Jacob backed into the rear wall but otherwise remained unmoved by Miriam's violence.

"You're a fucking asshole, Jake," chastised Miriam, the demon hemorrhaging emotionally. She bitterly counterattacked, "She fucking cheats on you again and again but you just can't fucking let her go. You're fucking pathetic, you stupid, weak fuck."

"*I'm* a fucking asshole?" Jacob snapped while sliding himself up the elevator wall and to his feet. Gesturing emphatically, he barked, "Sophie saw your little display this morning. What the fuck were you thinking, Mirry?"

Miriam, struggling with her emotions, gave Jacob a conflicted look. She trembled with rage and fright.

"Where is she?" inquired Miriam sharply.

"Safe from you, nut job," Jacob responded. Sensing her hostility towards Sophie, he added, "She's with Sarah."

Miriam's anger cooled. Resigned to her mission, she sought once again to tempt Jacob.

"There's something you should know about your precious Liz," counseled Miriam. She hesitated and contemplated how her revelation would devastate Jacob.

"What?" Jacob demanded. The dreaded hybrid sensation of anger, fear and embarrassment welled within him. He implored her, "What the fuck do I need to know?"

"She . . . she . . .," stammered Miriam, the *daimoniou* unable to injure Jacob's heart.

Jacob's terrified fury erupted. Unwillingly to tolerate Miriam's presence any further, he snapped.

"'I command you, come out of her!'" he bellowed with a crazed intensity. Fuming, he shouted again, "'Do not enter her again!'" (Excerpt from the Gospel of Mark 9:25).

Miriam screamed demonically, her very being scorched by Jacob's exorcism attempt. She sensed for the first time in her life as a *daimoniou* that her spiritual and material existences began to separate. Horrified, she fled into the spirit world.

Jacob exhaled.

"Jesus fucking Christ I need a drink," he lamented as he straightened his jacket.

• • • •

THE TRUNCATED SUMMIT of Chinese Peak appeared as if an immense knife sliced through the cylindrical tower. It housed The Thin Dolphin, a unique upscale restaurant of innovative design.

The first level of the restaurant housed the kitchen, an immense bar and a waiting area. The remainder of the restaurant consisted of individual platforms accessed by a network of elegant scaffolding and stairways. The platforms afforded each table its own private, secluded atmosphere and were scattered among several stories.

Jacob's and Elizabeth's table rested upon a platform nestled in the center of The Thin Dolphin. The other platforms were intermittently occupied by guests; however, the restaurant's unique design concealed them.

"We've never done this before," Jacob commented with a wry smile.

"Eaten dinner in an upscale restaurant?" retorted Elizabeth good-naturedly with her own amused grin. She scoffed, "I've taken you to the finest restaurants in Kaiser, my love."

"We've never been on a date when you weren't queen of the fucking world," Jacob facetiously replied. Elizabeth laughed, her eyes shimmering with lighthearted, girlish innocence. Realizing the volume of her chortle, she daintily placed the tips of her fingers over her mouth.

Jacob's spine tingled. Elizabeth rarely displayed such an expression, an expression that she wore in nearly all the pictures of her youth.

"There aren't any security personnel lurking in the background, no one's interrupted us to provide you with 'vital' information, Darby hasn't burst in wanting to kick my ass. . . need I go on?" continued Jacob, his countenance glowing with love.

"Point taken," conceded Elizabeth softly while lifting the bowl-shaped glass to her lips and sipping the red wine within it. Setting her glass on the table, she suggested cryptically, "I suppose we should take advantage of the opportunity."

"How's Mal?" queried Jacob, his guilt causing him to miss Elizabeth's odd tone. He thought of Vanessa and Mallory often since his impromptu departure from Kaiser and rued his failures as a husband and stepfather.

"Children are resilient, as the old adage goes," Elizabeth said sadly with watery eyes, "and Mallory is strong."

"Like her mother," interjected Jacob though Elizabeth ignored the compliment. The topic of his stepdaughters stirred Jacob's memory and he said, "I need to ask you something about Vanessa."

"Do you know something new?" Elizabeth inquired as her motherly instincts flared. Marshaling her composure, she asked eagerly, "You do, don't you?"

"Easy, Liz," assured Jacob while reaching across the table to tenderly grasp Elizabeth's hand. She let the moment linger before abruptly pulling her hand from Jacob's grip and placing her hands in her lap. A wounded Jacob absorbed the rejection and bluntly asked, "Does 'Ness have a heart condition?"

"She's had an irregular heartbeat on a few occasions but that was years ago," Elizabeth answered in puzzlement as Jacob's countenance grew dark. She titled her head and probed, "Why do you ask?"

"Vanessa's no longer possessed by Marcion," answered Jacob grimly as he sidestepped Vanessa's heart condition. Elizabeth began to rise, her intent to depart prompting Jacob to say, "Liz, sit down."

"I need to find Aaron," Elizabeth snapped.

"Liz, sit down and listen," replied Jacob with the utmost seriousness. Elizabeth froze. A sour expression on his face, he shook his head and uttered, "In fairness, Aaron may not have known."

Elizabeth lowered her eyes and gradually sat down. Adrenaline coursed through her veins and she trembled silently for twenty seconds. She then lifted her gaze to Jacob.

"It turns out my exorcism of Marcion took," explained Jacob, "but Vanessa's freedom didn't last long. Another demon possessed her."

"Oh my God," Elizabeth gasped as the tears streamed down her cheeks. Each one cut Jacob.

"Liz, I can get her back," said Jacob with a confidence that lessened Elizabeth's distress. He continued with a determined mien, "You don't need Aaron. I can get Vanessa and we can all go *home*."

Elizabeth wiped the existing tears from her eyes and no more fell. Mustering her defenses for Jacob's inevitable explosion, she spoke firmly and slowly.

"I, in exchange for Vanessa's safe return, ceded the slums of Kaiser to Aaron," she explained. Jacob, in the middle of drinking, choked on his whiskey. Plopping his glass down on the table, he forced several coughs to clear his throat as Elizabeth watched him with a startled expression.

"You," said Jacob while coughing several more times, "did *what*?"

"What was I supposed to do?" Elizabeth inquired harshly, her ire rising. Heightened emotion infusing her words, she asked, "Simply toss away the only opportunity I may have to get her back?"

"Liz," replied Jacob as he held up his palms in a sign of parley. Lowering his hands and grasping his glass, he said earnestly, "I'm not angry. You just caught me by surprise, that's all."

Elizabeth, however, appeared to be the one caught by surprise, the Constable rendered speechless by Jacob's measured reaction. She studied his face with a bewildered countenance. Her puzzlement gave way to an uncertain, muted grin.

"I'm impressed," Elizabeth remarked, her smile widening. The smallest of traces of resentment in her voice, she added, "I was expecting quite the battle."

"You did what ya' had to do," responded Jacob, "but I can get 'Ness back. We can cancel the deal."

The smile evaporated from Elizabeth's face upon Jacob's use of the word "we." Steeling her will, she prepared, as Darby would say, to "pull the trigger."

"And maybe we can fix us, too," said Jacob quickly before his wife could speak.

Elizabeth, while presenting an unruffled, noncommittal front, inwardly panicked. She perceived Jacob's burgeoning hope and sympathized with his plight but she knew their time together drew to a close. Her endless calculations, however, included a trump card.

"I thought you might say that," said Elizabeth as she set her purse on her lap and clicked it open. Jacob heard pills rattle inside a plastic pill bottle as she scooped it up and set it on the table.

Jacob looked at the familiar, translucent orange bottle with its large, white cap. He knew it contained lithium, a drug Elizabeth and Dr. Adai pushed on him since their marriage. She waited with baited breath and hoped Jacob would once again balk at taking medication.

Jacob's mind churned. He knew that the medication was tantamount to complete surrender of his vices and total submission to Elizabeth. Jacob scrutinized the bottle as he considered the offer and she watched him with unwavering attention. Waving the white flag, he looked to Elizabeth.

"Okay," he said, "I'll do it."

Elizabeth's heart plummeted into her stomach. She managed to muster a half-hearted smile as she pondered flight.

"That's wonderful," replied Elizabeth.

· · · ·

JACOB'S BODY WANDERED aimlessly around Chinese Peak while his mind wandered aimlessly around the world of his thoughts. Drowsiness crept over him gradually but he forced his eyelids open. Ambling clumsily down a hallway, he stopped as he noticed a mirror to his right. Placing both palms upon a high, narrow table beneath the mirror, he gazed into it and grinned a goofy grin.

"I got this one but she still wants to go with Aaron's plan first," he said to himself in disbelief. He noticed dark circles under his eyes and lifted his head to examine them. Satisfied that he appeared defeated, he dropped his head and explained to himself, "That's gonna come back to bite her on that hot little ass of hers."

Jacob felt his intoxication wearing off, his oncoming sobriety evidenced by his dry mouth, mild headache and decreasing elation.

"I bet that fuck already knows Assarion's got Vanessa," Jacob continued with an acrid expression.

"Hi, Jake," said Miriam uneasily, the demon appearing to Jacob's left. He cast an unwelcoming, sidelong glance at her before returning his eyes to the mirror.

"What the fuck do you want?" Jacob grumbled. Miriam trembled and struggled with her emotions.

"Aaron," she began while shuddering. Steadying herself, she said, "Aaron would like to see you."

"Demoted from temptress to messenger girl," Jacob jabbed as he stood up straight and turned towards her. Thrusting down his feelings for her and the pain they caused him, he continued bitingly, "Guess you've made *your* decision, huh? Oh, and in answer to your question, you're not a dog or a thorn. You're one of the fucking birds."

Jacob's slight momentarily paralyzed Miriam. She appeared as if she might faint but soon tensed as if she expected him to strike her.

"I'm going to get changed out of this ridiculous fucking monkey suit," Jacob advised as he surveyed his clothing with irritation, "so you can tell your asshole boss he can send *someone else* to get me in thirty minutes."

"'But no one can enter the strong man's house and plunder his property unless he first binds the strong man,'" stated Miriam with pain and sorrowful desperation etched on her face, "'and then he will plunder his house.'" (The Gospel of Mark 3:27).

Jacob furrowed his brow. Suddenly, the light bulb clicked on.

"'Therefore, be on the alert,'" he replied uneasily as he departed, "'for you do not know which day your Lord is coming.'" (The Gospel of Matthew 24:42).

• • • •

BRIGHT, WHITE LIGHT penetrated Jacob's corneas, the illumination causing him to wince and quickly avert his eyes. His sight soon adjusted to the intensity of the light which streamed from buzzing fixtures in the paneled drop ceiling. He stood in an empty, insipidly-decorated room of white walls and white-tiled flooring. Scuff marks and scratches covered the walls, the blemishes a sign of many years of heavy use.

"The best view of the plant is from this very room," Aaron commented, the demon highlighted by the sunglow-hued lights flooding through an observation window spanning the entire wall. Dressed in an immaculate, stylish suit, he gazed out the window and said, "Beautiful."

Jacob saw the ceiling of a colossal cavern, the sight confirming his suspicion that he was now within the heart of the mountain range behind Chinese Peak.

"And yet it was only an employee break room. Such a waste," he scoffed while folding his arms.

"Shouldn't you be fleecing my wife out of something?" asked Jacob, his tone pregnant with a mixture of disdain and amused resignation. Sneering, he added carelessly, "Or fucking my girlfriend?"

Aaron laughed a malevolent laugh. Jacob's skin crawled.

"Sex is such a trivial endeavor, a mere weapon to use against a sinful, lustful humanity," Aaron remarked. Entertained by Jacob's focus on sexuality, he said, "It ceased being a pleasurable experience for me long ago. You and I have much weightier matters to discuss."

"Like why you haven't told Liz that I gave Marcion the boot?" questioned an aggravated Jacob. He walked towards the window and asked, "Or that Vanessa's latest parasite is Assarion."

"That is none of your concern," Aaron answered dismissively. Jacob stopped in his tracks.

"Holy shit," gasped Jacob. The observation window overlooked a human aggrandizement of a colossal cave. A natural gas plant constructed within the cavern's confines bustled with activity, its workers moving about an intricate network of housings, pipes and tanks. Aaron noticed Jacob's astonishment with satisfaction.

"The earth beneath Chinese Peak contains abundant natural gas, enough to sustain its substantial energy needs for at least a century," explained Aaron. He gestured towards the cavern and said, "This entirely self-contained facility harvests, processes and delivers it."

"You'd better not tell Liz that. She'd kill to get her hands on that type of power," replied Jacob with a grin. His smile fading over a quiet thirty seconds, he turned to Aaron and stated blithely, "Ya' know, this isn't exactly like showing me all the kingdoms of the world."

"And you're not exactly Christ, are you?" Aaron countered sharply. Looking Jacob in the eyes, he continued, "But what *would* it take to seduce the brooding Jacob Gottschalk? A quiet, happy family life in Kaiser with a faithful Elizabeth, your inimitable emotional connection rekindled? Or an intense emotional and spiritual kindred with a God-fearing Miriam? The two of you mired in a symbiotic relationship where she defends you from material danger while you guard her from the perils of the spiritual world?"

Jacob's expression grew cold and grim as he attempted to ward off Aaron's temptation. The scrutiny of his competing desires unnerved him and he chewed the inside of his mouth.

"Too difficult to decide between your wife and your mistress? How about an uninhibited life of pleasure here at Chinese Peak, soaked in alcohol and surrounded by gorgeous, adoring women eager to please your every deviant desire?" Aaron questioned cunningly, his voice firm and unyielding. Jacob clicked the callous in his mouth several times. His imagination churned with the seemingly endless possibilities as Aaron said, "No worries or responsibilities . . . *no competition or pain* . . . just unadulterated gratification for the rest of your days."

Aaron lifted his left arm up and shook his finger in the air.

"What about all those aspects in one woman?" offered Aaron. He smiled cunningly and said, "I have quite a few perfect human vessels here, and, believe it or not, some emotionally-aware and precocious demons to pour into them. The younger ones are not quite as *hardcore* as their elders. The days of foaming at the mouth and convulsions are passing away, albeit gradually."

"Like Assarion?" Jacob chuckled as he stuffed his hands in his pockets and began pacing between the window and the door. The mention of the demon's name broke Aaron's oratorical momentum. He suppressed a grimace.

"*No,*" he growled, the faintest traces of his demonic voice bleeding into his human one. Aaron complained bitterly, "Unfortunately, that cunt operates independent of my authority."

Jacob stopped pacing. Assarion's alleged independence intrigued and confused him and he weighed the sincerity of Aaron's visceral response. He began pacing again.

"In any event, Jacob, it could all be yours," reaffirmed Aaron while watching Jacob expectantly, "in exchange, of course, for the revocation of your allegiance to God. Simply name your price. Perhaps even a younger version of your wife?"

Aaron's final specious suggestion broke his spell. The Holy Spirit coursed within Jacob and he stopped pacing. Feigning a lunge towards Aaron and firing him a stinging glance, he caused the demon to flinch.

"Fuck you, demon," snarled Jacob with a haughty smirk. He pointed his right index finger at Aaron and admonished him, saying, "You're a mother fucking liar and deceiver just like your asshole boss, and even if you weren't, *I belong to God.*"

Jacob turned on a dime. Exiting the room self-confidently, he was unaffected by Aaron's rancorous roar as it followed on his heels.

10

JACOB WALLOWED IN THE hot shower water though his stomach gurgled with hunger. Amazingly, he slept more soundly and peacefully than he had slept in months. God's morning light revealed the path Jacob should follow and the guidance eased his mind. A knock on the bathroom door wrested him from his thoughts.

"Breakfast will be ready in fifteen minutes," Sarah informed him with a raised voice. He chuckled.

"I think I married the wrong woman," joked Jacob aloud.

"I think that's pretty obvious," Sophie replied. Jacob started and nearly toppled over. Buttressed by the tiled shower wall, he regained his balance and searched his side of the curtain. Jacob found no one so he peeked out from behind it.

"What the hell are you doing, Sophie?" exclaimed Jacob as he saw her sitting on the toilet. She wore his wrinkled, red dress shirt from his dinner with Elizabeth, its sleeves folded up to her elbows and most of its buttons unfastened. Her white panties were around her ankles.

"Peeing," Sophie answered with flat affect, a fact soon confirmed by the splash of urine in the toilet water. Jacob grimaced.

"I mean what the fuck are you doing in here while I'm taking a shower?" asked a flabbergasted Jacob. Sophie writhed sensually and performed moves he had never seen from her.

"You held up your end of the bargain," answered Sophie while locking eyes with Jacob, "so I'm here to hold up mine. Literally."

Jacob's cock hardened and, through his shirt, he could see Sophie's nipples followed suit. The inner edges of her breasts were visible due to the unfastened buttons.

"Look, Soph, there wasn't any deal," countered Jacob as he tore his gaze from the enticing morsel before him and closed the shower curtain. His heart pounding and his erection throbbing, he continued, "Like you said: *We're just helping each other out during the shitstorm we're all in.* And, by some miracle of God, I've got a plan to get us *out* of the shitstorm."

Sophie failed to respond. Seconds later, she attempted to throw back the shower curtain but Jacob thwarted her and used it to cover his naked body.

"What if I wanna have sex anyway?" Sophie inquired as she stood face-to-face with Jacob. She grabbed his penis through the shower curtain and punitively squeezed it. Sexual sensation rippled through Jacob's body and momentarily paralyzed him. He wavered, his libido begging him to pull Sophie into the shower and make wet, soapy love to her.

"I'm going back to my wife, Sophie," advised Jacob after an internal struggle.

"Oh," Sophie said. She released his penis and stepped back. Crouching to the floor, she gripped her panties with both hands and pulled them on in one fluid motion. Jacob sighed and watched her walk to the door with swaying hips. She added a disinterested, "Bye."

"There's something wrong with that girl," muttered Jacob as he returned to his shower. Glancing at his engorged penis, he asked, "Now what the hell am I supposed to do with this?"

• • • •

SHOWERED AND SHAVED, Jacob glanced into the kitchen where Sarah simultaneously placed the finishing touches on breakfast and began the post-meal cleanup. Clad in jeans and a thin, white hoodie, she more resembled a housewife than a nun. There was no sign of Sophie.

A scrumptious feast covered the small kitchen table to Jacob's right. Two places were set while the rest of the table's surface contained plates of bacon, fried potatoes and scrambled eggs. Two glasses of orange juice and two mugs sat between the plates while a carafe of hot coffee stood guard at the center of the table.

Sarah swept into the dining room carrying a plate of fresh biscuits and a small tub of butter. She swiftly placed them on the table.

"I figured I'd bribe you for information with breakfast," Sarah said with a smirk. She sat down, passed him the shredded potatoes and added affectionately, "Dig in."

"Yeah," replied Jacob. He loathed the thought of rehashing the previous evening's events despite his new plan. Sarah noticed his troubled expression as he uttered, "Right."

Sarah waited patiently for Jacob to fill his plate and pour himself a cup of coffee. She pounced after he spooned sugar into his coffee cup and stirred it.

"Have you seen Miriam?" Sarah questioned in a worried, hushed tone. She lifted a forkful of scrambled eggs to her mouth.

"Yep. She ambushed me in the fucking elevator on my way to dinner last night," Jacob answered as he unfolded his napkin.

"What did you tell her?" Sarah inquired, her eyes widening with anticipation. She popped the eggs into her mouth.

"That I was going to dinner with my wife," Jacob said, his statement causing Sarah to cringe. He salted and peppered his potatoes and took a bite. Chewing his food, he said, "Damn, these are good. Anyway, she freaked when I said it, so I had to use a little Jesus Kung Fu on her. Then she took off."

Sarah pondered Jacob's intense encounter with Miriam while he greedily wolfed down his food. Pausing, he took a drink of his coffee.

"Don't worry, Sister Sarah," Jacob said as he set down his coffee mug. He took another bite of his breakfast before saying, "We ran into each other again. She knows what to do if she wants to abandon the dark side."

Jacob gorged himself on several huge bites of food and gulped down more coffee. Sarah ate as well as she patiently waited for him to expound on his theory.

"This is really damn good," remarked Jacob, the satiation of his hunger serving to calm his spirit as well. Setting down his fork, he continued, "She may or may not still be in love with the fucker, but either way, she's under Aaron's control . . . and I don't think that's gonna change for a while."

"That's terrible," Sarah said, the pitch of her tone rising with her disquiet.

"Maybe not," commented Jacob as he gestured in her direction with his coffee mug. Focusing on Sarah, he explained, "I should've taken your advice about Miriam. She's physically assaulted me twice now, and once in front of Sophie."

"Are you giving up on her?" Sarah questioned, the nun surprisingly hurt and disappointed by Jacob's words.

"Aaron, slippery fucker that he is, is probably gonna get Vanessa back for us," Jacob stated ardently, his blue eyes crackling with vibrant energy. His forward lean intimidated Sarah, her discomfort with his intensity causing her to press her back into the spokes of her chair. Unaware of her anxiousness, Jacob said, "Liz and I are getting back together, Sarah. She asked for some serious concessions, but I don't care, I'm making them, and I'm taking Liz and 'Ness back to Kaiser and we're going to be a family again. The days of all this demon bullshit are over, at least when it comes to *my* family."

"And Sophie?" Sarah asked. Jacob's cheeks faintly flushed and he bit his lip. She said, "She's a very troubled girl."

"I know," Jacob said in an unsettled voice. He took another sip of coffee and expounded, "I'd like you to take her under your wing for a while. We'll get St. Cyril rebuilt and the two of you can live there. Liz has Kaiser on the rise, Sarah, and there's a future there, *for all of us.*"

Dumbfounded, Sarah stared at Jacob. The news uplifted her heart but failed to quell the warning in her spirit. She offered Jacob a weak smile.

"*Miriam can't hurt us,*" Jacob rambled on, brimming with an odd, impassioned confidence, "because she'll be under Aaron's sway for a long time, and that's a good thing. A very good thing."

"You don't think she loves you as she claims and that you're destined to be her guide in the Spirit?" queried Sarah. She remembered Miriam's proclamations of her fierce love for Jacob and her own initial disbelief of those proclamations. Struggling to contain her sorrow, her eyes watered and she asked, "Were you and I wrong?"

Jacob took another swig of coffee and then clambered over Sarah's disturbing questions.

"Even if we weren't," answered Jacob, "it won't matter for a very long time."

· · · ·

WAITING IN THE UNNAMED lounge topping the waterfall in Chinese Peak's lobby, Jacob nervously scanned the crowds for Elizabeth. The couple planned a rendezvous at Vitoria for a late lunch during which she agreed to further discuss the end of their separation and the terms of Jacob's homecoming. Jittery yet excited, he fantasized about a return to happier, more peaceful days.

The hordes of demons skulking about Chinese Peak overloaded Jacob's spiritual radar and concealed the approach of a demon without a human host. The demon swirled around him at a distance of several feet and spoke to Jacob spiritually.

"Assarion wants to see you," the demon advised, Jacob hearing its deep, raspy voice within his head. He flinched and looked around himself with abrupt, twitchy movements. The demon instructed, "Follow me."

"Fuck you," replied Jacob angrily. Acquiring the demon's diffuse presence, he followed its circuit with his eyes and asked, "What am I on fucking call or something? Tell her I'm busy."

"The girl's dead," the demon stated flatly without emotion or sympathy. Jacob's elation over his reunion with Elizabeth vanished in a puff of smoke. Deeply saddened, he uttered a single word.

"*Fuck.*"

. . . .

CHINESE PEAK'S PREVIOUS proprietor constructed a morgue in a basement sublevel to deal with the many deaths that once occurred in his pleasure palace. Those deaths ran a broad gamut: older male patrons dying from overexertion during sexual dalliances, occasional mob hits and gory demonic murders in the days before Chinese Peak's demons walked openly among its human patrons. The death toll shrank significantly during Aaron's administration but sporadic deaths occurred nonetheless.

"In there," the gruff demonic voice said. Jacob sensed the demon's departure as he entered one of the morgue's smaller storage rooms. He found an antiseptic environment consisting of brown cement walls and a bank of hermetically-sealed, refrigerated drawers with silver, metal handles and placards identifying their occupants. A long, metal table occupied a space on the left wall.

The center of the bank, which contained a lone, open drawer, drew Jacob's attention. His feet refused to move forward as if the floor enveloped them and his heart thumped in his chest. Fearing the worst and unable to approach it, Jacob observed the drawer for several minutes.

Jacob's nerve developed at a snail's pace but his curiosity eventually surpassed his trepidation. He advanced towards the drawer by slowly placing one foot in front of the other. Stopping before his field of vision encompassed its occupant, Jacob shivered as the cold air flowed out if it.

"Please, God, don't let it be her," Jacob prayed. Gathering his strength, he traversed the distance between himself and the drawer. He repeated with little hope, "Please don't let it be her."

The color draining from his face and numbness wracking his body, Jacob stumbled and fell into the bank of drawers. Vanessa, the quintessential picture of death, lay motionlessly before him. A white sheet covered her naked body, part of it pulled back to reveal the pallid, bluish tint of her face and lips.

Moving to Vanessa, Jacob reached out his hand and rested it on her cold forehead. He struggled to restrain his emotions and prepared to pray over Vanessa. Her eyes popped open, however, and caused him to jump backwards, trip over his own feet and tumble to the floor. Sitting on the unforgiving cement with his arms stretched out behind him, a shocked Jacob gaped at the drawer with his chest heaving.

"Fucking cunt!" Jacob yelled in outrage over Assarion's prank. Sitting up in the drawer, she let the sheet drop and expose Vanessa's breasts. Jacob leapt to his feet and, gesturing emphatically, blistered Assarion, "Why the *fuck* would you do that?! And if you say old habits die hard, I'll cast your ass into the fucking Abyss right now! Bitch! Mother fucking bitch!"

Assarion hopped out of the drawer, wrapped Vanessa's body in the sheet and approached Jacob. He glowered at her, his face red with wrath.

"You have no sense of humor," Assarion said as she shook her head. The demon was unaffected by Jacob's ire.

"What the fuck do you want?" demanded Jacob. Desiring to strike Assarion but unwilling to harm Vanessa, he seethed and paced.

"I have something to show you," Assarion said in a foreboding tone. Her suddenly-grave demeanor thrust Jacob into a mental fog.

"Great," remarked a defeated Jacob, "just great."

• • • •

THE ELEVATOR DOORS sluggishly slid open and unveiled a dimly-lit, extravagant hotel hallway. Soft, soothing light wafted into the elevator, the glow emitted from two lines of equidistant, eye-level lights running to a three-way intersection.

Halfway down the corridor, an intertwined couple ardently kissed in the shadows. The woman, smaller in stature than her paramour, wrapped her right leg around his calf and sensually caressed the back of his leg with her foot. Their hands gracefully explored each other's bodies as the man lifted the woman and they disappeared into one of the suites. Worried about Assarion's imminent revelation, Jacob uneasily observed the couple.

"That could be you and Vanessa," cooed Assarion while leaning Vanessa's body into Jacob and batting her eyelashes at him. A subtle forearm shiver disrupted her advance while a stinging glance warned her not to venture another attempt. She acquiesced with a muted grin and taunted, "Well, what a prudish little Christian you are today."

She sauntered into the corridor, the demon content to lead Jacob forward wearing only the morgue sheet. He followed her and charily rested each foot as if the carpet concealed landmines. The elevator doors closed.

Sexual moans of pleasure arose from one of the suites as Jacob walked by its door. He listened intently as his chest tingled with anxiety and he attempted to discern if any of the moans came from his wife. His initial dread dissipated as he failed to hear his wife's distinctive tone.

Assarion and Jacob proceeded further down the hallway. Looking to his left, he noticed a door ajar. Inside the room stood an attractive brunette with long, wavy hair and milky skin. She desirously studied him with unremarkable brown eyes, her open, red-silk robe and the corridor's lighting exposing her enormous, fake breasts. Her sudden appearance stunned him and caused him to halt and stare at her beautiful body.

"Whoa," muttered Jacob. The woman offered him an inviting smile as a willowy blonde, obscured by the brunette and the shadows, emerged from behind her and erotically massaged her breasts. The palpable sexual tension aroused Jacob. He started as the door slammed shut without warning.

"Focus, Jacob, and stop thinking with your penis," instructed a mildly-annoyed Assarion with arms crossed. Memories of Miriam's similar counsel on the first night they met flared in Jacob's mind. He bit the inside of his mouth and held the callous in his teeth briefly while staring at the closed door.

"At least *he* always knows what he wants," Jacob said. Miriam faded from his thoughts as he pondered his surroundings, the deviant sexual lair exposing Assarion's intentions. He turned to her with his heart pounding and, with his fear and shame growing, he inquired, "So which one of these rooms is my wife in and who the fuck's she with?"

"I never said she was in any of these rooms," corrected a composed Assarion. Her eyes were riveted on Jacob as she added, "Nor did I say she was with anyone."

"Cut the bullshit, will ya'?" Jacob grumbled while thrusting his hands into his pants pockets. Angered, amused and inwardly beginning to panic, he expounded, "This floor is obviously some big fucking orgy, and my wife's somewhere in the middle of it. That's why you brought me here, right? To show me my wife's a cheating whore and I shouldn't reunite with her? Then once she's out of the way, you'll find some way to dispose of Miriam, and then I'm completely free to show you the way."

"So shrewd, yet so afraid," replied Assarion critically, the demon undaunted by Jacob's words. She smirked and purposefully strode up to him. Reveling in Jacob's mushrooming panic, she stated, "She's in room 1555. Down this hall, last door on the left. And I believe she's enjoying the company of a *very* handsome black man."

Assarion produced a key card and extended it to Jacob. He examined the card closely but failed to pluck it from her grasp. She could feel the anxiety radiating from him like the oppressive heat of a blast furnace.

"You know you want to use this, *Jake*," taunted Assarion coldly, her jabs more effective because of Vanessa's strong resemblance to her mother. Moving the card towards him, she continued softly, "Because, for *you*, not knowing is the greater torture."

. . . .

THE KEY CARD SHAKING in his right hand, Jacob held it up to the locking mechanism and hesitated. A fierce debate erupted in his mind over whether he truly wanted to cross the threshold of suite 1555.

"Would you like me to do it?" Assarion queried with sincerity in her voice. She placed a supportive hand on his arm.

"No," answered Jacob hoarsely while pulling his arm free from Assarion's grasp. A surge of adrenaline buttressed his resolve and he swiped the key card in the reader. The indicator light flashed green and the electric lock clicked open. Disregarding his own safety, Jacob opened the door and forged ahead into the room.

"I'll never forgive him for bringing them into our lives," Elizabeth said bitterly to Darius.

"I don't blame you," replied Darius, Elizabeth's lover leaning back in a hot tub as he soaked with arms outstretched on its marble base. Jacob strode into view.

"Jacob?!" Elizabeth exclaimed. Eyes wide with astonishment, she demanded, "How did you get in here?"

Jacob froze in his tracks in the middle of an ostentatious living room and stared down the barrels of two semiautomatic pistols. A separate room, entered through a high archway, contained a jetted hot tub set in a marble base and positioned in front of a window running from floor to ceiling. Seated upon the base, Elizabeth lowered her weapon. Darius followed suit.

"What the fuck is *this*, Liz?" demanded Jacob in an accusatory tone. Several tense moments followed during which only the din of the whirring hot tub jets and the churning water broke the silence.

Jacob glanced at a doorway to his left, which led to the bedroom, and surveyed the living room from left to right before returning his gaze to Elizabeth. She wore a long, casual dress of white with sleeves terminating at her middle forearms and a high neckline. A cocktail and a white handbag sat next to her on the marble.

Meanwhile, a shirtless Darius reclined at the end of the hot tub opposite Elizabeth with everything above his muscular torso visible. He held a drink in his left hand.

"We were only talking and, actually, I was about to leave to have lunch with you," Elizabeth finally said in response to Jacob's disapproving glower.

She scooted off the edge of the hot tub and onto her white pumps, adding, "Honestly, Jacob, I'm fully clothed."

"Yeah? And how fucking long was that gonna last?" questioned Jacob. Angered, he yanked a painting off the wall and hurled it into the bedroom with a crash. He then yelled, "Fuck!"

"Calm down, Jacob!" Elizabeth admonished him. She snatched up her purse, stuffed her pistol into it and zipped it closed. Irked, she approached her husband and explained with feigned-yet-flawless sincerity, "If I wanted to have sex with Darius, I could've simply stayed in Kaiser and done it there."

"What about the night after your dinner with Aaron?" asked Assarion innocently, her words causing a chill to ripple down Jacob's spine. Appearing behind him but obscured by the hallway shadows, she instantly caught Elizabeth's attention and the Constable noticed the claws on her left hand.

"Wonderful, Jacob," Elizabeth scolded him. She exhaled to vent her anger and sneered, "Human whores are no longer enough, so now you must traipse around with demonic ones. May *I* throw a painting now?"

"Maybe you'd better see this first," Jacob countered smugly. His cockiness disconcerted her.

"See what?" Elizabeth asked with a wavering voice. She knew Jacob held an ace in his hand and she feared its revelation.

"Assarion," beckoned Jacob with a forward gesture. She obeyed him and stepped into the light of the living room.

"Vanessa!" Elizabeth cried as her daughter appeared before her. She faltered but used a chair to keep herself upright.

"Assarion currently possesses your daughter, Liz," said Jacob haughtily, "and to this point she's shown no inclination of surrendering her. Isn't that true, Assarion?"

Elizabeth wept and trembled, her emotional strength shattered. Shocked into inaction, Darius watched the heart-wrenching scene in horrified disgust.

"That's correct," answered Assarion in her own voice. Elizabeth shuddered and bawled.

"*Please*," she begged, "please, I'll give you anything, anything you want. Just let her go."

"You don't have anything I want," replied Assarion matter-of-factly in Vanessa's voice. She turned and exited the room as Elizabeth screamed and reached out for her departing daughter.

"No!" Elizabeth bellowed.

Seconds later, Miriam appeared in the bedroom and remained invisible to human eyes. She growled upon seeing Jacob with his wife though the inaudible warning drifted away harmlessly. Elizabeth turned her gaze to Jacob.

"I'm sorry, Jake," Elizabeth mewled, "*I'm so sorry*. Please, just get her back. I'll do anything."

Miriam tilted her head and skulked into the living room just as Assarion retreated out of the suite. Forbidden to harm Elizabeth or reveal herself to Jacob, she ruminated over how to vent her burgeoning rage.

"*I'm working on it*," Jacob grumbled while feeling spiritually impotent in his quest to save his stepdaughter. He retrieved the lithium bottle from his inside jacket pocket and sneered, "Oh, and you can have these back."

He threw the bottle at Elizabeth but missed. The improperly fastened cap popped off the bottle when it hit the hot tub, the impact sending pills flying everywhere. Jacob then stormed out of the suite, his wife watching his exit with tears in her eyes.

• • • •

AN INFURIATED JACOB stomped out of Darius's suite and forcefully pulled the door shut. Assarion hid herself around the corner and peeked out as Jacob marched down the hallway and disappeared into the elevator.

Assarion returned her attention to the suite as Elizabeth flung the door open and rushed passed her, the Constable unaware of the demon due to her determined pursuit of Jacob. Miriam followed on Elizabeth's heels like a rabid dog.

"Slaughtering his wife won't win you his heart," Assarion called out spiritually. Miriam whirled around to strike but aborted her action when she realized Assarion stood before her. She lowered her arm, *daimoniou* warily watching *daimoniou* and remaining silent.

The ding of the elevator caused them to glance down the hallway. They postponed any discussion until Elizabeth boarded it and its doors closed.

"I don't need your help," Miriam snarled. She glowered at Assarion and, while moving into her personal space, threatened, "Maybe I'll just maim one of her daughters. Tear off an arm. Rip out an eye. Crush a knee."

"*No*," rebuked Assarion condescendingly, "because if you hurt one of her daughters he'll never forgive you. His guilt could bind him to Elizabeth permanently, even if she ultimately rejects him."

Miriam shrieked and shoved her away though she failed to utilize her demonic strength. Assarion calmly absorbed the contact and stepped backward to steady herself.

"Why do you care?" Miriam grumbled in her hybrid voice. She lazily lunged at Assarion again, swiped at her with her claws and added, "You're trying to take him from me."

"Begin using your mind," suggested Assarion as she dodged Miriam's strike and her question, "and not just your teeth and your claws. You must push both of them apart, not just one from the other, and you can't kill any member of Elizabeth's *family*."

Assarion waited patiently while Miriam spun her words around in her mind. A malicious smile of pointed teeth spread across Miriam's face.

"Darius," Miriam stated with devious delight. She looked to the open suite door and said, "An open nerve that Jake and Lady Lizzie share."

"Exactly," confirmed Assarion. Miriam began dematerializing but she held up her hand. The gesture caused Miriam to reappear in time to hear her warn, "But be *patient*."

· · · ·

THE PINNACLE SIDE OF Chinese Peak's summit housed the glass-enclosed restaurant The Thin Dolphin but the southern third of the tower was flat, its surface coated with white, lifeless concrete and dotted with air conditioning and other utility units.

Stepping onto the flat roof, Jacob spied an open corridor leading towards the southern edge of the building. Light fixtures lined the walkway, each one containing both a red and a green light and sitting atop a three-foot-high post. A Eurocopter EC 135, painted a crisp black, sat dormant on a helicopter pad constructed at the end of the corridor.

"Too bad I can't fly a fucking helicopter," Jacob remarked while momentarily indulging in an escapist fantasy. Looking to his right, he noticed a metal maintenance ladder bolted into the side of the building and ascending to the very zenith of Chinese Peak. He thought to himself, "Guess I can climb."

Jacob cautiously ascended the access ladder by climbing rung after precarious rung. His endeavor was perilous as plummeting to the roof below would result in certain death. The desire for total solitude, however, spurred him upward.

Pulling himself up onto the curved steel spine that formed the tip of Chinese Peak's zenith, Jacob held out his arms for balance. He then steadied himself and turned to the East.

The awe-inspiring view astonished him though the chilly and occasionally-swirling breeze caused him to shudder. The oncoming evening eagerly swallowed up the daylight, an occasional star winking into view. Mountains bookended the eastern landscape with lower, heights and forest-covered slopes in between them.

Jacob rotated one-hundred-eighty degrees. The mountain range dominated the northern landscape beginning on the west side of Chinese Peak and meandering east out of view. The striking palette of vibrant colors from the hidden sunset radiated around other mountain peaks further to the west, the intersections of yellows, oranges, pinks and reds blurred and nearly indiscernible.

"You sure as hell know how to make a sunset," Jacob lauded God, the faintest of grins coming to his face as he soaked in the ambiance. He walked to the center of the spine and seated himself upon it, Jacob setting his arms on his knees and clasping his hands in front of them. A measure of peace infused Jacob's veins like his own blood, the tranquility of shedding all human and spiritual presence, save that of God, centering, if not uplifting, his troubled spirit. Feeling unworthy of God's presence, he thought, "'Go away from me Lord, for I am a sinful man.'" (Excerpt from the Gospel of Luke 5:8).

Jacob's thoughts crept over Elizabeth and Miriam. He once considered relinquishing his wife to cling to Miriam but now his demonic paramour wavered in her alleged love for him and deferred to Aaron. Rekindling his turbulent relationship with Elizabeth was no longer an option as Darius held sway over her heart. He pondered a deal with Aaron for Vanessa's safe return but his "allegiance to God" was not something he could surrender.

"Enough of this love bullshit. Looks like it's time for me to get the hell out of Dodge," Jacob remarked discontentedly. Sighing, he let his eyes absorb the picturesque skyline as the prospect of tackling a dangerous, uncertain world on his own rippled across his mind. He quietly muttered, "*Again.*"

Jacob shivered as a chilling wind whirled around him, its fingers probing underneath his clothing. The sensation sparked his memory and he recalled Sophie.

"I can't take her with me," Jacob rebuked himself, his mood darkening as his libido reared its ugly head. He conceded in a defeated tone, "She's gotta go with Sarah . . . that's all there is to it."

Hankering for a drink, he paused and waited for divine confirmation of a fact he already knew. The wind died and all grew quiet and still. A star manifested itself faintly above him, its light struggling to twinkle against the fading sun. The Holy Spirit imbued him with a measure of hope and strength at the perfect moment and alleviated his doubt.

"*As you will,*" Jacob answered obediently.

* * * *

"YOU'VE BECOME QUITE skilled at disappearing," Elizabeth said, her arrival shattering Jacob's spiritual mood. She stood several feet away from where he sat on Chinese Peak's summit with her arms at her sides. The unceasing breeze tussled with Elizabeth's hair, the contrast of her motionless silhouette against the darkening sky giving her the ominous appearance of a movie villain. She scolded Jacob, "I searched for you all afternoon."

"Just fucking go away," grumbled Jacob. He glanced at Elizabeth and then returned his gaze to the sky. The overwhelming illumination of Chinese Peak replaced the sun, its glow insatiably feasting on the darkness. Stewing, Jacob growled, "Why don't you go fucking bust Tanner's balls?"

Jacob smirked.

"Oh wait," he added with sinister glee, "he's fucking dead. Maybe you could bust Darius's balls when you're done sitting on his cock."

"Jacob, *please*," Elizabeth replied, his wife struggling to restrain her ire. She approached Jacob and sat down next to him, saying, "I'm not here to fight."

"But we're so fucking good at it," retorted Jacob, his tone thick with sarcasm.

"I want to talk about *us*, not them," Elizabeth snapped before composing herself. Regardless of whether Jacob sought an argument, she wished to avoid any conflict.

"Ya' know, I only fell in love with a part of you," Jacob stated thoughtfully, his acrimony evaporating. Elizabeth observed him with wonder as Jacob expounded, "Not Elizabeth the Constable, or the mother, or the sister. I fell hopelessly in love with Liz, a woman who only existed when she and I were alone together and she wasn't supporting the weight of the fucking world on her shoulders. It's the only part I ever wanted. But I fucked up. It wasn't the whole you, and I shoulda' known that."

"You fell in love with a fantasy, Jacob," Elizabeth stated in a tone of rebuttal.

Jacob shook his head.

"The Elizabeth who irrevocably captured my heart exists, Liz," Jacob asserted while staring out into the night, "but it's impossible for you to be her all the time. Had I realized that, I could've saved us both a lot of time and heartache."

Jacob and Elizabeth sat in silence for several minutes, each spouse hesitant to travel down the path they tread. Elizabeth stirred first.

"I think it may be time to face the unfortunate truth," Elizabeth suggested reluctantly. The peculiar tone with which she spoke rattling Jacob's spirit, she said, "That . . . *wonderful* . . . *incredible* connection we enjoyed is simply gone, and living in one another's worlds has proven impossible."

"I'll be damned," said a stunned Jacob as his mind processed the import of Elizabeth's words. The color draining from his face, he asked, "You're ready to call it off, aren't you?"

Distressed, Elizabeth turned her head away from Jacob and fought off tears.

"Yes," she answered weakly. Jacob began chewing the inside of his cheek relentlessly and repeatedly popped the callous that his habit created. Reviving old defenses, he buried his feelings deep within his spirit and hardened his heart.

"Did you fuck Darius the other night?" inquired Jacob while thoughts of throwing himself, Elizabeth or both of them off Chinese Peak's summit percolated in his mind.

"Yes," Elizabeth confessed, the Constable softly crying as she did so. She whimpered, "I'm so sorry, Jake."

"Okie dokie," stated Jacob tranquilly with an unusual air. Reaching into his right jacket pocket with his left hand, he retrieved three folded sheets of paper. He unfolded the papers and handed them to Elizabeth who hesitantly accepted them.

"What's this?" Elizabeth queried quizzically as she studied the first page. Jacob pulled a pen from his pocket and held it out to her.

"Three copies of an Order of the Constabulary declaring that we're divorced," responded Jacob matter-of-factly. Keeping his eyes on the horizon, he continued, "One for you, one for me, one for the city clerk. All that's missing are your signatures."

Elizabeth's jaw dropped and she gaped at him. Her eyes darted to the pen and then back to Jacob.

"Why do you have these?" Elizabeth inquired in forlorn disbelief.

"Because I knew if we didn't work out, there was no fucking way I could stay in Kaiser," answered Jacob, "and you know me. I hate loose ends. I just never had the cojones to go through with it. Pretty fucking ironic that you did, huh?"

Jacob tipped the pen towards Elizabeth.

"It's your move, Constable," he said.

11

DARIUS WATCHED THE water of the hot tub churn relentlessly, the tedious nature of his assignment wearing on him. His ever-present pistol lay on the edge of the tub.

Darius'ss stay at Chinese Peak proved unremarkable, the visit livened up only by his sexual encounter with Elizabeth and Jacob's impromptu visit the previous day. Elizabeth confined him to his suite after Jacob's threat due to fear of reprisal for her infidelity. She even sought Aaron's assistance in barring all demonic contact with Darius, a strategy he vehemently opposed to no avail.

"That woman sure is a ballbuster," Darius remarked while laying his head on the tub's base and swiping his hand from this forehead to his chin to remove beads of sweat.

"Try being married to her," said Jacob as he aimed a sawed-off, double-barrel shotgun at Darius. Cognizant of the lethality of Jacob's weapon regardless of accuracy, he failed to reach for his pistol. He smirked and laughed.

"Where the fuck did you get that," Darius asked, amused by Jacob's audacity, "and how the hell did you get in here again?"

"You'd be astounded to know what's stockpiled in this place," answered Jacob with tension in his voice. He took several steps towards Darius and kept the shotgun trained on him the entire way, saying, "As to your second question, why don't you nudge that gun onto the floor first? Nice and slow, please."

"Okay," Darius replied. Unruffled by the threat of violence, he haughtily flicked his gun to the floor with the back of his hand. The gun clattered on the tile, discharged on impact and fired a round into the wall. Jacob started but kept his weapon on Darius. He clicked the callous in his mouth.

"You and your girlfriend never asked for the key back," said Jacob. He cautiously reached into his jacket and produced the key card given to him by Assarion. He held it between his middle and index fingers for Darius to see before flinging it into the hot tub. Improving his grip on the shotgun and pressing the butt into his shoulder, he added, "You should probably should give it to her . . . oh, wait, you already have."

Elizabeth's unfaithfulness fouled Jacob's mood. He paused.

"*Fucker,*" muttered Jacob with absolute hatred.

"Go ahead, Jake, call me a nigger," taunted Darius with a cocky grin. He straightened up, cracked his knuckles and said, "You just can't stand it that Liz chose a brother over your pathetic cracker ass."

"Ya' know, not every white person's a fucking racist," Jacob replied sharply. He adjusted his grip on the shotgun's handle and stated, "I don't give a fuck that you're black. I give a fuck that you've been sticking your cock in my wife."

Jacob chuckled fatalistically. His eyes glazed over.

"Or at least I used to," said Jacob.

"I don't know why you would," Darius stated, "because you're fucking that little demon bitch anyway."

Darius's accusation momentarily confounded Jacob, the allegation causing him to wonder about Miriam's sexual capabilities. He fell out of his funk and reacquired Darius in his sights.

"First, I don't even know if that's possible," Jacob uttered. Still bewildered by the prospect of intercourse with Miriam, he added brusquely, "Second, it's never happened."

"Buuullllshit," Darius replied while firing a scathingly-skeptical glance at him. Jacob took another step forward and readied to fire the shotgun.

"I should kill you," Jacob began crossly, "I *want* to kill you. Just fucking shoot you right now and be done with it. It'd be so simple, and I'd get away with it."

Jacob's anger cooled and was replaced with a strange, resigned sadness. His eyes fell to the floor. Darius furrowed his brow at Jacob's changing demeanor and remained silent.

"I shot Tanner," confessed Jacob, "several times. Mutilated the poor fuck. His face was unrecognizable. Didn't do a damn bit of good, though. Pain didn't stop. Elizabeth didn't stop."

Jacob lowered the shotgun and lifted his gaze to Darius.

"And what if I'm wrong?" argued Jacob steadfastly. Gesturing as was his wont, he reasoned, "*What if you're her answer?* What if she gets Vanessa back, and the three of you go back to Kaiser, and live a happy fucking life. Maybe have a kid of your own. I'd be ruining that. With one fucking pull of the trigger, with one hateful, evil act, I'd be ruining four people's lives. Maybe ending them for all I know."

Rendered speechless by Jacob's impassioned monologue, a wide-eyed Darius simply watched his assailant with puzzlement. Pity welled in his spirit, pity for a man crumbling before him. Jacob smiled.

"Of course, my Master won't allow it, either," Jacob continued. His eyes watered and he said, "'But I say to you who hear, love your enemies, do good to those who hate you, bless those who curse you, pray for those who mistreat you.' (The Gospel of Luke 6:27-28). I'd be failing him as I usually do. *But not this time.* He's kept me alive through mother-fucking Armageddon, dumb fuck that I am. 'For I was hungry, and He gave me to eat; I was thirsty, and He gave me to drink; I was a stranger, and He invited me in; I was sick and He visited me; I was in prison, and He came to me.'" (Derived from The Gospel of Matthew 25:35-36).

Jacob lowered his head and stood motionless and silent. Darius failed to realize it but he prayed.

"Jacob!" Darius called out, seeking to wrest him from his trance, "Jacob!"

Jacob's head jerked up and he looked at Darius stolidly. He walked up to the edge of the hot tub and placed the shotgun upon it.

"She's officially yours now," uttered Jacob. He turned his back on the shotgun and said, "*Good luck.*"

· · · ·

MIRIAM, PRESENT FOR Jacob's entire monologue, revealed her physical form to Darius as Jacob departed. An errant shadow obscured her demonic features, the ambient light revealing only her curly, golden locks, her petite frame and her red dress. Jacob cast a sidelong glance at Miriam, paused, and then left.

"Well, now, who are you?" Darius asked Miriam without missing a beat. Assuming Miriam to be a "gift" from Aaron, he stood up and moved to the center of the hot tub, the water beading on his muscular frame. He snuck a precautionary peek at the shotgun before saying, "You can tell Aaron thanks but no thanks. I'm spoken for."

Jacob closed the suite door.

"I'm not one of Aaron's whores," snapped Miriam in her hybrid voice, her demonic tone triggering Darius's memory. She remained perfectly still.

"Miriam," Darius said with distaste. Realizing the uselessness of a weapon, he returned to his seat and inquired, "What the fuck do you want?"

"Jacob," replied Miriam curtly and candidly. Angered, Darius licked his bottom lip and then bit it. Miriam ambled up to the edge of the hot tub as he saw her demonic features and said, "And you're going to help me get him."

"Bullshit," Darius asserted with fear fluttering in his heart.

"I thought it would've been enough," explained Miriam, her tone softening. She, though looking directly at Darius, saw nothing but Jacob's face and uttered distantly, "Elizabeth being such a cheating whore. Tanner, you, who knows who else. But she has some fucked up hold on him, like an infection. Killing her would feel . . . *so* fucking good . . . I would love to bleed her slowly, to kill her over hours, days . . . ."

Miriam paused and fantasized about slaughtering Elizabeth. Shaking off her murderous daydream, she refocused on Darius.

"But I'm not allowed to kill her," conceded Miriam, "and it wouldn't help anyway."

A terrifying, evil chill emanated from Miriam's spirit, the supernatural cold generated by her fierce hatred of Elizabeth and her intense desire for Jacob. Darius shivered as her malevolence washed over him.

"Fuck you, you sadistic bitch," Darius countered as he steeled his courage. Miriam refocused on him, smiled and revealed her jagged teeth.

"So, if I can't kill her," said Miriam, "we'll have to go with Plan B."

"Plan B?" Darius inquired.

Miriam instantaneously disappeared. Emerging from beneath the surface of the hot tub water to Darius's left, she wailed hideously. The horrifying screech momentarily paralyzed Darius, the nauseating sound rendering him unable to thwart Miriam's attack. She grasped his shoulder with her left hand and crushed it while gripping his head with her right hand. Forcing him downward, she slammed his face onto the hot tub seat.

"That's where I kill you," expounded Miriam coolly as she held Darius beneath the water, "and Elizabeth blames Jacob for it."

Darius raged unsuccessfully against Miriam's supernatural strength. The increasing pressure she applied to his skull crushed his cheekbone, his screams muffled by the water. Exhilarated by Darius's panicked struggle, she thrust downward and pulverized his head. He struggled no more.

Miriam squished Darius'ss skull and flesh in her fist and relished the feel of them as they oozed around her fingers. She then released his corpse and let it float to the surface of the hot tub. Nudging it away from her, Miriam caused it to bob gently in the water.

"Stupid fucking humans," griped Miriam. Sitting down on the hot tub seat, she said, "Always the hard way."

• • • •

"WELL, IF IT ISN'T THE moral paragon, Jacob Gottschalk," Aaron ridiculed Jacob while puffing haughtily on an expensive cigar. Grinning, he asked, "What can this 'mother fucking liar and deceiver' do for you?"

Jacob bristled, every fiber of his being revolting against dealing with evil. He journeyed through the immensity of Aaron's office, the recent divorcee dodging expensive furniture and invaluable works of art. Buttressing his will with his faith, he arrived before Aaron and spoke.

"I'm here to make a deal," admitted Jacob begrudgingly while loathing his capitulation to Aaron. Aaron's grin evolved into a smirk.

"Really?" Aaron asked with raised eyebrows. He withdrew the cigar from his mouth and said, "Let me guess, you're not willing to surrender your faith in God but you're going to offer me something lesser . . . in exchange for, say, Vanessa's safe return?"

"My wife . . . *Liz* already made that deal," sneered Jacob with a sad, contorted scowl. He looked away and fought off angry tears. Composing himself, he snarled, "May God cast you into the outer darkness if you don't get her back, you demon fuck."

"You need to work on your negotiation skills, you human fuck," Aaron replied blithely. He puffed on his cigar, held it away from his face and examined it. Turning his gaze back to Jacob, he inquired, "What is it that you want?"

"I want Sarah to walk out of here - *safely* - with Sophie," answered Jacob. Shoving his hands in his pockets, he continued, "No questions asked, no strings attached and – this is the important part – no one goes after them. *Ever.*"

"And in return?" Aaron queried with great interest. Jacob lowered his eyes, his mien one of shame.

"Anything short of my faith in God," he replied weakly. Remorseful disgust etched on his face, he added, "Demon's choice."

Aaron's eyes lit up and he slowly set his cigar in the notch of the gold ash tray on his desk.

"Miriam and Elizabeth," Aaron said with great satisfaction.

"What?" replied Jacob. Aaron's desired consideration perplexed him.

"You heard me," Aaron repeated with cruel relish. He eyed Jacob closely and said, "I know you've already lost Elizabeth but you must give her up as well. You cannot reunite if she suffers a change of heart."

"Why?" inquired Jacob between clenched teeth.

"So you'll be utterly alone," Aaron answered sharply. Jacob placed his hands on his hips and turned his back on him as the demon stated, "That's the deal, Mr. Gottschalk."

Jacob pondered Aaron's proposal. He wondered how Aaron learned of the divorce so quickly and debated with himself whether to address the subject. He decided to let sleeping dogs lie.

"I'll need transportation, supplies," muttered Jacob. He sighed in resignation and bit the callous inside his right cheek. Remembering the loss of Miriam's protection against worldly threats, he added, "And weapons."

"Of course," Aaron assured Jacob who turned to face him. He asked, "Do we have an agreement?"

"Yep," confirmed Jacob. He turned to depart.

"Oh, and one more thing," Aaron stated. Jacob stopped and listened to him request, "Please cease and desist from exorcisms for the rest of your stay at Chinese Peak."

"Sorry," grumbled Jacob, "that's above my pay grade."

. . . .

"WHAT'S THE HURRY?" Darby complained while trailing Elizabeth on the way to Darius'ss suite. The elevator doors closed behind them as she reasoned, "He's probably taking a fucking nap. House arrest is pretty fucking boring."

"Darius is not answering his telephone," answered Elizabeth anxiously, "and that's *not* like him."

Arriving at Darius'ss door, she pounded on it forcefully. Darby rolled her eyes and leaned against the wall opposite the door with arms folded. She lifted her right knee and placed the bottom of her boot on the wall.

"Darius!" beckoned Elizabeth. Continuing to loudly knock on the door, she called out, "Darius!"

Panicking, Elizabeth grasped the door handle and repeatedly attempted to force it open. Her efforts failed. Darby watched Elizabeth's attempts with an annoyed smile and a shake of the head.

"Move," Darby instructed. Elizabeth stopped and turned towards her sister with a baffled expression. Darby nodded to the right of the door and said again, "*Move.*"

Reluctant but obedient, Elizabeth slowly moved to the right. Darby's patience waned.

"*A little further,*" she stated in irritation.

Elizabeth moved further to the right and, before she planted her last step, Darby drew her fifty-caliber pistol. Firing three precise shots, she removed the handle and locking mechanism from the door.

Drawing her own pistol, Elizabeth kicked open the door while Darby made a tactical entry. The two women efficiently swept through the entry hallway and into the living room. Darby saw Darius first.

"*Holy shit,*" Darby said, Elizabeth's sister observing his mutilated body floating in a gruesome soup of bloody water and chunks of torn flesh. Elizabeth pushed her aside.

"Oh, God, not again," lamented Elizabeth, the Constable horrified by the gory scene. Tears welled in her eyes as she examined Darius'ss corpse and its surroundings. She noticed the sawed-off, double barrel shotgun resting on the edge of the tub as well as the bloodied key card floating in the water.

"*Jacob*," she whispered. Darby moved to Elizabeth to comfort her but her sister waved her off. Her tears disappeared and her face hardened. She holstered her weapon and marched out of the suite with Darby in tow.

• • • •

THE DOORS TO AARON'S office closed, the demonic presence of the unseen door wards causing the hair on the back of Jacob's neck to stand on end. Numbed by the daunting future ahead of him, he turned his gaze upward.

"So, what's next?" he prayed silently. Uncertainty and self-doubt plagued him.

"Jake?" asked Vanessa's innocent voice. Lowering his head and turning it to the right, he saw her standing several feet away. She watched him with the sad, weak stare of one exhausted by constant trauma.

"God damn it, Assarion, I-," Jacob began before he ceased talking and froze with an expression of bewilderment on his face. Vanessa shed a single tear.

"It's me, Jake," said Vanessa.

"You're . . . you're not . . . not . . . ," Jacob stuttered while searching for the right words.

"She's still in me," said Vanessa uneasily, "but she's letting me talk to you."

"*Why?*" Jacob queried with a ghostly-white face. Tears rolled down Vanessa's cheeks.

"I don't want her in me anymore," answered Vanessa desperately. She broke down and mewled, "I can't take it. I'm so tired, Jake, *so tired.*"

"Hey, hey," Jacob said as he moved to Vanessa and embraced her. Attempting to comfort her, he stated untruthfully, "It's all right, sweetheart. You're all right. This'll all be over real soon."

"*Please,*" begged Vanessa. Raising her muted green eyes to Jacob, she whimpered, "Help me."

"I can't, kiddo," Jacob said with Vanessa's emotion slicing into his heart. Struggling to respond, he explained, "I just can't do it. You'll *die* if I do it. Your heart's defective and if-."

"I already know," interrupted Vanessa, Jacob's former stepdaughter clinging to his body. Shocked into speechlessness, he merely stared at her. She shook him gently and continued, "But I don't care anymore. You have to cast her out. Please."

Overwhelmed by Vanessa's request, Jacob's mind ground to a halt and he relentlessly chewed on the inside of his mouth. Vanessa's eyes suddenly went black and she shoved Jacob away.

"What's the problem, Jake?" demanded Assarion impatiently. She shoved him again and chastised him, saying, "Why the indecision? You were hell bent on casting me out of her before. *She wants this.*"

A rage exploded within Jacob. He quelled it.

"What do want, Assarion?" Jacob asked. He shrugged and continued, "You could free her if you wanted so what's your angle? Can I get her back with a deal or is this whole thing just another subplot in the temptation of Jacob Gottschalk?"

"There may come a time when I trade her for your teaching but I'm not tipping my hand to the Master, not yet," expounded Assarion. Gazing at him gravely to underscore her point, she said, "But you have another problem."

"Is that so?" Jacob replied with a sneer and a chuckle.

"'If your eye causes you to stumble, throw it out; it is better for you to enter the kingdom of God with one eye, than, having two eyes, to be cast into hell, where their worm does not die and the fire is not quenched,'" said Assarion. (The Gospel of Mark 9:47-48).

"You've got some real balls, demon," Jacob snarled while thrusting a threatening finger at Assarion.

"It's come to my attention that I could be recalled by my Master at any time, and where I go, she goes," counseled Assarion, "so it's better that you throw me out of her so she can enter the kingdom of God than she be thrown into hell with me."

"Fuck," Jacob cursed. Conflicted by the apparent mutual exclusivity of Vanessa's spiritual and physical health, he realized that Assarion spoke the truth and it irked him terribly. Mulling over his options, he stated, "I need to run this by someone first."

"Need the ex-wife's permission, do we?" jabbed Assarion, the *daimoniou* vexed by Jacob's hesitation.

"No, *cunt*," Jacob replied. Tucking his right arm beneath his left arm and covering the lower half of his face with his left hand, he said, "I need a moral second opinion."

"Ah, the nun," said Assarion knowingly. Jacob slid his hand downward and grasped his chin.

"You know about Sarah?" queried Jacob.

"Of course. Every demon here senses her like a knife in the kidney," stated Assarion. She placed her hands on his chest and advised suggestively, "You see, her spiritual presence is second only to yours."

Tears began rolling down Vanessa's cheeks again, her predicament washing away Jacob's confidence. Taking her cold hand in his own, he looked on her with compassion.

"Hang on, 'Ness," he said solemnly, "just hang on."

· · · ·

"AH, MIRIAM, SO GLAD you could come," greeted Aaron with an arrogant grin. He carefully lit a cigar with a match before discarding the match in the ash tray on his desk.

"What the fuck do you want?" Miriam inquired harshly. Regardless of her hostility, she failed to completely conceal her guilt. Aaron exhaled cigar smoke in an ostentatious display.

"I understand you've been a very naughty girl," answered Aaron with disapprobation. Holding his cigar to the side, he said, "I never sanctioned your slaughtering of Elizabeth's lover."

"You don't care about the minor players," Miriam fired back hatefully.

"Not true," disagreed Aaron, continuing to enjoy his cigar, "though I must admit that Darius was quite expendable. Your obedience is the issue here, however, not his murder."

"I'm turning up on the heat on Jake," Miriam advised. She leapt onto a large bronze bust and perched upon it like a vulture. Tilting her head to the side, she said, "Lady Lizzie will freak when she finds out I killed Darius. She'll blame Jacob, they'll wage another ugly battle and she'll nudge him closer to me. It's all part of the plan."

"I see," said Aaron, his tone thick with condescension. He prematurely crushed out his cigar in the gold ashtray and indulged in his last puff before blowing the smoke high into the air. Aaron then advised, "I appreciate the efforts but they're no longer necessary. I have good news. You're going back to your old stomping grounds, to your old job tempting spurned lovers in Kaiser."

"I'd rather you cut off my legs and I walk on the bloody stumps to the Abyss," snarled Miriam, "and then drink rotten pus out of the Master's asshole."

She shuddered and appeared physically ill after the words passed her lips. Aaron scowled and bored into her with his eyes.

"Watch your tongue," he chastened her, "or that could be arranged."

"I'm not going back . . . to either place," Miriam said dismissively in a monstrous tone.

"Oh, yes you are," corrected Aaron sternly, "because Jacob Gottschalk is no longer your concern."

"You said I could have him," Miriam growled, the sound so guttural the bust on which she sat vibrated. She thrust a claw at him and in her demonic tone uttered, "That was part of the fucking deal."

"Unfortunately, I must alter the fucking deal," countered Aaron. Miriam's composure wavered as her abject fear warred with her anger.

"Please . . . don't do this," Miriam whimpered as the very will to exist bled from her spirit. Melting down, she hurled herself at Aaron. Landing on his desk but venturing no further, she growled desperately in her hybrid voice, "I'll lose Jake."

"I'm afraid that ship has sailed," stated Aaron, the demon unfazed by Miriam's aborted assault. He stood up, looked her directly in the eyes and said, "Earlier today, your beloved Jake traded you away for the young blonde. What is her name? Sophie, I believe."

"Bullshit," Miriam scoffed though the trepidation on her face betrayed her. Panic infused her spirit.

"Your time with Jacob Gottschalk is over," sneered Aaron mercilessly. He sat down and warned, "Don't visit him again or your next visit will be to the Master."

"You evil fucking megalomaniacs always underestimate your enemies," Miriam chided. Relishing every word, she continued, "I knew you'd renege. But when I crawl out from under your thumb – and I will – Jake'll be mine."

Stifling the terror of losing Jacob and the prospect of Ba'al Zeboul's punishment, Miriam gave Aaron the finger and faded from existence in the material world.

・・・・

JACOB BLINKED IN DISBELIEF upon walking into the tiny chapel, its presence in Chinese Peak completely unforeseen. An A-frame ceiling hovered above its taupe walls and three rows of short, oak pews. The small, raised apse contained no altar but a large cross hung on the far wall. Bookended by two large, stained-glass windows comprised of green, yellow, orange and red panes, the burnished metal cross sparkled despite the dim chapel lights.

"A chapel in a demon's den," thought Jacob. Sarah and Sophie kneeled on kneelers in the first row with their heads bowed in prayer. Jacob observed them for over a minute before permitting the chapel door to close. The resultant click caused Sarah and Sophie to abruptly turn their heads.

"What're we up to, ladies?" Jacob asked with muted grin.

"Sarah's teaching me how to pray," answered Sophie mechanically. She turned her head forward again and bowed it down.

"See ya for a minute?" Jacob asked as he motioned with his finger for Sarah to join him. Carefully standing up, she placed a reassuring hand on Sophie's shoulder and gently squeezed it.

"I'll be right back," Sarah said softly. Exiting the pew to the right, she traversed the length of the aisle between the pews and the wall. Jacob stepped into the narrow, dingy hallway outside followed closely by Sarah. He left the door ajar to keep Sophie in his line of sight.

"How did you find this place?" inquired Jacob while examining the neglected hallway. He looked back to Sophie and asked, "And how the hell did you get her to pray?"

"Surprisingly, Adedewe," Sarah said in a hushed tone. A smile on her face, she continued, "As far as Sophie, I have no idea but there's definitely something at work in her."

"We need to talk," said Jacob bluntly. Sarah's grin faded.

"What is it?" Sarah asked concernedly.

"For starters," began Jacob, "I just bought you and Sophie safe passage outta here and a demon-free future."

"What about you?" Sarah inquired after collecting her thoughts. Distressed, she glanced at Sophie praying silently with head bowed.

"That's not important," countered Jacob. Sarah sighed and looked on him with pity as he added, "You just need to get her the fuck outta here and Kaiser's your best bet."

"Perhaps instead you should join Sophie and I and lay your troubles at the feet of our Father," Sarah counseled firmly yet compassionately.

"Actually, I've got one to lay at your feet," said Jacob. He shook his head and said, "My stepdaughter, Vanessa, has a heart condition. She was seconds away from a massive heart attack when Assarion possessed her and, if I exorcise Assarion, Vanessa dies. But the kid's breaking . . . and she wants me to do it now, Sarah. *She wants death over possession.* Says she's tired."

Dumbfounded by the news, Sarah covered her mouth with her left hand. Jacob's agony was palpable.

"And that's not all," continued Jacob. A bitter expression on his face, he said, "Assarion, assuming she's telling the truth, said she could be recalled by her Master at any time. If that happens, we lose Vanessa forever anyway."

"What an evil choice," Sarah lamented with watery eyes. She hesitated but then embraced Jacob.

"Yeah, no shit," uttered Jacob. Sophie stirred and looked back at him with a penetrating gaze, her attention causing him to shiver and avert his eyes. Clinging to Sarah in a moment of emotional exhaustion, he exhaled and said, "Look, I've lost my wife, my family, my home and any hope of a normal life in a matter of months. Plus I've got the mother fucking 'ruler of demons' putting a full court press on my faith in God. Why he wants a fuckup like me I have no fucking idea but for some strange reason he's got a hardon for my downfall. And now I have to decide between demonic possession and death for Vanessa. It's just too much."

Sarah extricated herself from Jacob and gently grasped him by the cheeks.

"Then let Him make the decision for you," Sarah counseled Jacob in earnest. He turned away from her and put his hands on his hips.

"How the hell do I do that?" asked Jacob.

"Don't let Assarion force you into a decision you're not ready to make," Sarah answered. Her serious tone caused Jacob to turn around. Taking his hands in her own, she said, "Let her go."

"Abandon her?" Jacob queried sharply.

"I didn't say that," responded Sarah with a grave, sorrowful expression. Her body abruptly heaved with a sob but she stifled it and said, "May God be with you, Jacob Gottschalk."

Jacob abruptly took Sarah in his arms and passionately kissed her. She initially acquiesced but soon regained her senses, squirmed out of his embrace and moved Jacob away from her. Maintaining her grip on his arms, Sarah squeezed them and smiled.

"I may not be married," Sarah said as her grin melted into a forlorn expression and she released him, "but I've taken vows to another, Jake."

Disappearing into the chapel, she stifled another sob and closed the door. Jacob remained stationary and simply gaped at the spot where Sarah once stood.

"Cock-blocked by God," mused Jacob in defeat. Meandering down the hallway, he shrugged and said, "That's a new one."

. . . .

ELIZABETH STORMED INTO Vitoria's bar like an invading army and fired a round into the ceiling. An old, portly man in a powder blue suit and a petite, blonde prostitute cowered at their table, the unlikely pair startled by her pistol. Jacob, sitting at the bar with both hands wrapped around a tall glass of whiskey, remained still. A newly-opened bottle sat in front of him.

"The bar is closed," Elizabeth said in a commanding tone, her eyes boring into Jacob's back. Darby entered the bar and breathed heavily as Elizabeth barked, "Everyone get the fuck out. *Now.*"

The old man and his companion obediently scurried out of the bar while the raven-haired bartender swiftly departed into Vitoria's kitchen. Ignoring Elizabeth, Jacob drank from his glass while Darby turned to leave.

"Not you," Elizabeth said tersely. Reluctantly turning back around, Darby glowered at her sister but said nothing. Elizabeth motioned with her pistol towards the bar stool next to Jacob and directed, "Sit down."

A fuming Darby complied with Elizabeth's order and sat next to Jacob. He slid the whiskey bottle in Darby's direction.

"I think we're in trouble," advised Jacob while still staring into his drink, "so you'd better get a snort while you can in case she shoots us both."

"I would certainly like to shoot *you*," Elizabeth threatened Jacob. She took a few measured steps towards him and said, "And I would were you not now responsible for Sophie."

"Shoot me? Again?" replied Jacob without concern. He sipped from his drink and asked, "Why's that?"

"Your demonic jezebel slaughtered Darius," Elizabeth snapped. Overwhelmed by her emotions, her eyes teared and her face flushed. She rushed Jacob, pulled him off his bar stool and whirled him around. Grasping him by his lapels with her weapon still in her right hand, she shook him violently and cried, "Why?! Why did she kill him?!"

"I don't know, Liz," responded Jacob while allowing Elizabeth to manhandle him. Her assault fizzled out when she realized he failed to resist and she released him. Straightening his jacket, Jacob said, "I didn't have a fucking thing to do with it."

Battling tears, Elizabeth observed Jacob closely to assess his veracity. She composed herself and holstered her firearm.

"I'm sending Darby and Sarah back to Kaiser in the morning," Elizabeth stated, her conviction revealing she considered it a forgone conclusion. She looked to her sister and said, "I'll remain here until Aaron returns Vanessa."

"No fucking way," protested Darby while rising to her feet. She chastised Elizabeth with the intense fire of her crazed, light blue eyes and threatened, "You're not staying here by yourself."

"Yes, I am," Elizabeth said. She gazed on Darby with a staid expression and explained, "It was my intention all along to send you, Sarah and Darius back as soon as I found Jacob and Miriam. I failed Darius by not following through on that intention but I will *not* make that mistake again. You will return to the city with Sarah and-."

Darby interrupted her sister's monologue by barreling forward and upending a table and numerous chairs as she departed. Jacob and Elizabeth watched her wreak havoc on more bar furniture before she disappeared around a corner. Jacob shrugged.

"She took that well," he quipped. Unconcerned by Darby's tantrum, he returned to his bar stool and sipped his whiskey. Elizabeth sat down next to him in the chair Darby vacated.

"Always drinking," Elizabeth commented judgmentally. She studied Jacob while he studied his drink.

"I had him dead nuts, Liz," stated Jacob. He drank more whiskey and said, "All I had to do was pull the fucking trigger. But I didn't. I wanted to at first but I realized I'd just be hurting you and the girls. Who the fuck knows? Maybe he's your one. Unfortunately, Miriam had other plans."

Elizabeth pondered Jacob's words carefully for several minutes. The pair sat in silence, neither ex-spouse looking at or speaking to the other as Jacob continued to drink. Elizabeth finally turned her attention to him.

"Are you still . . . *with* her?" Elizabeth inquired gingerly, the Constable uncertain if she truly wished to know the answer. Jacob chuckled.

"Nope. Ya' see, just like you, she got a substantial dose of Gottschalk and then decided to go with another candidate," said Jacob apathetically. He glanced at her and continued, "So I traded her to Aaron for safe passage outta this hellhole for Sarah and Sophie. By the way, I need you to get them back to Kaiser for me."

Elizabeth viewed her husband with surprise and pity as she sensed the emotional pain he concealed beneath a thickening layer of apathy. She started to speak but Jacob beat her to the punch.

"So, if you'll excuse me," said Jacob indifferently, "it's time for me to get the fuck outta Chinese Peak."

Jacob drained his drink and slurped around the ice cubes to imbibe the remaining alcohol. He then set the empty glass on the bar.

"But what about poor Vanessa?" inquired Assarion, the demon walking up behind Jacob and Elizabeth. They both rotated their chairs around to face her.

"She's in God's hands now," Jacob replied defiantly, his faith struggling to overcome his fear. He slid off his chair and said, "I'd be taking a big fucking risk if I cast her out so I'm not doing it."

"What risk?" demanded Elizabeth as she grabbed Jacob's arm.

"Uh oh, somebody's been hiding something," Assarion said with particular relish. Throwing Jacob an impish glance with raised eyebrows, she taunted, "And that somebody is you."

Jacob shook with an adrenaline rush as Elizabeth drew her pistol and pointed it at his right temple. He flinched.

"She's got a defective heart, Liz," advised Jacob. Assarion's levity sparked a sudden rage within him that caused him to tremble. He continued with a pained look, "If I cast out Assarion, she'll go into cardiac arrest and, most likely, she'll die."

Elizabeth's eyes bulged with wrath and her entire body shook. She kept her gaze and her firearm trained on Jacob.

"Anything you want, anything at all," Elizabeth said calmly. Her trembling subsided and she offered, "I'll cage him for you and you can spend the rest of his pathetic life tempting him. Just come back to Kaiser with me and surrender her with doctors present."

"That's an intriguing offer," said Assarion with an elusiveness in her tone, "but I've decided to go in a different direction."

"No!" Jacob shouted as Assarion vacated Vanessa's body. It plummeted to the floor with a sick-sounding thud.

"*Vanessa*!" gasped Elizabeth, the Constable paralyzed with terror and grief. Jacob rushed to Vanessa's side and took her hand. Her cold, clammy skin prompted Jacob to press his ear against her chest to listen and feel for a heartbeat. Failing to perceive one, he examined her closely and realized she was not breathing.

"*Fucking cunt*," growled Jacob as his anger transformed into sadness. His bottom hip quivering, he said hoarsely, "She's dead. She was already dead."

Elizabeth dropped her gun and charged Jacob. Hurling him away from Vanessa, she broke down and bawled while hugging her lifeless child. Jacob crashed into two nearby chairs but, swiftly pulling himself up, he slumped against a table leg and watched Elizabeth mourn Vanessa.

"I'm sorry, hon," Jacob apologized, his heart shattered by the loss of Vanessa and his wife's grief. He crawled towards her.

"*Get out*," snarled Elizabeth amid sobs and tears, her vitriol causing Jacob to freeze. Hugging Vanessa's head into her shoulder, she swallowed hard and warned, "If I ever see you again, I *will* kill you."

12

JACOB AIMLESSLY WANDERED the halls of Chinese Peak as the minutes turned to hours. Shocked to his spiritual core by Vanessa's death, he paid no attention to his surroundings and soon became lost in the casino's mazelike enormity.

"What the hell does it matter?" thought Jacob as he considered Elizabeth's threat to kill him should they meet again. He meandered forward and said to himself, "I'm ready."

Jacob arrived at massive, golden-handled entry doors with butterflies churning in his stomach. He hesitated and listened to the music thumping beyond them. Enticed by shrill female voices, Jacob opened one of the doors and slipped inside.

"What have we here?" Jacob asked aloud. Illumined only in ultraviolet lights, nude, sylphlike women populated a converted theater. Fluorescent paint decorated their bodies with a multitude of designs and themes and they drank, socialized and danced erotically to peculiar, eerie music.

Two women to Jacob's right immediately captured his attention, their supple bodies intertwined as they shared an ardent kiss. A checkered pattern of interlocking yellow and blue diamonds decorated the women, their hair streaked with the same colors.

"Ho-ly shit," Jacob said with astonishment. The walls and two-story ceiling of the foyer emitted an ethereal, bluish glow. The right side of the foyer contained stairs leading to the balcony above and restrooms below. Large, square entranceways to the theater were situated on either side of a huge, four-sided bar with every libation imaginable amassed on a great, tiered island at its center.

"'Woe to the world because of its stumbling blocks,'" Jacob thought as he surveyed the pulsating festival of female flesh. (Excerpt of the Gospel of Matthew 18:7). A lissome woman caught Jacob's attention, her body painted with a multitude of glowing skulls. Enraptured, he lustfully gazed on her impeccably-toned body.

"'For it is inevitable that stumbling blocks come; but woe to that man through whom the stumbling block comes,'" echoed a voice in Jacob's head.

(Excerpt of the Gospel of Matthew 18:7). Whirling around, Jacob saw no one. He recognized Assarion's voice as she asked, "Or is it woe to the woman?"

"I need a drink," Jacob muttered. Proceeding through the left entranceway and gawking at the beautiful female bodies surrounding him, he entered the theater. Male, human patrons occasionally appeared among the painted women, each one indulging in the fantasy unfolding around him before disappearing into the crowd.

The main chamber occupied five stories with a balcony constructed above the foyer and bar. Large gradations, upon which sat high-topped tables and chairs, led down to a wooden dance floor. The rear of the theater housed a movie screen which displayed a warped, disturbing kaleidoscope of colors, shapes and patterns. Curtains emitting the ghostly, bluish light framed the top and sides of the screen while a stage formed its bottom border.

"Liz'll never find me in here," Jacob thought while maneuvering through the crowd. He arrived at a vacant, high-topped table, chose a chair facing the movie screen and watched it with rapt attention. He smirked and reasoned, "This place is fucking full of unadulterated, uncomplicated, no-strings-attached female attention. I don't have to be witty, or handsome or interesting. And no competition. Just the fucking way I like it."

Several shrill screams pierced the air and a commotion arose at the rear of the theater. Jacob's smirk faded and he rested his forehead on his left hand.

"*Fuck*," he complained.

• • • •

SAUNTERING INTO THE lobby of Chinese Peak, Tara removed her sunglasses and surveyed its luxurious immensity with rapacious eyes. Armed members of Kaiser's security forces fanned out behind her, the soldiers flooding into the lobby like ants. They were greeted by befuddled and startled stares from Chinese Peak's inhabitants and guests. An occasional scream ripped through the air. Mallory followed on Tara's heels like an abused dog, the teenager anxiously watching the gun-toting commandos secure the lobby.

"Keep up, Mallory," Tara ordered sharply, "and show a little backbone, please. Nicks women do not show fear . . . or feel it for that matter."

Emerging from the tunnel bisecting the lobby's waterfall, Darby strode purposefully up to Tara as security personnel rushed past her. Spotting Mallory, her eyes widened and she glowered at her mother.

"What the fuck's she doing here?" demanded Darby while pointing a finger at her niece.

"Having a little piss and vinegar pumped into her veins," Tara countered. She gestured for Mallory to approach her. Her granddaughter warily complied, her effort rewarded by her grandmother's arm wrapped around her shoulder. Tara asked, "It's what you wanted, isn't it?"

The urge to strike Tara flared in Darby but she repressed it. Instead, she grabbed a passing commando by the sleeve.

"There's a restaurant over there," Darby said as she pulled the woman towards her and nodded in the direction of Vitoria. She ordered, "Get one of your *female* comrades and get my niece something to eat. Two with her at *all* times, understood?"

"Yes, ma'am," answered the commando. She slung her assault rifle over her shoulder.

"Mal, go with her and get something to eat," Darby instructed. Mallory delayed compliance, the youngster frightened and dissatisfied with her options. A burgeoning, uncomfortable sympathy arose within Darby and she awkwardly hugged her niece. She then pulled away from Mallory but retained her grasp on her shoulders, assuring her, "I'm going to get your Mom and then we're getting the hell outta here, *together*."

Mallory nodded her head slowly at first and then more confidently. The commando reached out her hand and she took it, the unlikely pair departing into the bustle of the lobby. She glanced back at her aunt.

"I see your sister's not the only one who's gone soft," chastened Tara harshly as Darby forced a grin for Mallory. Darby threw daggers at her when her niece disappeared into the swarming crowds as her mother added haughtily, "It's a good thing Mommy's back in charge."

"You ever put that kid in danger again and I'll fucking kill you," Darby warned Tara as daughter moved into mother's personal space. The insane vigor in her eyes intensified into a psychotic, uncontrolled energy. Intimidated, Tara stepped back.

"How dare you threaten your own mother!" Tara scolded feebly.

"Fuck off, *Mother*," Darby snarled. Eliminating the space Tara created between them, she said, "I've gone along with all your bullshit and scheming because it's meant to save Liz and Mal. The second it puts either of them in danger, I'm out . . . and so are you."

"You have business with your sister and Jacob, tonight, Darby," Tara advised though still shaken by Darby's impassioned dissent. Quickly composing herself, she altered her approach and stated, "You finally get do what you've wanted to do all along, what you do best. *So get to it.*"

• • • •

BEADS OF SWEAT ROLLED down Elizabeth's face as she positioned her body underneath the hot, steamy water streaming from the shower head and it cascaded over her feminine curves. She repeatedly stretched her shoulders upward and then rolled them forward. Unable to find a perch for her pistol, she stowed it harmlessly on the edge of the vanity closest to the shower door.

Elizabeth, sensing danger, held up her head and listened carefully. She opened the shower door to retrieve her firearm as the bathroom doorknob turned. Her attempt failed, the moisture on her hand causing her to mishandle the pistol. It slipped from her grasp and slid forward into the sink as the bathroom door swung open.

"What the hell are you doing?" Darby asked with a puzzled expression. Elizabeth, wet and naked, stood before her with an outstretched arm as water dripped from her body onto the tile. Waterlogged strands of hair stuck to Elizabeth's face and neck.

"I was attempting to reach my gun," answered Elizabeth, the Constable perceiving an odd vibe from her sister. She hesitated but then shivered and retreated to the warmth of the shower. Darby closed the bathroom door and walked to the sink as Elizabeth scooped up a bottle, squirted shampoo onto her hand and said, "I trust that you're packed and ready to leave first thing in the morning."

Elizabeth began massaging the shampoo into her hair as Darby picked up her gun and stuffed it in her waistband. She exhaled.

"You know I love you, right?" Darby inquired, her uncertainty and uneasiness palpable. Elizabeth, though unable to open her eyes, turned her head towards Darby.

"I didn't even know you were capable of using the word," joked Elizabeth playfully. She ducked her head under the running water and rinsed the shampoo out of her hair.

"Just answer the fucking question," Darby barked. Her difficulty expressing emotion and Elizabeth's supercilious response frustrated her.

"I'm sorry, Darby," apologized Elizabeth. She used both hands to flip her hair backward and squeegee the water from it. Able to see her sister again, she assured her with an affectionate grin, "Yes, dear sister, I know that you love me. And I love you, more than you probably believe."

Elizabeth picked up the soap and began lathering her body. Glancing at Darby through the foggy glass of the shower stall, she furrowed her brow.

"What's the matter with you?" inquired Elizabeth.

"You're not staying at Chinese Peak, Liz," Darby stated while nervously fidgeting with the handle of her pistol.

"Excuse me?" said Elizabeth. She ceased washing her body and looked at Darby with a confounded expression.

"We're taking you back to Kaiser, *tonight*," Darby replied with conflict in her tone.

"You most certainly are not," said Elizabeth dismissively as she rinsed herself off. Annoyed by Darby's strange behavior, she questioned, "And who, may I ask, makes 'you' a 'we?'"

"I do," Tara interjected in a chilling voice that rattled Darby's very spirit. Elizabeth narrowed her eyes and scowled.

• • • •

WEAVING HIS WAY THROUGH the throng and attempting to ignore the nude, beautiful women pressing and rubbing against him, Jacob gradually progressed towards Miriam's murder scene.

"Where are ya', my vicious little pit bull?" he said as he forged ahead. The cacophonous music drowned out his words.

Jacob stumbled over a body lying on the floor in front of the bar. Jumping backward, he observed a man face down in a pool of blood. Jacob grimaced while sliding his shoes against the carpet to wipe the blood from his soles.

"Fuck," Jacob muttered due to his inability to completely clean his shoes. Studying the body, he discerned the outline of body armor beneath the man's clothing.

Swiveling his head and perusing the crowd, he caught a glimpse of Miriam's blonde curls moving into the foyer before she vanished. He searched the multitude of faces for the demonic towhead, her blonde curls soon reappearing at the top of the wide stairwell leading downward to the bathrooms.

"Mirry!" Jacob shouted while shoving his way through the crowd. Descending the stairs and hitting a landing, Jacob read a sign on the wall directing women to the right and men to the left. He hesitated, looked in both directions several times and chewed on the callous inside his cheek. Considering Miriam's penchant for disregarding rules, he made his decision and hurried down the stairs to his left.

Rounding the corner at the bottom of the stairs, he traversed a small outer room. He pushed open two large and padded black doors, each one possessing a leather veneer and an opaque, round window at head level. Entering an immense public bathroom illumined only by fluorescent lighting, he gawked at the glowing, white porcelain of the bank of sinks to his right and the urinals to his left. The tiny, square floor tiles, their original color indiscernible, emitted a dim, blue light that battled the luminosity of glowing red urinal cakes in the urinals. The tiles proceeded towards high stalls on the far wall.

"All right, Mirry," Jacob called out in frustration. The swinging doors came to rest, the dull thump of the music in the club the only sound in the bathroom. Walking to the center of the tiles, Jacob queried, "Where the hell are you?"

Quiet drips of water were all that interrupted the relative quiet. Jacob, unable to sense Miriam's presence, turned his attention to the urinal cakes. He laughed in amusement and approached them.

"Well, why I'm here," he said. Fumbling for the zipper on his pants but encountering difficulty in dislodging it, he muttered in annoyance, "Oh, fucking of course, now that I have to piss. Fucking beautiful."

"Talkin' about me?" cooed Miriam as she materialized behind Jacob, her right hand already clutching the right side of his neck and her right thumb claw pressed lightly into the base of his skull. She squeezed and Jacob felt the prickling of her deadly, elongated fingernails. Resigned to his fate, he let his arms drop to his sides.

"Nope," Jacob responded sharply while viewing Miriam in the long, wall-length mirror above the urinals. The romantic tension between them, fueled by the hopelessness of their situation, skyrocketed.

"I should just fucking kill you now," threatened Miriam angrily in her hybrid voice. Her wounded countenance weighed heavily on Jacob but he successfully hid his feelings. Her words dripping with disdain, she continued, "Now I know why Elizabeth wanted to do it all the time. Traded me away to save your own ass. *I hate you.*"

"You're a lot like her, always assuming it's my mother fucking fault," Jacob chided. Undaunted by Miriam's deadly grasp, he grinned mischievously and said, "Your new boyfriend probably didn't tell you that keeping Sarah and Sophie safe was part of the deal. Lying bastard. You two are fucking perfect for one another."

Miriam, her ire rising even higher, applied more pressure to the base of Jacob's skull and breached his skin.

"Go ahead, Mirry, do it," Jacob taunted her. He ignored the pain and the blood trickling from the puncture.

"You *want* me to kill you?" queried a baffled Miriam. She pulled back her thumb.

"No," Jacob answered matter-of-factly, "but *He* must because He's not stopping you. So what the hell? Just do it."

Fear momentarily struck Miriam as she recalled Jacob's spiritual field of force. She maintained her grasp, however, as it failed to appear.

"If you kill me, I'm going home to my Father," Jacob explained with complete confidence, "but when I do, where will you go, Mirry?"

An explosion rocked the theater above them, its force shaking the bathroom. An enraged Miriam shrieked and vanished. Several other screams, demon and human, rang out from the club.

"What the fuck now?" complained Jacob while reaching back to touch his wound. He approached the bathroom doors, gingerly cracked one open and leaned out. Submachine gun fire rang out in the foyer amid screams and authoritative shouts though the blaring music obscured them. Muzzle flashes reflected into the stairwell.

"Time to go," a female voice said in Jacob's ear, the sound of it triggering the memory of when Miriam used those very same words to rescue him from Darby at The Last Place. Jacob froze. The woman, just as Miriam had done months before, eerily added, "Darby's on her way."

Jacob marveled at the sight before him as he walked backward into the bathroom. Sophie followed him, a light-blue, fluorescent paint glazing her naked body and sufficiently masking her nudity. Electrical impulses of white tinged with blue decorated her entire form and, with the darker blue paint, created a shimmering, dazzling display.

Stunned and speechless, Jacob gawked at Sophie as more submachine gun fire erupted above them. She grabbed Jacob's arm and deftly maneuvered him to a stall in the far-left corner of the room. Stunned by her initiative, Jacob allowed her to do so. Sophie opened the door, pulled him inside and quickly closed it.

"Where the fuck did you come from?" Jacob inquired. Sophie's exotic appearance flabbergasted and aroused him.

"A peaceful little room in a drainage tunnel until you dragged me into this fucking mess," complained Sophie with sneer.

"*Nice,*" Jacob scolded her as he studied her body with desirous eyes. His adrenaline flowing, he queried, "So we're just gonna hide in a fucking bathroom stall?"

"Shut up and move," rebuked Sophie. She grasped a handle behind her and turned it. Opening a little know exit door, she yanked it open and ushered Jacob inside before slamming the door behind them. A burst of anxiousness coursed through Jacob's veins when Sophie locked it, the total darkness and close quarters stoking his claustrophobia. He extended his arms and felt the contours of the walls and the low ceiling.

"What about Sarah?" Jacob said, his heart pounding and his breathing heavy.

"What, want to dump me off on her again?" said Sophie with an unexpected, injured tone. Swiftly shrugging off her discontent, she tugged on Jacob's arm and said, "We'll get her. *Now move.*"

• • • •

BRINGING THE FULL BRUNT of her physical power against the apartment door, Darby kicked it several times. Her efforts severely weakened the bond between the door's hinges and the frame, the attack allowing her to rip the hinges out of the wall by recklessly throwing her body into the door itself.

She leapt over the wreckage, drew her fifty-caliber pistol and advanced into the apartment's main hallway in one fluid motion. Commandos cautiously followed at a distance, Darby's underlings unsure whether they feared the potential unseen dangers of the apartment more than their fearless leader.

A short, stocky blur moved in Darby's peripheral vision and darted from the kitchen into the pantry. She keyed on it while turning her head and her pistol in the direction of the movement. Firing three rounds through the space between the kitchen counter and the cupboards, Darby blasted chunks out of the door just after it was pulled closed. Seconds later, the sounds of falling foodstuffs and other unknown items accompanied the thud of something heavy hitting the pantry tile.

"Bedrooms," Darby ordered as the commandos swept past her and fanned out into a tactical formation. Her rigid focus on finding Jacob and neutralizing threats faded as she observed the holes in the pantry door. Wondering whom she killed, she remembered Sarah.

"Oh, shit," Darby uttered. Rushing to the door, she grabbed the handle but halted. Paralysis set in as she pondered if she truly wanted to learn the identity of her victim. Seconds rolled by yet Darby remained motionless. She trembled and stared through one of the holes in the door but it provided no view of the corpse inside.

"There's no one here, Ms. Nicks," advised a lanky male commando, his report causing Darby to start. Several quiet seconds passed, the silence prompting him to call out, "Ms. Nicks?"

Her senses regained, Darby holstered her gun, ripped the pantry door off its hinges and effortlessly chucked it into the living room. The impact of the door broke the coffee table and sprayed pieces of it several feet. Darby forced herself to look inside.

The color drained from Darby's face. An overweight maid lay crumpled in the corner of the pantry amid the food debris caused by her fall and several displaced shelves. Blood saturated her clothing around two massive bullet wounds in her back. Darby watched the blood stains slowly spread.

"Get out," Darby growled.

"Ma'am?" the lanky commando inquired.

"Get out!" she bellowed while drawing her pistol and aiming it at him. He and the other commandos swiftly obeyed and scuttled out of the apartment.

Seating herself on the floor and folding her legs beneath her, Darby laid her pistol on the kitchen tile between herself and the maid. Her troubled eyes were glued to the woman, the gears of her mind turning in ways they had never before turned.

"Maybe she's right," Darby remarked in a disturbed tone, "maybe I *have* gone soft."

• • • •

THE ACCESS TUNNEL THROUGH which Jacob and Sophie escaped emptied into a large, many-storied maintenance hub. Access tunnels intermittently honeycombed three of the walls, the corridors reached through a web of scaffolding and ladders, while the fourth wall contained three freight elevators. Work stations, maintenance equipment and large tool chests dotted the cement floor.

Jacob descended one of the ladders followed by Sophie. He struggled against his urge to gawk at her beautiful, painted body. Looking upward, he noticed the paint concealing Sophie's vagina began to wear away.

"Like watcha' see, old man?" Sophie tauntingly asked him. Embarrassed, Jacob averted his eyes from her genitals.

"Sorry," muttered Jacob while increasing his pace. He soon hopped off the latter and onto the floor. Dashing to a work bench, he fetched a work coverall and then jogged back to the ladder as Sophie's feet touched cement.

"Here, put this on," Jacob said, his head turned to the side as he held out the coverall. Sophie laughed and accepted Jacob's offer of clothing. He rotated around to give her privacy as she stepped into the coverall and tugged it onto her body.

"So, how do we get to Sarah?" Jacob inquired, his embarrassment fading as his thoughts centered on rescuing the Ursuline.

"Leave that to me," replied Sophie while sliding her arms into the sleeves of the coverall.

"That's not very reassuring," Jacob countered while suddenly suspicious of Sophie's motives.

"Relax, Jake," Sophie responded. She abruptly and fervently embraced and kissed him. His head reeled with sudden emotion.

"The Thin Dolphin," Jacob stated knowingly as Sophie released her lip-lock. The light bulb in his head clicked on and he said, "One of those elevators leads to its kitchen, doesn't it?"

"Yep," Sophie said with a smirk as she eyed Jacob mischievously, "and from here, all three descend directly to the basement, though getting outta there may prove a little tricky."

"Too bad you can't fly a fucking helicopter," Jacob commented blithely.

· · · ·

"THAT WIFE-O-MINE IS pretty fucking ruthless," Jacob said as the freight elevator creaked and groaned on its upward journey. He tapped the wall with his fist and continued, "Her daughter just died but she's still claiming the natural gas reserves of this place."

"Ex-wife," Sophie reminded him. The freight elevator doors opened to reveal a four-man special operations team standing in the kitchen of "The Thin Dolphin." Three pointed submachine guns at Jacob and Sophie while a fourth held Sarah by the arm. She squirmed defiantly in an unsuccessful attempt to break free.

"Fuck," Jacob sighed. He and Sophie stepped out of the elevator. Jacob raised his arms as the doors slid closed behind them.

"Damn it, Mirry, if there was ever a time," Jacob begged in his head while praying Miriam would hear his spirit calling to her. He knew only her murderous prowess could rescue them. Growing shame plagued him, however, as he realized he was powerless to save his charges.

Perched high above Jacob in the kitchen's rafters, Miriam perceived his call. Her jealous obstinacy peaked and, in tandem with Aaron's command, rendered her inert. She wrestled with the impulse to rescue Jacob and Sarah.

Miriam suddenly tensed. She felt another unseen, elusive presence in the kitchen as Assarion slithered her spiritual perception around Jacob's mind like a snake.

"'Do not be afraid any longer, only believe,'" Assarion whispered in Jacob's head. (Excerpt from the Gospel of Mark 5:36). His trepidation began to rapidly thaw like a cube of ice set in the rays of a sweltering sun. Assarion raised the volume of her voice in his mind and continued:

> "'. . . for truly I say to you, if you have faith the size of a mustard seed, you will say to this mountain, 'Move from here to there,' and it will move; and nothing will be impossible to you.'"(Excerpt from the Gospel of John 14:12).

"Let me protect them," Jacob prayed silently. Seconds later, the Holy Spirit flared and then detonated within him as it infused him with the very grace of God. Viewing Jacob from within the spirit world, Miriam shielded her eyes as he ignited with a dazzling white light.

"'. . . he who believes in Me, the works that I do, he will do also,'" Jacob stated with an authoritative conviction that stunned the commandos. (Excerpt from the Gospel of Matthew 17:20). His eyes passionately shimmered as if blue flames burned within them.

"*Jacob,*" called Miriam in a voice inaudible to the material world. She attempted to shriek violently at the Holy Spirit's intensity but found herself bereft of the ability to scream.

"Gentlemen, if you'll excuse us, we're leaving," Jacob advised firmly. The commandos became as dead men and simply stared at him. He calmly and quietly led Sophie towards the door that led to the roof of Chinese Peak with an astonished Sarah in tow.

• • • •

USING A METAL KITCHEN cart, Jacob attempted to bar the door. He cursed in frustration as he failed to wedge it underneath the handle.

"Mother fucking bitch bastard cart!" barked Jacob, his words barely audible over the helicopter's twin engines and twirling blades. Feeling slimy for using profanity after utilizing the power of the Holy Spirit, he lifted his gaze to the dark sky and guiltily uttered, "*Sorry.*"

Jacob abandoned his effort and his eyes darted to the helicopter as he shoved the cart aside. Sarah, sitting in the pilot seat, emphatically gestured for him to embark. He turned and jogged down the open corridor leading to the helicopter pad and passed the red and green lights lining it. Miriam appeared behind Jacob at its entrance.

"Jake," Miriam called out feebly, the din of the helicopter drowning out her voice. Failing to hear her, Jacob continued towards it. Miriam strengthened her voice with a demonic edge and once again called out, "*Jake.*"

Jacob spun around and froze. The sight of Miriam paralyzed him.

"Were Sarah and Sophie really part of the deal?" Miriam inquired with a sad expression and an elevated, somber tone. Jacob charily walked towards her.

"Yeah," yelled Jacob while breathing heavily. The helicopter rose several feet off the helipad as he added, "I didn't think I had a choice."

"You didn't," Miriam shouted back. Jacob continued to approach her cautiously and, to his surprise, she backed away from him and firmly pressed herself against the door.

Meanwhile, the helicopter drifted lazily towards Jacob. He looked back momentarily as the air swirled around him and Sarah gestured again.

"Get in!" she mouthed.

"He's keeping you here," said Jacob after closing the distance between he and Miriam.

"No," she answered. Her countenance bleak and pale, Miriam muttered in a chilling demonic tone, "Kaiser."

The mention of Kaiser caused the color to drain from Jacob's face so much so that his skin tone nearly matched Miriam's pallid countenance. The prospect of her return to her old way of life and her presence in the city with Elizabeth and Mallory pierced his heart.

"Back to temptations?" asked Jacob. Miriam shook her head in the affirmative as the wind tussled with her blonde curls. The helicopter hovered half-way down the corridor.

"Yeah," Miriam stated in a sad, human voice. She trembled and repressed a sob. Automatic weapons fire erupted inside the building, its jarring sound faint but unmistakable. Jacob ignored it as Miriam said, "I didn't think *I* had a choice."

"You did," Jacob stated. The cold, resigned look on Miriam's face disturbed him.

"I didn't know Sarah could fly a helicopter," Miriam said with a weak, forced grin.

"Makes ya' wonder if she's really a nun," replied Jacob. Someone turned the door handle and attempted to open it as Jacob reached out for Miriam. She thrust him away with one hand.

"You'd better go," she advised. Jacob hesitated. The person on the other side of the door kicked it twice though Miriam's demonic strength rendered the effort futile. Backpedaling with his eyes fixed on Miriam, Jacob retreated towards the helicopter. An explosion rocked the skyscraper's summit just as he clambered onto the left landing skid. He opened the rear cabin door and glanced back.

Miriam was gone.

. . . .

MIRIAM RENDERED HERSELF invisible to all human eyes while still holding the door fast. She perceived the thoughts of the commandos and their intent to place charges on its inside surface. Releasing it, she walked down the lit corridor.

The helicopter accelerated into the eastern sky just as an explosion blew open the door and a team of commandos flooded onto the roof. Several fired their AK-47 rifles at the helicopter in vain but one commando wielded a FIM-92 Stinger missile launcher. Dropping onto one knee next to Miriam, he carefully aimed the launcher at the helicopter.

"Launching!" he yelled.

Miriam glanced at the commando with scorn as his companions secured the roof. She placed her hand over the barrel of the launcher and crushed the muzzle closed at the exact moment the commando squeezed the trigger. The missile misfired and exploded inside the launcher, the blast killing the operator and several of his companions. The survivors dove for cover.

The prevailing winds quickly dispatched the smoke from the explosion and revealed Miriam standing amid fires, bodies and debris. She quietly walked to the edge of the roof, the demon despondently watching the helicopter grow smaller, turn north and then disappear into the mountains.

"I love you, Jake," she whispered though no one heard it.

. . . .

"WHAT *the fuck* happened up here?" Darby growled as she surveyed the destruction wrought by Miriam. Commandos carried the wounded on stretchers and covered up the remnants of their comrades who perished in the explosion. Metal and concrete debris littered the area near the missile launcher's demise.

"Gottschalk, the nun and the girl escaped in a chopper," explained a tall, burly commando in a deep voice. He lumbered up to Darby.

"Well, that's it then," Darby grumbled.

"We . . . we tried to shoot the chopper down," said the commando, Darby's underling uncertain of how to address her, "but the launcher misfired and exploded. We lost four."

"Probably Miriam's handiwork," Darby muttered with a disgusted mien. She surveyed the dead and ordered gravely, "Let's get them outta here."

Trudging towards the edge of the roof, Darby moved out of the zone of destruction and gazed into the night sky. She pulled her flask out of her jacket, unscrewed the stopper and held it aloft.

"Godspeed, Gottschalk, you slippery fuck," Darby said aloud before drinking from the flask. Gulping down the whiskey within it, she indulged in the burn and added, "Godspeed."

13

"HOW DARE YOU LAUNCH an armed assault on Chinese Peak!" Aaron lambasted Tara with traces of his demonic voice leaking into his human one. He approached her as she stood in the lounge atop the lobby waterfall, the Constable's mother hawking the movements of her commandos and appraising her newest acquisition. Impeccably dressed, Aaron wore an expensive three-piece suit and violet tie with a matching pocket square. He composed himself and continued, "There's been no official transfer of Chinese Peak yet."

"I just transferred it, so order your beasties to stand down," gloated Tara as she covetously enjoyed Aaron's undeniable sex appeal and masculinity. Aaron scowled at her, his reaction prompting her to purse her lips before stating, "Besides, I'm not tossing you out in the street. The old courthouse has been cleared of Agatha's rabble and your new home awaits you."

"And my *other* residence?" Aaron queried, his anger cooled by Tara's partial performance of her end of the deal.

"I told you you're going to have to wait for that," answered Tara sharply. Irritated by Aaron's inquiry, she said, "I'd think you have enough on your plate now that you've unfettered access to the entire city."

"I will handle my own affairs, Tara," Aaron said, the tension between he and Tara rising. He moved next to her, his shoulder mere inches from her shoulder, and folded his arms. Casually observing the commotion below, he inquired, "Have you brought Elizabeth into the fold? If she resumes her role as Constable and nixes the deal-."

"I'll let you handle your own affairs if you let me handle mine," interrupted Tara snidely. She tightly grasped the railing in front of her with both hands, her grip causing her knuckles to whiten as she said, "This deal supersedes your deal with Elizabeth so you needn't worry about her for now."

"And what of your granddaughter?" Aaron probed while carefully scrutinizing Tara's face.

"If you can save her then I expect she will be returned to us as a sign of your continuing goodwill," explained Tara emotionlessly. She released the railing and glanced at Aaron, adding coldly, "If that proves impossible, then it's unfortunate and I'll grieve Vanessa's loss."

"Your ruthlessness is admirable," Aaron commented with an evil grin. He turned his body towards Tara and said, "You would make quite a demon."

"That makes one of us," Tara jabbed as she threw Aaron a haughty smile. Spinning around, she marched off but was pursued by Aaron's hateful, hostile stare.

• • • •

FOUR KAISER COMMANDOS escorted Elizabeth through the waterfall tunnel and into Chinese Peak's lobby. Clad in a commando uniform with her wrists handcuffed in front of her, she walked at a strong, brisk pace. She wore an expression of unapologetic defiance, the Constable refusing to kowtow to Tara or surrender her dignity. A single word tore through her resolve.

"Mom!" Mallory shouted. She scurried from Darby's side as the two approached Elizabeth from the sitting areas.

"Mallory?!" replied Elizabeth with sudden distress. She knelt on one knee before Mallory crashed into her with a desperate, loving embrace. Elizabeth pecked her daughter on the cheek and asked, "What're you doing here?"

"Grandma brought me," Mallory responded sheepishly as she clung to her mother. They watched Tara advance towards them.

"Yes, I did, and I stand by the decision, Darby's objections notwithstanding," interjected Tara while firing a bitter, disappointed look at Mallory. Her eyes boring into Elizabeth, she bitingly added, "The women of this family need a serious dose of reality."

"Has she been up all night, Mother?" asked Elizabeth incredulously, her distress giving way to umbrage. She agilely rose to her feet with Mallory attached to her side. Stepping into Tara's personal space, she demanded, "Has she eaten? Or are you now withholding sleep and food to toughen her up?"

"I made sure she ate, and she's slept a little," Darby said before interposing herself between Tara and Elizabeth. Looming over them both, she shot a sidelong glance at Tara and added disdainfully, "Grandma and I also had a little talk, and this *won't* happen again, will it, *Grandma*?"

Tara and Darby engaged in a brief optical battle while Elizabeth pulled free of Mallory and stepped out from behind Darby. The teenager watched the three greatest female influences in her life with growing angst.

"Enough, both of you!" ordered Elizabeth, her commanding tone and struggle against her handcuffs garnering both Tara's and Darby's attention. Her dissent caused her escorts to discretely place their fingers on the triggers of their weapons and inch their firearms upward. Tara waved them off.

"Vanessa's dead!" Mallory shouted, her young eyes watering. Her proclamation concerning her sister's demise astonished all within earshot and caused Tara, Darby and Elizabeth to cease arguing. Crying and sniffling, Mallory fiercely expounded, "She's fucking *dead*, Mom. You can't save her. She's *gone*, and it's time for all of us to go home. You've been through a lot and you just need to come home. Let Grandma and Aunt Darby run things until you feel better. *Please*, I just want us to go *home*."

Her heart bleeding for her child, Elizabeth's strength evaporated. She suppressed a sob but could not staunch several tears that rolled down her cheeks. Walking to her daughter, she looped her arms over her head and hugged her. Mallory reciprocated as Elizabeth planted a kiss on the top of her head, mother and daughter indulging in a much-needed embrace. Tara remained unmoved but Darby observed the display with restrained love and pity.

"You're right, sweetheart," said Elizabeth as she looked down on her daughter and squeezed her snugly. Taking Mallory's chin in her hands, she confirmed gently in a wavering voice, "Your sister's gone."

"What?" Darby asked as her face whitened. Elizabeth broke down and bawled while Mallory entered a catatonic state, the sight of their palpable disquiet injuring Darby's very spirit. Tara remained silent and scowled.

"My beautiful girl is gone, Darby. She died of a heart attack yesterday," responded Elizabeth in a surprisingly-clear, composed tone. She untangled herself from Mallory and said, "The possession was just too much for her body."

Elizabeth wept openly. She allowed Mallory to lead her out of Chinese Peak while Darby and Tara watched them depart with grim faces.

"Take us home, Darby," Elizabeth called out.

"I guess that solves all of your problems," Darby remarked. She trembled with squelched rage and sadness.

"Except Jacob," said Tara without reacting to Vanessa's demise. She turned to Darby and asked, "Did you dispose of him?"

"Nope," Darby replied. She took great satisfaction in the failure of one strand of Tara's deceitful web and now her concern extended only to her sister and her niece. No longer yearning to kill Jacob, she sneered, "He bolted in Aaron's helicopter with Sister Sarah . . . and a little help from that demonic cunt. Apparently, nuns do know how to fly. But I doubt we'll ever see him again. He's got no reason to go back to K-town now."

"You didn't you pursue him?" asked Tara, Darby's mother frustrated by Jacob's escape. Fuming, she admonished her, "We brought a fucking Apache, didn't we? It has air-to-air missiles, Darby. Honestly, you're losing your edge."

"He's gone so get the fuck over it. I did," Darby snarled. Exhausted by Tara's constant, cutthroat scheming, she hurriedly walked away from her to catch up with Elizabeth and Mallory.

"Oh, he'll be back," muttered Tara. Resigned to Jacob's good fortune and content with her successful annexation of Chinese Peak, she turned on a dime and followed her family.

* * * *

"GOOD EVENING, DARBY," said Tara, the elder Nicks dressed in a blue, festooned kimono fashioned from fine silk. Seated in the sitting area of Elizabeth's office, she sipped a martini. Sören sat in a chair to her left, the Chief of Staff shuffling through several neatly-organized stacks of documents lying on the glass coffee table.

"You goofy old bitch," Darby said in disbelief upon seeing her mother's ostentatious kimono. She queried disrespectfully, "Where the hell did you get that?"

"Perhaps you should have a drink, my dear," snapped Tara as her good mood soured. Sören, discomfited by the antagonistic exchange, lowered his eyes and pretended to search for a document. Tara sipped her martini again and added, "It might improve your shitty attitude."

"Sorry, *Mom*, a shitty attitude is in my fucking DNA," Darby retorted as she accepted Tara's invitation and fixed herself a glass of whiskey at the butler. She asked, "You wanted to see me?"

"Yes, you and Sören," confirmed Tara as business trumped her emotions. Standing up, she held her drink in both hands, began meandering around the room and explained, "Elizabeth has always been under excessive pressure as Constable, and handled it quite well, but her divorce from Jacob and the death of Vanessa have pushed her over the edge. I'm afraid she's had a psychological breakdown."

"Unfortunately, I must agree," confessed Sören though plagued by guilt. Darby's mouth dropped open. Sören eyed her apologetically and said, "I will forever be loyal to your sister but her decision-making ability and focus have been in decline since her marriage to Jacob began spinning out of control."

"Which is why I propose that we continue our little triumvirate indefinitely," Tara suggested while continuing her circuit around the room. She passed behind Darby and explained, "Her grief will render her unfit to lead this city for the foreseeable future. We need to ensure continuity of government during her incapacity."

"I concur, but only temporarily," warned Sören. He retrieved a teacup and saucer from the table, took a drink of tea and said, "Once Elizabeth is of sound mind, she should be immediately reinstated as Constable."

"Of course," Tara said. Thrusting down her urge to assault Sören, she stated, "I have absolutely no interest in running this city permanently. When she regains her mental health, we'll reinstate her as Constable."

"Yeah, and who the fuck determines that?" asked Darby with angry skepticism dripping from her tongue. She drained her glass and then rapidly shook it. The ice cubes clinked against each other and the glass.

"Your sister is confined to the psych ward at the hospital and is under observation, as we discussed," Tara stated steadfastly. She completed her first lap around the room and began a second, explicating in a reassuring tone, "Dr. Adai is overseeing her progress, which includes treatment by the finest psychiatrist in the city. The two of them will make the final call. It will be a purely medical decision, without involvement by any of us."

"Until then, Sören will continue to administer the day-to-day operations of the city while I handle policymaking, external non-security affairs and any larger issues that come up. Darby, you will handle all security issues, both internal and external. Agreed?"

"Agreed," indicated Sören without apparent concern as he set his teacup and saucer on the coffee table. Darby poured herself another drink.

"So you've got it all figured out, huh, Mommy?" queried Darby mockingly. She loudly gulped down more whiskey and uttered, "Ahhhhhh."

"Yes, I do," Tara said with complete conviction as she glowered at Darby. Sören said nothing and patiently awaited Darby's answer. Ten tense seconds elapsed.

"Fine," acceded Darby as she set her unfinished cocktail on the butler. She winked at Tara and headed for the doors. Pausing before exiting, she said, "Oh, and Mother?"

"Yes, Darby," Tara responded, the Acting Constable annoyed in advance by the slight she expected from her daughter.

"*I'll* be taking care of Mallory," threatened Darby while glancing menacingly at Tara with her crazed eyes. She threw open the office doors and departed.

• • • •

ELIZABETH AWOKE FROM a vibrant dream in which Vanessa and Mallory were demons. Malicious, jet black eyes stared out from their teenage faces as they rent her with vicious claws and masticated her flesh with jagged teeth. She felt no pain as her daughters savagely murdered and consumed her though she still felt terror and called out for Jacob. He did not answer her summons.

Her horror quickly faded as she wiggled out of her grogginess, her sleep brought on by the sedatives administered by the psychiatrist. She would normally refuse medication of any sort, the Constable secretly fearing the loss of control it caused. She now, however, relished the ability to sleep peacefully and enjoyed the solitude of her room.

It resembled a small hotel room with beige walls, a white ceiling and sheet-vinyl flooring in a woodgrain pattern. A thick, reinforced window with a cross-shaped pane provided ample natural light beneath which was constructed a two-rowed, counter-topped shelving unit. The counter formed an L-shape at one end and created a small desk area with a chair slid underneath it. The room also contained its own bathroom and a modest closet.

The platform bed and simple foam mattress were a far cry from Elizabeth's king-sized bed yet they provided enough comfort for a restful sleep. Elizabeth snuggled into the mattress and her dark blue blanket as the last remnants of her disturbing dream vanished from her mind.

"I could sleep for days," she said aloud as she rolled onto her side and closed her eyes. Dr. Adai and her psychiatrist concurred that she was not a suicide risk, a determination that granted her more freedom within her room, but they confined her to it nonetheless. She tried to sleep as much as possible as Darby and Mallory planned a visit for later that evening. Mallory promised to bring Elizabeth her personal effects and clothing though she longed more for her daughter's smiling face than her toothbrush.

She opened her eyes. A security officer passed outside, his head visible through the two-foot, rectangular window embedded in her door. He peeked in but quickly disappeared when he realized Elizabeth gazed back at him.

Rolling onto her back, she stared into the white ceiling and replayed the events of the past few months in her mind. She examined each one and attempted to pinpoint when her mental health may have begun to decline. She contemplated her war of a marriage with Jacob, her bizarre and often dangerous encounters with the spiritual world, Vanessa's abduction and death and the enormous strain of building and maintaining a post-apocalyptic society while raising two children.

The moment overwhelmed her and she collapsed. Emotionally and mentally weary beyond comprehension, Elizabeth bawled. Eventually crying herself to sleep, she once again drifted into the frightening world of her dreams.

· · · ·

"SÖREN," TARA SAID, the Acting Constable acknowledging his entry into Elizabeth's office with a fleeting glance. Darby stood hunched over to Tara's right with her hand on the desk as the two women studied a large map of Kaiser.

Ignoring Tara's greeting, Sören marched to the desk where Tara sat like a queen on her throne. He tossed a dossier onto the map, his interruption drawing a stinging glare from Darby but no response from Tara.

"This file contains Elizabeth's medical orders," stated Sören in a serious, angered tone. Darby stood up straight and folded her arms. Intrigued by the mention of her sister's medical records, she allowed Sören to say, "The orders weren't kept in her main medical file but were instead in a *secret* file in her psychiatrist's office."

"And why should I care about that?" Tara inquired emotionlessly though her eyes conveyed malice. She removed her reading glasses and held them away from her face.

"You should care because the orders conflict with Dr. Adai's reports to us," replied Sören. Darby reached for the dossier but Tara pushed her hand away. His left eye twitching with restrained wrath, Sören continued, "Of more concern, however, is that her hospitalization is scheduled to continue for at least six months regardless of her progress."

Darby snatched the file from Elizabeth's desk and evaded Tara's hand. She scampered away with her prize and stopped in front of the balcony doors to leaf through it. Sören triumphantly watched Darby read the orders while Tara scowled.

"He's right, *Mother*," said Darby while slinging the file back at Tara and sending a spray of paper across the room. Ducking, Tara avoided the trajectory of file folder. Darby demanded with a horrid expression, "Why is he right?"

"Elizabeth's mental state is worse than any of us thought," Tara explained, the ire formerly etched on her face softening into a sly mien. She explained, "In fact, she may never fully recover, and *that* is information we don't want falling into the wrong hands . . . hence the separate file."

"I demand an immediate conference with the psychiatrist and Dr. Adai," said Sören determinedly.

"Yeah, so do I," Darby snarled while moving closer to Tara. She ignored Darby's comment and addressed Sören.

"Now is your opportunity to truly demonstrate where your loyalties lie," Tara counseled gravely, "because my daughter may never again be mentally well enough to be Constable. Your commitment to her remaining so, while admirable, is most likely futile. You're tremendously gifted in municipal administration, Sören, and an asset to this city-."

"I tender my resignation, effective immediately," interjected Sören curtly. Turning on a dime, he walked towards the office doors. Tara stood up, brandished a semiautomatic pistol with a silencer and fired a single bullet into Sören's back. The force of the impact carried him into the office doors. He bounced off them and landed on his back. His skull smacked the floor.

"Oh, shit," uttered Darby as she immediately drew her own pistol but failed to aim it. Stunned by Tara's actions and uncertain of her next move, she let it point harmlessly at one of the chairs in the sitting area as she watched her mother amble to where Sören lay.

"Resignation accepted," Tara advised him with derision. He gazed upon her with weak eyes and blood trickling from one corner of his mouth. Tara abruptly fired several shots into Sören's chest and sighed, "What a waste."

She examined Sören's dead body for several seconds before turning her disapproving countenance to Darby. Tara then walked back to Elizabeth's desk and returned to her seat.

"Put your gun away, Darby," Tara snapped while throwing a critical look at her daughter. Darby lifted her weapon to aim it at her.

"You hated the man," Tara reminded Darby tersely. She put her glasses back on and asked, "Have you forgotten about throwing him out of a moving car?"

"I'm not as fucking stupid as you think," responded Darby. Remarkably and uncharacteristically composed, she chided her mother, "You're finally moving in on Kaiser. Ya' just couldn't resist, could ya'?"

"Your sister's pregnant," Tara said. The news prompted Darby to lower her pistol and her jaw.

"What?" asked Darby several seconds later. Tara rose from her chair – the move causing Darby to step back into a defensive posture – and began collecting Elizabeth's medical records. Quickly scanning them page by page, she found the document for which she searched and offered it to Darby.

"Dr. Adai discovered it after a blood test. She's around five weeks pregnant," Tara advised.

Darby looked at the paper suspiciously but refused to take it. Tara held it out for ten more seconds before retreating to Elizabeth's desk chair.

"She can't run this city while expecting," Tara explicated while setting the papers on the map. Leaning back in her chair, she expounded, "Having children has proven to be a serious detriment to her governing abilities. She could very well lose the baby if she reassumes the role of Constable and she won't survive the loss of another child. Her focus will be on the baby, not the city. And as we expand our reach into the larger world, we'll get the attention of those who want what we have. If the demons taught us anything, it's that the first target of your sister's enemies will be her children."

Darby scrutinized Tara's face. Sören's murder disturbed her but Tara's claims and actions concerned her far more. She holstered her pistol.

"Does she know?" asked Darby, her face awash in distrust.

"Not yet," Tara answered, "but I planned on telling her today."

"I'm going to check on Mal," said Darby. She approached the office doors with firm footfalls.

"Before you go," Tara said, nodding to Sören's corpse, "be a dear and clean up that mess for me."

• • • •

PUSHING OPEN THE DOOR to Elizabeth's room, Tara furrowed her brow upon finding the bed empty and the bedding carelessly pitched onto the floor. The sound of Elizabeth forcefully vomiting erupted from the bathroom, the noise causing Tara's puzzled expression to change into one of disgust. She closed the door.

Elizabeth vomited again as Tara stepped over her bedding and stopped in the bathroom doorway. Dressed in dark blue sweats with her hair hastily tied in a ponytail, Elizabeth sat on the floor tile and hugged the toilet bowl like it was one of her children.

"I suppose you know you're pregnant now," Tara quipped, her words garnering a scowl from Elizabeth. Dark circles underscored her eyes as they stared out from her pale face. Grasping a towel lying on the floor, she wiped spittle and vomit from her mouth. An irritated Elizabeth then lobbed the towel in Tara's direction but her mother sidestepped it and said, "Horrible morning sickness is a Nicks family curse."

"Being pregnant at my age is a curse," growled Elizabeth while resting her forehead on the cool porcelain of the toilet bowl. She raised her arm with some effort and flushed the toilet.

"Who's the father?" Tara queried matter-of-factly over the swirling water.

"I'm not in the mood, Mother," grumbled Elizabeth, her foul demeanor permeating the room like the stench of her vomit.

"I know about your affairs, my dear," Tara said spitefully. Folding her arms and leaning on the door frame, she inquired again, "Who's the father?"

"It can only be Jacob's," answered Elizabeth as she raised her head to yawn. Satisfied that her stomach was empty, she slowly crawled towards her bed and shrugged off Tara's attempt to assist her. She struggled to heave her body onto her mattress but succeeded and collapsed in exhaustion. Tara quickly scooped up the sheet and blanket and covered Elizabeth with them.

"Now *that* is a curse," Tara scornfully remarked as Elizabeth snuggled into her pillow. She sat on the edge of her daughter's bed and placed a reassuring hand on her hip, saying, "I'm sure Adai can perform the abortion for you."

A groggy Elizabeth opened her eyes and lifted her head.

"I haven't made that decision yet and I'm not making it until I have a clear head," stated Elizabeth in a quiet yet firm voice.

"Why on earth would you keep it?" Tara admonished her. Elizabeth laid her head on her pillow and began drifting into a deep slumber while Tara said, "You've just rid yourself of Jacob and he's proven to be a terrible father figure. Why do anything to draw him back in? And if his little demon whore doesn't kill the baby, some other demon probably will. Aborting the poor child seems to me like the only humane thing to do."

Elizabeth's heavy breathing heightened into a snore and then fell again, the sounds alerting Tara that she no longer listened to her. She stood up and tucked in Elizabeth.

"I guess I'll have to make yet another decision on your behalf," Tara complained as she tenderly brushed Elizabeth's cheek with the backs of her fingers, "but at least this one's easy to make. You're not keeping Jacob's pathetic spawn."

"Oh, yes she is," countered Miriam in a voice inaudible to Tara. She sat with her legs hanging over the shelving unit and her hands gripping its edge. Disappearing as Tara exited the room, she left Elizabeth behind in a peaceful slumber.

14

DEPRESSING THE ACCELERATOR, Jacob increased the speed of the older-model cargo van as it trundled up a steep hill. It shimmied and groaned, the vehicle struggling upward but finally succeeding in its quest.

"Piece of shit," Jacob thought as the van crested the hill. He considered the alternative of no transportation at all and changed his tune. Glancing to the ceiling of the van, he prayed silently and earnestly, "I take that back. *Thanks*."

He and Sarah abandoned the helicopter early in their escape from Chinese Peak as Aaron's minions failed to keep its fuel tank full. A deserted, roadside gas station's parking lot provided both a convenient, makeshift helipad and the functioning van. They traveled in the van for two days, the pair using seldom-trekked back roads to avoid unwanted attention.

Sophie slumbered in the cargo compartment, swaddled in blankets, while Sarah sat in the passenger seat studying a map of the area. She knew of an old vacation chalet maintained by a former parishioner of the Church of St. Cyril and nestled in the forest to the northeast of Kaiser.

"I sure as hell hope we're close," Jacob said while eyeing the gas gauge's needle. His worry increased as the daylight decreased and he stated, "We won't find another abandoned car with gas out here."

"We're close," replied an undaunted Sarah, the nun closely scanning the roadside in search of her marker. She suddenly and excitedly jumped in her seat and instructed, "Slow down, slow down!"

"What is it?" Jacob asked. He obeyed her command and tapped the brakes twice.

"Did you see that big rock back there?" inquired Sarah as she watched the roadside with rapt attention. Jake glanced in the rearview mirror and caught sight of the massive rock as it dwindled into the darkening distance.

"Yeah, what about it?" Jacob questioned.

"That's our landmark," explained Sarah hopefully. Grinning, she added, "Turn right on the next road."

• • • •

"THANKS FOR THE RIDE," Jacob said as he slapped the side of the van twice in appreciation for its service. It sputtered and died twenty yards before the driveway leading to the chalet, its momentum permitting him to pull it off the narrow two-track road and into a small clearing amidst the trees.

Hauling as much as they could carry, Jacob, Sarah and Sophie walked the final twenty yards and turned left onto the driveway. The van's demise proved fortuitous as brush and large branches hid the driveway and made detecting it difficult from a vehicle. The last light of the sun waned so Jacob clicked on a flashlight and led Sarah and Sophie onward.

The driveway proved to be a long, winding uphill journey of nearly two miles interrupted by three downed trees and Jacob and Sophie complained bitterly during their ascent. Sarah, however, remained silent, the nun eventually taking point and relieving Jacob of his flashlight privileges. They finally arrived at the chalet nearly an hour later, the wooden dwelling built in the Swiss style with a heavy, gently-sloping roof and wide, sturdy eaves. Sarah marched forward.

"Shouldn't I check it out first?" Jacob inquired as he snagged Sarah by the shoulder of her shirt. His tug unexpectedly spun her around and he caught her in his arms. She smirked and lingered there before Jacob politely set her back on her feet.

"There's no one in there," said Sarah confidently. She proceeded up the front steps and onto the chalet's wrap-around porch. Jacob hesitated.

"Ah, what the hell," he muttered. Walking forward with Sophie at his side, he said, "If we survived Chinese Peak, we sure as fuck can survive this place."

• • • •

JACOB SAT IN AN ANTIQUE oak chair, his elbows resting on his knees and his hands folded in front of him. The chalet bedroom in which he sat reeked of rustic, country charm, the furniture constructed of oak and the curtains and bedding consisting of patchwork squares of multi-colored fabric. Its appearance reminded him of the mansion's breakfast nook and the times he spent there with Elizabeth and the girls. He wiggled free of those painful memories and buried them deep.

Fatigue clung to Jacob's bones, his exhaustion the result of the harrowing flight from Chinese Peak and the challenging journey to the chalet. Sophie's recent dearth of words concerned him, however, and he wished to question her about it.

"This place is no Chinese Peak," commented Sophie disappointedly as she inspected her bedroom. A cup of hot tea, prepared by Sarah, steamed on her night stand.

"Do you miss the demons or the death more?" Jacob snapped with an incredulous expression. Sophie failed to react. Instantly regretting his temper, Jacob hung his head and said, "Sorry, kid. I'm pretty burnt right now."

Sophie sauntered up to Jacob and playfully bumped into him with her leg. He looked up to her and saw the wry smile on her comely face.

"Ya' know, the nun said the solar panels on this place are operational and it's got a well," advised Sophie. She plopped into his lap and said seductively, "Why don't we take a nice, hot shower and then go to bed?"

Raising his hands to avoid touching Sophie, Jacob guiltily squirmed under the wonderful sensation of her young body. She cuddled into him and wrapped her arms around his neck. His enjoyment of her affectionate attention made him feel slimy and he imagined Miriam's gory retribution if she caught them in such a compromising position.

"Look, you're at least a decade younger than I am," reasoned Jacob as he tried to lift Sophie out of his lap. She resisted his efforts with a mischievous grin, the young woman twisting to meet his hands with her buttocks and thighs.

"Decade and a half," countered Sophie as if taking pride in the age difference. Her perilous blue eyes blunted his efforts to escape but he continued to squirm uncomfortably beneath her. Sensing his anxiousness, she abruptly released him and stood up.

"You sure can turn it on and off easily," Jacob said as he rose to his feet.

"I know you want Sarah," replied Sophie without the ire Jacob expected. Unfastening her jeans, she slithered out of them and revealed the traces of blue body paint still visible on her lean legs. Jacob turned his back to her and stepped away.

"I don't want *anybody* right now, kid," Jacob countered in tired frustration. He cautiously shuffled towards the door and uttered, "I just want *sleep*."

"I saw the pass you made at her," said Sophie blithely. Climbing into bed, she slid under the covers, fluffed up the pillows and leaned into them.

"Did you see her shoot me down, too?" grumbled Jacob. He placed his hands on his hips and turned around.

"I'm going drink my tea now," said Sophie pointedly, her idiosyncratic manner kicking into full gear. Baffled by her penchant for oddity, Jacob exhaled.

"You do that," Jacob said. He hesitated as his libido made a final plea for Sophie. Dashing its hopes, he collected himself and said, "Sleep well, Soph."

Sophie picked up the tea cup and sipped from it. Jacob moved to exit the room and grasped the door handle.

"Jake?" inquired Sophie. He stopped.

"Yeah?" Jacob responded. He held his breath in anticipation of her next bizarre statement.

"You need to stay with me until I fall asleep," said Sophie. Jacob paused, glanced back at Sophie and studied her. She looked at him with flat affect and waited patiently for him to comply with her wishes.

"Sure, what the hell," Jacob relented. Releasing the door handle, he returned to his chair. The pair sat in silence, Sophie drinking her tea and Jacob fighting off sleep.

* * * *

JACOB CLOSED THE BEDROOM door and stepped out into the living room of the chalet. Lingering in a haze of exhaustion, he closed his eyes and massaged the radix of his nose. The distinctive scent and crackling of burning wood forced open his heavy eyelids.

The flames of a healthy fire licked the ceiling of the fireplace, their light bathing the room in a soothing, orange glow. Two long, tall candles flickered on either end of the mantle. Sarah sat upon a plush couch facing the fire with only the silhouette of her slender shoulders, neck and head visible. She lifted a glass of red wine to her lips and sipped from it as shadows danced wildly throughout the room.

"How is she?" inquired Sarah, a compassionate concern evident in her voice.

"Sleeping, amazingly. What the hell did you put in that tea?" Jacob inquired. Sarah snickered but failed to answer his question. He studied her closely and noticed that she wore her hair down.

"I took the liberty of fixing you a drink," said Sarah as she stared into the fire. Jacob remained rooted to the floor and turned over her strange behavior in his mind. The flames suddenly shifted, their light falling on Sarah's shoulders and revealing that they were bare save for two spaghetti straps.

"Please, come sit with me," she requested kindly while turning her head to catch Jacob in her peripheral vision. She drank from her glass again and said, "I haven't had the pleasure of wine and idle conversation for some time."

Jacob's suspicion ebbed as Sarah returned her gaze to the undulating flames. He exhaled with a shiver.

"Ah, what the hell . . . I could use a little hooch," Jacob admitted with a sigh. Relaxing his body and ambling over to the couch, he stopped abruptly when he rounded the right end table. Sarah wore a slinky, forest green nightie and light, tastefully-applied makeup. The nightie was cut at the middle of her thigh and, much to Jacob's surprise, revealed her cleavage.

"Jesus, is there something in the water here?" Jacob murmured uneasily. Trying to focus his gaze on Sarah's blue eyes instead of her inviting breasts, he asked, "Little heavy on the sex appeal there, huh Sister Sarah?"

"Just trying to be comfortable," assured Sarah with an inviting pat of the couch cushion next to her. Sarah nodded to a glass of whiskey and ice sitting on the coffee table next to an open bottle of red wine. Condensation coated the glass, the moisture caused by the heat radiating from the fireplace. Sarah cooed, "Come. Relax. Drink."

"Ya' know, if Miriam showed up right now, she'd kill you," Jacob advised earnestly as he hoped to ward off Sarah's bizarre attention with Miriam's name. He desired nothing but a single drink and then deep sleep.

"And why would she do that?" asked Sarah coquettishly, the nun grinning before sipping her wine.

"Because you're not dressed for idle conversation," Jacob countered. He indulged his lust and briefly gawked at Sarah's shapely form. Her smile faded as she glanced away and fingered the seam of the couch cushion.

"Miriam can be overwhelming at times," acknowledged Sarah. A poignant expression came to her face when she reacquired Jacob in her vision.

"At times?" Jacob replied with a chuckle. His eyes fell to the ground and glazed over as he contemplated Miriam's volatile nature. Sarah examined Jacob's countenance meticulously, the Ursuline seemingly reading his facial features like tea leaves.

"You still have feelings for her," remarked Sarah knowingly as she rose to her feet and placed her wine glass on the coffee table. Sauntering over to Jacob, she lifted his chin with her index finger, locked eyes with him and expounded grimly, "But you're worried that she's making no progress in her relationship with God. I must say, she was much more passive in her evil prior to your entry into her life. Yet that's no longer the case. She continues to slaughter anyone who comes close to you or threatens your wellbeing, be it physically or emotionally. I'm still hopeful that her insatiable love for you will draw her towards our Lord but I'm by no means certain of it. You'll have much difficult work to do if Aaron ever paroles her from her vocation as temptress."

Sarah's probing insight stoked Jacob's confusion and distracted him so much so that he failed to register her comment about Miriam's return to her "vocation." His mind churned and he chewed the inside of his mouth.

"I don't know," Jacob said. Intimidated by the apparent sexual energy radiating from Sarah, he broke eye contact and walked towards the fireplace. He plucked the glass of whiskey off the coffee table, raised it to his lips and gulped twice.

"Her efforts to welcome God into her life are brief and superficial," Jacob confessed in a distressed tone. Gawping at the fire, he took another swig of whiskey and continued, "She still kills without thought or remorse, unless I'm there to stop her, and I wonder how long even that will last. But . . . ."

"Yes?" questioned Sarah with the slightest trace of impatience in her voice.

"What we shared seemed so deep at times . . . and real. Vividly real. I just don't fucking get it," Jacob explained. Clearly conflicted, he paused and then exploded with rage, shouting, "FUCK!"

Jacob hurled his drink into the fire, the alcohol causing a small eruption of flame amid the shards of broken glass. Sarah remained motionless though a strange light in her eyes rapidly glimmered before evaporating. Jacob grimaced and exhaled in frustration.

"I just don't fucking know," he muttered.

"What you do know, Jacob, is that when we are troubled, we must turn to Scripture for guidance," Sarah began somberly. Her hands falling to her sides, she glided to Jacob and said, "This may be difficult for you to hear but you must consider it:

> 'You will know them by their fruits. Grapes are not gathered from thorn bushes, nor figs from thistles, are they? So every good tree bears good fruit, but the bad tree bears bad fruit. A good tree cannot produce bad fruit, nor can a bad tree produce good fruit.'" (The Gospel of Matthew 7:16-18).

"I think she loved me, though, Sarah," rebutted Jacob in a feeble tone. Sarah's wise confidence rattled his faith in Miriam's redemption but he repeated, "I think she loved me."

"Jacob, you must know in your heart that her efforts were merely meant to curry your favor," Sarah replied. She grasped his arm reassuringly and said, "I, too, believed that Miriam could be saved. It's such an encouraging thought, that our Lord would redeem even a demon."

Sarah paused and smiled warmly. Her smile melted into a grim countenance.

"So very encouraging," she continued, "but remember, Jacob: 'Every tree that does not bear good fruit is cut down and thrown into the fire.'" (The Gospel of Matthew 7:19).

Sharp pains radiated through Jacob's chest and his stomach ignited as he contemplated Sarah's erudite reasoning. Disconsolate, he droned:

"'Therefore just as the tares are gathered up and burned with fire, so shall it be at the end of the age. The Son of Man will send forth His angels, and they will gather out of His kingdom all stumbling blocks, and those who commit lawlessness, and will cast them into the furnace of fire; in that place there shall be weeping and gnashing of teeth.'" (The Gospel of Matthew 13:39-43).

"*Miriam is lost,*" Sarah said softly while tightening her grip on Jacob's arm. Locking onto his eyes with her own, she stated affectionately, "But *we* are not."

• • • •

JACOB IGNORED THE UNUSUAL, biting chill of the night air and took a swig of whiskey from the bottle. The comforting warmth of the liquor flowed down his throat and into his chest. He set the bottle on the wooden railing of the chalet's deck though it remained firmly clenched within his fist.

Clouds tinged with the silvery light of a hidden moon meandered across the dark sky to the music of rushing wind and rustling leaves. Glittering stars littered the dark splotches of night amidst the clouds, their twinkling reflections dancing on the undulating waves of the lake. The door leading to the deck opened.

"I don't need any fucking company right now," grumbled Jacob. He lifted the bottle to his lips once again, the sloshing of the whiskey within it audible as the breeze died. He gulped from it and set it back on the railing with a jarring clunk. Worming its way into his blood stream, the alcohol ushered in the slightest measure of elation. The deck door closing echoed across the lake, the sound rolling to the opposite shore.

"God sent an angel to me, Jacob," Sarah advised, her countenance serious yet expectant. She enfolded herself in a flannel blanket to ward off the cold night air. Closing half the distance between them, she stopped and waited.

"Oh, yeah?" snapped Jacob as he turned to face Sarah. His arms outstretched, he smirked and proclaimed, "He sent me a fucking demon."

Memories of Miriam exploded in Jacob's mind and the smile drained from his face as he gradually lowered his arms. He took another swig of whiskey and shivered.

"And then He took her away," Jacob stated dejectedly. Sarah approached him, the nun's eyes brimming with adoration.

"But He also sent you *me*," she pleaded.

"You've spent months busting my balls about Miriam," scoffed Jacob angrily while raising the bottle briefly and thumping it on the railing. The whiskey within it splashed against its sides as he ranted "*'Put the girl out of your mind, go home to your wife and never again come to this place.'* Remember all that fucking bullshit? *'I may not be married but I've taken vows to another, Jake.'* I remember it! Tell me Sister Sarah, what the fuck's changed?"

Jacob inhaled to unleash more fierce chastisement upon Sarah. Casting off the flannel blanket, she aborted his fury by placing his hand on her firm stomach. Stunned, Jacob wished to pull away but the conviction with which Sarah held his hand to her belly paralyzed him.

"His favor is upon you, Jake, and from you . . . from *here* . . . will raise your child," Sarah declared ardently. She gently pressed Jacob's hand into her belly and said, "*That* is what the angel told me. I didn't see it before yet it is perfectly clear to me now. The angel said it would soon be time for Miriam to leave and for me to '*take on another.*' I thought the angel meant another demon but I was wrong. *I was meant to take on your child.*"

Jacob's head reeled partially due to the whiskey and partially due to the unbelievable shift in his destiny. Sarah began to involuntarily shake, her thin nightie no match for the falling temperature.

"E-e-everything that has occurred u-until now has led us to this very m-moment in time, to the p-p-perfect opportunity to serve our Lord and f-f-fulfill his p-plan," concluded Sarah determinedly through chattering teeth, her muscles beginning to shiver violently. Extracting himself from his astonishment, Jacob set the whiskey bottle on the railing. Quickly scooping up the blanket from the deck, he wrapped Sarah in it. He rubbed her shoulders and arms to warm her.

"You've been pursued by demons and ungodly women for far too long," Sarah counseled him while gazing on him lovingly. She insinuated herself into his arms and, though uncomfortable with her affection, Jacob allowed her to remain there. Sarah explained with conviction, "God is rewarding your faith with a loyal, God-fearing woman and with her you shall consummate His will."

"Having a child in this world is risky and dangerous, and you'd be a high-risk pregnancy as it is," warned Jacob gravely. Despite detecting no falsity in Sarah, the course she suggested simply felt wrong. The Holy Spirit provided him no guidance.

"But what if it guides Sarah?" Jacob asked himself. God undoubtedly blessed her with the Holy Spirit and no one knew more of His designs than her. Sarah extricated herself from Jacob's reluctant embrace and walked several steps towards the chalet door.

"Jacob," called Sarah tenderly while extending her hand to him. He hesitated and pondered her offer. She beckoned, "Our daughter awaits us."

A long-buried emotion surged within Jacob and he battled tears. His blue eyes vibrantly glistened.

"Our daughter?" he queried in disbelief.

"You have always desired a daughter, haven't you?" asked Sarah with an odd elation. Reveling in her intimate knowledge of the subject, she expounded, "*Yes*. You've always sensed it. In dark times you buried it deep, doubting it, even fearing it at times, but you never completely surrendered your belief in it. You saw her spirit on the way to Hanahan, didn't you?"

Tears welled in Jacob's eyes as Sarah stretched her hand out further to reinforce her offer. He nodded in the affirmative.

"It's been revealed to me as well," cooed Sarah "so it *must* be His will."

Emotionally and mentally drained as well as physically exhausted, Jacob succumbed to Sarah's beautiful, hopeful vision. Taking her hand, he ceded his destiny to her and followed her into the chalet.

* * * *

MAKING LOVE TO A WOMAN other than Elizabeth for the first time in many years, Jacob reveled in the physicality of Sarah's body and the touch of her soft, smooth skin. She proved active yet submissive, the Ursuline allowing Jacob to dictate the positions and pace of their lovemaking.

Lastly, Jacob moved her into the position he enjoyed most with Elizabeth; however, his ex-wife did not breach his thoughts as he engaged in coitus with Sarah. Lying on her back as he repeatedly thrust his penis into the silky, wet warmth of her vagina, he stretched his arms underneath hers.

They continued to copulate passionately with hands clasped, Sarah moaning each time Jacob pushed deeper into her. He occasionally kissed her back and neck.

Jacob reached climax, and, unable to withstand the sensation any longer, ejaculated inside Sarah. Her body answered with an orgasmic shudder of its own as they continued to grind against each other, the pair intent on wringing every last drop of sexual pleasure out of their dalliance. Gradually relenting, Jacob let his weight fall on Sarah with one final thrust. He kissed her neck and cheek tenderly as they both breathed heavily. Jacob closed his eyes.

"Let's see Miriam do that for you," said Sarah with a sinister sensuality foreign to her character. Jacob's eyelids popped open. He suddenly rolled over and hurled Sarah's body off the bed in one flailing motion. She hit the floor with a resounding thud.

"'What is your name?!'" Jacob demanded. (Excerpt from the Gospel of Luke 24:39). Sarah pierced the air with a jarring screech and glared at Jacob with black demonic orbs. Her splayed limbs lifted her off the floor like a spider and she bared sharp teeth at Jacob. Undeterred by Sarah's demonic warnings, he again barked, "'What is your name?!'"

"Assarion!" admitted the *daimoniou* ferociously. Leaping onto the far wall, she affixed herself to it and shrieked again.

"You cunt!" Jacob chastened. Standing up, he held the sheet over his nakedness with one hand and pointed at Assarion with the other. Jacob, filled with the Holy Spirit, ordered, "Come out of her!"

Flushed out of her earthly host by Jacob's spiritual fervor, Assarion fled. Sarah once again fell to the floor with a thud, the nun striking a dressing table below her. Jacob rushed to her side.

· · · ·

SARAH AWOKE IN THE bed she and Jacob shared the night before, her body aching and sore. She wore men's flannel pajamas, the garments oversized on her womanly frame but comfortable nonetheless. Rays of the morning sun streamed in from the window and they provided both light and heat. Sarah yawned while wallowing in the warmth and comfort of her bedding and stretching her muscles to alleviate her soreness.

Jacob knocked and entered the room. He carried a tray containing a mug of hot coffee and a plate of corned beef hash. Sarah smiled at him but his face remained sullen.

"Good morning," offered Sarah, her spirits clearly rising as she sat up in anticipation of her meal. The aroma of the corned beef hash wafted through the air, its smell causing her to remember her hunger and her stomach to growl. Sarah hurriedly placed two pillows behind her to support her back. Jacob waited patiently for her.

"It's all they have," said Jacob apologetically, "though they sure as hell have a lot of it."

"It is fine, thank you," Sarah stated. She allowed Jacob to place the tray on her lap. Sensing his palpable distress, she laughed a carefree laugh and picked up her fork.

"We'll see how fucking funny it is in nine months," he snarled. Despite Jacob being anxiety-ridden over the prospect of a demonic child, Sarah's smile grew. He grimaced and uttered, "How the fuck-."

"Language," Sophie scolded Jacob with a smirk as she slowly passed by the doorway. He walked to the door and slammed it shut.

"How the fuck did I let her snow me like that?" queried Jacob in a low, harsh tone. Furious with himself for falling into Assarion's snare, he gesticulated frantically and growled, "I'm so fucking stupid!"

"*Jacob.* I've sought God's forgiveness for my broken vow of celibacy, and I will do a penance, but we must not be too critical of ourselves," explained Sarah as her expression became serious. Jacob froze. Sipping on her coffee and then taking a bite of her breakfast, she reassured him, "There was also one critical flaw in Assarion's plan. *I'm infertile.*"

"What?" replied Jacob, his disquiet waning. He carefully contemplated Sarah's words and sifted through the events of the past week. She swallowed her food.

"I have what is referred to as a luteal phase defect," Sarah stated. She sipped her coffee again and continued to ravenously eat and chew while saying, "I secrete inadequate amounts of the hormone progesterone during my menstrual cycle. The lining of my uterus doesn't form properly and my eggs can't implant in it. My vocation obviated the need to treat it, so I never did. I'm *not* pregnant."

"She knew about Vanessa's Brugada Syndrome," countered Jacob, the gears of his mind still turning. He narrowed his eyes and asked, "So how did she miss your 'luteal phase defect?'"

"Arrogance, perhaps," Sarah answered with a shrug of her shoulders. Setting down her coffee cup on the night stand, she continued, "Maybe I was simply at a stage in my menstrual cycle when she couldn't sense it. I don't know. But, most importantly, we are *not* the parents of a demonic child."

Jacob chewed on Sarah's words as she chewed on her food. His countenance brightened and his anxiety disappeared.

"One more question," Jacob said thoughtfully. He sat down in an oak rocking chair in the corner and inquired, "Could you fly a helicopter before she possessed you?"

"No," replied Sarah with a sly smile.

15

A LIGHT, STEADY BREEZE found its way through the trees, around the chalet and across the lake. The sun shined brightly in the light blue sky and rapidly warmed the early afternoon air. Sitting on the flight of broad steps leading to the chalet's wrap-around porch, Jacob and Sophie watched the trees sway in the wind.

"So what level of hell is reserved for nun-fuckers?" Sophie asked. The inappropriate question wrested Jacob from his thoughts.

"That was a mistake," blurted Jacob with a sour look. Irked by Sophie's penetrating gaze, he growled, "A *demonically-induced mistake*. And it's none of your fucking business, anyway."

"Oh, you were possessed, too?" Sophie countered with mock innocence. She reached out with her right index finger and flicked a ladybug off her knee.

"Fuck off," snapped Jacob. The chalet's front screen door suddenly banged shut, the jarring noise causing him to start and jump to his feet.

"Sorry," apologized Sarah as she crossed the porch and dried her hands with a white dish cloth. She wore an old purple sweatshirt and faded jeans with her hair styled in its usual bun. Raising her voice, she announced, "Lunch is ready."

"Thanks, *Sister* Sarah," Sophie said while eying Jacob. She rose to her feet, walked into the house and let the door slam behind her.

"We need to fix that door," suggested Sarah as Sophie disappeared. She slung the dish cloth over her shoulder, grinned at Jacob and asked, "Coming?"

Jacob winced at her choice of words but Sarah missed it. He ascended the stairs.

"Yeah," Jacob answered. Plagued by a flourishing infatuation with Sarah, he moved close to her and indulged in the sexual tension between them. Miriam materialized but remained invisible to human eyes, the demon perched like a hawk atop a post at the foot of the porch stairs.

"Did she hear anything last night?" asked Sarah, the Ursuline feebly attempting to change the subject. She blushed but failed to retreat.

"She knows we . . . ya' know," replied Jacob. Sarah meticulously studied him and recognized the burgeoning adoration and yearning on his face. He stepped within her personal space and the romantic energy between them crackled to life. Miriam perceived that energy, her trepidation and wrath rapidly growing like ugly, tangled weeds. Jacob added, "I think she might be, well, jealous."

"She's becoming pretty attached to you, even if she doesn't always show it," said Sarah with both emotional and physical sensations stirring within her. Miriam's eyes widened and she trembled with fearful rage.

"Yeah," Jacob responded as he tilted his head and moved his lips towards Sarah. Miriam screeched.

"I was only with you in body last night," countered Sarah as her own head tilted, the nun resisting Jacob's advance with her words but not her actions. She continued, "You've been through a romantic wringer for months - *for years* - and I can understand how last night confused-."

"Haven't you spread enough seed, dick bag?" Miriam taunted Jacob as she revealed herself. He spun around and nearly toppled off the porch before Sarah pulled him back from the brink.

"Spread enough seed?" Jacob asked angrily. Shaking off his surprise, he descended the stairs and inquired, "What the fuck are you talking about, Mirry?"

"You're gonna be a daddy, Jake," advised Miriam in a mock congratulatory tone. Jacob and Sarah exchanged flabbergasted glances before he glowered at Miriam.

"How the fuck do you know that?" Jacob demanded while reaching out to grab her. She evaded him by vanishing into the spiritual world. Jacob whirled towards Sarah and chastised her worriedly, "You said it couldn't fucking happen!"

An utterly-shocked Sarah apologetically shook her head with mouth agape. Reappearing on the opposite post, Miriam smiled with devious satisfaction. Jacob approached her with a hostile finger pointed in her direction.

"How the fuck do you know?!" Jacob demanded again.

"Your mother-in-law told me," said Miriam without emotion as she relished the snail's pace at which she revealed information to Jacob. The way it made him squirm pleased her as did the way he gaped at her with bewilderment.

"How fuck would Tara-," Jacob trailed off as he realized that Miriam knew nothing of his tryst with Sarah. His mood darkening, he uttered, "Oh shit."

"Oh shit is right," said Miriam while squatting down to bring her face closer to Jacob. Reaching out to him, she lifted his chin with the claw of her index finger and, speaking slowly, she explicated, "Listen very carefully, Jake. Tara's holding Lady Lizzie in a psych ward at the hospital. She's also trying to get her to abort the baby, and I think she just might do it."

Jacob's head reeled. Leaning into him as if she might kiss him, Miriam longingly studied his face.

"Your baby's in danger, dumb fuck. If Lady Lizzie doesn't kill it, Tara will," warned Miriam.

Jacob grasped her hand and stared into her eyes with such sincere desperation that it crushed Miriam under its weight. His fear permeated the entire area like a thick fog, his trepidation so great that even Sarah felt it. She shivered.

"It's on you until I can get there," Jacob earnestly begged Miriam. Enraptured by his passionate plea, she nodded her head in the affirmative and departed into the spirit world.

• • • •

"WHAT THE FUCK DO YOU want!?" Miriam roared, the *daimoniou* infuriated by Aaron's untimely and inconvenient summons. Her grasp on Jacob remained tenuous and she needed to return to Elizabeth's child.

"Your spirit should be destroyed for your disobedience," said Aaron calmly. He stood on the roof of Agatha's former headquarters and observed the vastness of Kaiser as it sprawled out to Mount Borgia in the West and Mount Baldwin in the East. He continued, "I overlooked your final goodbye but I will not overlook your latest visit."

"Lady Lizzie's pregnant," Miriam said in her human voice while seething underneath a veneer of deference. Aaron rotated around slowly. Troubled by the news, he listened as Miriam added, "All I did was tell him she's thinking about an abortion."

"Pregnant?! Pregnant?!" squealed Marcion as he appeared to Miriam's right and studied her with black, slightly-distended eyes. He still inhabited the body of the young, dark-haired girl.

"Yes, pregnant, you little douchebag," Miriam replied.

"Where's Mallory?" demanded Aaron angrily.

"Don't worry, she's in good hands," said Marcion with a devious sneer, "or should I say the good hands are in her?"

Marcion cackled. He, Miriam and Aaron formed the points of a demonic triangle, each one suspiciously scrutinizing the others as their minds churned the new information and the possibilities it presented. Marcion smiled knowingly after several tense moments of silence.

"'He's a God damn woman when it comes to his emotions,'" quoted Marcion smugly while using Darby's voice to speak Darby's words. He grinned with jagged teeth and added, "'A kid's the perfect bait.'"

"Absolutely not, you fool," stated Aaron. He approached Marcion but halted several feet from him.

"Why?" Marcion responded shrilly as he took a step back.

"I don't need Gottschalk traipsing around Kaiser performing exorcisms and spreading his Biblical filth," began Aaron while gesturing towards Kaiser. All three demons became uneasy upon Aaron's mention of "Biblical." He recovered, however, and declared, "I want him out of my city."

Miriam hopped onto an air conditioning unit and tilted her head in her usual animalistic manner. She dreaded Aaron's impending revelation of her role in his latest scheme.

"You will possess Mallory Nicks as planned," instructed Aaron. He pulled a cigar from his jacket pocket and continued, "And then, using your new host, you will lead Gottschalk out of the city. He's a slave to Catholic guilt so if you flaunt Mallory's possession, he'll follow. Prolong his pursuit and keep him out of Kaiser. In the meantime, Miriam will kill Elizabeth and her unborn child."

A horrible, painful tingling wracked Miriam's body. She could obey only one master and make only one choice: spare Jacob's child or murder it. Marcion, meanwhile, squinted his bulbous eyes and contemplated his orders.

"Have I made myself clear?" asked Aaron. Marcion nodded his head but, when Miriam failed to respond, Aaron inquired, "Miriam?"

"Crystal," she answered. Fading slowly into nothingness, she stated in a harsh, demonic tone, *"Lady Lizzie must die."*

. . . .

"FUCK!" YELLED JACOB as the car's engine sputtered. He turned the key in the ignition three more times as the vehicle struggled to start. Finally, on his last attempt, it rumbled to life.

The pale-yellow jalopy, upon which he stumbled while traveling on foot, had been recently hidden in a pile of brush. Stepping out of the vehicle, he motioned to Sarah and Sophie. They emerged from a thicket carrying as much gear and food as they could manage. Jacob returned to the thicket to retrieve the remainder of their cargo as Sarah and Sophie quickly packed the old clunker.

"Three quarters full," said Jacob. Looking to the sky, he added with gratitude and a sigh, "Keep 'em comin.'"

Fortunately, Sarah's former parishioner was a survivalist and his preparations for a second doomsday included a store of gasoline. The fuel that remained at the chalet permitted them to travel a full day in the cargo van before it was expended. Kaiser still lay many miles away, however, and they travelled the bulk of the day on foot.

"The Lord provides yet again," Sarah remarked with an encouraging smile as Jacob pulled onto the highway and accelerated. He kept his eyes on the road. Sophie kept her eyes on him.

"He always does," said Jacob. He had remained morose for most of the journey from the chalet and responded to Sarah's hopefulness with half-hearted, sad smiles. He glanced in the rearview mirror for other vehicles and said, "Whether I deserve it or not."

"So, what's next?" Sarah questioned, the nun deftly sidestepping Jacob's pessimism.

"We'll run into one of Elizabeth's roving security units before nightfall," answered Jacob, "and when her goons realize who I am, and if Miriam was telling the truth, we'll be ushered right to Tara. And then the fucking fun begins . . . ."

"I meant for you," Sarah countered. She was still in the process of reconciling her vocation and her newfound feelings for Jacob. He shot Sarah an amused look and chuckled.

"If you're asking about Elizabeth, nothing," said Jacob, his brief jovialness fading. He returned his attention to the road and shifted in his seat, explaining, "It's taken a while for me to figure out what really happened with Liz and I, but I finally got it. A baby won't change a damn thing between us."

Jacob stopped speaking. Sarah waited for him to resume but, when he failed to do so, her curiosity spurred her forward.

"So what happened?" asked Sarah. She tensed and subtly leaned towards Jacob in anticipation of his reply.

"She stopped loving me months before Mirry even entered our lives," Jacob stated, his emotional wounds throbbing and bleeding as he ripped the scabs off them. He commented with hazy eyes, "It wasn't Mirry's fault."

"What makes you think she stopped loving you?" Sarah queried. She was no longer content to learn Jacob's theory at his annoyingly-gradual pace.

"Who the fuck really knows?" Jacob answered, his pain palpable despite being repressed beneath his emotional surface. Resentfulness slowly building in his voice, he said, "It was always a turf war with her, especially with those kids, and any misstep on her territory always turned into an ugly confrontation. But something changed towards the end, she became more protective of them, and more critical of me, which made me angrier, which made her more protective and critical, which made me angrier . . . and it just spun out of control. At that point it was too late . . . I was forever diminished in her eyes. No longer good enough."

Peeking into the back seat via the rearview mirror, Jacob noticed Sophie nodded off. He felt a nagging sexual desire for her but repressed it.

"Unfortunately, she also hit it off with a new door guard right around the same time," confessed Jacob, the resentment transforming into jealous ire. He began chewing the inside of his cheek and occasionally popping the callous there as he said, "I discovered the two of them chatting in her office a couple times and it seemed like I was interrupting something. I don't think she fucked the guy - at least I hope not - but she probably wanted to. *She cheated emotionally*. Shit. What the fuck does that even mean? I'm fucking pathetic, that's what it means. I guess she just found somebody better. Or maybe it was the other way around. Who fuck knows? So it doesn't fucking matter now, baby or no baby."

Sarah grasped Jacob's hand tenderly. Seeking to redirect him yet again, she broached a new topic.

"Have you considered how Miriam may respond to a new love in your life, albeit a different kind of love?" Sarah inquired cautiously.

"I'll fall off that burning bridge when I come to it," uttered Jacob in a defeated tone. Neither he nor Sarah spoke again, the pair spending the remainder of their journey in silence.

• • • •

DARBY PEEKED THROUGH the rectangular window of Elizabeth's psych ward room nervously and observed Mallory help her mother pack. She relieved the door guard as soon as they arrived with the intention of springing Elizabeth from custody.

"C'mon!" Darby mouthed as she tapped on the window. She glared at Elizabeth and hissed, "Move it!"

Darby's body abruptly careened across the hall, through an open doorway and into a vacant room. The impact knocked her unconscious and the door slammed shut as her limp body crumpled to the floor. Puzzled by her sister's sudden disappearance, Elizabeth looked through the window. A chill flowed down her spine.

"Mallory, we have to go, right now," ordered Elizabeth urgently, her knuckles white as she grabbed the door handle. It failed to turn. Elizabeth rattled it in frustration and uttered, "Damn it. Locked."

Mallory turned her back to her mother, drew a semi-automatic pistol from her coat and aimed it at the other side of the room. Determined and poised, she steeled her will and resisted the urge to flee.

"If you want Jake, then take Jake," Mallory said aloud. She instinctively stepped backward and warned, "Just leave us alone."

"Mallory, what the hell are you doing?" said Elizabeth. Stunned by her daughter's possession of a firearm, she asked, "Where did you get that?"

Miriam appeared in front of Mallory and punched through her chest, her fist spraying a gory glaze of blood, tissue and bone onto Elizabeth. She retrieved her hand from teenager's wound, snatched the gun from her and shoved her to the ground. Holding the firearm awkwardly, she squeezed the trigger and pumped a round into Mallory's right eye.

"Mallory!" bellowed Elizabeth sorrowfully. Devastated by the instantaneous death of her child, she fell to her knees. Miriam dropped her hands to her sides and tilted her head with a frown.

"You've been a serious pain in my ass for far too long, Lady Lizzie," Miriam complained while tossing the pistol into the bathroom with a clatter. Continuing matter-of-factly, she stated, "It's time to rid the world of *all* Nicks women."

"Miriam, please," begged Elizabeth with desperate tears streaming down her face as she viewed her dead child. She implored Miriam, "You can have Jacob. I'll let him go and never interfere in your lives again. I swear it. And you can kill my mother. Please kill my mother. But spare Darby. *Please.*"

Elizabeth bawled and her mascara smeared. Ignoring her peril, she lunged towards the body of her lifeless child and scooped Mallory into her loving arms.

"You e-evil bitch," snarled Elizabeth through her sobs as she held Mallory tightly. Miriam smirked at her as she threatened, "You *will* pay for this."

"No, I won't," Miriam said in a sour tone. She scowled and said, "It's over now. Stupid fucking cunt."

Miriam, with blood on her dress, pried Elizabeth from Mallory and effortlessly set her on her feet. Elizabeth instinctively placed one hand over her stomach and retreated into the wall.

"Remember when I told you you'd never see it coming?" Miriam inquired with a mischievous grin. She lunged towards Elizabeth who cringed and lifted her arms to block the blow. Miriam, however, halted before connecting. She snickered and said, "I was wrong."

"Then do what you came here to do," said Elizabeth fatalistically. Standing straight up and holding out her arms in surrender, she conceded, "You win, Miriam. Enjoy the spoils."

"Oh, how I'd love to torture and kill you," Miriam replied, the urge to do so festering in her blood. Her face contorted with hatred and she uttered,

"I've thought about it every day since I met Jake. In fact, I'm *supposed* to do it. But while he'll heal from losing your brats, and even you, he'd never heal from losing *her*."

Miriam's revelation prompted Elizabeth's eyes to widen with utter shock. The demon's hand flashed forward with supernatural precision and she shoved Elizabeth's head straight into the wall. The crack of her skull impacting the stud echoed in the room.

Elizabeth fell into Miriam's arms and the demon carefully laid her limp body on her bed. She then touched her stomach and smiled.

"Hang on, little one," Miriam said in a comforting tone. Leaving behind a small scratch, she added, "Help is on the way."

Miriam stood up and rapidly exited Elizabeth's room. Reaching out, she grabbed the door of the room in which Darby lay, ripped it off its hinges and tossed it aside like a soiled napkin.

"Get up, Darby!" bellowed Miriam in her demonic voice. She pounded on the wall and yelled, "Your sister needs you!"

"What the fuck?" muttered a dazed and disoriented Darby. Her foggy, double vision nauseated her as she struggled onto her elbows.

"Get up!" Miriam shouted. Alarms suddenly screamed throughout the hospital as she turned and paused to survey her handiwork. She sighed and, before dematerializing, griped, "The things I do for that man."

• • • •

JACOB PACED ANXIOUSLY in a holding cell within the north wall checkpoint as Sarah and Sophie sat on a bench with exhausted expressions. Walking to a small, square window in the steel door, he looked out into an empty hallway. Reinforced concrete formed the walls, ceiling and floor.

"This is really fucking weird," Jacob said. Placing his hands on either side of the window, he complained, "We've been here for almost two hours. Even if Liz's still running the show, she wouldn't have waited this long."

Jacob looked in both directions and strained to catch sight of a guard. He scowled in frustration and resumed pacing.

"I'm sure everything's fine," assured Sarah. She patted the bench next to her and said, "Come sit down."

"Something's wrong," Jacob countered while shaking his head in disagreement.

Footsteps in the hallway drew Jacob's attention and he whirled around quickly. The guard's face appeared in the window and, upon locating all three detainees, she unlocked and opened the door.

"What the fuck's taking so long?" Jacob demanded. He was unaccustomed to his loss of clout in Kaiser.

"Mr. Gottschalk, you are to come with me immediately," the guard informed him. Normally, Jacob would have keyed on her attractiveness, her long, dark hair and her lean muscularity but he presently failed to notice. Two more guards appeared in the hallway.

"Bullshit," snapped Jacob as he stepped forward. Preparing to resist attempts to move him, he set his feet and said, "I'm not going anywhere without them."

"You needn't worry about them, Mr. Gottschalk," the female guard said firmly, "because they're going to the same place you are. You're just not going together."

"*Where* are we going?" inquired Jacob. The guard's odd demeanor troubled him.

"To the hospital," the guard stated bluntly, "to see your wife."

. . . .

"HOLY FUCK," JACOB UTTERED despondently. Elizabeth lay motionless before him in a hospital bed, his wife cloaked in a deathlike slumber. A respirator breathed for her and the color of her clammy skin resembled the white bandages wrapped around her head and underneath her chin. He feebly called, "Liz?"

Elizabeth failed to respond, her inaction prompting Jacob to move to her side. He gingerly lifted a chair as he approached her, turned it around and set it next to her bed. Slumping into it, he trembled as he touched the cold skin of Elizabeth's cheek. He jerked his hand back. His attention then turned to her stomach.

"Why didn't you tell me, babe?" Jacob queried. Distressed by the daunting odds Elizabeth and his unborn child now faced, he gently ran his hand over his ex-wife's belly before burying his head in her chest and weeping.

"It's my fault," said Darby remorsefully. Jacob's head popped up and he wiped away tears. Darby stood before him, her eyes bleary and puffy and a scowl etched on her face.

"What the hell are you talking about?" Jacob inquired. Darby's presence agitated him and fouled his mood.

"Liz. Vanessa. Mal," answered Darby. She folded her arms and grumbled, "They're all dead because of me. They're dead because I couldn't kill you."

"Mal, too?" Jacob asked with a heavy heart. He fought off a sob and then wept.

"Your demon cunt punched a hole through her chest," snarled Darby, Elizabeth's sister itching to draw her pistol and kill Jacob immediately. She continued with a muted, malicious smile, "You're going to die, Jake, but not before you experience pain like you never have before. And I've got plans for Miriam, too."

Jacob rose to his feet but maintained his grasp on Elizabeth's hand. He squeezed it.

"This family's seen enough death," Jacob said. He warned grimly, "If you kill me, *she'll kill you.* If you torture me, *she'll kill you.* If you go after her, *she'll kill you.* You can't stop her, Darby."

"Oh, I disagree," responded Darby. Reaching into her shirt, she produced the Rosary she wore around her neck and let it fall to her chest. Pressing her palms and fingers together as if praying, she said mockingly, "You'll be happy to know I've found Jesus, Jake, thanks to my new spiritual guide."

Stepping into the envelope of light surrounding Elizabeth's hospital bed, Sarah looked on Jacob with somber eyes. She wore her traditional Ursuline garb and held a Bible in her hands.

"Sarah?!" Jacob exclaimed. He gently set Elizabeth's hand down on her bed and asked, "Where the hell's Sophie?"

"She's safe," confirmed Sarah with an expression of sincere pity. She glanced at Darby deferentially and said, "Darby has promised Sophie and I permanent sanctuary in the city in exchange for spiritual protection."

"See, Jake, even *I* can be reasonable," interjected Darby with a confident grin. She lumbered up to him and insinuated herself into his personal space, saying, "But what does that matter to a dead man?"

"So, when my daughter asks how her father died, are you going to tell her the truth?" asked Jacob unabashedly as he glared at Darby. Her eyes widened and crackled with crazed energy. She lunged towards him, grasped him by the jacket with both hands and slammed him into the wall.

"How the fuck do you know that?!" yelled Darby. Shaking him roughly, she yelled again, "How do you know?!"

Unfazed, Jacob sternly met Darby's gaze. He let her twist in the wind for ten seconds before speaking.

"You and I are the only real family she has left in this world, Darby," Jacob advised. The import of his words struck her like a sobering slap to the face as he continued, "And she can't afford to lose you because you're right. *I'm a dead man.*"

Her hostility faded and she released her grip on Jacob. The two unlikely allies carefully studied one another.

"Now get the fuck outta here," Jacob insisted, "and let me say goodbye."

• • • •

THE ENTRY DOOR TO ELIZABETH'S hospital suite clicked shut as Jacob studied her comatose face. He sensed no life or vitality in her and perceived her body to be no more than an empty shell from which her spirit fled. Try as he may, he could not feel the presence of his child.

Reluctant to touch Elizabeth for fear of miraculously awakening her, he put his hands on his hips and paced in front of her bed. The systematic beep of her heart monitor and the whirring of her ventilator interrupted the silence. Jacob exhaled.

"Do you remember the night before our wedding?" Jacob asked Elizabeth. Unable to look at her as he paced, he folded his arms and said, "You were working late that night to wrap up a few things so you could spare a few uninterrupted days for our honeymoon. You *demanded* that I leave you alone so you could focus on your work."

Jacob grinned warmly yet mischievously. Fondly recalling the passionate desire for Elizabeth that infused his very spirit during their courtship, he chuckled.

"I, of course, wanted to fuck, so I paid you a little visit anyway," Jacob continued. He remembered how Elizabeth detested him stating he wanted to "fuck" her, so he puckishly added his usual, "Fuck you *with love*, I mean."

The smile on Jacob's face evaporated. A pained, angered expression replaced it.

"I'll never forget the look on your face when I opened your office doors," he uttered, each word tearing at his heart. Faint traces of the hybrid emotion of fear, anger and embarrassment arose and strengthened within him. Jacob turned his back on Elizabeth.

"Shocked guilt," he said, the resentment in his voice building, "though you buried it deep and recovered pretty quickly. And, then, when I asked what you were doing, you became indignant. The fucking 'Tanner defense.' Little did lovesick, hapless, dumbfuck Jake know, his bride-to-be was looking at pictures of her old fiancée, perpetually incapable of letting go of her romantic past."

Jacob's smile returned though without its former warmth. He rotated around to observe his wife, the sight of her a bittersweet reminder of their failed love affair.

"It was our first evil, ugly fight," Jacob reminisced as if recounting their first date. He grabbed the back of the chair and continued, "You tried to jam the pictures into your shredder so I charged your desk and kicked the fucking thing over. We both dived on the floor, yelling at each other as we wrestled over those stupid fucking pictures. I finally ripped one out of your hand . . . but not before you smacked me in face, though."

Jacob's blood boiled with jealousy, his foray into that fateful night rending open the infected scabs of old wounds.

"You and that bristly-mustached fuck, laughing and raising your glasses in a nice little 'fuck Jake' salute. You said you were just saying a final goodbye," said Jacob. He punched the wall and yelled, "Fucking cunt!"

Repressing his ire, he walked to Elizbeth's side and grasped her cold, limp hand. The physical contact cooled his enragement by dousing it in a flood of remorse.

"That was it, Liz, that was my warning," Jacob stated. He sat down and mused, "That was my sign from God, and I fucking ignored it. Hell, even you suggested we postpone the wedding. If I would've had the balls to bail, 'Ness and Mal would be alive today."

Mortified tears arose in Jacob's shimmering blue eyes, one rolling down his left cheek despite his efforts to repress it. He wiped it away and his voice wavered as he spoke.

"Y-You'd be alive, and our little girl wouldn't be fighting for her mother fucking life," he said. Grief-stricken, Jacob planted one last, loving kiss on Elizabeth's inert lips and squeezed her hand.

"We were a train wreck, Liz. A fucking plane crash on top of a train wreck. I don't know why God put us together just so we could fall apart," Jacob lamented. Letting go of her hand, he sighed, "All we can do now is save our daughter. You've got to keep her alive, babe."

Jacob bowed his head sadly and walked to the door. He stopped before exiting and lifted his chin ever-so-slightly.

"If I don't find someone else to cleanse me of my love for you," Jacob said forlornly, "then that love will haunt me until the end of my days . . . though that end's probably not far off."

16

"LOOKS LIKE WHISKEY'S not the only thing we have in common these days," Jacob quipped as he accepted the flask Darby offered him. He eagerly took a swig, swallowed it down and indulged in the burn as it trickled down his throat. He handed the flask back to Darby, who ignored his comment, and added, "Thanks."

Jacob sat in the passenger seat of Darby's black sedan, the vehicle sheltering him from the pouring rain of the thunderstorm passing through Kaiser. The car, parked in a lot adjacent to the San Joaquin River, idled as the unrelenting rain pelted it from above. Lightning danced intermittently throughout the city, the flashes trailed by rumbles of thunder.

Darby retrieved the flask and gulped from it twice. Reaching into the back seat, she offered the flask to Sarah.

"How 'bout you, Sister Sarah?" Darby inquired.

"No, thank you," responded Sarah while remaining otherwise motionless. Darby pulled back the flask and drank from it a third time.

A bolt of lightning struck a tree on the far bank of the river followed by a deafening clap of thunder that erupted above them. The strike broke a thick, warped branch and caused it to plummet into the swirling waters. It was soon washed away in the torrent.

"Other than Adai and his staff, who I've already threatened, only the three of us and mommy dearest know about the kid," Darby began as she stared forward into the rainy night. Her focused-yet-troubled levelheadedness surprised Jacob as she expounded, "Liz's brain dead, and that's it. There's no coming back from that. But her heart's still functioning properly, and so are her lungs . . . with a respirator, anyway."

Darby again drank from her flask and handed it back to Jacob. He partook of its contents as she sighed.

"The odds fucking suck, but it's possible they can keep her ali- . . . *functioning* for several months," Darby said while struggling to mask her sorrow. Jacob grew pale and slumped in his seat but Sarah remained silent and stared out into the storm. Darby continued, "She's about six weeks pregnant now. The kid can hack it on her own at about 24 weeks but getting her to at least 28 weeks substantially improves her chances. The longer the bun's in the oven, the better."

"Eighteen weeks," muttered Jacob skeptically. He again took a swig from the flask and said, "Eighteen mother fucking weeks."

"The longest Adai's heard of a pregnant mother successfully giving birth after brain death is four months," Darby stated. Scowling, she added, "But those babies were much further along than our little bundle of joy."

Darby shook her head and snatched the flask from Jacob's grasp. She glared at him with a horrid maliciousness.

"It's a good fucking thing your fucking demon cunt botched the job," Darby growled through clenched teeth.

"She didn't botch the job," corrected Jacob as he craved more whiskey to dull his pain. Darby's head jerked sideways to glower at him with puzzlement. Nauseated by the excruciating emotional ache prompted by Elizabeth's demise, he explained with difficulty, "Miriam left Liz alive to *save* the baby."

Darby's hatred waned and she guiltily looked away. Jacob staved off tears.

"In her warped mind, rendering Liz brain dead served two purposes," said Jacob. He shifted in his seat and explained, "It ended any chance of Liz and I reuniting but at the same time preserved the life of my child. Apparently, Liz was going to have her aborted."

"Oh, Miriam," gasped Sarah, the nun openly weeping over Miriam's descent into unmitigated evil. Darby seethed.

"But that doesn't mean the baby's safe from her," Jacob replied sternly. His conflicted feelings for Miriam tormented him.

"Why the hell is that?" asked Darby incredulously. She glowered at him and snarled, "You just said that bitch *saved* the baby. Why the fuck would she kill her now?"

"Miriam's love is desperate, unrelenting and savage," Jacob said, "and it doesn't tolerate competition. That's why she destroyed my family, to eliminate any threat to her claim on me. See, she doesn't consider the baby a threat right now. But if the baby and I developed any type of relationship, Miriam'd become jealous of her. It'd slowly eat at her, infect every ounce of her being, until that jealousy exploded in her usual homicidal rage. If she even suspects I love the baby as much or more than her, she'd eventually kill her, without thought or remorse."

"He speaks the truth," Sarah confirmed, her arms grasping her shoulders tightly as if she embraced herself for comfort. She added, "Miriam won't suffer anyone to divert his love and affection."

Darby groaned and punched the steering wheel. Her violent outburst caused both Jacob and Sarah to start.

"Can't you use that fucking Jesus bullshit on her to cast her into hell or something?" barked Darby while leaning towards Jacob threateningly.

"Not permanently, at least I don't think so," Jacob grumbled, his ire with Darby rising. He composed himself in an attempt to mask his indecision and said, "And Sarah or I would have to be with the baby twenty-four hours a fucking day to protect her."

"That's not our only problem," confessed Darby in shame. She hesitated before explicating, "My mother wanted me to kill you at Chinese Peak, Jake, and she wanted Liz to abort the baby. She'll kill anything with Gottschalk blood."

Sarah looked on Darby with great concern while Jacob remained still. Thirty silent seconds elapsed.

"So what the fuck do we do, asshole?" questioned a frustrated Darby. Jacob swallowed hard.

"We kill anything with Gottschalk blood," he said.

• • • •

"*Thank you*," Jacob gushed as he eagerly accepted a steaming foam cup of coffee from Darby. Drinking from it greedily to ward off the exhaustion that hung on him, he muttered, "Four fucking hours of broken sleep. Fuck."

"Stop your bitching, pussy," grumbled Darby. She retrieved her flask from her jacket and poured whiskey into her coffee before drinking from her coffee cup. Noticing that Jacob watched her closely, she held out the flask and said in a feigned polite tone, "Cream and sugar?"

"This better be important," Jacob warned while ignoring Darby's offer. He slumped on a couch in Elizabeth's hospital suite, the repetitive beeping and whirring of the medical equipment lulling him towards sleep.

"You can sleep after I kill you," sneered Darby as she stowed her flask. Dr. Adai, a tall, gray-bearded black man, abruptly strode into the suite wearing his usual white lab coat. He immediately approached Jacob with hand extended. Darby closed the suite door.

"Jake, how are you?" greeted Dr. Adai fondly with a smile. Jacob stood up, set his coffee cup on the window ledge and shook his hand. Dr. Adai nodded at a returning Darby and said, "Darby."

"Doc," Darby gruffly responded. She squirmed uncomfortably. Dr. Adai's smile disappeared.

"I'm glad to see the reports of your demise were greatly exaggerated," Dr. Adai continued in a serious tone. Glancing at Elizabeth, he said, "I'm so sorry for your loss. Your wife was a tremendous woman and this city will sorely miss her . . . as will I."

"Yeah," Jacob responded with uncertainty as his eyes darted to Darby and then back to Dr. Adai. He caught her shaking her head in the negative in his peripheral vision. Recovering, Jacob added in a dubious tone, "She was loved by many."

Noticing his weariness, Dr. Adai motioned for him to be seated. Jacob plopped onto the couch as Dr. Adai sat on the edge of a recliner. Darby swept up a chair, spun it around and sat on it with her arms folded upon its top rail.

"I trust Darby has explained the situation to you," said Dr. Adai. Leaning forward and resting his elbows on his knees, he folded his hands solemnly.

"Yeah," Jacob replied, the distraught father limiting his words in an effort to hold back his grief. He bit his lip. Darby watched him without emotion save for the intensity sparkling in her eyes.

"She's informed me of what you intend to do," stated Dr. Adai. Jacob's expression soured and he glanced at Darby.

"And?" Jacob asked brusquely. He was highly suspicious of Darby's motives and concerned by Dr. Adai's knowledge of his plan.

"I think I can help," said Dr. Adai bluntly, his revelation causing a stunned Jacob to gape at him. The doctor rose to his feet and said poignantly, "Meet me in surgery suite four in twenty minutes."

Jacob stood up and watched Dr. Adai with astonishment as he exited the suite. Turning his attention to Darby, he attempted to speak but could not find the words.

"I've already lost Liz, 'Ness and Mal," stated Darby, her eyes watering. She growled through clenched teeth, "I'm *not* losing anyone else. Except maybe Tara."

"I think Tara's right. You've gone soft, Darby," Jacob commented in jest. Darby suddenly lunged at him while drawing her pistol. She pinned him to the suite wall and stuck the gun in his mouth.

"Oh, yeah, fucker?" snarled Darby, her anger stoked by Jacob's lighthearted accusation. She moved her face close to him, smirked and said, "How about I feed you a fifty-caliber sandwich? How's that for fucking soft, huh? Fuck you and my mother."

Seething, she withdrew the gun from his mouth, holstered it and stormed out of the suite. Jacob, after watching Darby depart, shook his head, straightened his jacket as if nothing happened and threw himself into the recliner. Leaning back and closing his eyes, he exhaled.

"Twenty minutes of peace," he said softly. Drifting into a light sleep, he repeated, "Twenty ... minutes ...."

• • • •

STATE-OF-THE ART SURGICAL equipment crowded three of the four walls of the surgery suite. Ranging from sternal saws and blood pumps to high-definition televisions and computers, the equipment served only the elite of Kaiser and only two of its several surgeons were permitted to use it. A single lamp shone in the suite, its light focused on a body lying on a raised surgical table and covered with a blue sheet.

"Come on in, Jacob," Dr. Adai said, his voice transmitted by speaker into the suite's observation room. Jacob stood at the observation window, his attention riveted to the body on the surgical table. Darby stood to its left with her arms stoically folded while Dr. Adai rolled back the sheet to reveal the brunette woman beneath it. Jacob's skin crawled and he felt nauseous but he managed to steel his will and hesitantly enter the surgical suite. He approached the cadaver but halted several feet from the foot of the table.

"She was brought in this morning," Dr. Adai said as both he and Darby studied Jacob closely. He simply looked at the woman with watery, inert eyes and a mien of saddened disgust.

"Another female corpse," uttered Jacob, a fatalistic grin emerging on his face. He chuckled hauntingly. "The Gottschalk curse strikes again."

"And they think I'm a sick fuck," Darby muttered. Dr. Adai gazed on Jacob with mild disapprobation.

"This woman was in a car accident this morning, Jake," Dr. Adai explained. Placing his hand on her bare shoulder, he said, "She suffered the same injury as Elizabeth, as well as others, and they caused her death before she arrived at the hospital."

Jacob knowingly glanced at Dr. Adai. He walked to the foot of the surgical table and examined the woman's motionless face.

"The brain surgery should lead to facial swelling, which in turn should conceal the facial and age differences," Dr. Adai continued.

"Ah, the misfortune of looking like Liz," commented Jacob with a chilling smirk. Darby glowered at him in disbelief as he added, "That would be the Nicks curse."

"Does she look enough like Liz or not, stupid fuck?" demanded Darby with a threateningly-pointed finger.

"No one will ever match your sister's beauty," Jacob said nostalgically. He drifted away and stood silently for several seconds as images of Elizabeth flashed in his mind: images of her peacefully slumbering to dancing at the wedding of Sören's daughter. Dr. Adai and even Darby patiently waited for his reverie to end. Finally, he uttered, "Yeah, she'll do."

"We need to act quickly," Dr. Adai advised. He removed his hand from the woman's shoulder and said, "We'll rush Elizabeth into emergency surgery within the hour. The surgery will be successful but she will expire due to post-surgical complications. I'll declare her death sometime tomorrow."

"Isn't it dangerous to move her?" inquired Jacob.

"We're taking a calculated risk but the best of my staff and I will personally oversee her transfer," Dr. Adai answered. He pointed to a wide door in the wall behind Darby and said, "That door leads to other surgical suites. Elizabeth will be in this room for all of twenty seconds."

Jacob carefully contemplated Dr. Adai's plan as he walked up to the woman and studied her countenance. He ran his hand over his face before making his decision.

"Thank you," Jacob whispered. Pitying the woman as he took her cold, lifeless hand and raised his eyes to heaven, he prayed, "Guide her home, God. Guide her home."

Darby walked up to Jacob and roughly poked his shoulder. He looked at her in annoyance.

"If you're finished kissing God's ass," Darby said, "we've got another problem."

• • • •

DARBY PROVIDED JACOB and Sarah a quaint ranch in an older, quiet section of the city. Constructed with greyish-brown bricks and titivated with flower boxes and white shutters, it formerly belonged to a recently-deceased senior citizen. Meeting Jacob at the front door like a jealous, overbearing wife, Sarah glared at him.

"Where in God's name have you been all day?!" she lambasted him. Her demeanor changed radically when she saw the dark circles around his eyes and his fatigued countenance. Sarah asked worriedly, "What happened?!"

"What, I fuck ya' once and all of sudden you get to chew my ass out when I'm a late?" countered a grumpy Jacob.

"How dare you!" Sarah exclaimed, a wounded expression washing across her face. She stomped away from him, her ire prompting Jacob to lunge forward and grab her by the arm. He spun her around.

"Sorry. I'm sorry," said Jacob quickly.

"I broke my vows to God when we had sex," Sarah said, the nun distressed and ashamed. She struggled within Jacob's grasp but failed to break it as she asked, "Why would you be so callous?"

"You were possessed by a fucking demon when it happened," Jacob replied. He grasped Sarah's other arm and pulled her towards him. She resisted as he assured her, "I think He'll give you a pass on that one."

"Jacob, please," Sarah pleaded while wiggling to free herself. He attempted to embrace her but she again resisted and scolded him, "We've discussed this."

"Yep," snapped Jacob while rebuking Sarah with a light shove.

"What happened to put you in such a foul mood?" Sarah asked. Jacob's rude treatment surprised her.

"We did it," replied Jacob as he walked into the living room. Dropping himself into a recliner, he sighed, "We fucking did it."

"Did what?" inquired a puzzled Sarah. She rebuked him with a smack on his shoulder as she passed him and seated herself on the couch opposite the recliner.

"By this time tomorrow, the city will mourn the loss of its Constable," answered Jacob blithely. He closed his eyes and paused as if he fell asleep but soon reopened them and continued, "And as her funeral procession moves through the streets of Kaiser, she will lie in a hospital bed, clinging to the last vestiges of life . . . to save our fragile little girl . . . against all fucking hope."

Jacob battled tears but was unable to compose himself in the face of despair and exhaustion. Touched by his vulnerability, Sarah approached Jacob and knelt before him. She reassuringly took his hands in her own.

"'Do not be afraid any longer, only believe,'" recited Jacob with an irked steadfastness. (Excerpt from the Gospel of Mark 5:36). Standing and lifting Sarah with him, he said, "He sure as fuck makes that difficult to do sometimes. Fuck this fucking bullshit. I've made a mother fucking mess of everything, Sarah, and people've died because of it. That fucking ends today. I'm going to start cleaning up those messes. *Today*."

Sarah tolerantly endured Jacob's profanity-laced tirade. She also raised her finger to her lips to remind him that Sophie lingered in her bedroom.

"Elizabeth's gone, but the baby's as safe as I can make her," continued Jacob passionately though in a lowered tone, "especially with her crazy, dangerous bitch of an aunt on the scene. Mal and Vanessa are gone, too. That sick fuck Aaron had some of his goons steal their corpses. *But fuck him*. God's given me the power to fucking get them back and properly lay them to rest . . . and I'm gonna do it if I have to spill every last drop of my blood."

Tears welled in Jacob's eyes and he paused, his raging emotions overwhelming him. Sarah watched him closely with a mix of intense adoration and empathy on her troubled face.

"I'm going to get the girls' bodies back," vowed Jacob while successfully holding his tears in check, "and harry those demonic motherfuckers to the end of my days."

"What about Miriam?" Sarah gingerly queried, the Ursuline loathing to broach the topic but unable to resist.

"Fuck if I know," said Jacob bitterly. Lifting her chin with an index finger, he released his bitterness and leaned in to kiss Sarah. His lips, however, never reached her.

· · · ·

REELING, JACOB SHOOK off the cobwebs in his head. An unseen force smacked him in the face before he kissed Sarah and knocked him back into the recliner. His blurred vision cleared and revealed Miriam standing to Sarah's left. She held the Ursuline's entire jaw firmly in her right hand.

"No, no," Miriam scolded Jacob as he attempted to stand. Pushing up Sarah's head, she smirked and warned, "Try anything and I'll crush her fucking jaw."

"You do that and I'll cast you right into the Abyss, Mirry," threatened Jacob. Miriam bristled at the reference but maintained her composure.

"So, what about Miriam, Jake?" Miriam inquired in a sinister tone as she mocked Sarah. Her words saturated with disdain, she continued, "What the fuck's she supposed to do now that you've abandoned her for Sister Sarah? Elizabeth, Vanessa, Assarion, Sarah. Who the fuck's next, Jake? That cunt Darby?"

"Mirry, you killed Mal and left Liz brain dead on a fucking ventilator," growled Jacob. He asked in disbelief, "Why the fuck would I stay with you?"

"Because I'm the only one who'll ever love you for exactly what you are," Miriam replied with confidence and conviction. She explained with an underlying snarl, "You're broken, Jake. Hopelessly fucking broken. But I want to wallow in your brokenness. And as a spiritual being, I love spiritually . . . your physical being means nothing to me. No more worrying about the Dariuses, Tanners and Stevens of the world."

Miriam's reasoning rendered Jacob speechless. His eyes studied Sarah and Miriam, one choice moral and safe, the other immoral and risky yet teeming with potential. Sensing Jacob's indecision, Miriam swooped in for the kill.

"Jake, *I* saved your daughter," Miriam said earnestly. Maintaining her death grip on Sarah, she continued, "Lady Lizzie was going to abort her. But I stopped her, and your little girl is still alive because of me. *Me*, Jake."

Utilizing the weariness and sorrow he already felt, Jacob forced his eyes to water. He chewed the callous inside his mouth and frowned.

"What's wrong?" Miriam asked, the demon alarmed by Jacob's reaction.

"She's gone, Mirry," uttered Jacob with difficulty.

"Who's gone?" Miriam replied quizzically while abruptly tilting her head to the side.

"Both of them," answered Jacob. Punctuating his performance with a cracking voice and a quivering lip, he said, "Liz died and there was nothing they could do for the baby. She couldn't survive on her own. You didn't save her, you killed her."

The news paralyzed Miriam as it eviscerated her final play for Jacob's heart. She surrendered to old, evil instincts and pressed her claws into Sarah's skin. Her face bled.

"Miriam, please don't do this," Sarah begged as she squirmed in pain.

"Is the baby still in her?" Miriam queried eerily. Lowering her head, she kept her spiteful eyes fixed on Jacob. Her tone caused Sarah to shiver.

"You're pissed at *me*, Mirry," said Jacob. Grasping the arms of the recliner with whitening knuckles, he implored her, "Don't take it out on Sarah. It's *me* you want to kill."

"Is the baby still in her?!" barked Miriam in a monstrous voice.

"Yes, damn it!" answered Jacob. Miriam's bizarre fixation on the baby's location bewildered him.

"Then that's where it should stay," droned Miriam. Her skin crawled and her demonic instincts warred against her love for Jacob but she showed no emotion.

A sudden surge of spiritual energy flung Miriam backward as the spiritual force fields of Jacob and Sarah erupted simultaneously. She crashed into the far wall. Seizing the opportunity, Jacob leapt to his feet and charged after her.

"Miriam!" yelled Jacob in a commanding tone, the Holy Spirit exploding within him and stunning her. He instructed her grimly, "I command you, go back to the Abyss and do not return here again."

Miriam attempted to shriek but could make no sound as she perceived nothing but intense, searing light. Losing complete control of her spirit, she involuntarily vanished into nothingness.

17

ORANGE LIGHT FROM A late-day sun drenched everything in Kaiser and cast Elizabeth's private funeral in an eerie glow. The ceremony, originally planned for the morning, proceeded in the late afternoon due to unexpected thunderstorms that rolled through the city earlier in the day. The rare and relative quiet permeating the metropolis deepened the bizarreness of the setting.

The mansion's former owner constructed a small, hedge-enclosed cemetery within its walls though he never interred anyone beneath its rich, green lawn. Its meticulous landscaping and colorful flowers faded under the overwhelming-orange rays of the sun. Floral displays surrounded the coffins of Elizabeth, Vanessa and Mallory which, accompanied by a thin, black wooden podium, rested upon a raised dais. Three rows of six black, wooden chairs were placed in front of the podium where an aged, gaunt minister presided over the service.

Tara and Darby occupied the middle two chairs of the front row, mother and daughter flanked by key members of Elizabeth's inner circle and dignitaries who also occupied the second and third rows. Security personnel, clad in suits and ties, positioned themselves at the entrance to the cemetery and in each of its four corners.

Jacob lurked in the entranceway partially to avoid human contact and partially to keep an escape route open. He attended the funeral only at Sarah's urging, the reluctant attendee fidgeting often under the confining fit of his suit and the uncomfortable lack of a friendly face. The minister droned tediously and periodically adjusted his spectacles as his oratory meandered beyond tediousness.

Flashing into existence like lightning, Miriam appeared on the dais. No one moved or reacted, the lack of response prompting Jacob to believe that she hid herself from human perception. She grinned evilly at him.

"Shit," Jacob thought. He glowered back at her and shook his head in stern warning. He then searched unsuccessfully for a way to reach her without disrupting the ceremony.

Flipping Jacob her middle finger, Miriam's devious smile melted into a jealous sneer. She slithered around the coffins and manipulated their locking mechanisms before returning to her original position.

"No!" Jacob screamed as Miriam unexpectedly and effortlessly flung the coffins forward in turn and they hurtled towards the ground. Hitting the lawn with resounding crashes, the coffins rolled and ejected the bodies of Elizabeth, Vanessa and Mallory. The minister dropped earthward and huddled in fear as the crowd scattered.

Jacob charged straight towards the coffins amid the horrified screams of startled attendees and flung chairs aside as he waded through the chaos. Arriving at the dais, he realized he stood alone. Whirling around several times, he saw no one. The faint cry of an infant rang out and he slowly rotated around to once again face the coffins. He started upon seeing them back upon their stands.

"What the fuck?" he uttered in astonishment.

• • • •

A STINGING SLAP TO the back of Jacob's head woke him from his dream. He examined his surroundings and caught sight of Darby hurriedly exiting the cemetery. A handful of mourners lingered near the entrance and quietly regaled each other with stories about Elizabeth. The coffins remained unspoiled in their original positions and no trace of Miriam existed.

"Sleeping at your ex-wife's funeral," Tara admonished him jokingly as she watched Darby disappear. She uttered with disdain, "If you weren't nùmero uno on Darby's shit list before you sure as hell are now."

Ignoring Tara, Jacob stepped onto the dais and listened intently. No sounds emanated from the coffins, their surfaces tinted orange by the hazy sunlight. Jacob lowered his left ear to Elizabeth's coffin.

"You're the strangest man I've ever met, Jacob," Tara commented harshly, "and I've met some very strange men in my time. What my daughter saw in you I will never know."

"Well, you don't have to worry about me fucking up her life anymore," said Jacob while continuing to listen for the cries of an infant. Hearing nothing, he dismissed the crying as nothing but the stray strand of a dream and straightened himself. He looked to the peak of Mount Borgia as the sun sank behind it but continued to bathe Kaiser in orange light.

"Oh yes, mission accomplished," Tara sneered, her hatred for Jacob breaking through her initial attempt at civility.

"Save the bullet, Tara," suggested Jacob. Turning to face her, he said, "Elizabeth's gone and I'm leaving the city anyway. You know me. I'll be dead in a week."

A peculiar expression appeared on Tara's face but she swiftly repressed it. Smirking, she approached the dais.

"Is that so?" Tara asked while folding her arms in the familiar manner of Nicks women. She chided, "Now that you've killed my daughter and granddaughters, I figured you'd stay, given that you're sticking your cock in the nun. Perhaps ruin her life. Darby's still alive, too. You could get her killed."

Tara's accusations rankled Jacob and he threw her a caustic scowl. Slithering out of her abhorrence, he tenderly touched Elizabeth's coffin as if to say one last goodbye. Saddened yet satisfied that their book had closed, he hopped off the dais and proceeded to the entranceway.

"Enjoy being Queen of the World, Tara," said Jacob sarcastically. He exhaled and added, "You've got a tough act to follow."

· · · ·

JACOB'S HEART LEAPT and fluttered as the beam of his flashlight fell upon the sepulcher. The pristine, white stone remained as he remembered it, the small grains of luminous minerals embedded in it twinkling like stardust. The meticulously-manicured lawn angled upwards around the sepulcher and ran towards Mount Borgia's peak. Backlit by the ambient light escaping from Kaiser, the peak jutted out from the dull, purple haze and into the black, star-dotted sky above its tip.

"What is this place?" Sarah inquired, the Ursuline equally awed by its spiritual energy and its stunning views.

"The place you'll bring my daughter when she's old enough to appreciate it," instructed Jacob. He paused to soak in the ambiance and walked up to the sepulcher. Reverently placing his hand upon it, he added, "To connect with It . . . with Him."

"You can bring her here yourself," Sarah countered. Irritated by Jacob's insinuation, she approached him but stopped short of his reach and said, "Whether you free those girls or not, you'll be back. I don't understand why you need to leave in the first place. I'm sure they'll come to you, to taunt and tempt you."

"I need to shift the battle away from civilians, away from the little one," argued Jacob in an annoyed tone with his back to Sarah. He reasoned, "There's been far too much collateral damage in this war and there's no guarantee I'll survive it."

"Nonsense. The Holy Spirit guides you always and our Lord has never left your side," Sarah counseled compassionately as Jacob turned around. His forlorn, fated expression chilled Sarah's spirit but she pressed on, saying, "Even the *prospect* of losing a child is devastating. Your fear and grief are causing you to be pessimistic. *You will be back for her.*"

"If Vanessa and Mallory taught me anything, it's that my pathetic ass was never meant to be a parent," Jacob admitted fatalistically, the admission tearing at him like Miriam's claws. He muttered, "Even where she is now, that kid's better off without me."

"That's ridiculous," Sarah stated firmly but to no avail. Reading the grim determination on Jacob's countenance, she surrendered and suggested gently, "You should give her a name."

"Does it really matter now?" asked Jacob forlornly. Sarah did not reply but patiently watched him. He contemplated a name for his only child.

"I would name her after her mother but I'm not sure that burden should be laid on her. I did know a perfect soul once," Jacob stated as he fondly recalling the image of the buxom, blonde teenage girl from his youth. He looked to Sarah and said, "Other than you, of course."

Sarah blushed and shook her head to deflect his praise.

"Her name was Autumn," Jacob said.

"Autumn Gottschalk," stated Sarah approvingly with a warm smile. Jacob fumbled in his jacket pocket for several seconds before producing a single silver key. He held it out to her but, after glancing at it, she waved it off.

"*Take it*. If not for you, for Sophie and the baby," Jacob said as he moved the key closer to Sarah. She reluctantly complied as he explained, "It doesn't matter where the fucking money came from. Just use it to buy your way out if it ever comes to that."

Sarah, unable to vocalize her thoughts, simply nodded her head in defeated agreement. Jacob locked his eyes on her.

"Please take care of my daughter," he implored her. He trembled and stated dejectedly, "And after the two greatest commandments, teach her this: 'Do not call anyone on earth your father; for One is your Father, He who is in heaven.'" (The Gospel of Matthew 23:9).

• • • •

TARA WATCHED THE VENTILATOR breathe for her daughter, her chest rising as it pumped oxygen into her lungs and then falling as it withdrew carbon dioxide from her body. She stood at the foot of Elizabeth's bed, her arms folded and her face devoid of emotion or concern.

"Darby, you underhanded little cunt," Tara said disappointedly as she surveyed Elizabeth. A sneer slowly developed on her face and she grumbled, "Faking your sister's death and trying to hide it from me. Your punishment will be severe."

An emotionless Sophie abruptly materialized out of the shadows. Wearing a full surgical outfit, her entire body was covered save the area around her blue eyes and the back of her neck. Tara started and turned her body to face the unexpected visitor.

"How did you get in here?" Tara demanded with wrath. She seethed at the intrusion but, without knowledge of the intruder's identity, she maintained her ruse. Tara snapped, "And how dare you disturb my daughter in her condition."

"I know the whole story," Sophie droned while examining Tara with eerie meticulousness. Kaiser's new Constable assessed the veracity of her claim and, deeming it to be true, she smirked. Sophie, with a long knife in her hand, remained cold and said, "And I know you care very little for your family."

"I chose to live in the face of my granddaughters' and daughter's inevitable deaths," Tara replied scornfully as she focused on Sophie's knife. Her smirk became a scowl and she declared, "I still love them dearly."

"As much as your ambition will allow," countered Sophie.

"Who *are* you?" Tara inquired. Her calculations did not include Sophie and it irked her.

"It doesn't matter, at least to you," responded Sophie with continued flat affect.

"Fuck you, demon," a flustered Tara snapped. She took a moment, partially composed herself and warned, "Your boss and I have an accord and you're fucking it up. I don't imagine he'll be pleased about that."

"And how would you know who my boss is?" asked Sophie, her chilling tone causing Tara to tremble. Hesitating to ponder Sophie's identity, she rued her lack of knowledge and the unforeseen monkey wrench in her machine. Tara waited patiently for the right moment to draw her pistol.

"Who are you?!" Tara demanded as her panic and desperation flared.

"I take it you silenced the alert tones on her medical equipment?" inquired Sophie. Tara nodded in shocked disbelief. She took a few steps towards the Constable and backed her into a wall while stating calmly, "And I take it you know the computer system running the security cameras on this floor is undergoing routine maintenance for the next fifteen minutes so no one will see or hear anything. Oh, and thanks for disposing of the nurse. That'll give me plenty of time."

Tara moved to Elizabeth's right side. She pecked Elizabeth tenderly on the cheek, gazed lovingly on her daughter and caressed her bandaged forehead. She then lifted her eyes to Sophie.

"Will you at least tell me why you're doing this?" Tara asked. Sophie grimly shook her head in the negative.

"No," replied Sophie.

Tara reached for her gun but her discombobulation caused her to fumble it. Sophie, however, charged her with precision and stabbed her in the stomach. Tara emitted a truncated groan as she twisted the blade but her voice faltered when Sophie stabbed her several more times. She then let the elder Nicks crumple to the floor and turned her attention to Elizabeth.

Sophie abruptly ripped the breathing tube out of Elizabeth's mouth. Tossing it aside, she hacked Elizabeth's throat several times and sent out a gruesome spray that painted the wall in gore. Sophie's eyes darted to Elizabeth's stomach and the slightest trace of anger came to her youthful face.

Slicing a swath upward from Elizabeth's abdomen and across her pregnant stomach, she ripped her hospital gown, penetrated her skin and opened up her uterus. She thrust her left hand inside Elizabeth's womb, carefully grasped the tiny fetus between two fingers and mercilessly-yet-precisely cut it free from her body.

Her homicidal surgery complete, Sophie dropped the tiny fetus on the floor and ground it into the tile with her booty-covered shoe. The resultant squish was sickening.

"Three more down and just one left," stated Sophie matter-of-factly. Laying the knife across Elizabeth's mutilated throat, she said, "To kill Darby or not to kill Darby. *That* is the question."

• • • •

SUMMER REASSERTED ITSELF and the night proved warmer than average, the high temperatures ushered in by a steady southwest wind. The turbulent atmosphere herded stratocumulus clouds northeast across the sky.

"God, I fucking hate this heat," Jacob complained bitterly, the sweat lightly beading on his forehead as he tossed a bag in the trunk of Darby's sedan. Suddenly realizing he used God's name in vain, he added quickly with a glance to the sky, "But you already knew that, didn't you?"

"Let's go, asshole," barked Darby before twice pounding on the outside of the car door with her fist. Jacob slammed the trunk shut.

"Wait for me," Sophie said with a raised voice as she ambled towards Jacob. She walked down the sidewalk wearing her usual garb with a bag in one hand and a new baseball bat in the other.

"Where the hell were you?" said Jacob as he examined Sophie.

"I needed a new bat," responded Sophie as she made a move for the car. Jacob blocked her.

"You're *not* going," Jacob scolded. He was enheartened by Sophie's desire to accompany him but dismayed that he had to leave she and Sarah behind.

"Yeah, I am," countered Sophie. She pounded the trunk twice with her fist and, surprisingly, Darby opened it for her.

"Are you fucking nuts?" Jacob inquired sharply as Sophie tossed her bag inside the trunk. He reasoned as she slammed it shut, "You wanna leave the safety of Kaiser for the shitstorm the outside world's become? And now the shitstorm's got demons, too."

"*Now*, Jake," Darby angrily ordered. Jacob shot her a hostile glance as Sophie disregarded his objections and climbed into the backseat.

"'Go, behold, I send you out as lambs in the midst of wolves,'" Sarah stated as she appeared behind Jacob. She continued, "'Carry no money belt, no bag, no shoes; and greet no one along the way. Whatever house you enter, first say 'Peace be to this house.' If a man of peace is there, your peace will rest on him; but if not, it will return to you. Stay in that house, eating and drinking what they give you; for the laborer is worthy of his wages. Do not keep moving from house to house. Whatever city you enter and they receive you, eat what is set before you; and heal those in it who are sick, and say to them, 'The kingdom of God has come near to you.' But whatever city you enter and they do not receive you, go out into its streets and say 'Even the dust of your city which clings to our feet we wipe off in protest against you; yet be sure of this, that the kingdom of God has come near.'" (The Gospel of Luke 10:3-11).

Sarah's blessing caused Jacob to simply gape at her. Her face quivered with repressed sorrow

"If you leave her here, she'll follow you," Sarah advised. She forced a pained grin and reasoned, "At least this way, you can keep an eye on her."

"' . . . for I will give you utterance and wisdom which none of your opponents will be able to resist or refute,'" Jacob replied. (The Gospel of Luke 21:15). His eyes watering, he wrapped his arms around Sarah as she kissed his cheek. Turning away, he quickly embarked into the car and closed the door. Darby hung a quick U-turn and the car sped away as Sarah watched it dwindle into the distance.

• • • •

DRIVING WITH HER USUAL reckless abandon, Darby said nothing and kept her eyes on the road. Jacob permitted her characteristic aloofness as he decided to instead ponder his impending foray into the dangerous outside world. His Bible sat on his right leg with his hand atop it. Sophie sat silently in the back seat and stared out the window.

"Sarah'll take care of the kid," Jacob began before Darby scalded him with her eyes. Her inaudible criticism failed to daunt him and he stated, "But you still need to be involved."

"The nun's got it, asshole," muttered Darby uneasily, the child's reluctant aunt irked by Jacob's attempt to engage her in uncomfortable conversation about family matters. She retrieved her flask from the dashboard. Driving with her knees, she unscrewed the cap, took a pull and then screwed the cap back on, grumbling, "Besides, Liz never trusted my parenting skills so why should you?"

"She needs her own flesh and blood, Darby, and you're her last, best hope," Jacob said. Darby tossed the flask back onto the dashboard and returned her hands to the wheel.

"Fuck you, Jake," snapped Darby, her ire and her speed increasing. She ran a red light and narrowly avoided a collision with several vehicles amid the screech of tires and the blaring of horns. Extending her middle finger to scrambling pedestrians who protested her reckless driving, she continued, "There's no more room on my back so get the fuck off it."

"It's what Liz would've wanted," Jacob said in a serious tone. Darby's face quivered as she struggled with her grief over Elizabeth's death. Repressing her emotions, she abruptly slammed on the brakes and the car skidded to a halt. She stared forward, stone-faced and perturbed.

"Get the fuck out of my car," replied Darby. Jacob opened the car door and stood up. He tossed his Bible onto the front passenger seat.

"Here, you need that more than I do," Jacob said before slamming the door. Darby shifted the sedan into reverse, which, in a cacophonous display, hurtled backward, turned one-hundred-eighty degrees and then sped off. Sophie stood opposite Jacob with only her baseball bat and a blank stare.

"Fuck," Jacob cursed with an annoyed expression. Placing his hands on his hips, he griped, "The bitch took all our stuff."

• • • •

JACOB AND SOPHIE STRODE out of the south wall checkpoint. His old sedan sat across from its entrance. A drop of sweat rolled down the side of his face as he grinned.

"Aren't you a sight for sore eyes?" he asked. Sophie observed the car with apathy as Jacob remarked, "Maybe there's a little luck coming our way after all."

"Hello, Jake," called out Assarion.

"Or not," Jacob sighed. He recalled the first time he heard the sinister seductiveness and wisdom of Assarion's youthful voice and shivered despite the heat. He swiveled around.

"Holy fuck," Jacob uttered feebly, his heart overwhelmed by grief and nauseated by the hideous sight before him. The corpses of Vanessa and Mallory watched Jacob from a distance, the younger sister doing so through one eye. Sophie let her bat fall to her side and its head clanked on the ground.

Mallory's right eye was replaced by a fleshy, bloodied gunshot wound. The blood that once saturated her clothing had dried and her chest contained a gaping hole ringed with torn flesh and broken bone. Jacob forced down vomit as he observed Mallory's innards, her demonic possession freezing her wounds in time much like Miriam's spider bite. Vanessa's body remained intact but the pallor of death hung on her like the sagging, gray flesh on her bones.

"You fucked up, Gottschalk," squealed Marcion with delight, "you fucked up!"

"You sick fucks," bellowed Jacob. Shaking off his horror, he charged the unlikely allies. His efforts proved to be in vain as they immediately vanished. Jacob screamed in a profanity-laced tirade and gesticulated wildly during his vitriolic rage. Sophie waited for it to fizzle out and then quietly approached him.

"You realize that was just the baiting of the hook, right?" asked Sophie. Her words took the air out of Jacob's sails, the pariah scowling as she added shrewdly, "And that Assarion just took your old girlfriend's job?"

Jacob fumed. He walked around the front end of the car and opened the driver side door as Sophie stood motionless. Pausing, he glowered at her.

"Get the fuck in the car before I change my mind," Jacob ordered. He entered the car and pulled the door shut. Obeying his demand, Sophie embarked and the sedan rolled away into the deepening night.

18

MIRIAM HUDDLED IN THE soul-draining emptiness of the Abyss, the demon wallowing in perpetual, disheartened trepidation. The viscous evil of Ba'al Zeboul's realm coated her like petroleum and oozed to the very core of her spirit. Pained cries and a cacophony of bizarre clicking noises echoed in Miriam's soul.

Miriam shuddered. Succumbing to hopelessness and contemplating a complete surrender to the Abyss, she permitted it to overwhelm her, absorb her and forever imprison her in despair. It seemed her only option. All was lost.

"'Therefore I say to you, all things for which you pray and ask, believe that you have received them, and they will be granted you.'" (The Gospel of Mark 11:24).

Miriam trembled with pain and elation. The words of Christ scorched her but she was heartened by the sound of Jacob's voice in her spirit. Two pinpricks of light arose in the darkness, the star-like points blazing with a fierce intensity and warring against the evil blackness of the Abyss.

"He's mine," Miriam demanded amongst the evil discordance raging around her. Battling despair and fear, she whispered deferentially, "Please . . . give him to me."

Miriam realized that only sincere repentance and unyielding faith offered parole from her spiritual prison and a chance to reclaim Jacob's heart. She surrendered to God and forsook the Abyss.

The Holy Spirit suddenly washed over Miriam, a flash of searing heat like scalding water rushing through her inert veins. Desperately searching her mind for the proper prayer, she recalled the words provided by Christ millennia ago and began reciting them despite their injurious nature:

"'Our Father who is in heaven, hallowed be your name, your kingdom come, your will be done, on earth as it is in heaven. Give us this day our daily bread. And forgive us our debts, as we also have forgiven our debtors. And do not lead us into temptation, but deliver us from *evil* . . . .'" (Excerpt from the Gospel of Mark 11:24).

THE END

OTHER WORKS BY
JOSHUA R. FIELDS

A DOG RETURNS TO ITS Own. Months after banishing his demonic lover, Miriam, to the Abyss, Jacob Gottschalk travels into the frigid Canadian wilderness to rescue the corpses of his possessed stepdaughters and properly lay them to rest. The violent and insatiable Sophie lures him from the narrow way, however, and, blinded by his waning faith, he fails to detect the terrible secret she hides. His fortunes seemingly improve upon his arrival at New Oneida, an esoteric Christian settlement located in a pristine river valley. Its leader, Dr. Irinushka Zhukova, tempts Jacob with many beautiful vessels of spiritual purity and seeks to create in him a wellspring of the Holy Spirit. Unbeknownst to them all, a greater spiritual storm stains the skies of their future and threatens all those who dwell upon the face of the earth. Facing a terrible new evil and the destruction of everyone he loves, a stoic Jacob holds on desperately to the words of Christ: "But the one who endures to the end, he shall be saved."

 • • • •

THE MILLSTONE CRUSADE. *". . . but whoever causes one of these little ones who believe in Me to stumble, it would be better for him to have a heavy millstone hung around his neck, and to be drowned in the depth of the sea." The Gospel of Matthew 18:6.*

Shocking abductions of ones they hold dear unite Catholic teenagers Judas Trent and Ursula Baumé and thrust them into the evil world of human trafficking. Mentored by a whiskey-drinking, cigar-smoking priest, the headstrong psychokinetic and the disfigured healer lead their friends against a local sex-slave operation in Southeast Michigan and Northwest Ohio.

Together, Judas and Ursula take the fight to those who would harm and enslave children and score early victories against their enemies. Yet as the dangers of their Millstone Crusade against human trafficking increase and their feelings for one another are continually frustrated, they are forced to consider one simple question.

Can they stay together?

• • • •

'85 LOVE AFFAIR. Ten years after the unexpected and tragic deaths of their parents, siblings Elliott Warden and Emma Hastings enter 1985 in very different places. Emma, as matriarch of a loving family and owner of the successful club Johnny Dubs, prospers but Elliott, lost in a meaningless career and a sea of shallow relationships, flounders.

The return to Michigan of his high school sweetheart and her best friend, Donna, provides Emma the perfect excuse to intervene in her brother's love life. Her machinations quickly go awry after the arrival of a pretty, young waitress with a heart of gold and a vivacious, talented and beautiful musician with a soon-to-be fiancée. Believing Elliott to be courting romantic disaster with the younger women, Emma makes several risky plays to finally set him on the path to wedded bliss with Donna. Elliott has other ideas, however, and seems destined to make 1985 one hell of a year.

www.ingramcontent.com/pod-product-compliance
Lightning Source LLC
Chambersburg PA
CBHW071257250626
47159CB00004B/1217